SOULSHIMMER

THE VEILED KING TRILOGY

DAWN MERCHANT

EBURNEAN
BOOKS

To Sherene, who casually said I should write a book—and accidentally changed everything.

CONTENTS

PRONUNCIATION GUIDE

- **Aeralith** (AH-ree-lith): A tiny, winged species of Embers.
- **Aren** (AH-ren): The world in which the story takes place.
- **Aridan** (AH-ree-dan): The Dazzling Deity and creator of Aren.
- **Elaryn** (eh-LAR-ee-in): An ethereal, light-bound species of Embers.
- **Lerain** (LEE-rain): A sea-dwelling species of Embers.
- **Luxari** (LUX-ah-ree): The rulers of each Sphere.
- **Mora** (MOH-rah): Creatures that lure victims to their death with dreams.
- **Starvane** (STAR-vayn): A seaborne species shaped like stars.
- **Thresk** (THRESSK): A hybrid species with scales.
- **Virellith** (vih-RELL-ith): A serpentine species that dwells in the sea.
- **Colette Darroway** (koh-LET DAIR-oh-way)
- **Edur** (EH-door)
- **Kazimir Arid** (KAZ-ih-meer AHR-id)
- **Nerian Summit** (NEER-ee-en SUM-it)

To my Starry Flicker,

Sometimes I wish I could live on my own,
Where the people I knew would forget me once more.
My past a myth,
My future unknown,
My present left to be explored.
The one thing I treasured
Would always be with me:
My SoulShimmer,
My Love,
My bonded soul.

Queen of the Daze Sphere

NOTE TO THE KING

My King,

Here are the sealed Aren Archives from the Hush Sphere's library. Because of improper timing, I was only able to grab Volume I. I hope it helps.

Your trusted friend,
W.G.

1

AREN ARCHIVES
VOLUME 1: ORIGINS AND ORDER

I. Creation and Governance

Aridan the Dazzling, the supreme deity, created Aren. Five circular landmasses known as the Spheres make up our world. A Luxari governs each Sphere—a king or queen chosen by Aridan—except the Bleak Sphere. A Luxari Council, appointed by the Luxari, helps govern their respective Spheres.

II. Law of Lineage

All inhabitants inherit their magical or non-magical abilities from their lineage. A symbol showing the strongest bloodline marks the person's wrist.

III. Ari Souls

Magic comes from Ari Souls, which are pure souls. After death, half stays in Aren; the other half moves to "The Unknown." The Retired Luxari performs the Ari Ceremony at Soulari Hall. At age 28, the Luxari and the Luxari Council gain immortality. The Void harbors the Soul Snatchers and Rogue Embers.

IV. The Sphere Quests

Once a year, Aridan summons Questlings to take part in the Sphere Quests, held during Spice Season. Refusal results in social ruin, as Aridan punishes anyone who declines, branding them forever as a coward. However, success can earn one a seat on the Luxari Council—or even the gift of immortality.

SPHERE CLASSIFICATIONS

SPHERE CLASSIFICATIONS

The Hush Sphere

Class: Embers (individuals with magic abilities)
Magical Discipline: Charmers—water manipulation, charms, healing
Luxari & Council: Queen Catalina Cove, Council of 15

5

The Scorch Sphere

Class: Embers (individuals with magic abilities)
Magical Discipline: Enticers—fire manipulation, super strength, beauty
Luxari & Council: King Kazimir Arid, Council of 10

The Daze Sphere

Class: Embers (individuals with magic abilities)
Magical Discipline: Swayers—wind manipulation, mind control, mind reading
Luxari & Council: King Oak Piers, Council of 5

The Still Sphere

Class: Embers (individuals with magic abilities)
Magical Discipline: Shifters—earth manipulation, animal shape-shifting, Sphere Jumping
Luxari & Council: Queen Nerian Summit, Council of 12

The Bleak Sphere

Class: Dims (non-magic folk)
Magical Discipline: None
Luxari & Council: No Luxari

SOULSHIMMER

CHAPTER
ONE

Flames engulfed the Dreary Den. As people rushed out the main door, terrified screams erupted around me. Ink-black smoke billowed from the shattered windows, the heat making it hard to breathe. Glass shards, blood, bodies, and splintered wood scattered the ground.

I tried to hold back vomit as the stench of burning flesh and death surrounded me.

A Dim lay motionless on the dirt, his body drenched in crimson and his legs twisted and mangled.

A low hiss filled the air.

The hairs on my arms rose; my heart threw itself rapidly against my chest. I needed to get out of here before—

A tall Soul Snatcher lurched from the blistering flames. Its head pivoted in my direction. Where eyes should have been, there were two gaping holes of darkness. Paper-thin, rotted skin stretched across the mummified skull. Its frame was skeletal, draped in decaying sinew and taut, desiccated flesh clinging to sharp bones. The Soul Snatcher opened its mouth and dark globs of blackness fell from it, staining the ground in ink as it let out a high-pitched wail.

Panic welled in my throat. I spun around, frantically scanning the crowd as they fled down the patchy hill—but Will, my childhood best friend, was nowhere to be seen. Dread washed over me.

"Somebody help me!" a desperate voice shrieked from behind me.

I glanced over my shoulder. The Dim I'd served earlier was on his stomach, dragging his body forward, away from the Soul Snatcher. His hair was clumped and greasy, matted to his forehead as he grunted, hauling himself across the dirt.

The creature crouched next to a dead man, its mouth wide open as midnight-black sludge rushed out, coating the body entirely.

The tar hardened, and the Soul Snatcher raised its long, bony fist and brought it down with a wet crunch.

Shimmering golden dust—his soul—forced its way from the fissures, shooting upward, straight into the Soul Snatcher's nostrils. A low, chilling hiss escaped its mouth as it inhaled the soul. Its skin pulsed with a red hue as it lifted its voided gaze and let it fall on the Dim.

Nobody deserved that fate. Before I could stop myself, I sprinted toward him.

"Can you stand?" I panted, fighting to keep the tremor out of my voice.

Sweat coated his skin, black splotches blooming across his forehead. His eyes were wide with fear. I gripped his arm and hauled it over my shoulder, his weight slumping against me. My steps faltered as I dared a glance back.

The Soul Snatcher rose, its desiccated, towering body hovering over its victim. We had seconds. I gritted my teeth and pressed forward, dragging the weakened Dim along, step by shaky step. He groaned as he inhaled shallow breaths.

Then his weight shifted. I looked right, and a flicker of hope flared in my chest.

Will.

His soft, hazel-brown eyes were full of determination.

"I've got him, Coco," Will murmured. "Go." And in a flash of smoke, both of them vanished.

My shoulders ached and chaos roared around me, but I had to keep moving.

Fire nipped at my heels as I ran down the steep hill toward the valley. I looked back and froze.

The Soul Snatcher effortlessly flung bodies out of its way as it followed me.

Fear gripped my chest as flames blazed behind me, searing the air. I inhaled, and my mouth filled with dark smoke. Sweat streaked my forehead, my body burning from the heat and the strain of running.

A creamy, cloudy mist billowed in front of me, rolling off Will as he stepped forward and snatched my hand.

"I'm not losing you, too—let's go!" Will panted. A sharp ache slashed across my chest with the reminder that Milo was gone. Will dragged me down the hill, my feet scuffing against rocks and snagging on roots.

A distant, eerie wail pierced the night. Will yanked me to a stop and wrapped his arms around my waist, pulling me close.

"Hold on tight. You might get disoriented for a second."

I laced my arms around his neck.

Pearly gray smoke encompassed us in a thick cloud and a twirling sensation filled my stomach.

Nausea bloomed, tightening deep inside me. I had only Sphere Jumped twice, and the experience had left me queasy and disoriented. Wind whipped around us, and everything blurred. I squeezed my eyes shut, hoping it would ease the churning in my belly.

The temperature dropped. My feet landed on something soft. I looked down as they sank into the snow packed on the ground.

My mouth hung open in shock, heart pounding against my ribs. What had just happened? Why did a Soul Snatcher come to the Den?

But I shoved the fear down. Will would never leave me if he thought I was in danger.

He studied my face, his onyx hair shaved to the crown of his head, accentuating his sharp features.

I lifted my chin and met his eyes. "I'll be fine. Go check on your family."

Will hesitated, his jaw flexing as he searched my eyes. He gave me a curt nod and disappeared in a swirl of pearly gray smoke.

The crisp, frigid air numbed my fingers. A glimmer of golden dust danced across my palm, then vanished. I blinked, unsure of what I'd just seen.

Lifting my gaze, I scanned the snow-brushed mountains of the Frosted Peaks.

THE DAZZLING

AREN FOLKTALES

Aridan the Dazzling
Created Aren in Spheres—
Landmasses circular, warm, and sincere.
But Aridan loved games—
Quests, if you may.
He believed nothing came free—only
    earned through sheer will
So Aren grew—
With Embers and Dims.
And in each Sphere,
They gamble, they challenge, they
    persevere.

CHAPTER
TWO

I stood before my distant cousin's three-story mansion, nestled between towering pine trees. With every breath, a cloud of steam puffed into the frigid air. I didn't like showing up unannounced, but given my current circumstances, I didn't have much of a choice.

The snow crunched beneath my boots as I trudged up the long, winding walkway to the knotty alder door. My bare knuckles felt like ice, and each knock against the hardwood threatened to shatter them. The door groaned open, and Edur's wintry, ice-blue eyes met mine.

"Coco, what brings you here? We weren't expecting you until Crisp Season," he asked, his voice filled with surprise.

Ava joined his side, her smile welcoming as she motioned for me to come into the warmth. Her blonde hair, now a few shades darker since moving to the Frosted Peaks, framed her face gently.

"The Void attacked the Bleak Sphere," I said, exhaling into

my palms and rubbing them together, trying to warm my frozen fingers.

I stood in the entryway, taking in the festive red bows that were tied to the banisters. Ava and Edur both wore their finest, and a twinge of guilt crawled up my spine. Obviously, I was interrupting something.

Edur's brows furrowed. Without a word, he flicked his wrist, slamming the door shut behind me and ending the chill creeping up my back. I envied the ease with which he commanded objects. *Magic.* It was a gift he, and so many others, had—but one I lacked.

"What happened?" Edur asked, his eyes sharp with worry.

"The Void attacked the Dreary Den. But Will... Will saved me before the situation worsened."

My cousin grabbed my right hand, her brows knitting in sympathy.

Edur's eyes widened. "Why would the Void attack the Bleak Sphere?" Edur paused. "They've been more active, bringing conflict throughout Aren." He ran a hand through his short, ash-blonde hair.

A wave of surprise hit me. Were people in other Spheres so disconnected from the Bleak Sphere that they didn't know the Void had been attacking for years? The taste of annoyance lingered in my mouth, bitter with the ignorance of that comment.

"They're after Ari Souls," I said, and surprise flashed on Edur's face. I regretted my harsh tone, but everyone was aware that the Void desired magic. I cleared my throat. "Anyway, I'm just thankful Will was there." Ava squeezed my hand.

"I was wondering if I could stay the night," I said. Discomfort filled me—I hated asking for help. It seemed like a weakness. My father's words to the effect echoed in my mind.

Ava's fingers lifted my chin.

"Of course you can, Coco. You can stay as long as you need. The offer has always been open."

Their compassion filled me with gratitude, especially since they had taken me in after Milo's death.

Edur nodded in agreement, but his thoughts were still elsewhere. "I wonder if the Void attacked the Bleak Sphere because—"

Ava didn't let him finish his sentence.

"Oh, let's not dwell on conflict and mayhem when we have guests showing up within the hour," she said. She turned to face me. "Coco, as always, you look beautiful." She scanned my dress from top to bottom. I saw disapproval cross her face and knew she hated it. "I don't know if you're attached to this dress..."

"It's my work dress," I replied.

Relief flooded her face. "Oh, great! It'll need to go. I have the perfect gown for you to wear."

She grabbed my arm and led me toward the grand staircase. As we passed, I glimpsed the ballroom to my right, festively decorated.

"Wait. A ball gown?" I asked, my thoughts racing. I knew I had interrupted something, but dressing up for the evening was the furthest thing from my mind.

"We're having our annual Snowfall Ball tonight," she replied giddily, clasping her hands together.

Knots of anxiety twisted in my stomach. I glanced around, searching for an escape, but Edur just smiled and shrugged.

Leave it to my cousin to have me in a fancy dress within ten minutes of arriving at her house.

"We're getting ready, Edur! Keep an eye on Holly and North for me. The kids are in the ballroom. We'll be back soon." Ava ran up the rest of the stairs, pulling me behind her.

I stood in front of the floor-length mirror in the hallway. My mother's sea blue eyes stared back at me, wide in the reflection. The pale blue-gray gown clung to my frame— a shocking contrast to the girl who had just fled a Soul Snatcher. I tucked a loose wave of caramel hair behind my ear, drew a deep breath, and stepped into the ballroom.

The air smelled of peppermint, and tiny white snowflakes drifted from the ceiling, vanishing before they touched the floor —the perk of having a Charmer for a husband, I supposed. Gorgeous pine trees, draped in ribbons and bows, filled every corner of the room. Guests sat around tables, the cheerful buzz of conversation filling the air.

A huge orb hung from the ceiling like a chandelier trapped inside a blizzard. It exploded into a flurry of sparkling shards that swirled together. They wove themselves into a towering ice sculpture of Aridan, the deity. A groan escaped my lips despite myself.

Aridan's serene face glowed with soft blues and whites, intricate frost patterns tracing his robes. His outstretched hands seemed ready to bless the crowd with magic. Polite applause filled the room as people praised Edur's "beautiful display."

I could not stop myself from scoffing at how the Hush Sphere worshipped Aridan. Of course, they loved the God who had gifted them magic. But growing up in the Bleak Sphere, born a Dim—many saw Aridan as a symbol of prejudice. Yet, despite everything, I prayed to him because he offered me hope, even if he wasn't meant for people like me.

"Coco!"

I turned just in time to catch Holly, whose golden curls bounced as she ran toward me, her dark green bow a perfect match for her dress. She threw her arms around my legs, and I grinned, scooping her up.

Holly leaned back in my arms, smiling at me.

"You're so pretty, Holly," I whispered, my heart swelling. She pressed her little fingers to my cheeks.

"You're more prettier, Coco." She placed a wet kiss on my lips, then wiggled to get down. As soon as her tiny feet touched the floor, she ran after her brother, North, whose hands were covered in chocolate.

The sound of laughter caught my attention. Edur and two men walked through the archway, drawing the eyes of everyone in the room.

But my gaze went straight to North. The two-year-old

dragged an entire cookie platter away, with no intention of giving it back. I chased after him.

The wind cooled my flushed skin as I stood on the terrace and rested my hands on the iron railing, my heartbeat still racing from my wild dash after North.

The Frosted Peaks of the Hush Sphere were captivating. Pine trees, dressed in snow, crowded a frozen lake. The reflection of the stars and the moon in the water made it seem as if the lake itself held them.

The stillness of the moment made my thoughts drift back to the conversation I'd heard just before slipping outside.

I shouldn't be bitter, but I couldn't help it. An elderly couple joyfully announced that they had received news from the Retired Luxari: their son had moved on to the Unknown.

Knowing a family member had moved on to the next stage of life after death was the closure every family needed. Why hadn't I received word of my brother's ascension yet?

Jealousy bubbled inside me. All I wanted was to know if Milo had moved on to the Unknown. The silence from the Retired Luxari gnawed at my nerves.

Souls last only three years after death. Without the ceremony, they dissolve into nothing. Milo had been gone for two years—I only had one more year left to hear from the Retired Luxari before his soul turned to dust.

The brisk air sent a chill through me. My fingers stiffened from the cold. I wiggled my toes, attempting to rouse them from their numbness.

A strange prickling sensation swept across the top of my right hand. It seemed as if someone was scraping a fingernail across the surface. I frowned and glanced down.

Gold, shimmering dust floated lazily above my skin, almost like pollen. A prickle of fear skittered down my back.

No. No. No.

This couldn't be real.

My heart slammed against my ribs as I stumbled, raising a trembling hand beneath the pale moonlight.

A golden swirl bloomed on the top of my hand, faintly glowing.

Panic surged through me. No, this had to be a mistake. I wasn't an Ember. I was a Dim. Dims rarely competed in the Sphere Quests.

The air vibrated with magic, causing the hairs on the back of my neck to rise. A tiny, faint spark—no bigger than a thumbnail—appeared between two pine trees, hovering in the air. It pulsed, growing into the shape of an orb the size of my clenched fist. The transparent sphere filled with water, mimicking the sea in a deep shade of cobalt blue.

Without warning, it burst, sending raindrops of sparkling blue particles falling in slow motion around me. An enchanting, sharp, feminine voice filled the space, as clear as if she stood before me.

"This is Queen Catalina Cove, Luxari of the Hush Sphere and appointed Chancellor of Aren."

A brief pause. My breath hitched in my throat.

"Colette Darroway, congratulations on your summoning to the Sphere Quests by the Dazzling Aridan of Aren. You will report to the palace of the Hush Sphere tomorrow at noon, where we will review and outline the schedule and regulations of the Sphere Quests. Transportation will be provided at dawn."

The roar of the ocean filled the air. The blue sparkles poured down, quickening to normal time, glimmering underneath the stars. I stood frozen, staring at the shimmering dust that frosted the ground, each mote a mocking reminder of what had just happened.

Me? A Dim. Summoned to the Sphere Quests?

Icy horror numbed me from the inside out, as if a blizzard stormed through my veins. Bitter anger coated my tongue. Aridan's cruelty—summoning a Dim to compete against Embers—churned in my mind.

A soft click echoed behind me. The door to the terrace creaked open. Panic jolted through me.

I frantically pulled at the hem of my dress, yanking the light fabric over my hand to hide the new, glowing mark. Dragging the heel of my shoe across the marble floor, I tried to kick the shimmering blue dust under the railing.

I stood quickly, forcing a calm expression as if I hadn't just been summoned.

"Mind if I join you?" a husky voice asked.

I turned around. One of the men who had walked into the ballroom with Edur grinned at me.

23

His flaxen, shoulder-length hair glistened under the moon-light. The light color of his hair was a stark contrast to his deep tan.

"I don't see why not," I mumbled, annoyed and a little out of breath.

He braced his forearms on the railing, his muscles straining against his white tunic. His sleeves were rolled up slightly, exposing a sun marking on the inside of his wrist. He turned his face toward me. It was a work of art, as if Aridan himself had sculpted it.

His emerald eyes met mine. "What's a beautiful woman like you doing out in the cold while there's a ball going on?"

"I just needed some fresh air," I said, hoping he'd take the hint and leave.

I cursed Aridan for summoning me at the worst possible moment.

We stood in silence.

"So," he said, breaking it, "where are you from?"

"The Bleak Sphere."

I didn't ask him in return, hoping that he would get the hint to leave me alone.

Instead, he stepped closer. "Do you plan to attend the Sphere Quests?"

I blinked, startled by the question. A surge of panic flashed through me. *Could he know?* There was no way. He couldn't possibly know I had been summoned. Even so, I glanced down, instinctively checking to ensure that my dress covered my new marking—thankfully, it did.

Play it cool.

"Me?" I scoffed, forcing a careless grin. "No way. I'm from

the Bleak Sphere, so I have traveled little." I tilted my head, keeping my voice light. "Will you attend the Quests?"

"What kind of question is that? Of course I will—every single one."

"You'd attend all four Quests?" I stared at him in astonishment.

"Yes, indeed. Why do you appear so taken aback?"

"Well, first..." I started counting off fingers as I tried to make my point. "It's time-consuming and excessive. Plus, it seems like an awful lot of traveling."

"Excessive?" He blinked at me, then shook his head. "Surely you're at least a little curious about what lies beyond your own Sphere. You haven't truly lived until you've swum in the Cobalt Sea or let the red sands of the Scorch Sphere run through your fingers."

"You left out the Still Sphere and the Daze Sphere," I added, a little peeved that I lacked the money and magic to visit other Spheres. But I wasn't about to reveal that to a stranger.

"If you enjoy mystic woods, Aeraliths, and lush foliage, you'd surely adore the Still and Daze Spheres. As for me, I favor the heat and the ocean."

He didn't have to tell me he preferred the heat; his golden tan skin said enough.

A spark of excitement flickered at the thought of seeing more of Aren.

"Plus, it's great fun," he continued, pressing his point. "Watching the finest Embers compete for a place on the Luxari Council is pure entertainment."

"I don't get why people care so much about being on the Luxari Council."

His jaw dropped as he straightened, angling his body closer to me. "You must be joking."

He smelled of citrus—fresh and tangy.

"I just don't see why you'd want to live forever," I said.

He slung an arm over my shoulder as he looked out into the distance. "Imagine living for eternity—never aging, always beautiful."

The heat of his body pressed against me.

He raised his hand as if painting a picture. "Power, prestige... and secrets no one else knows. The Ceremony of Immortality. The sealed archives beneath Soulari Hall. And the *Ari Report*—the true list of souls who have moved on to the Unknown. These are all mysteries you uncover when you accept the offer to join a Luxari council."

My body stiffened in shock at his words.

"What did you just say?" I stepped back, keeping my eyes on him.

He smirked. "Which part, exactly?"

"The *Ari Report*. There are records of people who have moved on to the Unknown?"

"Of course there are. Only the Luxari have access to it, but every Luxari from each Sphere has a copy of the *Ari Report* in their private libraries."

A surge of emotion coursed through me.

"Kaz," a voice purred.

A woman stood on the terrace, one hand resting confidently on her hip while she examined her nails. A form-fitting gown hugged her pear-shaped body, and long, rich auburn hair cascaded in waves past her shoulders.

"If you're here, it can't be good," Kaz muttered, then sauntered off to greet the woman.

My heart pounded violently against my chest with this new information.

Then, an idea struck me like a blow to the head: if I participated in the Sphere Quests, I could gain access to the palaces of the Luxari. More importantly, I could access their private libraries, where the *Ari Report* was kept.

A wave of excitement spread through my veins as a plan formed. Being summoned to the Sphere Quests could benefit me. If Milo's name was on the *Ari Report*, I would finally get the closure I needed. But if his name wasn't on that list...

No, I couldn't think that way. His name had to be on the report. Every fiber of my being hummed with the conviction that Milo was an Ari Soul.

CHAPTER
THREE

I climbed the grand staircase, exhaustion weighing me down as I trudged down the darkened hall. But I needed to be ready for what tomorrow would bring, tired or not. And that meant research.

With a quiet sigh, I walked to the end of the hall and climbed the spiral staircase leading to the library. Bookcases covered the walls in the oval room, reaching up to the vaulted ceilings. Only one wall lacked books, instead, a fireplace stood along it with two high-backed, maroon chairs facing it.

I made my way to the ladder and rolled it over to the History section. I scanned a few titles until I found what I was looking for: *The Sphere Quests: Luxari Council & Immortality*. Of course, the book I needed was perched on the top shelf—where else would it be? With a soft grunt, I lifted the train of my dress and began to climb the ladder. The book was just out of reach.

I adjusted my stance, grasping both the rung of the ladder and the edge of my train with my right hand. Stretching, I pinched the hardcover between my fingers, but as I tugged, the ladder wobbled beneath me. My balance faltered, and I fell.

Strong arms caught me just before I hit the ground. The book landed gently in my lap as the arms slowly eased me back to my feet.

"Do you typically climb ladders in long gowns?" a deep voice asked.

I turned around. Standing before me was the most mesmerizing man I'd ever seen. I clutched the book to my chest.

"Do you typically wait for damsels in distress so you can swoop in and be the hero?" I shot back.

Humor flickered in his eyes. "I mean, I wouldn't call myself a hero, but thank you." He bowed, a curl falling over his forehead as he straightened. His lips parted in a dazzling smile, revealing straight, white teeth. His hair was the color of rich coffee, short on the sides with wavy curls on top.

"Now, I'm surprised by your book choice," he teased. "I would've pegged you for romance novels."

"Oh, really? Is that because I'm a damsel, risking my life for a romance novel?" I replied, my tone dripping with sarcasm.

"I would say it depends on the novel—some may be worth risking your life for," he said, chuckling. "What are you doing up here?"

"Just wanted to do some light reading before I turned in for the evening," I replied.

He smiled, a dimple emerging on his right cheek. "Would you like to join me?" He gestured toward the fireplace.

I nodded before my mind could react.

I walked forward and sank into one of the chairs, grateful to finally be off my feet. A book lay open on the table between us, as if my fall had interrupted his reading. A steaming mug sat beside it, and I inhaled the sweet, delicious scent.

"Would you like some?" he offered.

"Yes, thank you." Surprised at my automatic response, I realized that I had barely eaten since yesterday. With everything that had happened, food had fallen to the bottom of my priorities.

I watched him walk to the table. He was tall, muscular, and his skin glowed under the light. Magic seemed to zip through the air with each step he took. He returned with the mug and set it between us. I picked it up. The foam had formed into the shape of a pine tree.

He grabbed the book he'd been reading before I interrupted. The cover read *Aren Folktales*.

"Your fall, actually, was perfect timing for what I was reading," he said, a smirk tugging at his lips. Clearing his throat, he began to read aloud:

> *There once was a damsel in distress*
> *Who found herself in a mess.*
> *She struggled with fear*
> *As the night brought near*
> *A victor to wrangle her foe.*
>
> *There once was a damsel in distress*
> *Who suffered through tears and woes.*
> *He swept her away*
> *As she prayed through the day,*
> *Thanking her God for a man.*

"What do you find amusing?" I asked, curious.

"The story," he replied, his eyes still glinting with delight.

"You've never heard of 'The Damsel in Distress'?" I raised an eyebrow.

"Of course, I have. It's just... a little different where I come from," he said.

"And where might that be?"

"Far from here," he answered.

Well, that was vague. Clearly, I wasn't going to get more out of him on that topic. I took a sip of my drink. "So, what brings you to the library while there's a party downstairs?"

He sank into his chair, leaning forward, his forearms resting on his legs as his gaze fixed on the fire. The flickering flames danced across his sharp jawline and sun-kissed skin.

"I find crowds overwhelming at times," he said quietly, his voice a low rumble, his gaze still fixed on the fire.

I took another sip, eyes still on him.

"Do you like it?" he asked, tilting his head toward me.

"Are you kidding?" I couldn't help but laugh. "This is the best drink I've ever had."

"I figured you would, considering your nickname is Coco," he said casually.

The fact that he knew my name caught me off guard. I stiffened, setting my mug down between us.

"How do you know my name?" I asked, narrowing my eyes.

He chuckled, his grin widening. "Stop staring at me as though I'm some creature spawned by the Void."

"You didn't answer my question."

"Edur," he said with a smile.

Why was Edur speaking to this man about me? I had to be one of the least interesting Dims in Aren.

His eyes, gray as marble, met mine with intensity.

I cleared my throat. "Speaking of names, I don't know yours."

"It's irrelevant," he said, looking away from me toward the fire.

"Excuse me?" I couldn't keep the surprise out of my voice.

"I doubt our paths will cross again after tonight. Names are of no consequence." He shrugged.

We sat in silence for a few moments as the firelight danced across his face. I sipped at the drink, trying to find a new topic of conversation.

"Have you heard about the Sphere Quests? No one's been summoned yet," I said.

He scratched the inside of his wrist. My gaze flicked there for a second, curious about the markings, but the angle of my chair made it hard to see.

"I've heard," he murmured.

"I haven't even seen a member of the Luxari Council in real life. Have you?"

His gaze met mine.

"To answer your first question, yes, it's strange. Summonings usually happen at the beginning of Spice Season. We're well into the season, and no one's been called yet." He paused. "And yes, I know a member who serves on the Luxari Council for the Daze Sphere. Her name is Nikolette. She was summoned at 18."

"So, how did she react to her summoning? Did she choose immortality? She must've passed all the challenges, or she wouldn't be part of the Luxari Council." The questions spilled out before I could stop them. Now that the Quests were part of my future, I couldn't silence my curiosity.

"I'm telling you this because Nikolette's an open book," he continued. "If she were here right now, she'd answer all those questions for you, probably in much more detail." He chuckled to himself. "Nikolette's a very powerful Swayer—one of the best I've ever encountered. She was thrilled when she was summoned, though I wasn't surprised."

He leaned back, watching me closely. "She passed the challenges with ease and joined the Luxari Council for the Daze Sphere. She chose immortality."

"Do most of the Luxari Council choose immortality?" I asked.

"It's a personal choice," he shrugged. "After you accept the Oath of the Luxari Council, you have the option of immortality at the age of 28."

"Gusty, let's go!" A voice yelled from below.

He stood. "I enjoyed speaking with you," the man said, his tone respectful. "Goodnight, damsel."

Before I could think of a clever retort, he was gone.

ARI SOULS

AREN FOLKTALES

When Aridan created Aren,
He wanted magic for the land.
"Magic must be earned," he said,
"Or else the Spheres will bend."
An Ari Soul
Holds the way
For fates to carry on.
A soul that's pure,
Mature and sure,
Will bring the light of dawn.
The souls of those whose hearts are full
Will miss the kiss of death.
Half the soul will roam the globe,
While the rest will greet the end.

CHAPTER
FOUR

I paced back and forth in the guest room, wearing my thick wool socks. I couldn't sleep.

My eyes drifted down to the swirl etched into my skin. Everything was about to change, and that scared me. Thick fear coursed through my veins, like the dark globs of darkness oozing from the Soul Snatcher's mouth. I was terrified to participate, but what choice did I have? Refusing meant certain social ruin. Joining the Quests would make me an easy target to mock—the Dim girl from the Bleak Sphere—but also an easy Questling to eliminate quickly from the competition. Yet, having access to the *Ari Report* was my only chance to find some kind of answer.

I closed my eyes, and a vivid image of Milo filled my mind —my brother, my best friend, the strongest and most fearless person I had ever known. A hot ache grew in my throat. I missed him more than anyone could comprehend—more than the cool relief of water on a scorching day, more than food after days of hunger, more than the infectious laughter that shook my entire body, more than the warmth of the sun, more than the comforting embrace of safety and love. I would give up everything—my life—just for ten more minutes with him.

Of all my cherished memories together, one stood out above the rest.

The small wooden home was a blazing, roaring fire of death. Black smoke churned through the air, turning the bright blue day into a dismal night.

"Is anyone else in there?" Milo shouted, dropping his bag without hesitation. He sprinted toward a woman clutching her baby, wailing, unable to speak. Her wide-eyed fear told him everything. He didn't pause. He bolted inside. I screamed his name, but I could only hear the roar of the fire in response. The unbearable heat slicked my skin with sweat, while icy dread crept over my insides.

The crackling fire, the billowing smoke, and the ashy taste on my tongue were the only things I could focus on while he was gone. Then, glass shattered, and a dark figure came hurtling out of the window—Milo.

I lunged toward him, my heart hammering against my chest, and dropped to my knees beside him. Milo lay curled on the dirt, covered in blackness, as if he'd stepped into a pool of soot. My breath caught as he slowly opened his arms, revealing a small boy, no more than two, crying but alive.

Milo had always been courageous. Now, it was my turn.

A surge of hope and fiery determination swelled inside me like a wave. I would give the Quests my all, and nothing—not a Soul Snatcher, not a Lerain, not some globe-smashing idiot—would stand in the way of me finding the *Ari Report*.

At dawn, a sleigh waited for me in front of Ava and Edur's mansion, seeming to know exactly where to pick me up—just like the message had magically found me. I hadn't even said goodbye. Instead, I simply left a note that explained everything. I could barely process being summoned, and I didn't want to burden anyone else with it. It was happening, whether I was ready or not.

A Hush Sphere guard, cloaked in ivory, helped me into the sled and said, "Queen Catalina would like to remind all Questlings that any family or friends wishing to attend the Sphere Quests must arrange their own lodging and transportation."

I nodded. I didn't have anyone to bring. Even if I had invited Edur and Ava, I knew Edur had several galas with high-ranking Charmers he wouldn't miss, and Ava would've felt responsible for staying home with Holly and North.

He then climbed into the driver's seat and took the reins. A fur blanket lay on the seat, so I wrapped it around myself to shield my body against the frigid air. We glided across the snow, moving westward into the Hush Sphere.

I was grateful for the time alone. It gave me precious time to try organizing my thoughts as a swirl of emotions filled me.

First, there was the anticipation for the Sphere Quests, but more pressing was the need to come up with a plan to infiltrate the Luxari private libraries without detection.

I was headed to participate in the Sphere Quests, the most highly anticipated event in all of Aren, in which I was lacking the one quality they showed off most in the Quests—magic. My cheeks stung from the brisk breeze, and I blew into my numb fingers as we passed lines of pine trees and brick-and-stone homes.

An hour or two passed; it was hard to keep track when everything in sight was a blinding white canvas. But in the distance, patches of green and brown began to appear through the melting snow. The Frosted Peaks were enchanted to remain in Frigid Season permanently, but the charm wore off the further you moved out. My legs started to sweat beneath the warmth of the fur, and I pushed the blanket aside.

A long, pearl-colored carriage pulled by cream-colored horses rolled into view, its windows fogged from the breath and bodies inside. A small group of guards stood at attention in blue and ivory long-sleeve uniforms, each adorned with the Hush Sphere's bright blue wave stitched onto their chests.

My sleigh came to a halt. As the carriage door swung open, I stepped forward, straightening my dress before climbing in beside the others already seated—some staring out the windows, others whispering nervously. It was safe to assume, by the golden swirls etched into their hands, that they'd been summoned too.

We rode for an hour. I pressed my forehead against the pristine window, the throbbing pain from my nerves slicing across my forehead. It wouldn't subside. Anxiety kept me from holding still; I was closer than ever to finding out if Milo was at peace. The thought of him not being in the Unknown fractured my heart. It was unfair enough that death had claimed him so young, but the possibility that his soul wasn't accounted for filled me with unease. The *Ari Report* was the only thing that could give me resolution. I thumped my head lightly against the glass, hoping it would knock some ideas into me about how I would compete in the Sphere Quests and break into the Luxari's libraries.

The temperature rose and I fanned my face with my hand, trying to ignore the stuffiness of the carriage. Palm trees emerged from the ground, and the sun broke through the clouds as we headed into the village.

This would most likely be my only chance to travel to all the Spheres in Aren, so I wanted to make sure I took in every detail. Off-white granite homes with balconies and verandas lined the streets, adorned with colorful boxes of flowers—some I recognized from books, like dewbells and tideblossoms. But seeing them in person was different—almost too bright for my senses. The sweet floral scent of brineberry shrubs drifted through the warm, humid air, heavier than I could have imagined.

The farther we rode into town, the more pale Arenwood stalls lined the streets, their thin, jointed beams curving gracefully overhead as they sold rows upon rows of fruits bursting with vibrant color. My mouth watered as I scanned the assortment of sunberries, silka pods, star plums, and sparkling juices in crystal cups, sealed with Arenwood corks. I wondered if they tasted as incredible as they looked.

A parchment, painted in soft pastel shades, read: "This

Frigid Season, join the Frost Quests—sculpted ice figurines await."

I let out a harsh laugh, earning a few glares from the people around me. But it sounded so dignified—especially coming from the Bleak Sphere, where the only Quests involved seeing how many grogs you could keep down before throwing up or passing out.

Children, neatly dressed in sundresses and tunics, entered a Hall of Knowledge made of light gray slate. Growing up, I had always dreamed of going to school, which was something only wealthy families could afford in the Bleak Sphere. Milo had taught himself to read by sitting beneath our local Hall of Knowledge's window, and then he'd taught me. That's when my love for books had begun.

The ride grew smoother as the wheels moved from dirt to paved roads. White-painted wooden shops with wide glass windows displayed books, fine silks, and elegant clothing. The sun radiated off seashells woven into exquisite jewelry.

I couldn't help but smile as a memory surfaced in my mind.

"Coco, how I wish you could have been there. The Hush Sphere is just beautiful." Milo's blue eyes danced with excitement. He tucked his honey-blonde hair behind his ears.

"I brought you something," he said, a grin already growing on his lips.

I couldn't believe it. With the money he had just earned from joining the Hush Sphere's army, he'd bought me something. "Milo, you shouldn't be spending money on me," I protested. "You should be saving it so you can get out of this place."

He gripped my hand. "So we can get out of this place," he

corrected. *"But that doesn't matter. I promise I didn't spend much. Now, hold out your hand."*

The anticipation sent a rush of giddiness through me, like a cold shower on a hot Spice Day.

"There," he said. I peeked into my palm, gasping.

A small ring, crafted entirely from delicate seashells, rested there. Each shell was in shades of ivory and soft pink.

"It's beautiful, Milo," I whispered, my heart swelling with emotion.

He smiled widely. "I'm glad you like it."

I stared down at the ring he gave me, twisting it around my finger as a far less pleasant memory surfaced.

"Calm yourself, girl. You're an embarrassment," Father barked.

Milo had spent the last year on duty, stationed near the Depths of Delusion, trying to contain the rise of Soul Snatcher attacks.

I looked down at the dark brown leather sheath that held a small knife made of pure silver. The handle was woven into vines, ending in an onyx stone. I had spent the past year taking every shift I could at the Dreary Den to afford the knife I'd once seen Milo gaze at longingly through a shop window in town.

In the distance, dust began to rise, and a jolt of happiness shot through me. I flung open the wooden door. "Colette, you—" I didn't hear the rest of what my father said as I sprinted toward the horse coming up the dusty path. But my steps faltered when I saw the figure atop the horse—it wasn't Milo.

Dread coated every part of me as I shook my head. No. If a guard was coming, that meant... Milo was—

The carriage stopped, abruptly pulling me out of the memory.

Low voices murmured around me as I pressed my face to the window, where a small group of soldiers stood. I strained to catch a glimpse of what lay beyond, only to be met with the back of a guard's head. I reached for the door handle, but before my fingers could grasp it, the guard turned, his bright lavender eyes catching mine. He swiftly opened the door and offered his hand, but I ignored it, stepping down and inhaling the sea air. I gaped at what stood before me: the Hush Sphere's Palace.

A fountain, larger than the Dreary Den and carved from polished limestone, stood in front of the palace. Dolphins, sea turtles, whales, and many other sea creatures were carved into the smooth stone. At its center, Aridan stood within a gigantic conch shell from which pure, silk-blue water erupted, cascading into a rounded pool below. It was filled with turquoise, coral red, and green fish, while starfish clung to the glossy stone.

A smile spread across my face. The Hush Sphere was a far cry from the Bleak Sphere. I felt as though I had just walked into a Sphere of pure paradise. But beneath the awe, something twisted in my chest. My brother had died serving a Sphere that would never offer us this kind of beauty or peace. Places like this were never meant for people like us.

I slowly walked around the fountain, my gaze drawn to the grandeur of the Hush Sphere Palace before me. Towering marble and moonstone pillars rose every ten feet, and hundreds of oval, glassless windows covered the palace walls. The sun was so bright that I squinted. The hem of my borrowed periwinkle sheath gown brushed the sleek stone walkway.

The Cobalt Sea's crystal-clear waters lay to the right of the palace, sparkling under the sun. Palm trees dotted the perimeter, swaying gently in the breeze. There were no doors at the entrance—just wide, open arches lined with guards, whose uniforms were the same as those of the guards from earlier: a wave stitched onto the front of their tunics, but with short sleeves replacing the long ones.

I suddenly felt my confidence slipping away like the tide rushing back to the sea. Everything was happening too quickly. I had gone from being a nobody Dim barmaid to being a Questling in one of the most significant events in Aren.

Be brave like Milo, a voice whispered.

A slight nod from a guard greeted me, and he motioned for me to follow. I stepped onto the crystalline stone flooring, passing large pillars that stood between the guards. Turquoise chandeliers made from sea glass hung from translucent beams, and luxurious stone fountains decorated the halls in place of paintings. The sound of gurgling water, like a small creek, was comforting.

The guard led me to a room bare of furniture. I walked toward the arched windows that overlooked the Cobalt Sea.

The tranquil blue water rushed gently against the sandy shore. It was exactly how I had imagined it—only louder, brighter, and more potent than I could have ever expected. Far more beautiful than the muddy ponds scattered across the Bleak Sphere. I took a deep breath, letting the ocean mist spray against my face, carrying the scent of salt and seaweed.

The mist was cool against my skin, refreshing and grounding me. *I can do this.*

For a moment, I allowed myself to soak it all in—the vastness of the sea, the sound of the crashing waves. But then, the nagging thought of the library pulled me back.

I heard a gasp and turned. Will stood in the middle of the room, his wide eyes locked on me. A million thoughts collided in my mind, and a piercing splash of shock ripped through me.

CHAPTER

FIVE

Will was here? How was this even possible?

"Coco!" He ran to me, pulling me into a tight hug. He squeezed so hard I could hardly breathe.

I patted his back, my arms aching as I held onto him. After a moment, he released me, his hands lingering on my shoulders. Even though I'd seen him just yesterday, it felt as though a year had passed. So much had changed in such a short time.

I took his right hand in mine, both of us now marked by the same golden swirls etched into the tops of our hands.

The shock made the words wedge in my throat. This couldn't be happening. Only a handful of Embers from all of Aren were summoned, and not just any Embers—the most powerful. Most Embers had only one ability, but those summoned, like Will, often possessed multiple.

Why—*in Aridan's name*—would I be summoned?

Will brushed his thumb over the golden swirl now branded

into my skin. I hadn't noticed a marking on his skin last night. Did it happen after he had dropped me off?

"Usually, only Embers are summoned. What are the chances of both of us getting chosen?" His voice mixed awe and disbelief as he shook his head, as if trying to wrap his mind around it.

I didn't have an answer. For a moment, I felt like someone would step out from the shadows and laugh, revealing this whole thing as a joke.

I shoved the shock down into the pit of my stomach, forcing myself to speak. "Well, I'm not surprised you were summoned. You can shift into more animals than any other Shifter I've ever met, and Sphere Jump, too."

"I don't know about that," he replied humbly.

He looked up, and a flame of concern sparked in his eyes as his demeanor instantly shifted.

"You shouldn't have to participate." His voice was steady, but there was an edge of protectiveness in it.

The thought that he cared about my well-being made my chest tighten.

"I don't have a choice, do I?" I forced a shrug. "It's this or disgrace."

He ran his hand across his face and his gaze met mine, fear glimmering in his eyes.

He knew. Aridan made sure no one had a choice. Ruin—and the Ashen Death—awaited anyone who refused. We were both going to participate in the Sphere Quests no matter what.

Will's protectiveness, his fear, wafted off him like steam from a hot bath. But I needed to reassure him. I needed to say something, anything, to make this all feel less impossible.

"Don't be so glum. Everything's going to be fine," I said, forcing the words past the lump in my throat. I forced a soft smile.

Was that for him? Or was it just to convince myself?

"Thank you for getting me to Ava's house after the incident at the Dreary Den," I added.

"It was the least I could do," he replied, a trace of guilt crossing his features.

"You need to stop blaming yourself," I said, my voice firm.

"It was my fault."

"Milo's death was not your fault," I said, shaking my head. "The only blame goes to the Rogue Embers. I hate seeing you blame yourself for something that was out of your control."

We both fell silent for a moment. I needed to change the subject.

"Where did you go after dropping me off at the Frosted Peaks?" I asked.

"I went to get my family and Elizabeth out."

He looked as if he had accidentally let the word slip.

"Elizabeth?" I said, trying to keep the surprise out of my voice. "Who is she?" I couldn't believe he'd kept a girl a secret from me—he usually told me everything.

His lips twitched as if trying to find the right words.

"She went to school with me back in the Still Sphere. When my dad was offered a position to open a meat processing station in the Bleak Sphere, we kept in touch."

I'd forgotten that the only reason Will's family ended up in the Bleak Sphere was for work and more gold. No one would willingly move to the Bleak Sphere—boring and full of Dims—unless they had a strong reason, like Will's father did.

Will continued, "She came out to visit, and... well, things escalated faster than either of us expected."

"I'm happy for you, Will," I said. He deserved happiness more than most. He always put others first, and he had been an even better friend—and brother—to Milo.

"Thanks, Coco." Kindness filled his eyes.

His gaze drifted toward the arch. I dropped his hand as more than a dozen people entered the room.

They had to be the others who had been summoned. I scanned them quickly. Their presence screamed power. I felt a slight knot form in my stomach as all of us stood silently, sizing each other up.

My eyes swept over a petite woman. Her deep tan complemented her golden amber eyes. Thick, creamy blonde hair hung just past her shoulders.

I glanced at her wrist, noticing the sun—the marking for the Scorch Sphere. A lump formed in my throat as I looked down at the square marked on my wrist, a brand of shame. I quickly pressed my palms against my dress to hide it, but what was the point? They were going to find out soon enough that I was just a Dim.

An image of Ava appeared in my mind, her words ringing clear.

I looked in the mirror, wearing a gorgeous yellow gown Ava had picked out for one of Edur's galas, as she stood behind me and fussed with my hair.

"Only Embers will be here," I said, wringing my hands together. "I really don't think I should be attending."

Ava dropped her hands to her hips.

"Coco, you forget I'm just as much a Dim as you are, and I

married an Ember. I'm constantly surrounded by magic folk when I have none, but I don't let it get to me. I lift my chin and show them I'm confident, smart, and beautiful. I belong in this world. You need to do the same."

The memory faded as I lifted my chin with forced confidence—though I didn't feel it, I knew I had to pretend that I did.

A woman wearing a crown of shells glided into the room. Her hair, the color of sun-bleached sand, fell just below her shoulders in tousled curls, and her dress was covered with peach-colored sequins. She opened her arms wide.

"Welcome, cherished ones, to the Hush Sphere," she exclaimed.

A girl with a darker complexion, no older than 16, started clapping. I blinked, unsure of the protocol, but everyone else remained silent.

"That's not necessary," Queen Catalina replied, but her amused lips suggested she enjoyed it. "As Chancellor of Aren, it is my honor—as always—to host the opening of the Sphere Quests. Now, I don't want to waste time with pleasantries, so let's get right down to business."

She stood in the center of the room, surrounded by all of us in a circle, and my head buzzed like a swarm of bees. As she spoke, she moved slowly around us.

"As you know, Aridan has summoned you to participate in the Sphere Quests. To defy Aridan's summons is to invite the Ashen Death, a fate I am pleased to see that you have all wisely avoided by complying."

Queen Catalina's voice was like silk as she continued, "I commend you for accepting the summoning, and let this serve as a stark reminder of the price of defiance—of what it truly means to refuse Aridan."

She gave a tight smile.

A ripple of murmurs stirred the room as a striking woman entered, flanked by two guards. Her hair, a deep red like fine wine, tumbled over her shoulders. She walked with pride, chin lifted, gray eyes burning with hatred as they locked onto Queen Catalina's.

Her midnight blue gown flowed gracefully to the marble floor, the sleeves so long they brushed her fingertips.

Queen Catalina stepped forward. "May I?" she asked, raising a single brow.

The woman rolled her eyes before extending her arm.

Without laying a hand on her, Catalina swept her fingers through the air, charming the sleeve to curl back toward the woman's shoulder and reveal her bare arm.

It was a landscape of horror, from the shriveled tips of her fingers to the crook of her elbow. Her skin was rotting. The flesh had withered into gray-black sinew, twisted and decayed.

"The Ashen Death," Queen Catalina began, her voice calm and commanding, "is the price of defiance—the consequence of refusing a divine summoning."

The room fell into silence.

"It brands the skin, rots the flesh—slowly, irrevocably—until it consumes the entire body. It does not kill. It lingers, winding its decay through every limb as a relentless reminder. And it speaks to all of Aren: this soul stood in defiance of Aridan."

Her gaze sharpened.

"But the punishment is not merely of the flesh—it is of the

soul. Those who refuse a summoning shall never bear an Ari Soul. That path is closed to them." She fixed her gaze on the woman. "You may leave now."

The guards stepped forward, seizing her by the elbows and escorting her from the chamber.

My chest tightened. I felt like I couldn't breathe. Why did that woman defy Aridan? The consequence—never being able to move on to the Unknown—I couldn't fathom it.

"Now then," Queen Catalina said, her tone smooth as silk, "let us continue."

She clasped her hands together.

"What an honor—that Aridan deemed you worthy to compete, to be observed by the Luxari, and to be considered for a coveted spot on their private council, with the chance to be offered immortality. You will compete in a series of challenges to be offered a spot on one of the Luxari Councils for the Hush Sphere, the Daze Sphere, the Scorch Sphere, or the Still Sphere. Not just anyone can be summoned to the Sphere Quests— usually, only the most powerful Embers are called. Embers who not only possess one magical ability, but several. Amongst you, we have Charmers, Enticers, Swayers, and Shifters. But this year, we have a special contestant: a Dim."

A ripple of murmurs spread through the room.

Her eyes cut to me, sharp with curiosity, and everyone turned to look. I wanted to wave at everyone, saying, "Hi, guys. Yup, I'm a Dim. You can stop gawking now." But instead, I dropped my gaze to the floor. Will leaned in closer to me, his presence offering comfort.

Looking up, I made eye contact with a man with ash-blonde hair in a bun. He looked like he could be Edur's cousin.

They both had ice-blue eyes that seemed to pierce straight through you.

He met my gaze and nodded, as if to say it was okay to be a Dim. It was both surprising and oddly comforting.

"Now, for those of you unfamiliar with the Sphere Quests," she said, casually tossing a glance my way, "thirty of you have been summoned. Only ten will move on to the official Sphere Quests."

Shock tore through me. A buzz of excitement rippled through the crowd.

"Did you know this?" I whispered to Will.

He shook his head, eyes narrowed, jaw tight.

This was bad. I'd assumed we were all heading straight into the Quests—multiple chances to find the *Ari Report*, enough time to fail and recover. But now, only ten spots? Against Embers?

My chances had just plummeted.

My heart sank deep in my belly.

"To make the best use of our time and energy," she continued, "the other Luxari haven't yet appeared for the official opening. They will—once the ten competitors have been chosen."

"So," she said with a smile, gesturing toward the beach, "shall we begin?"

My feet suddenly felt heavy. The only reason I moved was because Will nudged me forward.

I didn't have time to plan. Or even think.

This wasn't how it was supposed to go.

No. No. No.

Milo's soul was at risk. I had one year before it vanished.

The only way to save him was by checking the *Ari Report*—and I'd never get near it unless I qualified for the Sphere Quests...

I swallowed my fear, even as my hands trembled. I had to pull myself together. There was no other choice.

We stepped onto the beach, the sun beating down and making me squint as the salty air filled my lungs. Grains of sand brushed against the hem of my dress. I glanced around.

Some women wore gowns, others wore breeches. Most of the men were already dressed to compete.

Too late to change.

"I can't compete in this," I muttered.

Will raised an eyebrow. "Then why'd you wear it?"

"I was trying to make a good impression," I hissed.

He gave me a half-smile. "Oh, you'll leave an impression, all right."

I elbowed him in the ribs. He chuckled and slung an arm around my shoulders.

"Dress or not, you're Colette Darroway. I've seen you win brawls in a gown. This is just another row—look at it that way."

"I wasn't picking a fight. Those girls—"

He hooked an arm around my neck and rubbed his knuckles against my head.

"Coco, you love to fight. Hence the argument we're having now."

I shoved him off, laughing—

And nearly ran into the people in front of us. We'd stopped.

I looked up.

Thousands of people sat and stood on Arenwood platforms dotted with dome huts, all floating just above the sea's surface.

Between them, it looked as if someone had carved out the ocean itself—an invisible barrier held the water back. The divide stretched all the way to a massive sea stack rising in the distance.

My hands trembled and sweat dripped down my spine, pooling at my lower back.

Queen Catalina ascended a few marble steps leading to the broad base of a fountain that spilled vibrant blue water. She turned, her eyes sweeping over us. Raising her palms skyward, she slowly lifted her arms.

Behind her, glowing orbs of various colors rose from the water. Inside each, chalk-like swirls danced. They hovered around her, glimmering softly.

She plucked a green sphere from the air. It fit perfectly in her palm, resembling a bubble filled with spinning paint.

"The task is simple," she announced. "There are ten Lumen Orbs—pure sunlight captured and condensed. They pulse with power and can be very temperamental."

Murmurs rippled through the contestants, but Queen Catalina continued with grace.

"Questlings who catch one and deliver it to the resting Lumina Pool at the top of the sea stack will earn entry into the Sphere Quests. Only ten will advance. The rest will go home."

A tremor ran through my fingers; anxiety twisted in my stomach like seaweed.

"Now, there are guidelines, regulations, and restrictions I expect you to follow. So, to the giggling group near the back—hush, if you please."

The air fell still. The only sounds were the waves lapping at the shore and the low murmurs from the floating Arenwood platforms.

I locked eyes with her, fear tightening my chest.

"There are ten shades of Lumen Orbs," she continued. "Blush, gold, azure, seafoam, violet—"

Each sphere she named pulsed and shot into the sky like a comet, disappearing into the ocean canyon.

"—amber, frost, platinum, crimson, and obsidian."

"That's it? We just have to return a silly orb to a pool?" The voice came from the petite blonde woman from earlier. Her slim fingers tapped impatiently on her waist, as if bored.

"Yes," Catalina replied unfazed. "Once you've caught an orb, you must climb the sea stack and place it in the Lumina Pool at its top. That will secure your place in the Sphere Quests. There is no time limit—only the first ten to retrieve a sphere and deliver it will advance. All magic is allowed."

I could feel raw energy pulsing through the crowd. Sparks crackled from a bulky man standing beside me, as if he couldn't contain his excitement. His sun-shaped marking seemed to burn with living flames, rippling across his skin.

"Killing another Questling," Queen Catalina tilted her head as she spoke, "will result in immediate expulsion and consequences governed by the Sphere they hail from."

Most of the players nodded, but a few Charmers and Enticers rolled their eyes. I made a mental note not to anger those ones. That kind of arrogance practically radiated off Embers.

Dims made up the smallest part of the population, Embers the majority. Among them, Charmers were the largest group, followed by Enticers, Shifters, and then Swayers. I could practically smell the hierarchy in the space.

My gaze shifted back to Queen Catalina. It was always the same—Dims were punished more harshly, held to impossible standards, while Embers got a pass. The Luxari ruled every Sphere —except the Bleak. That one fell under the Chancellor's jurisdiction, though Queen Catalina rarely intervened. More often than not, she let Embers "handle" Dims who stepped out of line.

"You will be observed... by creations of my own." She snapped her fingers, pulling me from my bitter thoughts.

In the distance, flickering emerald dots appeared—glowing flecks that swarmed through the air like bees. They zipped toward us.

Queen Catalina extended her thumb, and one landed delicately on it. "Hold out your hands," she commanded.

We all obeyed.

A single speck settled into my palm. At first, it looked like a dewdrop—but when I leaned closer, a wide grin spread across my face.

They were adorable little creatures, covered in soft, mossy fuzz. As it wandered across my skin, it left trails of sparkling moisture that lingered in the air.

Off in the distance, one chirped. Then another. Soon, the entire swarm was chirping in a chorus of rhythmic tones, communicating with each other.

Queen Catalina clicked her fingers once more. The swarm rose, flying to her and hovering just behind her.

"They are called Mosslings. They will be observing you and reporting back to me throughout the Quest," she said.

With that, the Mosslings streaked toward the canyon like an emerald cloud and vanished into its depths.

"Now, walk with me."

I hadn't realized how comforting the Mossling had been, but as they disappeared, my nerves tightened their grip. I clutched my stomach, trying to stop the nausea rising within me.

We approached the beach. The canyon's opening stretched wide, just enough for us to line up.

A trickle of fear formed in the back of my mind.

"Take your stance. Now, on deep."

My fingers twitched as I gripped the fabric of my gown, trying to steady myself. I bit my lip hard enough to taste blood.

"Breathe, Coco," Will whispered, leaning close.

I inhaled slowly, the sharp tang of sea spray filling my lungs. I tried to steady my reeling mind.

"Charm the calm."

A shimmering wall of water rose from the sand, forming a barrier between us and the canyon.

"Splash the wave."

Others crouched lower; the anticipation was nearly suffocating.

"And dive deep!"

The watery veil crashed down, drenching us in a cold wave. Salt stung my eyes and burned my lips. My first taste of the sea.

I wiped my sleeve across my face, blinking hard—only to realize the others were already inside the canyon.

My legs refused to move—but Milo didn't have time for my fear.

I ran forward, heart pounding, as I entered the seabed.

CHAPTER
SIX

It felt strange to walk across sand, seaweed, smooth pebbles, and rocky outcroppings—all completely uncovered by water. I was used to muddy ponds and flat prairie fields, not this sea-carved terrain.

In front of me, the water arched into dozens of glimmering tunnels, as if the ocean itself had parted to make a path. You could walk right through, untouched by the waves.

But which one should I take?

Goosebumps prickled my arms.

I glanced up at the spectators hanging over the Arenwood railings, glasses of champagne in hand, eager for a better view.

A streak of yellow light zipped past me, vanishing into one of the arches.

"All right," I murmured. "I guess I'll follow that one."

I wasn't used to the humidity—it licked at my neck and curled my hair at my temples.

Further down the arch, I spotted the orb slowing, drawing nearer.

It plunged into the watery barrier, hovering like a seahorse. Vibrant blue, green, and red fish darted around it.

In the distance, soft, rounded creatures bobbed gently— with velvety forms like baby seals. Their skin shimmered like rainbows, catching the light in waves of color.

Before I could think twice, my hand slipped into the water.

The Cobalt Sea was refreshingly cool, crisp but not too cold, and silky smooth to the touch.

The orb darted back, taunting me, spinning in tight circles.

Frustration gnawed at me.

I dove in. The ocean was thick, like swimming through jelly. I kicked hard, reaching for the orb again, but it zipped backward and retreated the way I'd come.

I stumbled out, soaked and gasping, and collapsed onto the sand. My dress clung to me, dripping. A strand of kelp was wrapped around my arm—I yanked it off in frustration.

"You think this is funny?" I snapped at the orb. I was yelling at a glowing ball of light. I had officially lost my mind.

"I think it's *very* funny," came a sly voice behind me, "watching a Dim entertain the idea that they can compete. It's like watching ice trying not to melt in the Scorch Sphere."

A feeling of dread washed over me. Clenching my fists, I turned slowly.

A tall man with golden red, tight curls stood with his hands on his hips. He wore leather, and his sun-darkened skin told me everything I needed to know: he was an Enticer.

No surprise that he'd mock Aridan's summoning. Enticers were known for their sacrilegious views—only paying tribute when they desperately wanted something. But refusing the Quests? That would mean the Ashen Death.

I shook my head at his arrogant remark.

The orb hovered between us now, suspended in the air.

A wicked smile tugged at his lips. Flames erupted from his palms.

I gritted my teeth, my heart slamming against my ribs. If he threw fire at me, I'd have to dive back into the jelly-thick sea.

He reared back and launched a bolt of molten energy straight at the orb.

"No!" I shouted.

It nicked the sphere. Dark smoke coiled into the air as the yellow light flickered, dimming. The orb drifted downward like a wounded Aurefly.

He scoffed. "Flames of Aridan, spare me. You're absolutely pitiful."

My jaw clenched. Anger roared in my chest.

There's no damn way in all of Aren I'd let him take the Lumen Orb.

He stepped closer, eyes narrowing. "What's the matter? Burn bright, or back off."

Think. Enticers are weak in water. They have limited air capacity. He wouldn't jump in—not unless he was a full-blown, globe-smashing idiot.

Milo's voice echoed in my head:

"The key is to mislead it. You want the Soul Snatcher to think you'll strike here—" He twisted and feinted.

"—but really, you dive here."

Then he head-faked and juked his body, proving the move in action.

I shifted right, pretending to lean on the watery veil.

"Enough of this," the Enticer growled, lunging.

I feinted. He slipped right past me, straight into the water.

I dove in after, shoving him deeper before I spun and swam out fast, my limbs slicing through the jelly sea.

I emerged gasping, hands on my knees, the sharp tang of salt burning my lungs. Water dripped down my temples.

When I looked up, I realized my mistake.

A short girl with a wild grin and wind-tossed brown hair had already snatched the yellow Lumen Orb—and was sprinting down the arched tunnel.

I broke into a run to keep pace.

A flicker of emerald light crossed my vision and landed gently on my hand—a Mossling.

"What are you up to?" I asked between quick breaths.

It chirped and perched on my shoulder just as the girl ahead halted. She summoned a gust of wind that lifted her into the air. She soared upward, carried by the breeze toward the sea stack.

I reached the edge of a massive circular basin and understood why she'd flown. My steps faltered.

The entire seabed was covered in slimy kelp and scuttling crabs. A foul stench of fish and sulfur filled my nostrils.

Eight archways ringed the basin's edge, each filled with a competitor. In the center, hovering in midair, floated the silver, crimson, and black orbs.

A Shifter sprinted forward, morphing into a hawk mid-run. Wings sliced the air as he launched toward one of the orbs—

But the kelp rose like serpents.

Slippery strands wrapped around him mid-flight and

yanked him down. He shifted back into human form with a gasp, limbs flailing, tangled in green. The kelp dragged him under as crabs crawled over his skin.

Will stood frozen in one of the arches, panic in his eyes. He raised his hands, trying to move the kelp—but nothing happened. Something was wrong.

Others turned away.

But I couldn't. *Milo wouldn't.*

Without thinking, I leapt into the basin.

Kelp surged around my ankles. I kept moving.

It wrenched me down hard. Pain shot through my entire body.

I fought back, tearing at the slimy vines, their texture slicing my fingers like splinters.

They continued to engulf me, creeping up to my knees.

With raw hands and burning lungs, I reached the Shifter. I ripped the kelp from him strand by strand, each pull sounding like a fish being torn apart.

The vines coiled up to my waist, tightening around me, stealing my breath.

I felt a prickly, damp sensation on my legs and glanced down. Crabs swarmed and clambered up my gown, their claws so rough I felt them even through the fabric. An alarm bell screamed in my mind, but before uneasy thoughts could fully cloud my brain, they scattered. Strong hands seized my waist, yanking me upward.

It was Will. He'd simply commanded the crabs to leave. Together, we battled the cursed vines, and with the half-conscious Shifter between us, we stumbled into an archway, my blood thrumming with adrenaline.

"Thank you," the Shifter croaked.

I looked up. The Lumen Orbs had vanished—except one. It shimmered faintly, drifting through the watery barrier like a sea turtle.

Will plunged in, his body shifting mid-dive into a sleek shark, cleaving cleanly through the sea.

That's when I noticed the emerald sparks fluttering around my shoulders.

I turned. The Mosslings trailed behind me with green light.

I didn't know why they were following me, but I didn't stop to ask, and I knew they couldn't answer.

The arch opened into a ravine swarming with competitors fighting each other and reaching for the spheres. Orbs zipped through the sky like fire-lit lightning bugs. The crowd above roared, cheering from Arenwood platforms that rimmed the canyon.

I watched a Charmer summon a wave that hurled him toward a purple orb. A grin split his face—until the sphere veered away at the last second.

Pure, unfiltered rage crossed his features. That's when a crimson orb shot toward him. He caught it, stunned.

It had moved toward his anger.

My gaze darted between the Questlings. The spheres weren't moving at random; they were reading us.

The crimson orb darted once more to someone boiling with fury.

They were attracted to emotions.

A silver sphere shimmered in the air, glowing like flecks of moonlight.

It sped toward me and I reached out, letting it fall into my palm. Its chrome specks seemed to wink—like a glimmer of wisdom, assuring me I was right.

If I wanted to keep it, I had to stay sharp.

I looked ahead. The sea stack towered in the distance, but too many competitors stood between me and the finish. I could swim, but not that far and not fast enough.

I glanced up. The spectators clinked their champagne glasses and watched us like we were insects crawling through their garden.

They stood on Arenwood platforms stretched like planks across the water, all the way to the sea stack.

That was my path forward.

Gripping the orb, I dove sideways into the water, kicking hard toward the surface.

Then I heard it: a whispery voice, like wind chimes humming a lullaby.

The water above swirled together, taking the form of an Aurefly, sunlight glimmering off its delicate wings. It continued to sing as bubbles streamed softly from its mouth.

Coco, Coco, brave and bright,
Don't fall behind—turn and fight.

It dissolved back into the sea and vanished like it had never been.

I shook my head, chest tight, lungs burning. I didn't know what that was, but I had no time to wonder.

I broke through the surface, sunlight warming my face. I treaded water for a moment, caught my breath, then pulled myself toward the nearest platform.

With one arm over the edge, I gripped the Arenwood and hauled myself up—emerging between two silky, turquoise chairs occupied by Charmers. They glanced down, startled.

The platform creaked beneath my feet as I stood.

The Mosslings followed behind me like an emerald train on a gown.

I nodded to the Charmers, who looked at me as if I were as disgusting as a Soul Snatcher, then bolted—ducking between tables, chairs, and startled Embers.

Gasps rippled through the crowd.

"Can she do that?" someone shouted.

It was too late to ask for permission—not that I'd ever been good at it in the first place.

I didn't care. My eyes were locked on the sea stack.

Losing wasn't an option.

Milo needed me.

I couldn't let him down.

Attendants scattered as I sprinted past, yelling "Excuse me!" more times than I could count.

My shoulder clipped a tray, launching crabkin cakes and suntide skewers everywhere.

"I'm so sorry!" I dropped to the ground, grabbing the attendant's silver platter. We both reached for the same crabkin cake. His hand brushed mine, revealing a square mark on his wrist. He held my gaze with bright eyes.

"I've got this," he said gently. "You go win. Show these Embers what we're capable of."

My throat tightened. I gave a quick nod and sprinted toward the sea stack.

"Dim! Dim! Dim!" a chant rang out from one of the rear platforms. Their voices pushed me forward.

I ran harder.

Sweat burned my eyes. My vision blurred. My chest rose and fell in ragged gasps.

Hang on, Milo; I'm almost there.

I reached the base of the sea stack. Up close, it was beyond intimidating. I craned my neck to see the top, dizzy from the height.

Competitors were already scaling it. An eagle soared above, shifting into a human at the top.

I could climb, too.

And if I fell—well, it was just water... unless I hit a wooden platform on the way down. *Not the time for worst-case scenarios.* I shook off the thought, exhaling hard.

Where was I supposed to keep the orb? I couldn't hold it while climbing, and my gown was too tight to tuck it anywhere.

"I'm sorry about this," I whispered, then gently opened my mouth and held the sphere between my lips. It tasted like white wine and mint.

My fingers grasped the slippery, rough surface of the sea stack, and I made sure my feet were planted before I pulled myself up. There were crevices and dips in the rock, making it easier to climb. I moved slowly to make sure I didn't make any mistakes.

The higher I scaled, the slicker the stone became. Fear coiled in my gut. My arms started to shake, the pressure to move faster mounting. And the dress—Aridan help me, the dress. Heavy and clinging, it dragged me down like an anchor.

My left hand slipped. All my weight jolted to the right and

pain lanced through my wrist. I swung my legs and managed to grab a jagged rock, steadying myself.

My jaw ached from clenching the orb between my lips.

Sweat gathered on my brow and streaked down my neck. A flat ledge came into view. I hauled myself onto it and finally took the sphere from my mouth, rubbing my jaw.

"You're barely a spark."

I turned toward the voice.

It was *her*—the woman with creamy blonde hair and a perpetual snarl. She leaned casually against the rock, as if she'd been waiting for someone to hand her a victory.

Before I could react, her grin widened. With one graceful motion, she nudged me.

I gasped. Her hair flashed past me as she darted forward and—smiling sweetly—knocked the orb from my hand and gave me a hard shove.

I stumbled, arms windmilling for balance.

She lifted a hand under her chin and blew me a kiss. But instead of air, flames shot from her lips.

I leapt back to dodge the fire—and fell.

The air jumped from my lungs. My stomach dropped as the wind whooshed around me.

But I never hit the water.

The Mosslings caught me in a glowing net of green, their bodies like soft, wet petals, and gently pushed me back toward the rock.

They had saved me.

"Thank you," I whispered, voice shaking.

I climbed again, more slowly this time.

The orb was gone.

The taste of failure lingered, sharp and bitter in my throat.

But I kept going.

I scraped over the final ledge, hands raw, knees trembling. Blood smudged the rock beneath my palms. My breath came in shallow gasps.

I met the gaze of the Enticer with gold-red curls and that same wicked grin. A black Lumen Orb pulsed in his fist, its surface twitching as if trying to escape.

Black. Death. Grief.

He stood smiling at me. I smirked back, but my thoughts were nowhere near happy.

I thought of Milo's death—the sorrow and the grief I lived with every day.

The orb quivered violently in his palm. He clutched tighter —but it shot out.

And it flew into mine.

I dove forward and plunged the sphere into the pool. Its indigo blue, swirling surface swallowed it immediately.

The Enticer shoved his arms into the water, as if he could scoop out the orb, but it was already gone.

He roared in fury.

"You." Hatred dripped from his lips like drool.

I stood my ground, clenching my fist in case he wanted to see just how well I could punch.

But it didn't come to that. Teal mist spiraled up from the ground like smoke, curling around me in shimmering coils. The sensation was similar to Sphere Jumping, but this vapor sparkled like twinkling gemstones.

My feet braced in the sand and the ocean roared in the background—except as the mist disappeared, I realized it wasn't the ocean. It was the crowd. And they were cheering for me, a Dim.

CHAPTER
SEVEN

Attendants moved through the crowd, handing out towels. I sank onto a bench near the fountain, happiness blooming in my chest and filling every corner of me. *I'm coming, Milo.*

"Coco!" Will's voice rang out.

He rushed over, swept me up into his arms, and hugged me tight.

"I *knew* you could do it—though you do smell like a sick Lerain wrapped in kelp."

I flicked his neck. He laughed, set me down, and pinched my nose in return.

"Did you do it?" I asked.

He grinned. "Do you even have to ask?"

We dried off. He pulled a piece of seaweed from my hair, and I caught a glimpse of the others—the ones who hadn't made it. Their disappointment stung more than I expected. I looked away.

"Those who completed the task," Queen Catalina called, emerging from the crowd, "please follow me."

We trailed her into an arched, airy, open room.

"She cheated!" the blonde-haired menace shrieked, jabbing a sharp finger in my direction.

Queen Catalina didn't even slow. "How so?"

"*How so?* Your Mosslings helped her!"

"They did," Catalina said coolly, "which is... interesting. You see, Mosslings have a mind of their own. They're not easily persuaded."

The queen glanced over her shoulder. "And one might say *you* cheated—waiting at the top of the sea stack for someone else to bring you an orb."

I let out a short laugh. The woman's head snapped toward me and sparks literally flashed in her eyes as her jaw clenched tight.

"This way, please," Queen Catalina said smoothly. "Don't dawdle."

Queen Catalina stepped onto a raised platform while the ten of us who had completed the Quest gathered around her in a circle.

"Congratulations are in order." She smiled before continuing. "Competing in the Quests can earn you an offer to serve on one of the Luxari Councils—in the Hush, Still, Daze, or Scorch Sphere—and a chance to achieve immortality, a gift granted only to Luxari and their council members. Each of you will participate in four Quests over the next two weeks, and the first challenge will take place right here in the Hush Sphere."

A tall, muscular, blonde man whooped, raising his giant fist in the air. With that amount of muscle, he had to be from the

Scorch Sphere. By Aridan's breath, he looked as if he could crush any of us as if we were no more than bugs. With short hair and olive skin, he looked like a force of nature.

"The second challenge will take place in the Scorch Sphere, the third in the Daze Sphere, and the fourth in the Still Sphere. The Quests will unfold over several days. After each Quest, you'll have a day of travel to reach the next location. Once you've completed the third Quest, you'll get an extra day to rest and recover before traveling again for the final challenge. At the end of the challenges, if you've made an impression on the Luxari and if there's an opening, you may be offered a position on the Luxari Council by any of the four rulers."

"Let me remind you, spots on the Luxari Councils only open when there is a demand. Some members who choose not to become immortal eventually pass on naturally, freeing a place. Others who do become immortal might later move on to the Unknown, creating vacancies as well. Sometimes, the Luxari themselves decide to expand the councils for their own reasons. During the Quests, they're watching your magical abilities and skills closely. Winning a Quest doesn't guarantee a spot on the council, but it helps you stand out. Think of it as your chance to showcase your greatest strengths and abilities in each challenge." She cleared her throat. "As an added incentive, the top five to complete each Quest will receive a vial of Ari Dust to enhance their magical prowess."

The announcement sparked murmurs throughout the room, instantly capturing everyone's attention. Yet for me, it held little excitement—how could it, when it would do nothing for my Dim blood?

The scuff of boots against marble echoed through the hall. We all turned as two men entered through the archway.

It felt as if time had stopped. The air was sucked out of the room, and a ringing bell echoed in my ear.

Surprise hit me, and I wrung my hands together.

"I wasn't expecting you until this evening," Queen Catalina said, struggling to hide the irritation in her tone. "Questlings, the rulers of each Sphere will be joining us for the Sphere Quests—though, apparently, some of them think arriving early is the new trend."

Great. Just great. My gaze bounced between the first man and Kaz. Both wore loose tunics, breeches, and boots. Kaz wore light colors, while the other wore dark.

"These are King Kazimir of the Scorch Sphere and King Oak of the Daze Sphere," Queen Catalina said with a hint of annoyance.

Of course, both men I happened to speak with last night turned out to be the most powerful rulers in Aren. By Aridan's breath, why were they at the Snowfall Ball? My face burned with embarrassment as I tried to remember every word I'd said, hoping I hadn't sounded like a globe-smashing idiot.

Just then, I glanced down and let out a low groan. I smelled like a sick Lerain and looked like a half-decayed fish.

Kaz nodded as people bowed. I realized a second too late that I was the only one not bowing. It felt as if someone had struck a match against my cheek, setting my skin on fire. This was beyond embarrassing. Kaz's eyebrow arched, and a smile tugged at his lips. I quickly followed the others' bows with my own.

"Are you okay, Coco?" Will whispered, placing a hand on my elbow.

I need to focus.

"Yes. It just got hot in here," I replied, my voice a little shaky.

Wiping my sweaty palms on my damp dress, I took a deep breath.

"You will complete the second and fourth challenges with an alliance. The first and third will be individual challenges. All of you have been grouped into two alliances. The Globe Alliance consists of Amabel, Rodor, Aldo, Cecille, and Severin. The Ellipse Alliance consists of Will, Tada, Otto, Hugh, and Colette. Aldo will be the leader for the Globe Alliance, and Will the leader for the Ellipse Alliance."

My thoughts paraded around my head. What were the chances of meeting King Oak and King Kaz, and being summoned to the Sphere Quests, all in one night? It couldn't be a coincidence. It was as if Aridan himself had stepped in to rattle my life around for his own entertainment.

"Tonight, we will have a celebration for the summoning of the Sphere Quests. All of you are expected to be there and stay for the entirety of the party. King Oak, Queen Nerian, King Kazimir, and I will be attending. Some of their Luxari Council will also be attending."

My pulse leaped with determination. A ball would provide the perfect distraction for me to slip away.

"One last thing." Queen Catalina's tone sharpened. "It's rare for death to occur during the Sphere Quests, but there have been instances where it has. We would like to see all of you finish the Quests, but there is a risk of death during the challenges, so please be advised."

A chill ran through me. I couldn't help but think the comment was directed at me.

"Please get acquainted with one another," Queen Catalina finished.

She strolled out of the room with Kaz and Oak, leaving the rest of us to "bond."

"Well, it seems as if introductions are necessary," said a beefy man, stepping forward. "My name is Aldo. I'm 24, from the Still Sphere, and I'm a Shifter."

Thanks to Will, I knew a lot about Shifters. They could shift into any animal at any time, control Earth elements, and even travel between Spheres. My mind raced as I tried to think of how I could contribute to my team.

Will took a step forward. "I'm Will. I'm from the Still Sphere. I'm a Shifter, 24."

His eyes locked on one of the Questlings—the one who had clapped earlier—and for a moment, it felt as if something passed between them. Then he stepped back, maintaining his usual cool demeanor.

"What was that?" I whispered.

Will gave a quick nod. "Nothing."

His tone made it clear—there was nothing more to say.

Aldo clapped his hands together. "Let's break out into our alliances so we can get to know each other."

The group split into two smaller circles.

I wasn't supposed to be here. Looking at the Embers and comparing their strengths to mine, I couldn't think of anything I had to offer besides endurance and book suggestions. I wanted to stand on my own, without relying on others. But more importantly, I had to find the *Ari Report*.

A tall, bulky man stepped forward and waved enthusiastically. "I'm Otto!" he exclaimed.

A grin involuntarily spread across my lips; his energy was infectious.

"I'm an Enticer from the Scorch Sphere," he continued.

Enticers were known for their beauty, and Otto's muscular frame only added to his appeal. He flexed a brawny, warm brown arm.

"I'm 18 and single," he added, winking at a girl with pink streaks in her chin-length hair. She scowled in response.

I tried to suppress a giggle, not just at him and his obvious flirting, but also at the frown from the girl.

"I need to win—because who wants this masterpiece," he gestured to his whole body, "to get old? Immortality, baby." He stepped back with a grin.

There it was again—the promise of living forever, of never aging. It seemed to tempt everyone but me.

Someone cleared their throat. "My name's Hugh. I'm 16, from the Daze Sphere. I'm a Swayer."

His dark brown hair was tousled, his eyes downcast, and the way he spoke made it clear he wasn't as confident as the others.

But anyone who could manipulate thoughts and control the wind was an asset—and my alliance needed every advantage it could get.

A girl with bright violet eyes stepped forward next. Her chin-length, ash-blonde hair streaked with pink complemented her fair skin tone.

"I'm Tada," she said. "I'm from the Hush Sphere. I'm 21—half-Charmer, half-Enticer."

Gratitude rushed through me. I'd been worried we wouldn't have a Charmer in our alliance, which would've been a serious disadvantage. They could heal, manipulate water, even move things with their minds.

Bloodline determined magic, not birthplace. Since both my parents were Dims, I was one, too. People like Tada—with two abilities—were rare. Some considered it a gift. Others called it a corruption of the bloodline.

Finally, it was my turn. I took a deep breath.

"I'm Colette, but my friends call me Coco."

I turned to Otto, who had the friendliest face among the group. "I'm 22, from the Bleak Sphere, and I'm a Dim," I said, trying to sound confident.

"That's so crazy you were summoned. But hey, if Aridan believes in you, I do too." Otto winked, then rubbed his hands together. "So... when are they going to feed us?"

The group laughed, but mine was forced. The last thing on my mind was hunger. My eyelids fluttered as I whispered a silent prayer to Aridan. *I hope I can at least pass one challenge.*

Standing just outside the ballroom, I glanced at my reflection in the floor-length mirror. Queen Catalina had chosen our clothes, and my dress didn't feel like me.

The aquamarine, one-shoulder, sequined ball gown definitely made my eyes stand out, but it was awkward to move in. My hair was pinned in a curly bun to the right side of my face.

Tada's reflection appeared beside mine.

"I hate this dress. I look like a rainbow," she spat.

A giggle escaped my lips. The empire-waist dress she wore did have every color of the rainbow.

"What are you laughing at? You look like a Lerain's tail," she snarked.

I couldn't stop laughing. Was it her remark about my dress, or the whole ridiculous situation?

"Before the next celebration, we should get ready together," Tada said, her violet eyes gleaming with amusement.

A rush of excitement tingled up my spine. Growing up, I'd only ever been surrounded by boys, never truly having a friend who was a girl. Maybe Tada could be my first.

She continued. "That way, we can warn each other about how ridiculous we look. Plus, I'm pretty sure I'm in the room next to you. Do you like yours? I feel like if I breathe too deeply, I'll stain all the white-themed everything."

My guest room was a landscape of snow—the sheets, the comforter, the furniture, and the bathroom all pristine and polished. The drastic change from living at the Dreary Den, to Ava's, to the Hush Sphere's palace was overwhelming.

"I feel the same way. I'm pretty sure just a glance from me will soil the rug," I joked, earning a laugh from Tada.

"I mean, I'm from the Hush Sphere, but I even feel out of

place here. So, let's just feel out of place together." She tucked pink hair behind her ear.

It was comforting to know I wasn't the only one summoned who felt this way. But curiosity got the better of me, and the question slipped out.

"What exactly can you do?"

"I can do charms, heal, control water..." She hesitated, then added, "and because my father's an Enticer, I'm somewhat resistant to heat."

She shrugged like it was nothing to have abilities from two bloodlines.

Her wrist caught my eye—a wave, the marking of the Hush Sphere, stamped into her skin.

"Why don't you have a sun marking, too?" I asked. "If you're half Enticer."

She shrugged again. "When someone is of mixed lineage, one side usually comes through stronger. My mother was a full Charmer—so were her parents. My father's folks had a mix of bloodlines, but the only thing that passed to me from his side was the Enticer magic. Still, the Charmer side runs stronger in my blood than the Enticer."

I envied her. I would kill for just one ability, especially now that I was participating in the Sphere Quests.

"But I mostly take after my mother," Tada continued, a smile curling at her lips. "My poor little brother is quite jealous. His only magic is little charms." She shrugged. "But I think he's the lucky one. I'm here, and he's home."

My brow arched in surprise. "You're not happy that you were summoned?"

"It's not that I'm unhappy—I just didn't have a choice. It

was either this or the Ashen Death. And after seeing that woman Queen Catalina showed us earlier, I'm glad I came. But I've never wanted immortality, or to serve on the Luxari Council."

I nodded, understanding more than I wanted to admit. "I feel the same way."

A delicate cough drifted from behind me. The woman from earlier appeared in the mirror. Her white silk dress barely covered her breasts, with two slits up to her hips and a gold chain resting low on her waist.

Beside her stood the hulking blonde man. His broad shoulders pulled his tunic so tight that it looked like it was about to tear.

"We didn't have a chance to introduce ourselves," the woman said, her gaze sweeping over me with a blatant lack of interest. "My name is Amabel." She gestured beside her. "This is Rodor."

Tada crossed her arms loosely across her chest, her eyes narrowed slightly as she turned to meet Amabel's gaze. "I'm Tada, and this is Coco."

A prickle of unease ran down my spine. Amabel had her condescending look mastered. She studied every inch of my face and body, her gaze lingering in a way that made my skin crawl.

She scoffed at me as she glanced toward Rodor, shaking her head as if to say, *pathetic, right?* A familiar heat rose in my chest. Clearly, she saw me as nothing more than a Dim.

"Is there something wrong?" I asked, stepping forward.

Her perfectly sculpted brow lifted. "Of course not. I was merely observing that our alliance barely has any competition.

No offense to you, Coco." Her gaze flickered over to Tada. "But being saddled with a Dim must be rather... unfortunate."

A muscle twitched in Tada's jaw.

"Really? Because I caught two orbs, and you had to steal one," I shot back, lifting my chin higher. Rodor, meanwhile, was stepping away from Amabel, trying to move into the ballroom.

Amabel's glare burned brightly, but quickly twisted into a smirk. "Yes, but I hardly had to lift a finger—I let you do all the grunt work. Besides, my skills alone are more than enough to win every Quest."

I tilted my head. "I can't decide which is your greater weakness: arrogance, or a distinct lack of social grace."

Her eyes blazed and her stare sharpened.

"Word of advice," I laced each word with venom as I stepped closer, "if you pull any shit like that again, you won't walk away unscathed. And if you want other Questlings to like you, don't cheat them out of victory. That leaves a bitter impression."

"Whatever." Amabel tossed her hair over her shoulder. She strutted forward, deliberately bumping me as she swept past me into the ballroom.

Tada let out a low whistle. "That right there is a pure, bona fide bitch. Let's thank Aridan she isn't in our alliance."

It felt as if my blood was boiling with anger. I couldn't believe Amabel was able to get on my nerves so quickly.

"Come on," Tada said, wrapping her arm through mine. "Let's get this over with."

CHAPTER
EIGHT

We walked under the wide, arched entryway. Bubbles descended from the ceiling and, like Edur's snow, disappeared before they hit the floor. The room was filled with hundreds of people eating, conversing, and laughing. It smelled of sweat and the ocean breeze.

I tried to ignore the stares and whispers that broke out the moment I entered the room. The attention was inevitable—I understood that. A Dim being summoned to the Sphere Quests was bound to cause a stir. But being gawked at, knowing most of them were probably mocking me? That was harder to ignore.

I needed to try my best not to let it bother me, so I focused on my surroundings instead.

To my left stood the main entrance to the ballroom. Straight ahead, more archways led outside to the palace's private beach.

Directly to our right stood two solid gold thrones on a raised dais. Dolphins, sea turtles, and other sea creatures were intricately carved into their gleaming surfaces. Queen Catalina sat perfectly straight in her seat, her wife beside her.

Tada mumbled under her breath, "They say she's a stickler for the rules. That the Sphere Quests, Soulari Hall—even Aridan himself—are her religion. She'll always put them first."

She shook her head slightly, as if to say, *Can you believe her?*

I wasn't surprised. Everything about Queen Catalina—her posture, her clipped tone, the precise way she smiled—radiated control. Even her elegance couldn't mask the truth: she needed power like most people need air.

I noticed a tall woman with dark brown skin standing near her. That had to be Queen Nerian. Her gold crown sparkled on top of her short hair. Queen Catalina's Luxari Council lined up against the wall, watching the crowd. They bore the mark of a Luxari Council—a dark swirl right behind their ear.

Could I ever be a part of the Luxari Council? The thought came and went so quickly that I almost wondered if I was teasing myself.

"That"—Tada pointed to the young girl with a darker complexion I had seen earlier—"is Cecille. She's a Charmer."

I watched her tight, coiled curls bounce as she spoke to the man who resembled Edur. She was the one who had shared that brief, curious exchange with Will.

Tada nodded toward the man with Cecille. "And that is Severin. He's also a Charmer."

"When did you have time to figure all of this out?" I asked.

She flashed a bright smile at me. "I'm very efficient when I want to be."

I chuckled. "Of course you are."

The celebration was inviting and magical, almost like an illusion. Coming from the Bleak Sphere to here was such a drastic shift that I almost felt like I was sleepwalking. I didn't mind observing, though. I loved taking in the ballgowns, the intricate details, and the variety of food. Was it excessive? Yes. Was pointing it out going to change anything? No. So, I might as well take it all in.

Tada immediately headed toward the refreshments. I followed.

Having Tada next to me all night was going to make my plan much harder. I needed to escape to the library to search for the *Ari Report* without anyone noticing.

As I scanned the room looking for Will, my eyes landed on Amabel. She stood next to the wall, her hand on a golden tan chest that I recognized—Kaz. Half of his flaxen blonde hair was pulled back into a bun, and a thin, obsidian crown sat on his head. He wore tight, light-colored leather pants tucked into boots and a loose tunic.

He leaned against the wall, clearly enjoying Amabel's presence.

Kaz's eyes flicked to mine, his gaze sweeping over me. A blush crept up my neck and I quickly looked away, startled by my own reaction.

Distracted, I turned, colliding with a powerful body.

"I'm so sorry!" I cried, stepping back and looking up.

Oak's gray eyes stared down at me, and the air around us seemed to electrify. His gaze was sharp and assessing, bordered by a serene sea-blue ring around his pupils, with gold flecks scattered across the gray. A slight shudder ran through me from the closeness of our bodies. I inhaled his scent—coconut and fresh rain.

He looked at me intently, then strode around me to the dance floor without saying a word. He met a woman with bronze skin and tight, curly hair. The two turned their backs and walked toward one of the arches, clearly not wanting anyone to overhear their conversation.

"Well, that was rude." Tada joined me, holding a plate full of sea creature-shaped pastries.

She took a big bite.

"Agreed. He at least had manners last night," I mumbled, my thoughts still lingering on the exchange with Oak.

Her head snapped in my direction so quickly that I thought I heard a crack in her neck. Her eyes lit with curiosity.

"You were with him last night? Can I have some context?" she asked, her full mouth spraying crumbs on my dress and the floor.

"Later. I need to get some air." I waved her off, eager to escape and find the library.

"Come on, Coco, don't leave. You're going to miss out on pastries and bubbles," she argued.

"Oh, pastries and bubbles? Now I'm definitely staying." I smirked as I turned and walked toward the exit.

"You're a sarcastic ass," she called after me.

I smiled to myself. I really liked Tada—I needed her easy-going nature and bubbly personality right now.

The moon shone through the glassless windows, illuminating the empty hall.

"Wait!"

I turned to see Kaz jogging to catch up with me.

I couldn't stop the rush of nerves jolting through me as he got closer. He had been easy to talk to last night, but that was before I knew who he really was—a Luxari. Not only that, but sneaking away was turning out to be a lot more difficult than it needed to be.

"Yes?" I arched an eyebrow, then bowed awkwardly, unsure of the proper protocol.

"How come you didn't tell me last night that you were summoned?" he asked.

"How come you didn't tell me you were a Luxari?" I shot back, then stood stunned by my own bluntness with a king. "I'm sorry—I shouldn't have said that."

Kaz smiled, but it vanished quickly as Oak came into view, striding toward us.

The air thickened with the power that radiated from two Luxari. Kaz carefully used his arm to move me aside, and I felt my back hit the wall. The tension in the hall grew with each passing second, causing my pulse to soar. I had never been this close to so much magic, and I barely dared to breathe.

"By the shattered spheres, what blasphemy is this?" Oak spat, his words sharp as shards of glass, fists clenched at his sides. He stalked toward Kaz.

"You dare to move your Flameborne Legion into the Delirium Sea without my permission!" Oak shouted.

I stiffened at his words. What was going on between the Scorch and Daze Spheres? Had living in the Bleak Sphere really left me this out of the loop?

Kaz didn't move, standing his ground just inches from Oak.

Both of them were tall, well-built, and exuded a commanding presence.

Kaz's right arm swung back, and—

SMACK.

Kaz punched Oak square in the jaw.

CHAPTER
NINE

My brain was still trying to catch up to what had just happened as Oak slid across the smooth floors of the hall. He lay on the ground, laughing. He sat up, wiping the blood from his mouth onto his tunic, and rested his forearms on his knees.

"Your punches have improved," Oak said as he spat blood over his shoulder onto the floor. He stood. "I'm glad you've finally taken some of my advice."

I couldn't believe this. They were actually providing the best possible diversion for me, but I was stuck. I didn't have anywhere to go. Both of my exits were blocked.

"Roll off, Oak," Kaz sneered, turning to walk away.

"Why did you move your Legion into my Sphere?" Oak's deep voice echoed through the hall.

Kaz stood there, breathing heavily, his nostrils flaring. His eyes narrowed as he slowly turned around. Oak kept walking toward him. *Oh, Aridan,* I thought, watching them. They were just getting started. The tension between them was palpable, as if a riot of thousands of people were fighting, and not just two men.

Kaz swung his fist for another hit, and I couldn't help but flinch. Oak gave a curt nod, and a gust of wind sent Kaz flying across the hallway, the force of it unraveling my hair from its bun and sending chairs and tables skidding and crashing to the floor. I pressed farther against the wall, shutting my eyes tightly against the wind.

His body slammed into the marble wall, leaving a giant crack. I winced at the sound. Kaz threw his head back and let out a bitter laugh as he attempted to get up.

"Stay down," Oak's voice dripped with authority. The sharpness of his tone and the power emitted from his words sent a humming vibration through the air, chilling me to the bone.

Kaz looked like he was fighting Oak's compulsion.

"Don't you use your cowardly mind tricks on me," Kaz growled.

Reading and hearing about a Swayer's power was a hell of a lot different than witnessing it. The absolute control Oak had over Kaz, with just words, was terrifying.

Oak crouched down in front of Kaz. "I will, when you're acting like a child. You will remove your Legion by the end of this week, or I will set the Lerains on them," he said with cool authority.

"You have proven yourself untrustworthy," Kaz hissed through clenched teeth.

"Is that so?" Oak taunted in a mocking tone. The emotion within him bled through the air, frosting my skin with fear—

the fear of angering a Luxari like Oak.

Kaz's whole body turned into a blazing fire, heating the entire hall like someone had opened the door to an oven. Sweat ran down my temples and my unbound locks plastered to my skin as smoke filled my mouth. An audience had gathered. The woman who had been with Oak in the ballroom stepped forward, her tight, dark curls falling neatly across her forehead.

Oak made eye contact with the woman. "Niko, you know what to do."

She nodded and turned to face the crowd.

"Very well, everyone. There's nothing to see here. Please return to your previous activities," Niko commanded. Her words rang just as strong as Oak's.

I didn't see what happened next. My body moved on its own, as if I were a puppet and Niko held my strings, pushing me to where I had left off before Kaz had stopped me.

Niko had used her mind compulsion to disperse the crowd. I had never been under compulsion by a Swayer before—never lost control of my body, let alone my thoughts. Even if I wanted to stop, my feet refused. As powerful and incredibly impressive as it was, it also absolutely terrified me.

After Niko sent me away with the crowd, it took me a few moments to regain control of my body. As the others began to gossip about the fight, I shook off my fear and headed towards the stairs. I needed to find the *Ari Report*, and no one was going to stop me this time.

The library was on the second floor, at the end of the hall. It was eerily quiet and dark. No candles flickered, and no sounds came from the arched rooms. A sense of foreboding made me hesitate, but I shooed it aside and continued down the dark corridor. My heart pounded loudly against my chest.

Suddenly, blood-curdling screams erupted from the first floor, shattering the stillness. Panic clawed up my throat as my gaze snapped toward the cries. A wave of fear washed over me —Will and Tada were down there.

But this was also the perfect time to sneak into the library. I hesitated, then moved.

My pulse raced, driven by the overwhelming need to act. My eyes darted to the iron rod holding the curtains above the arched window. Without thinking, I yanked it down and grabbed the rod, then sprinted down the steps.

Blood painted the floor in scarlet. Bodies splayed across the marble ground. I swallowed the vomit threatening to rise in my throat.

Party guests poured out of the ballroom—some fighting, others fleeing in panic. Dozens of Soul Snatchers and Rogue Embers chased after them.

How had they infiltrated the celebration so easily? I shook my head. That wasn't my problem, not right now. My problem was helping those who couldn't defend themselves. I gripped the rod and followed the stampede of chaos.

A yelp came from the beach just beyond the palace archways. I ran toward the sound.

Mayhem unfolded on the beach. Amabel, Rodor, Tada, Otto, and—much to my relief—Will, along with pretty much everyone who had been summoned, were still alive. They fought against the Soul Snatchers and Rogue Embers—marked by the crimson swirl carved into their cheeks. But a girl, no older than fifteen, sat in the sand, her shaky arms covering her head from a pudgy Rogue Ember.

I approached the Rogue Ember from behind. *Please, let this be enough.* I flung the iron rod into his back with all the force I had, aiming for his heart. The contact jolted my body, rattling my teeth. The man howled in anguish.

But the hit wasn't strong enough to kill. The Rogue Ember snapped his head toward me. His ruby-red eyes blazed with hatred. His hands burst into flames.

Shit. I had picked a fight with an Enticer.

Panic flooded my veins. I tried to pull my weapon from his back, but it was lodged in. The Enticer halted my movement by placing a fiery, iron grip on my wrist. My skin burned. I roared in agony as the sickening smell of charred flesh took over my senses. The Enticer's lips twisted into a smile.

I slammed my head into his. My brain rattled against my skull, but it worked. It caught the Enticer off guard, and he released my wrist. I tackled him, pain lancing up my arm from the impact. His body slammed against the ground, and the rod tore right through his chest. The sound of metal being shoved through muscle and organs was sickening—a squelching, tearing rip. Blood pooled down his stomach.

I began punching his face with my uninjured hand.

Although I knew the rod had done the fatal damage, I couldn't stop. I couldn't stop thinking of Milo and everyone else they had killed. I continued hitting him until his eyes were swollen shut. Scum like him were the reason good people were dead. Bubbles of blood foamed from his lips.

Strong hands circled my waist. I choked on a scream, thrashing, kicking out, and flinging my head back.

I came face-to-face with Oak. His hair, damp from sweat, clung to his sun-kissed skin.

"I wasn't done with him," I shouted.

"Yes, damsel, but he is done with you." He jerked his head to the swollen Enticer, covered with blood and sweat.

My burn pulsed as I tried to hide my scalded flesh behind my back, blocking it from his view. But I was too slow. His expression hardened as he saw my wrist.

I hissed as pain screamed through my arm. My flesh bubbled with blisters, exposing swollen pink muscle twisting around white bone. I shook my head, vomit rising in my throat.

"I'll be fine," I mumbled. But he still focused on my wrist.

I couldn't afford to appear weak, not from the very start, not in front of a Luxari, and not before the Quests even officially began. Weakness was not an option. And fear? I couldn't show that either.

"Just hold still." His voice was low, and the shadows cast by his dark eyelashes across his cheekbones were damn distracting.

He bent down, examining my skin.

A dark curl slipped forward, resting on his forehead. I felt a cool brush of his fingers on my forearm. I could hear my heartbeat pounding in my ears.

To distract myself, I studied the Daze lily etched into his skin: the marking of the Daze Sphere. Its intricate petals curled like swirling wind currents, edged with a faint shimmer of gold.

The pain dulled, then completely vanished. I blinked in astonishment as I looked at my wrist—it was healed. Swayers didn't have healing abilities like Charmers did. Was this a secret power only Luxari had? Or was it some kind of mind trick?

He gently lowered his hands.

"How did you do that?" I whispered, unable to hide my shock.

He casually shrugged. Then someone yelled for Oak from further up the beach. Without a word, he sprinted toward them.

I stood there, stunned, staring at my wrist. It had been burned to a crisp just moments ago, but now, it was flawless. All because of Oak.

THE HUSH SPHERE
AREN FOLKTALES

Hush, the water whispers.
Be discreet, do not bicker.
Charms and waves
Storm across the bay
As the Hush Sphere beams and flickers.

CHAPTER
TEN

Surprisingly, the Quests weren't delayed by the attack and were set to move forward as scheduled. I tried to find answers, but Queen Catalina kept her lips tight and shut down any conversation about it. It didn't reflect well on her—how easily the Hush Sphere had been breached—but instead of acknowledging it, she chose to ignore it. I could only hope Soulari Hall had better protection.

Sitting at the long, wooden table in the airy palace room, listening to Will drone on about teamwork, was slowly lulling me into a daze.

I stifled a yawn, regretting that I'd stayed up all night gossiping with Tada—even if it had been the most entertainment I'd had in years. After Oak had healed me, I'd made my way back to my room only to find Tada sprawled on the bed, waiting for me. She'd shared what she knew about the attack, which turned out to be as much as I knew. But she had then proceeded to tell me her life story for the next several hours.

Tada had grown up in the Hush Sphere. She was an identical twin, but her twin passed away at three months old.

Knowing that Tada had also lost a sibling made me feel closer to her. Not that I wished that on anyone, but unless you had been through it, you couldn't truly relate. I found myself lowering the walls I had built since Milo's death. I silently thanked Aridan for summoning Tada, who was turning out to be the companion I needed to keep my morale up.

Will had woken us at sunrise for a meeting with our alliance. He'd found us both fast asleep, the drool on my face staining my pillow.

The meeting had been going all day as Will analyzed and detailed each of our strengths and weaknesses.

"Coco, you've been really quiet," Will said, snapping me awake.

Tada, Otto, and Hugh's eyes all fell on me. I sat up.

"Well, I get going over our strengths and weaknesses, our magic abilities and lack of them," I joked, shrugging. Otto laughed, while Tada elbowed him in the rib cage. "But I don't even know what to expect from the challenges. I've never seen them."

"Me neither," Will added.

Otto shot up to his feet, palms spread flat on the table. "You guys are missing out. I've seen several, and the most epic challenges always take place in the Scorch Sphere." He started punching the air, kicking out, fighting invisible demons.

Tada tried and failed to hide the smirk on her lips. "Otto, Coco wants to know details—like what they're actually about."

She looked at me and rolled her eyes.

"Ah, yes, I see." Otto plopped down in his chair, his hair still wild. "Well, I can't say for certain, but from what I've seen in the past, the alliance challenges are usually a game, or they involve completing a daunting task."

I mean, I'd imagined as much. It was the individual challenges I was worried about, and I thought Otto could read it in my expression.

"Now, individual challenges are a bit more... unpredictable," Otto said, leaning in. "They usually take place away from the audience, so it feels more isolated—like you're alone when you face whatever mystical"—he wiggled his fingers as if casting a spell—"creatures and obstacles they've placed for you. But I'd argue it's reasonable to expect they'll resemble the Lumen Orb Quest."

A knot of apprehension twisted in my stomach. I hadn't even considered the isolation part of it. The idea of being separated from the group and left to face the challenge alone filled me with a growing sense of dread.

Will nodded, taking in every word. Hugh just traced circles with his thumb on the table, lost in his own thoughts.

By the time we finished, the sun was already setting. I had only an hour to prepare—mentally and physically—for the first challenge. The thought of it sent a frantic flutter through my chest.

I walked along the sandy shores of the Cobalt Sea with the other Questlings, tension gnawing at my stomach. This was the first challenge of the Sphere Quests, and all I could think about was failing.

A strand of hair blew into my mouth, and I immediately tasted the salty sea.

The Cobalt Sea was breathtaking during the day, but under the moon, the water turned a churning dark gray—a darkness that could swallow you whole, never to be found again.

I shivered as I trailed beside Will. His presence offered some comfort.

I could feel his eyes on me. "You're staring, Will," I murmured with a smile. He didn't return it. The crease between his brows deepened.

"Coco, you're smart. And your endurance—especially for a Dim—is remarkable."

I tilted my head. "Why do I feel a pep talk coming on?"

His voice dropped quieter, gentler. "I promised Milo I'd protect you. But I can't do that during the individual challenges. I just need to know you're going to give it everything you have."

Something about the way his worry clung to him made me reach for his hand. I gave it a squeeze.

"I will," I said. "I promise."

He nodded, and we kept walking.

After a moment, I glanced at him sideways. "Where were you last night? During the celebration? Before the attack?"

"I was there," he said, too quickly.

I raised a brow. "Oh? That's weird. I didn't see you."

Instead of answering, he picked up his pace, eyes fixed straight ahead.

I watched him for a moment, suspicion crawling up my spine. Where had he been—and why didn't he want me to know?

Ahead, Queen Catalina stood next to Queen Nerian. Oak and Kaz's towering figures were unmistakable even in the shadows, their faces obscured by the night. Two attendants with lanterns illuminated Queen Catalina's features as she explained the rules.

"The first task will take place at Moonlit Grotto. We'll take two boats there, and once we arrive, each of you will have to retrieve a chest with your initials on it—and the key to unlock it."

The tension in my stomach grew. I prayed the trunk wouldn't be too heavy.

"You will have one hour to retrieve your chest and the key. At the sound of the gong, you will jump into the sea, swim to the grotto, and retrieve your chest along with the key. The second gong will announce when an hour has passed. Regardless of whether you have the chest and key or not, you must return. You will be judged on speed and completion. Water Elaryns will be observing your progress and will report back.

"Shall we?" Queen Catalina motioned toward a very small boat.

There were about four benches. As all ten of us loaded onto the boat, our bodies pressed together. The Luxari boarded a much bigger vessel that rocked next to ours.

I had no idea what we would encounter in the grotto, but fear and anxiety gripped my stomach. The seasickness, combined with the anxiety of the task, was going to kill me before any creature had the chance. I went to spin the ring Milo had given me, something that usually brought comfort. But as I reached for it, I remembered I'd taken it off for the Quest—so it wouldn't get ruined—and all I felt was bare skin.

Water sprayed my face as we sailed across the waves.

Will's hand found mine, his grip reassuring. "You're shaking the whole boat, Coco," he said softly, a hint of concern in his voice.

I looked down and, sure enough, my leg bounced back and forth. I halted the movement, trying to take a deep breath. The constant rocking of the vessel left me feeling nauseous.

I knew how to swim—not well, but enough. I thought of the darkened depths of the Cobalt Sea and the monsters lurking beneath the surface. I shook my head. I needed to banish every negative thought, because it wouldn't help me with the task at hand.

"Are you just going to Sphere Jump to the grotto and back?" I asked Will.

"If only it were that easy," Will replied, shaking his head. "First, I can only jump from one Sphere to another. So, I'd have to leave the Hush Sphere, say, go to the Bleak Sphere, and then come back. But the bigger issue is that I can only Sphere Jump to places I've already been. Since I've never been to the grotto..." He trailed off with a sigh. "It would be pointless."

I'd never really considered the limitations of a Shifter's abilities. Maybe magic wasn't as all-powerful as it seemed.

I scanned the boat. Amabel studied her nails, as if she had other places to be. Everyone else seemed quite calm, except for me.

The oarsmen rowed in unison, cutting sharply through the sea.

"You have nothing to worry about," Will murmured in my ear, offering reassurance once again.

"Unless you run into Thresk," Cecille said, locking eyes with Will. His lips pressed into a straight line.

"Who?" I asked, my voice rising despite my effort to stay calm.

"Thresk is just a myth—a sea creature said to dwell in Moonlit Grotto," Severin answered before Cecille could speak. He waved a dismissive hand. "Just a story. No proof. It's never been seen."

I nodded, even as my pulse quickened. Just a myth.

The oarsmen then began to sing—a low, soft, enchanting tune:

> *Down in the depths of the sea*
> *In the grotto where moonbeams gleam,*
> *You'll find the lair of the creature of scare,*
> *Drifting along like a dream,*
> *Roaming the sandy bed,*
> *Scales like jewels*
> *And eyes like lead.*
>
> *Breath soft and curling,*
> *Smooth as smoke and swirling,*
> *The monster roams at night,*
> *Kissing the waves*
> *As it lingers at bay,*
> *Waiting for prey in its sight.*

Its swirling silver smoke
Can freeze your breath and make you
　　choke—
It turns the living cold and still,
To sterling silver, against their will.

Now a gulp of air
Can break the snare,
But only with care.

And so it is said,
When kids go to bed,
They're warned by whispers from the sea:
Swim in the ocean,
With heart and devotion—
But fear the springs that glow
Beneath the moonlit sea.

The words struck something deep inside me and made anxiety pool in my stomach.

My heart pounded so loudly that I could feel it thudding in my ears.

The grotto appeared ahead, a blue glow pulsing from the cave's mouth. Suddenly, an attendant tossed an anchor into the sea, and the boat lurched to the left.

We rocked back and forth outside the darkened cave. My eyes fixated on the blue glow and the task at hand. I dampened my lower lip with my tongue, tasting the salty sea again.

Queen Catalina's voice filled the humid air. "You will all go at once."

Water Elaryns emerged from the dark depths, hovering above the crashing waves. I had never seen any type of Elaryn before. Their translucent skin ranged in hues of pale blue and silver. Long, wispy hair, resembling strands of water, rippled with each movement. Their luminous eyes glowed like the moon above. The Elaryns glided through the air, their delicate limbs flowing gracefully in the breeze.

Aldo was the first to stand, rocking the boat as he tore off his shirt. The rest of us rose hesitantly—I worried the vessel might capsize if we all stood and jumped out at once.

My legs shook—whether from fear, the cold, or a mix of both, I couldn't tell. A gong appeared beside Queen Catalina as she struck it. A bright, clear tone echoed across the waves. I felt the vibrations of the gong through the air, and without a second thought, I jumped into the sea.

The icy water sliced through me as my body submerged into the violent waves. I started to kick, propelling myself to the surface. The crisp air stung my cheeks as I began swimming toward the grotto. As it neared, I focused on the glow of the water. It was a sharp, electric blue, and the air seemed to hum with magic. I sensed the presence of the glowing Water Elaryns streaming behind me.

Suddenly, a fin glided through the water and disappeared beneath the waves, then a second one. It was safe to assume that they were Aldo and Will.

I glanced around to see how the others were faring. Amabel, Otto, and Rodor were struggling—their intolerance to water was weakening their strength. I felt a pang of sympathy for Otto and Rodor... but not a single ounce for Amabel. She had pushed me off the sea stack, after all.

I slipped past them with ease.

Tada, Cecille, and Severin were already at the grotto, the water becoming one with them and carrying them forward effortlessly.

Even Hugh had summoned a breeze, shoving him ahead.

I swam under the arch and into an underwater cavity. To my surprise, the others had vanished from view. They were likely already beneath the surface, hunting for their chests.

My goal was to find the trunk first, then worry about the key.

I couldn't see the ocean floor. I took a deep breath and plunged beneath the glowing water, toward the sandy seabed.

Silvery specks floated in the water. They were humming and creating the glow of the sea.

The hum grew louder as I neared the bottom. They brushed against my skin, clinging like moss. I swiped at my arm, but they wouldn't budge.

The seafloor was just seaweed and sand.

My chest began to ache, and the desire for air burned through my body. My feet touched the sandy floor as I pushed off, soaring toward the surface.

My head burst through the waves. I sucked in air, panting as if I couldn't get enough. I bobbed for a second, catching my breath. A Water Elaryn hovered a few feet away from me, her luminous eyes making me feel exposed. I inhaled a final breath before diving back into the glowing water. Out of the corner of my eye, I saw two Water Elaryns gliding through the sea as gracefully as fish. The silver specks were everywhere, but now they did more than hum—they were speaking.

Coco.

The voices were just the specks, trying to distract me from the task. I plowed through the water, propelling myself toward the bottom.

Coco, Milo misses you.

The voice came from a tunnel against the cavern wall. I closed my eyes. *This is part of the Quest. The specks are there to distract me.*

Coco... Coco... Coo...

The voices grew louder and louder, pounding in my head as if Queen Catalina had hit me with the mallet she used on her gong. The specks stuck to my skin, making me feel slimy.

Dim Girl... Dim Girl... Inadequate, small, and frail... What can you offer, besides beauty and bite? Give up, Dim girl, and fall into the night...

Each word felt like a slap to the face. The accuracy rang in my head.

What was I doing here? I wasn't going to be able to compete. Even the fact that I was attempting it was completely laughable.

My head throbbed, my skin felt slick with slime, and my chest ached. I shoved off the seafloor, breaking the surface. I gulped down the humid, fresh air.

I treaded water, weighing my options. I had no idea how much time had passed. The ocean waves sloshed around my neck. I wasn't sure where to look. The chest could be anywhere on the bottom of the sea in the grotto, and it was too big an area to search. Exhaustion began to grow in my legs, spreading like wildfire through my body.

A thought grew louder than the pounding in my head. A memory of Milo flashed through my mind, his voice telling me to never give up. My heart thundered in my chest as I clenched my fists. I couldn't stop now—not after coming this far. I had to keep moving.

I plunged back beneath the surface. The specks still hummed, calling my name. But I saw a dark shadow sweep in front of me, spreading out like ink poured into the ocean.

My instinct was to follow it. It spread toward the seafloor. I followed. But I only had a certain amount of time, and it was leading me exactly where I had already looked.

Once the shadow hit the sandy floor, it bolted toward the cavern wall. I kicked hard, trying to keep up. The pressure of the water elicited a throbbing sensation that grew in my ears. As I neared the wall, a glimmer of wood caught my attention— there, at the base of the cavern, a wooden chest was wedged between two rocks. I yanked the trunk from the rocks, the initials *C.D.* carved into the soft wood. Pure joy and adrenaline helped me to kick off the seafloor and pull my body towards the surface, the chest clenched tightly against me.

Waves greeted me, slamming me against the rocky walls of the cavern. An ache grew in my ribs from the way my body hit the jagged stones.

A sudden jerk on my ankle yanked me downward, cutting off my circulation as I was dragged swiftly through the water. Instead of a scream, desperate bubbles burst from my mouth. My gaze dropped, and I froze in terror.

ELEVEN

Below me, a creature pulsed with sickly light the color of bile, its body stretched long and wiry like a ribbon. Through its semi-translucent skin, I could faintly make out the dark shapes of its organs.

Panic clawed at my throat as the creature hauled me deeper. I was utterly helpless.

It slammed me onto the sandy ocean floor.

A shadow loomed closer. Another creature, glowing like mine, pulled Hugh toward me through the water. He frantically tore at the rotting flesh, desperate to rip the eel-like creature from his ankles, but they were binding our legs. They burrowed into the sand, as if collecting us for someone—or something.

It coiled around his legs once more, and its needle-thin snout opened, revealing rows of ashy teeth. In a surge of panic, I shoved my wooden chest towards Hugh. He met my frantic gaze, caught it instinctively, and began using it to pound the eel's snout. Blood oozed from its beady red eyes.

Then Otto plummeted from the surface, thrashing, another one of those creatures already coiled around his ankles. Sparks flickered and died at his fingertips as his body went eerily still. His lungs wouldn't last much longer.

Otto's eel demon plunged into the sand mere inches from where I floated.

Think! I roared internally, my lungs burning. The creature's body kept wrapping around my ankles, working its way up toward my arms.

My eyes darted and snagged on a flash of deep royal blue, speckled with periwinkle. The sight triggered a sudden memory:

Milo and I lay by the pond. He held a book in front of his face, shielding himself from the sun as he read:

"With no air, surrounded by Lerains, she knew this was the end. But then—a splash of color. Could it be exactly what she needed? A Starvane."

Hope flared. I lunged for the five-limbed starfish, clawing through pebbles and sand, hands trembling with desperation. My vision began to blacken at the edges—but I couldn't give up.

Otto and Hugh needed me.

I pinched the starfish between my fingers and ripped it free, immediately hauling it to my lips. Air rushed into my lungs as it sealed itself over my mouth and nose. It was wet and uncomfortably warm, but I didn't care. I gulped one last breath from it, then peeled it off and pressed it against Otto's mouth. As he gasped, my eyes scanned the seabed for anything sharp. My fingers closed around a jagged rock, and I began to saw frantically at the eel-like creature.

With one strand severed, Otto glanced at his other leg, then ripped the creature in half with newfound strength; the air from the starfish was clearly reviving him.

He tore the creature that was wrapped around me to shreds. I swam up, pulled the starfish from his lips, and turned to help Hugh, but he was already free and just inches away. He grabbed my hand and Otto's, and the Starvane slipped through my fingers as Hugh used the current to catapult us upward.

We burst through the surface.

"What in the scorcher's sun was that sphere..." Otto began, but a crashing wave cut him off, splashing us in the face. That's when a chilling realization hit me: Hugh didn't have my chest. I groaned in frustration.

I dove beneath the surface, keeping clear of the sickly creatures while searching desperately for my chest. My gaze locked with golden amber eyes framed by creamy blonde hair.

Amabel held two trunks, one with my initials, and had a Starvane pressed to her lips. Anger boiled inside me as I surged toward her. She was faster than I'd given her credit for, easily swimming ahead of me. But a jellyfish shot out, wrapping its tentacles around the arm carrying my chest, and stung her.

My chest slipped from her grasp. I lunged, clutched it tight, and kicked hard for the surface.

The water above me swirled together, just like it had during the Lumen Orb Quest. Once again, it took the form of an Aurefly with Nightsparks glimmering on its wings. Bubbles streamed from its mouth as it softly sung:

Coco, Coco, brave and bright,
Don't fall behind—turn and fight.

You hold the fate of those now gone,
And you'll be the one to right the wrong.

It burst, dissolving into tiny particles that drifted down into the depths of the sea.

Was this part of the Quest? To me, it felt like a jumble of nonsense thrown together. I didn't have time for it—I needed to find the key.

Breaking through the surface, I rolled onto my back, resting the chest on my stomach as water filled my ears and I caught my breath.

I hadn't seen any keys or the other Questlings with theirs, and the sandy sea floor was empty besides the snake-like creatures. The only chance I had was following the shadow.

It was worth trying. I tucked the chest against my side and began swimming back toward the ocean floor, but instead of searching for the key, my eyes sought the shadow.

A dark, inky shape drifted along the rocky cavern wall where I'd found the chest. I followed it, kicking fiercely despite the burn in my lungs and the ache in my muscles.

The rocks grew bigger, sharper, and glossier, jutting out further into the ocean. The shadow slipped around one of them, vanishing from sight.

I kicked harder, just in time to see it dart beneath a narrow crevice in the cavern wall. I pushed off the ocean floor and broke the surface with a gasp of air, the salty breath filling my lungs. Only then did I realize I was barely outside the grotto, the open sea stretching wide before me.

When I felt like I had enough air, I dove back down to

where I had seen the inky splotch disappear. Tucked between spiky rocks, a narrow tunnel stretched into the darkness.

I forced myself in; the rough stone bit into my skin and panic curled tightly in my throat at the thought of getting trapped. But I pushed through until I emerged into another grotto that was bathed in the same pulsing, glowing, blue water.

Instead of a sandy floor, glossy stones shimmered in deep purple, blue, and black—like polished obsidian and scattered sapphires on the ocean bed.

Above me, pale beams of moonlight filtered through the water, casting a soft glow over silver keys sprinkled across the stones, each one softly shining.

But which one was mine?

A flash of bright, creamy blonde caught the corner of my eye. Amabel floated nearby, her smug smirk concealed behind the Starvane attached to her mouth. She clutched her chest tightly beneath her arm. She had followed me—and judging by the others emerging from behind her, she wasn't alone.

Will, Aldo, Rodor, and Severin emerged from the tunnel one by one. I needed to act fast.

I dove, cutting through the water toward the ocean floor—only to find Amabel deliberately blocking my path. She slammed into my side, shoving me off course and sending a sharp pinch through my ribs.

I had to focus my energy on the key—or I would surely lash out at Amabel. Forcing my mind to stillness, I pressed onward toward the ocean floor.

As I drew closer, I spotted the keys scattered across the stones. Each was etched with delicate curls that intertwined into letters. My eyes darted frantically until they locked onto my initials—*C.D.*—swirling into a crescent-shaped handle.

I pushed myself harder, a forest fire raging in my lungs as I reached out to grasp the key.

One of the stones scattered across the ocean floor stirred, revealing a solid silver eye—molten and unblinking.

The entire floor shifted suddenly, ripping upward like a sheet torn from a bed. I lunged back, hands trembling and heart hammering in my chest.

The creature moved with terrifying speed, and my body froze, unsure of what to do. I was trapped, surrounded by jagged rocks.

Its tail whipped toward me. I snapped aside just in time. The water churned with the force of its strike. As the massive form shifted, the "stones" of the ocean floor rippled and peeled back. They weren't stones at all; the entire seabed was the monster's hide.

Then came the most horrifying sight: its massive, angular head lunging straight at Rodor.

Crowned with ridges like molten stone cooled into obsidian, its mouth stretched wide, revealing rows of razor-sharp teeth that reminded me of bones jutting from the earth.

Luckily, Rodor had a Starvane on his lips. Without hesitation, he surged forward, using his Enticer strength to clamp the creature's jaws shut. His biceps bulged as the rest of the monster thrashed wildly.

Nearby, I caught sight of Will and Aldo diving for the keys where they hung on the purple scales. Rodor struggled to hold the beast in place—though he couldn't hold on for long.

I needed to act fast.

Instead of reaching for the key, I swam to the surface, breaking through the water with a gasp. The crisp, chilly night air clung to my skin.

Peering over the rim of glossy rocks, I spotted a figure swimming toward the boats—it was Hugh. He must have already retrieved his key.

My brow furrowed as a sudden realization clicked—the oarsmen's lyrics echoed in my mind:

Now a gulp of air

Can break the snare.

If one of us got caught, air would be the key to survival.

Without hesitation, I dove back down, eyes wide at the chaos below.

Aldo and Severin had grabbed their keys and darted toward the tunnel. Will clutched his own, but I saw him reach for mine. I surged toward him, ready to warn him off—just as the creature shifted its gaze toward us.

Its mouth opened, and a hissing cloud of molten silver ink burst forth. Thick and metallic, it crackled and shimmered, spreading like liquid starlight through the water.

Sparks flew straight toward Will.

I rammed into him, driving him against the cavern wall before shoving him into the tunnel.

Ice-cold pain shot through my elbow, sharp and piercing. It stiffened, frozen in place.

The monster slammed into the wall, dislodging a boulder that crashed onto the sandy seabed, blocking the tunnel.

I glanced down at my elbow—it looked like gray stone, petrified and immobile. I could only move my wrist and shoulder.

Air would fix it—but how was I supposed to get my key now?

Amabel and Rodor tried to get their keys while the monster's gaze locked onto me, its jaws opening to finish me off.

The creature let out a sharp hiss, and its neck snapped back.

Blood pooled from the raw flesh where a scale had been. Amabel's blade had carved it off for her key, and now bright crimson gushed, spilling like ink to paint the water.

I darted around the creature, eyes scanning for my key as Rodor did the same. Amabel kicked toward the tunnel—I smirked, knowing she'd have to find another way out. Her eyes burned with fury as she faced the beast.

It thrashed violently, the motion dizzying. An idea sprang to my mind.

I glanced down at my elbow, shot towards the surface, and lifted my arm, making sure it broke through the water first. Cracks spidered through the stone that encased it, chipping away in heavy flakes that fell into the sea.

What if...

I dove back down and whistled sharply to draw the creature's attention. Its silver eyes snapped toward me, glowing fiercely.

I planned to turn its own defense against it.

Bolting for the surface, I zigzagged through the water, praying to Aridan that my movements would keep me clear of its petrifying, smoky coils.

My head broke the surface, and I moved toward the boulders rimming around the crater's edge. I swam toward the nearest one, reaching to haul myself onto the sleek rock—just as water erupted around me like a volcanic explosion.

The creature hissed. When I glanced back, its smoky breath twisted into the air, curling over its scales and freezing the beast mid-motion like molten silver.

It began to sink.

I plunged back beneath the waves, watching as the heavy, immobilized creature crashed onto the ocean floor, sending clouds of sand bursting upward. Encased in gray stone, its massive form lay motionless.

Through the petrified casing, the outlines of the scattered keys remained visible.

Amabel slammed into my side—my ribs ached, as if crushed beneath a weight. Her eyes gleamed with malice as she darted toward the surface.

Anger surged through my veins, but there was no time to waste. I needed the key.

This was the moment—my only chance to seize the key embedded in the creature's scaled hide. Who knew how long the petrification would hold?

I dove deep, lifting the chest above my head, then rammed it down onto the stone, aiming for the sharp corner to pierce it. A satisfying crack followed as it gave way, revealing the gleaming key beneath.

Rodor caught on immediately, smashing the creature with his fist to free his own key. He shot me a quick nod before launching toward the surface.

I slipped my key into the lock—not turning it, just securing it so I wouldn't be burdened with carrying two objects.

I hauled myself from the water and scrambled over the slick boulders before plunging back into the vast, open ocean. The boats floated in the distance, and I pushed toward them.

Water Elaryns floated above me, soaring back to the boats, their wispy hair glowing in the night sky. The crisp ocean breeze turned my cheeks to ice. I didn't have time to be cold—I had to make my way back. The sea surged against me, forcing me back onto my stomach as I kicked toward the vessel.

I struggled to swim back, gasping for air and clutching my chest with trembling hands. As I neared the skiff, my hands shook as I tossed the chest over the side. I pulled myself up, my drenched tunic dragging me down. I rolled onto the floor of the boat and sat up as a wave of dizziness washed over me. Will helped me onto the seat.

"Well done," Queen Catalina called, clapping.

Water Elaryns whispered into her ears just for her to hear. Hopefully, they were leaving out some details. I didn't want all the Luxari to know I had slammed into the cavern wall—or what the silvery specks had said.

I exhaled, relief flooding through me. "How long...?"

"58 minutes," Will answered, wrapping an arm around my shoulder. My body molded to the warmth of his arm.

Severin's ice-blue gaze met mine.

"Just a myth, you say?" I panted.

His lips trembled, like he was trying to suppress a laugh, and he shrugged.

"I'm so sorry, Coco," Will said, drawing my attention back to him. "I tried to get back through the rocks."

He shook his head, but I raised a hand to stop him.

"You have nothing to apologize for. You don't need to baby me. See? I got out all right."

He gave me a faint smile.

I looked around at the other Questlings, all of us soaked. Tada and Otto had their backs to me. Hugh stared down at the chest in his lap. I was curious how he'd gotten back himself, but we weren't close enough for me to ask.

Cecille gazed up at the stars, her legs short enough to swing back and forth. Rodor sat motionless, eyes fixed on his hands, clamped tightly together. Aldo and Severin were deep in conversation about something I couldn't hear. Amabel was fussing with her hair.

I was the last one back—but not all of them were holding a chest.

The boat lurched forward, heading back to the Hush Sphere's palace.

A bolt of shock went through me. I had actually done it— barely, but I had done it. The pride of finishing in time quickly faded, replaced by the bitter coldness of the ocean breeze.

Will's finger brushed against my damp skin, flicking away the tiny glowing specks that clung to me.

"What are those?" I asked, my voice breathy.

"Nightsparks. Distracting little buggers," he said, his eyes scanning my skin where they left behind a faint glimmer. "I'm sure they were just excited for the company, away from the gloomy Sea Phantoms."

"Were those the shadows?" I asked, my voice hoarse from the cold, my body trembling with exhaustion.

"Yes. Sea Phantoms are the shadows of souls swallowed by the sea," Will said.

He spoke so casually, like everyone knew what they were.

Growing up in the Bleak Sphere had made me more ignorant than I realized.

"And those demon snake things?" I asked.

His eyes widened. "I didn't run into those."

"Well, you should thank Aridan for that." The mere thought set a shudder through my body.

"But I did hear Amabel had a nasty run-in with a jellyfish," Will said with a smirk.

I glanced at Amabel—her entire arm swelled with a purplish-blue bruise.

"Maybe she shouldn't shove my friends off sea stacks," he mused with a quirk to his lips.

My head snapped toward him. "That was you," I whispered.

He lifted one brow. "I have no idea what you're talking about, Coco," he said, but his mischievous grin said it all.

"Have I told you you're my favorite?"

"Not today," he chuckled, squeezing my leg just above the knee.

"Well, you are. And hey, if I can complete the first Quest, who knows? Maybe I can complete the next one."

"Coco, I'm calling it now—you're going to dominate every Quest and get offers from every Sphere. Colette Darroway, the first Dim offered a spot on the Luxari Council."

A grin spread across my face before I could stop it. Honestly, I was surprised at how much I liked the sound of that.

All the Questlings stood on the beach, drenched and cold, watching as Queen Catalina disembarked from the boat. The other Luxari joined her.

"Congratulations to Hugh, Will, Aldo, Severin, Rodor, Amabel, and Colette for completing the task in the time frame allotted. The time it took you to retrieve your chest represents the place you took in this first challenge of the Sphere Quests."

That meant I took seventh place. I groaned as I trembled from the cold, wishing for a towel.

Cecille and Otto hadn't found their chests in time. I wished more than anything that I could have helped Cecille. The sadness in her deep brown eyes made my heart ache. Tada hadn't been able to find her chest, so she had decided to head back to the boat early. Otto had gone on a rant about a "sea monster" he'd had to battle—one different from the eel, and one that nobody else had faced.

Queen Catalina opened her hand, palm to the sky, and a shimmering vial appeared, filled with swirling dust. Inside, gold and silver specks floated like sunlight and starlight captured in glass. It pulsed with raw energy.

She plucked the vial with her other hand, holding it delicately between her thumb and forefinger.

"This is Ari Soul Dust," she said. "It fuels the magic in Aren. As an Ember, if you consume it, it will slightly increase your magical abilities. To what extent, and how it will register in each individual... I cannot say. But it is yours to use as you please."

Amabel's face scrunched with anger, her skin turning a blotchy red.

I couldn't stop the smirk that spread across my face—at least Amabel didn't place.

Queen Catalina handed one to Aldo, then four more appeared as she distributed them to Will, Severin, Rodor, and Hugh.

Rodor uncorked his vial and tossed the contents into his mouth. He grinned, then slammed the empty vial onto the sand. It shattered instantly. He wiped his lips with the back of his hand.

Aldo took his vial and drank, while Hugh raised his hesitantly, tilting his head back to sip carefully.

Severin and Will both pocketed theirs without a word.

"Now, for those of you who recovered your chests, you will find inside a reflection of your character. Hugh, since you took first place," Queen Catalina said, motioning toward his chest.

He pulled out a candle.

Oak spoke for the first time that evening. "Candles symbolize unity, love, and family."

Hugh nodded in appreciation.

Will slid his key into the lock and turned it to the right. A soft click sounded, and he opened the chest and pulled out a small wooden figurine of a wolf.

A small smile tugged on my lips. To me, wolves stood for loyalty, guardianship, and strength—everything Will was.

Aldo's chest held a compass, and in the time I'd spent with him, it made sense. Balance, stability, decision-making—traits of a leader, which he clearly was. He had the natural ability to take charge; his presence among all of us was grounding.

Severin had a book in his chest. Books could represent a million things, but the Luxari stayed silent, not offering an explanation like Oak had for Hugh.

Rodor had a shield in his chest, which he grinned at. Obviously, his shield represented defense and duty, and I had absolutely no doubt that the man had courage. Every bulging muscle on him screamed, "Come at me."

Then there was Amabel, who pulled out a mirror. I had to bite my tongue to prevent the laughter that would surely spill out if I opened my mouth. It couldn't have been more fitting. She was completely self-absorbed, and as if on cue, she lifted the mirror to check her hair.

"Coco, fix your face," Will whispered to me. "It's your turn, and Amabel saw you smirking at her. She looks one second away from lighting your hair on fire."

I quickly wiped the smirk off my face, pulling it into a bored expression, and glanced down at my chest.

My eyes were drawn to the intricate markings on the wood. Turning the key, I lifted the lid. Iridescent, shimmering gold and silver dust filled the space. I frantically scooped through the sand, searching for an object, but I felt nothing but the velvety grains.

My chest was full of literally nothing but dust. I had fought a sea monster for this?

Disappointment, confusion, and annoyance filled me. I could feel several gazes on me, but I couldn't tear my eyes away from the shimmering dust. Everyone else had an object that clearly symbolized characteristics of themselves, but no—I, a Dim, got dust.

I looked up, met Oak's intense gaze, and quickly looked away as I felt a rush of heat race across my cheeks. I swallowed hard, my thoughts spinning.

"That concludes the first challenge of the Sphere Quests. Now, this Quest was the easiest out of all of them. Let's just say we wanted to get your feet wet." Queen Catalina smirked at her own joke, and dread filled my stomach. If this was the easiest task, I was surely doomed. "Leave your chests. Our guards will carry them back for you. We look forward to seeing you in the Scorch Sphere."

She clapped her hands as the group began to walk the shoreline back to the palace.

Amabel came straight at me, her fiery amber eyes flaring with malice. She stopped inches from my face, but I wasn't going to move. This was what she wanted—for me to be scared of her—and I would not give in.

"Isn't that cute?" she purred. "You won't make it through the Sphere Quests, and all that will be left of you is dust." Her sultry voice couldn't conceal the hate behind her words.

Rage and fury bubbled in my veins, but I took a slow breath, telling myself to stay calm. She wanted me to fall apart, to show her my weakness—and I wasn't going to let that happen.

"How unfortunate," I said, meeting her gaze, "that the only reflection of your character is your vanity."

Her eyes narrowed into slits, and smoke began to steam from her skin.

"Amabel, you're literally setting yourself on fire," Tada said, looping her arm through mine and tugging me away. "And honey, if your face burns up, what will you have to offer? Your one good quality will be fried."

We both erupted into laughter.

"Thanks for saving me, Tada."

"Girl, you didn't need saving. You had everything under control. I just wanted to join in on the fun," she said, giving me a playful shove as her violet eyes sparkled with mischief.

Otto emerged from behind us, wrapping an arm around Tada's shoulders.

"Well, it's probably good I couldn't find my chest," Otto said.

"And why's that?" I asked, raising an eyebrow.

"It was probably too large. You know, because I have too many amazing characteristics to hold in one small chest."

Tada and I immediately started laughing again. It felt good —like my heart had been holding its breath and finally exhaled. I hadn't even noticed how tense I'd become since the summons.

"Well, tomorrow we go to the greatest Sphere in Aren!" Otto hollered, breaking through my thoughts.

"That's not biased at all," I said, rolling my eyes.

Otto's face broke into a wide grin as he burst into song:

> *The best of the best*
> *Come from the west,*
> *Where the sand dunes cry*

With no water supply.
Who cares for the grog,
Or the big hulking hog,
When the finest and prime
Are the Scorch's Divine?

THE SCORCH SPHERE

AREN FOLKTALES

Of beauty and fire
Is born the fighter—
Filled with strength and power.
They entice by day,
And seduce by night,
Scorching paths beneath the sun.

CHAPTER
TWELVE

The next morning, we sailed across the Cobalt Sea to the Scorch Sphere—a journey that took about four hours. Upon arrival, we mounted Sundraks for the ride into Kaz's Kingdom, where his palace awaited.

It was my first time on a Sundrak, and I made a mental note never to repeat the experience. I told Will that now he'd visited the Scorch Sphere, if I ever needed to return, he could Sphere Jump us back without the need for a horrible Sundrak ride. The heat was overwhelming. The red desert stretched endlessly, and my eyes stung from the sand.

Tada pulled me through the bustling streets, alive with Ashgoats and Cindrils. We passed mud brick buildings and homes with clay-tiled roofs and courtyards filled with Dunebristles. Colorful fabric awnings in stripes of brown and blue provided shade for baskets filled with bloodpearls, amber roots, and molani figs. I was surprised by the variety of food in this harsh climate—they had more options than my village in the Bleak Sphere.

A cloud of dust brushed the hem of my billowing pants. Tada swore that the daffodil yellow of my cropped top made me more beautiful than an Enticer. I couldn't stop the faint blush that crept up my neck at the compliment—it was either from that, or from the bright sun.

Queen Catalina had given all the Questlings new clothing and a small bag of gold coins. Mine hung from a string at my waist.

Stone-baked bread and sticky buns sat temptingly on display, surrounded by jars of spices and herbs.

My mouth began to water, and I sensed Tada's did too.

"I have to get some," she said. She stomped under the awning into the shop and left me under the blazing sun.

I pressed a cloth to my mouth, shielding myself from the sand.

Bright amber canopies caught my attention, and tables covered in glass showcased twinkling gemstones—ruby, sapphire, diamond, topaz, opal, and turquoise.

I walked toward the shade, and that's when I saw them: two children in rags. Their cheeks were sunken, and their hungry eyes were locked on the sticky buns behind the vendor's screen.

My heart clenched. They reminded me of Milo and me.

I was pulled into a memory.

We stood outside the Hall of Knowledge, our stomachs aching with hunger, watching the other children skip out of the building, each holding an apple dipped in chocolate and caramel.

Milo and I had spent the afternoon crouched beneath the open windows, trying to catch snippets of the lessons inside. We weren't allowed in, but we still wanted to learn.

That was when we first saw Will.

He walked out of the Hall, but instead of heading off with the others, he turned toward us.

He smiled—soft and sure.

Then he did something I'll never forget.

He handed us his apple, saying it was too sweet for him, and walked away without waiting for thanks.

The next day, he brought part of his lunch to share.

The day after that, he let us borrow a couple of books.

And not long after, he brought us home to meet his family. That's where our friendship blossomed.

Will's kindness changed the way I saw the world. It reminded me that goodness—real goodness—still existed.

The memory faded.

I untied the velvet pouch from the string at my waist and stepped toward the children.

The boy—no older than six—stared at me with wide eyes as I pressed the bag into his hand.

His little sister clung to his leg with her gaze fixed on the ground.

Before either of them could speak, I turned and walked away.

Tada was nearby, laughing as she held two sticky buns. Otto leaned in to whisper something in her ear, and her cheeks turned the color of the desert before he tugged her down a shaded passage between tents.

That might take a while.

I wandered beneath the awning, browsing gemstones. I wasn't watching where I was going and bumped into a basket of pearls, scattering them across the rugs that covered the sandy floor.

Flushed with embarrassment, I dropped to my knees and started picking them up, one by one.

Beside me, a sun-kissed hand reached to help.

Oak's gold-flecked eyes met mine, his face breaking into a devastatingly irresistible smile.

"Hello, damsel. I'm beginning to think you're terribly clumsy," he said.

My stomach flipped. Why did he always have to find me in the most humiliating situations?

"Har har," I scoffed, quickly scooping the pearls toward my knees so I could gather them into the basket. I glanced up at the vendor, who was already scowling.

"We'll take care of it," Oak said smoothly.

Recognition flashed across her face. "Oh, Your Majesty, I can—"

He cut her off with a shake of his head. "No need. Consider it done."

Turning back to me, a faint smile tugged at the corner of his mouth. "If I might offer some unsolicited advice: stay away from ladders. And baskets."

A spark of humor lit his gaze.

I couldn't help the smile that slipped free. "Noted."

We finished scooping up the last of the pearls. As I stood, Oak stepped in front of me, blocking my way.

"Yes?" I arched a brow as I looked up, suddenly reminded of how tall he was.

"I saw what you did back there," he said softly, his voice low. His ocean-blue eyes studied mine, the gold flecks swirling like light deep beneath the sea.

I shrugged and glanced down at the ground.

"That was incredibly altruistic of you."

"Altruistic?" I echoed, biting back a grin.

He smirked. "Surprised by my vocabulary?"

"No," I said a little too quickly. Heat bloomed in my cheeks. "That's not what I meant."

Why did I speak without thinking? This was a Luxari, a being who could not only kill me instantly but likely read my mind or control my very will. I wanted to take it back, but it was too late.

His laugh was low and warm. Something in my chest fluttered.

Then his eyes locked onto mine, unblinking.

"Someone who has little, yet gives more than they keep for themselves, is..." His voice was smooth, but it did nothing to calm my nerves. I knew exactly where he was headed—and I hated compliments.

"Umm, not to argue, Your Majesty"—I made a half-awkward curtsy—"but how do you know I have little? Maybe I'm swimming in gold, handing it out in my free time."

He took a step closer, and the scent of fresh rain and coconut flooded my senses again.

His lips twitched, as if he were trying to suppress a smile. "Swimming in gold?"

"You've... never tried it?" I asked, my voice trembling slightly. "Oh. Um, that's—well, that's a shame." I gave a tentative gesture. "Would you—uh—mind stepping aside?"

"Wait." His voice froze me. He lifted a finger and lightly traced my cheek, brushing sand from my skin. His touch was feather-light but sent an unexpected surge of excitement coursing through me.

"It's fine," I said, stepping back and nervously wiping my face. "Maybe... I want it there."

His lips twitched with a barely contained smile.

I cleared my throat. "So, um, if you could please move..."

"If she said to get out of her way, I'd get out of her way— she throws a mean punch," Will's voice came to my rescue.

I was shocked that he would speak to a Luxari like that, and yet it didn't even seem to faze him. Was that courageous, or stupid?

Oak turned to reveal Will standing casually, unfazed.

Oak looked at Will, then back at me, and stalked off.

"Thank you, Will."

He grinned and reached out to pluck something from my hair—a pearl. Sphere shit—had that been in my hair the entire time I was talking to Oak? I felt like a globe-smashing idiot.

I eyed his waist, where Queen Catalina's money had been hanging earlier.

"Where's your gold?" I asked.

"Same place yours is," he said over his shoulder. I followed him to join Aldo and the others, who had begun to gather.

I glanced toward where I'd seen the children earlier, and sure enough, the little girl clutched a small pouch in her hands.

Warmth spread through me. The kindness, the goodness inside me—it came from him. He made me who I was, and every day I aspired to be more like him.

Tada and I walked through the village, but she was moving much faster than the others. I struggled to keep up.

"Remind me why you have so much energy this morning?" I yawned. Her grip tightened on my wrist, forcing me to match her pace. My muscles ached from swimming in the first trial last night.

She cleared her throat, as if preparing to speak in front of thousands of people. I couldn't help but raise an eyebrow at her.

"The Scorch Sphere's palace is the only underground palace in Aren. It has an arena that can fit thousands and a skylight dome ballroom. They say you can see every star at night."

"You're way too giddy for this hour, Tada," I grumbled.

Tada halted.

The Scorch Sphere guards stood in front of a wide, sandy staircase that led downward into darkness. Their faces were concealed by headwraps, leaving only their eyes exposed. Their glittering pupils unsettled me, like spiders crawling up my spine. One wrong look, and our corpses would be left to rot under the unbearable heat.

They wore thin, cream-colored tunics, black pants, and boots. I didn't know how they wore so much fabric—I felt like I was about to pass out, and I could feel trickles of sweat pooling at the base of my neck.

Two massive scorpions stood on either side of the steps. Carved from polished obsidian, they gleamed under the brilliant sun, standing in sharp contrast to the red, dusty sands. Their curved tails arched high, poised to strike at any moment. *Subtle,* I thought. If Kaz was trying to show how intimidating the Scorch Sphere was, it was working.

Tada took a step forward, and each guard reached for the sword strapped to their side. My stomach plummeted. I jerked her back, my attention momentarily distracted by the dagger handles—obsidian, with pigeon-blood red rubies adorning them.

"Hello, hazel eyes," Tada said, stepping forward and slipping from my grasp before I could stop her. My breath hitched. I could already smell our rotting corpses.

She waved her hand in the air like an Aurefly, palm facing inward, displaying her golden swirl mark inches from "hazel eyes."

The guard was easily over six feet tall, while Tada was barely five feet. He looked down at her and sheathed his sword —not before I noticed the crinkles at the corners of his eyes. He wasn't angry. He was amused.

I straightened my spine, visualizing the imaginary spiders sliding off my back—everything was fine.

The guards stepped aside in unison, allowing us to pass. I

could already feel the slight breeze of cool, damp air rising from beneath the dunes. We slowly descended into the pitch-blackness.

I had to admit, Tada hadn't exaggerated the extravagance of the Scorch Sphere's palace. It was a complex web of tunnels that led to luxurious rooms, each one decorated with black silk and satin and accented by ruby-red tones.

My room, connected to Tada's, was accessible through a narrow marble hallway. The entrances were covered with sheer, midnight-black fabric. Throughout the palace, billowing tulle hung in corners, obscuring the view of small, soft benches draped with silk pillows. I could faintly make out the silhouettes of people kissing, which lit my skin on fire, so I quickly looked away. The blatant display of intimacy was something I wasn't used to.

Statues made from precious stones stood throughout the palace. They took the form of desert animals and reptiles. Sometimes, if you took a turn too sharply, you'd come face to face with a snake made of emeralds—ten times the size of a human.

A sacred, darkened chamber housed a statue of Aridan,

where you could light a candle and place it at his feet in gratitude or in hope of a blessing.

One area was dedicated to self-care and relaxation. Dozens of mud baths lined one wall, while a small triangular opening led to a steam room. Gold doors led to the skylight dome ballroom, but they were locked. I practically had to haul Tada away before she could damage the door with her powers by trying to get in. I reassured her that at some point during our stay, I was sure a ball or celebration would be thrown in that room.

As we continued through the palace, I noticed tall, thin doors made of volcanic rock. An attendant passed by, carrying books inside—the library. Excitement and anticipation blazed in my chest.

The Hush Sphere had been a bust, but maybe I'd get lucky and find the *Ari Report* here with ease. My eyes were locked on the door, and I probably would've made a very ungraceful attempt to break in right then and there if Tada hadn't been with me. I made a mental note of its location for later.

After an hour of touring, we headed toward the arena. We walked down a darkened tunnel, torches flickering on the dirt walls to light our way. Laughter and chatter echoed ahead as we emerged into the largest room I had ever seen. Thousands of people crowded around a sandy pit enclosed by a wooden wall, with seats rising in tiers all the way to the rock ceiling. Shrieks of laughter, cursing, and boisterous conversation bounced off the cavern walls. The event was supposed to start soon. I glanced down at the glass-enclosed rectangular box for the Luxari Council that sat at the edge of the pit. The box was already filled with people.

"What about this fight is intriguing?" I shouted over the roaring of the crowd.

"Well, I've never seen one personally, but it's something you can only see in the Scorch Sphere," Tada replied. "During Spice Season, they hold the Sunfire Quests—a series of high-intensity trials—and this is one of them. Otto said the winner takes home more gold than most people see in a lifetime, so the motivation is clear. You can see just how invested everyone is," she said, gesturing toward the crowd.

They were loud and confident, their enthusiasm just a bit too much for my comfort. In the Hush Sphere, the Charmers perched on the Arenwood platforms had looked down at me as if I were nothing more than a pebble stuck in their shoe. The entire kingdom was polished to perfection—no one had a hair out of place or a speck of dirt.

But here, the arrogance was still present—only meaner, rougher, and far more dangerous.

"Tada, I don't even know if we'll be able to find a seat!" I yelled over the noise.

"That won't be a problem," a throaty voice from behind us answered.

Tada and I both turned. I inhaled a little too sharply—hopefully, she didn't notice.

An overwhelmingly beautiful woman stood in front of us, her slender fingers tapping her hip. A wave of self-conscious-ness washed over me. Her ivory-smooth skin glowed with pale gold undertones. Her facial features were delicately carved, her nose exquisitely dainty. Thick charcoal hair fell to her hips, slightly curling at the ends. She was slim, with curves hitting all the right places.

"I'm Sabina," she said, her eyes piercing mine. They were sage green, with a shade of caramel highlighting her pupils.

"Kaz asked me to grab the two of you. You're the only ones missing," she said, her voice cool, with a touch of irritation.

Without waiting for a response, she turned and briskly walked away. Tada and I exchanged a look, and after a beat, we followed her into the darkened tunnel.

CHAPTER

THIRTEEN

We emerged into the box overlooking the pit. Already, the sound of laughter and the clink of glasses filled the air as people drank champagne and devoured smoked meats and sausages.

A hog hung over glowing coals as an Enticer ignited the flames with a single touch. Unbothered by the heat, he turned the pig by hand, his bare palm pressing against the sizzling skin. A jagged scar ran from his temple across his eye and down to his chin—and, fittingly, a tattoo of a pig was inked onto his bicep.

Will, Aldo, and Severin had claimed seats near the front, while Amabel and Rodor whispered quietly in a corner.

A woman with warm bronze skin lounged on a chair, drinking from a gold-rimmed goblet. Otto's face was practically smashed against the glass, eagerly anticipating the fight. Will made eye contact with me from across the room and gave me a small smile and nod.

Kaz wrapped his arm around Sabina's slender shoulders.

"So, I see you've met my little sister," he drawled.

They were siblings? I hadn't seen that coming.

"Sister?" I blurted out.

"Unfortunately," Sabina said, her tone dry.

Okay, that wasn't exactly the warmest sibling reunion.

She lifted his arm and stepped out from under it, glancing around the room as if she were looking for someone.

"Sorry for her mood. You know how younger sisters can be." Kaz winked.

Sabina's eyes widened, her raspberry lips parting into a smile. I followed her gaze. Oak smiled at her from across the room. He wore brown breeches and a light blue tunic with billowing sleeves.

Sabina practically danced into his arms, hugging him tightly as he wrapped an arm around her slim waist.

The tiniest pang of jealousy flickered through me—vanishing before I had time to dwell on it.

Kaz looked amused as Tada complimented him on the design of the palace, speaking quickly and excitedly. He leaned down to hear her better. It was sweet of him.

He wore sleek, leather black pants, boots, and a sleeveless tunic. His sharp, obsidian crown rested on his flaxen hair, which had been pulled into a bun at the nape of his neck.

His Scorch Sphere marking, which began as a sun at his wrist, had been extended with fiery orange, red, and yellow flames that twisted and wrapped around his muscular arm, covering his entire right side. I'd heard that some Luxari embellished their marks with elemental designs—purely preference, a way to show off their power or style.

Otto gave me a wide grin, jumped from his chair, but didn't come to me. I realized too late that the grin was for Tada. He grabbed her hand and dragged her to the window overlooking the pit.

"Coco, you look stunning," Kaz said in a low, husky voice.

My throat went dry. I had no idea what was happening—a Luxari thought I was beautiful? A *Dim*? I almost laughed in his face, but instead, I fumbled for something to say.

"Uh... Kaz, you look good too."

"Good?" he scoffed. "I'll accept sexy, dazzling, deeply attractive. But 'good' hurts my feelings." He attempted a frown.

"What feelings?" The woman who had interrupted our conversation at the Snowfall Ball appeared beside Kaz, an eyebrow raised.

I said a silent prayer of thanks to Aridan for allowing me a moment to breathe. I couldn't seem to think properly.

"I have feelings," Kaz whined.

"Yes, but they're all limited to one part of your body," she said, her eyes flicking to his crotch.

I tried and failed to suppress a giggle.

Kaz grinned, flashing his flawless teeth.

"Coco, this is Eda. She's part of my Luxari Council and serves as my Emissary for Spheres and Trade."

Eda stepped closer to Kaz, her voice steady. "Queen Nerian wishes to speak with you." She flipped her auburn hair over her shoulder, and her jade eyes silently judged me.

"I'm sick of arguing about trade with that woman. She probably had to close a dozen cattle ranches after all the meat I just bought," Kaz grumbled, turning on his heel and striding toward Queen Nerian. Eda followed suit.

The only open spot in the box was next to the woman with the goblet. She was the one who had dispersed the crowd after Oak and Kaz's spat.

She lounged in her chair, glass in hand, feet propped up on the seat in front of her. I slid into the space beside her. Her eyes flicked to me, filled with surprise.

She leaned forward, a smirk tugging at her lips.

"You look like a lost puppy," she drawled.

"I'm not lost. I just don't want to sit alone."

She shrugged casually and dragged her thumb over the rim of her glass, revealing the Daze lily etched on her right wrist.

I studied the golden swirl, the mark of the Luxari Council, which was barely visible behind her ear, hidden mostly by her tight dark curls.

"I'm Nikolette, but I go by Niko," she said. "I make it my business to know everyone's name who participates in the Quests. And since you're a Dim, yours was one of the first I memorized."

Nikolette. The Luxari Council member Oak had said he "knew"—or he could've just admitted right then and there that he was Luxari. I let out a slow exhale of frustration.

"Um... so, Niko, if you don't mind me asking... What exactly is your role on the Daze Luxari Council?"

"I am the Emissary of Spheres and Oak's right hand. So, in other words, I take on whatever job King Oak needs me to," she answered, her gaze never leaving the pit.

Until a few minutes ago, I hadn't realized there were specific duties assigned to the Luxari Council. It made sense, though—running a Sphere smoothly had to require both work and management. But like most people, I'd always assumed the appeal of the Luxari Council was immortality and the chance to work alongside a Luxari.

It made me wonder—what role would I want to have on a Luxari Council? But the thought was gone as soon as it came. There was no way the Luxari would offer a Dim a spot on the Council, even if I had managed to complete the first Quest successfully.

Fifteen Enticers, some shirtless, walked into the pit. Tanned and covered in bruises, scars, and cuts, they all bore the mark of the Scorch Sphere: the bright sun on the inside of their right wrist.

They formed a tight circle around a crate. I leaned forward, intrigued.

"It's Crate Brawling," Niko said, her tone indifferent.

"I'm from the Bleak Sphere... so, I'm sorry, but that doesn't really mean much to me."

"Fifteen Enticers are put in the arena. No fire allowed. They can only use their bodies and whatever's in that crate. The last one standing wins."

Shock ripped through me, my stomach tightening. I snapped my head toward her. "You mean they kill each other?"

"No. Well, sometimes they do. There's a pretty hefty fine if you kill someone. You're only supposed to knock them out," she explained with a hint of amusement.

"Oh, well, that makes it all better," I sniped. I couldn't believe Kaz would allow this to happen in his own kingdom—then again, I barely knew him at all.

"What's in the crate?" I asked.

"Now that's where the fun is. Nobody knows. Each brawl,

there's an unknown object in the crate. It reveals itself once the match starts."

The walls of the crate crashed to the red sand with an invisible force. A sudden dust cloud billowed and dissipated. In the empty space, a wooden ladle waited.

"There is only one?" I asked.

"Exactly." A mischievous glint lit her eyes. "Let's see who gets to it first."

A roar from the crowd signaled the start of the match.

Niko threw back her head to finish her drink. She set the glass down and rubbed her hands together.

A burly man lunged for the ladle, swiping it just before a fierce brute barreled into his ribs. The force sent him crashing onto crimson ground. A grunt escaped his lips, but the ladle stayed locked in his grasp. Another Enticer tumbled onto the gritty scarlet sand, somersaulted forward, and slammed into him like a boulder smashing down a cliff. A muffled thud reverberated through the pit. He sprawled out, his fingers unclenching from the ladle in his palm.

The Enticers circled the fallen. Their eyes shone with predatory anticipation, as if they were waiting to step in once some of their competition was eliminated. Then someone dove for the ladle, and it was as if a cork popped. A guttural growl ripped through the pit as they surged forward, a mass of sweat-slicked limbs and straining muscle. They piled onto each other, creating a mound of bodies, the air thick with grunts and curses. Red sand frosted their tangled forms and flew into their eyes.

A crisp, sickening snap of bone, followed by a chorus of

grinding crunches, made me look away. Bile rose in my throat, but I was soon distracted by nearby movement.

Oak stood, holding Sabina's hand as they walked out of the box.

I couldn't help but feel curious about their relationship—Sabina being Kaz's sister, after all.

A loud yell from the arena caught my attention, and my eyes fell back to the fight.

Clumped bodies lay, sand clinging to their damp skin, while one brute rammed the ladle into his opponent's eye. A bright spray of blood erupted, splattering those around him red and coating the glass window that separated us from the pit. Blood ran down the glass like rain against a windowpane.

This was getting too brutal for me. Maybe talking to Nikolette would be a good distraction.

I wanted to know more about Kaz and Oak's relationship—I think everyone did, after all the physical and verbal punches they had exchanged. But was I brave enough to even mention it to someone on their Luxari Council?

What did I have to lose? The worst she could say was no.

Taking a deep breath, I asked, "Since you serve on the Luxari Council for the Daze Sphere... would you mind giving me some context about what happened at the celebration?"

"What happened?" she replied innocently. She met my eyes, but hers darted away after just a moment.

I raised an eyebrow. "Oh, King Kaz punched King Oak."

"Ah, yes, that," she replied smoothly. "To put it succinctly: first, never become romantically entangled with anyone on your own Luxari Council. And second, never allow pride to cloud your judgment." Her voice took on a sharper edge.

Her response only stirred more questions within me. I opened my mouth to ask, but she raised a hand, silencing me.

"I must apologize, but that is all I am at liberty to share at the moment," she said, her voice tinged with sadness.

My attention drifted back to the brawl. They were still fighting like savage animals: biting, punching, kicking, choking, and wielding the ladle like a club. I winced before looking back to her.

"Why doesn't someone just leave the Luxari Council if they're having issues with one of the others?" I asked, curiosity causing my loose tongue.

"You can't. Once you take the oath, you can't leave. You'll die. Even immortals can die if Aridan deems it."

Die if you leave? The thought made me shudder. Was joining any Luxari Council worth it if you had to bind your life away? It was a lifetime commitment with no exit. A slight throb began to pound at my temples.

Could I ever take an oath like that? To bind myself to something so unbreakable? The very idea unsettled me, the weight of it too much like the loss of Milo. How could I ever promise forever when nothing—especially life—was guaranteed?

Finally, only one man remained standing. It looked like the aftermath of a battlefield, and he stood victorious. Dark blood dribbled down his elbow, dripping off to form a puddle beneath him. His eyes were swollen shut. He looked directly into the booth and smiled, revealing a tooth had been knocked out. He raised the ladle in the air and let out a primal cry. The crowd unleashed screams and chants, shaking the walls of the underground palace.

Niko stood up, stretching her arms and legs.

"I eagerly anticipate witnessing your skills tomorrow."

I scoffed. "What skills?"

"Oh, spare me. You're a Dim who's managed to survive the Bleak Sphere this long—I'd say your odds of coming out of this are higher than you think."

The compliment sent a jolt through me. Before I could respond, Niko added, "Good luck tomorrow, Coco." She smirked and sauntered off.

CHAPTER
FOURTEEN

I had planned to visit the library after Crate Brawling, hoping to make up for lost time. But Kaz had intercepted me on my way out. That didn't mean I couldn't still try to make some kind of progress.

Now, Kaz and I walked side by side through a darkened tunnel. Torches flickered along the damp dirt walls.

My nerves raced. Being alone with a Luxari was intimidating—I couldn't fathom what game he was playing by indulging my company.

"Tell me about your library," I asked, keeping my tone casual.

"Library?" He arched an eyebrow. "There are far more exhilarating pursuits in this palace than dusty old books."

"I love to read," I smiled. A twinge of guilt crawled up my spine at how casually I was flirting in exchange for information.

He glanced down at me, the corner of his mouth quirking.

"I have quite the collection. But most of it is private—records, reports, that sort of thing. Only my Luxari Council has access."

I thought back to the person I had mistaken for an attendant, now realizing she was probably on the Luxari Council.

"So, is it under lock and key?"

Kaz chuckled. "Lock and key? You truly are from the Bleak Sphere. It's charmed—only I and my Luxari Council may enter."

Disappointment surged through me. At every turn, I felt like I was failing Milo. My first attempt to get into the library at the Hush Sphere had been interrupted by the surprise attack from the Void, and now my second attempt was being blocked by a charm. But maybe I could find a way around it.

"What do you enjoy reading?" Kaz asked, his voice softer now.

"History, Starlight Tales, folktales," I said. "My brother loved books. Will, our best friend, had a library, and the three of us would spend entire days lost in stories..."

I was surprised at how easy it was to talk to him, and I felt my nerves begin to calm.

"Do you have any other siblings?" Kaz asked, as we kept walking down the darkened tunnel.

"No. It was just me and Milo," I paused. " He passed away."

I hesitated, swallowing the ache that rose in my throat.

Sympathy swam in Kaz's eyes.

"What about you?"

"Just Sabina and me."

"Are you close?"

"We fight as viciously as those in the Crate Brawl, yet we still remain close. I'd go to great lengths for her."

His sentiment seemed sincere.

A cold draft shot through the tunnel, and I rubbed my arms instinctively for warmth.

"Cold?" Kaz asked. The firelight flickered across his sharp, tan features.

By Aridan's breath, nothing got past him.

"I'm fine," I said, trying to brush off the goosebumps on my skin.

"Of course you are," he replied with a smirk. "Luckily, we're here."

"Here?" I raised a brow in confusion, as embers of anxiety flared within me.

"My rooms," he said, a mischievous glint shining in his eyes.

My face burned. I hoped he didn't have any expectations. Sweat gathered at the back of my neck and in the palms of my hands.

Why was the King of the Scorch Sphere leading me to his rooms? I swallowed hard, trying to soothe my dry throat.

He led me up a staircase carved from solid gold. Two massive doors, made of obsidian, glossy and sleek, stood at the top. A guard on either side bowed and pushed them open without a word.

The room beyond sent a jolt of shock radiating through my core. It wasn't what I'd expected from him.

Unlike the rest of the palace, drenched in crimson and midnight, Kaz's room was soft and inviting. The floor was gray marble, covered with rugs woven with gold thread. At the far end, a canopy bed stood with beige curtains drifting gently from its posts, the sheer fabric embroidered with delicate flames in orange stitching.

The intimacy of it hit me all at once. My heart raced. My skin buzzed with warmth.

I tried to shake it off by moving around the room.

Along one wall, glass cases displayed objects like relics: a broken sword, a crushed helmet, a wrinkled map marked with faded ink.

But it was the soft glow from the opposite wall that drew my gaze.

A large glass tank stretched across the wall. Inside, pale, fire-lit fish flickered like embers in water. The tank arched into a tunnel overhead, allowing you to walk beneath it. Beyond it, the back wall glimmered with dancing electric-blue flames.

Kaz crossed the room and opened a chest near the wall. He pulled out a folded blanket and walked back to me, wrapping it gently around my shoulders. The fabric was smooth and smelled faintly of oranges.

His touch was careful—almost hesitant—and the gesture awakened something within me.

"Care for a game?" Kaz asked.

I turned toward him. He stood next to the tank, beside a low cherrywood table shaped like a tray and filled with deep red sand.

"A game? You have me alone in your room, and that's what you want to do?" I laughed, surprised by my own boldness. Kaz had a reputation with women—something I was quickly starting to learn since arriving here.

Kaz shrugged, clearing his throat. "We have time for both," he muttered, looking away as a faint blush rose to his cheeks.

What was that supposed to mean?

"What's the game?" I stepped closer.

"*Flame Spiders.*"

A spider was carved into each corner of the table, its blackened outline etched deep into the wood. Kaz pressed his finger to one of the engravings, and a spark leapt from his skin. Flames erupted outward, forming a fiery barrier around the tray of sand. Tiny yellow spiders began to emerge from narrow slits in the wood, glowing faintly as they skittered across the rust-colored grains.

Kaz reached beneath the table and unhooked a small black satin pouch. He opened it, revealing polished stones the size of grapes—some a rich emerald green, others a vivid cerulean blue.

He picked up a green stone, leaned over the table, and squinted toward the sand. Then, with a snap of his wrist, he launched the stone. It struck a spider dead-on, which immediately burst into green flames.

He grinned, grabbed another stone, tossed it, and this time —nothing happened.

"If you miss, it won't ignite. But hit one, and it erupts in the color of your stone. The one who lands the most wins."

"What's the prize?" I smirked. "I don't do anything for nothing."

He contemplated, arms crossing over his chest, biceps flexing as he looked me over.

"If you win, your opponent answers one question. No lies."

That could get dangerous—fast. But if I won, I could ask him how to get around the charm in the library.

"Deal." I held out my palm.

His eyebrows lifted. "You agreed much faster than I expected."

I shrugged, setting my blanket down. The fire's warmth had chased away the chill.

He dropped the cerulean stones into my hand. I studied the sand, biting my lip. Then I threw one.

The stone hit a spider, and it exploded into blue fire. I jumped, squealed, and spun to face Kaz, throwing my hands into the air in celebration.

He chuckled. "Don't get too cocky now."

He closed his eyes in confidence and launched the stone. It struck true—green flames flared where it landed.

"Hmph." I narrowed my eyes at the sand.

We went back and forth, trading tosses and bursts of flame. In the end, he won—by one. But I couldn't believe how much I was enjoying myself. For once, I was having fun—without worrying about the Sphere Quests or the *Ari Report*. It felt nice.

"What's your question?" I asked.

He studied me for a long moment, as if weighing every possible option—then, with a smug tilt of his lips, said, "How many men have you been with?"

"What?" I blinked, caught completely off guard. Heat rushed to my cheeks before I could stop it.

He gave me a cocky grin, eyes sparkling with amusement. "What? It's a valid question."

"That's not even getting to know me," I said, folding my arms. "And it's completely irrelevant."

His grin only widened. "Fine. You show me how it's done."

I rolled my eyes but couldn't help the small smile tugging at my lips. "All right, then. What's your favorite place in all of Aren?"

"Easy," he said, stepping a little closer. "I'll show you."

"Right now?" I asked. He nodded, taking my hand in his.

My nerves raced as a frantic flutter stirred in my chest. The rough calluses on his palm scraped against my skin as he gently led me toward the glimmering electric-blue fire along the wall.

He could have walked right through without harm—but I would've been fried to a crisp.

His hand rose, and he brushed the flames aside as though drawing a curtain back from a window.

Beyond lay a small circular room with a floor carved from jade. A round settee occupied the center, draped in shades of emerald green and honey gold. Against the far wall stood a white marble desk.

But what was truly remarkable was the ceiling.

Above us, a domed skylight revealed a perfect view of the stars that shimmered like jewels across the sky.

The beauty and comfort of the room were not only enticing, but reassuring.

This was the room that mattered—not for show, not for court, lovers, or power plays.

Just for him.

The outer room seemed to be a mask, like his smirk and swagger.

But this one—this soft, starlit sanctuary—was Kaz when no one was watching.

Pressed petals and letters on faded sheets of brown paper were pinned to the walls.

I stepped closer to one. It read,

I sleep in sparks and wake in flame.
Love, Eda.

I had no idea what it meant, but clearly, it was important to him.

Everything hanging on these walls was important to him. It felt like taking a glimpse into his soul—his heart.

I turned to face Kaz. His expression was tense, like he was caught in an internal battle—torn between speaking or moving.

"I must say, Coco, I find you intriguing."

"Why would you say that?"

"I've been with a lot of women," he said.

I rolled my eyes, but he continued, "Every one of them defines their happiness by wanting something—immortality, influence, power. You act like you couldn't care less. You're a Dim, competing against Embers—and you finished the first Quest without magic. That's impressive. Most would've called it a fool's errand, yet here you are. And you're not swayed by riches or immortality. Not even a seat on the Luxari Council. I don't get it."

I shrugged. I wasn't sure how to explain it.

"Why is that?" he asked again.

"I don't know," I said, voice low. "Life is already hard enough. Why would I want immortality just to endure pain and hardship forever?"

He didn't speak.

We stood there in silence, bathed in starlight.

"Life has more to offer," he said at last.

"I know." I looked up and met his eyes. "But so far, all it's offered me is grief... and poverty."

The silence, the anticipation, the anxiety about him making a move made me speak quickly, saying the first thing that came to mind.

"Any advice for tomorrow?" I asked, raising a brow. I kept my tone steady even as a slight tremble crept into my hands. I tucked them behind my back before he could notice.

I didn't know if the tremble in my hands came from being alone with Kaz... or from what tomorrow might bring.

Maybe both.

"Leverage your strengths," he said.

I scoffed. "Seriously? That's it?"

"Oh, be sensible. Everyone has their strengths. Surely you can boast a little. What are you particularly good at?"

I gave a half-smile. "I'm fast." I ran my hand along the settee as I walked around it, the fabric silky and cool beneath my fingers. A citrusy mint scent wafted off the pillows, filling my senses.

He nodded. "The thing about Embers is that we lean too heavily on our magic. But from my experience, some of these tasks? A Dim could handle them just as well—no powers required. And when they underestimate you..."

He paused, locking eyes with me.

"Because they underestimate you, they fail to see you as a threat. That's precisely when you become your alliance's secret weapon—with that remarkable speed of yours."

He offered a slight smile. "Use it to your advantage. And, naturally, be confident."

He stood there, watching me.

I gave a short laugh. "Easy for a Luxari to say."

He just stared at me meaningfully, the corners of his lips quirking slightly.

"I'm not the only one. Everyone's speaking of you, Coco—a Dim who actually made it through the first Quest. My people say every inn and tavern is fully booked. Visitors are pouring in from all over Aren just to catch a glimpse of you."

My stomach twisted into tight knots.

If he was trying to help, he was only making me feel more anxious.

"Why?" I wrapped my arms around myself. "They weren't even there during the first Quest..."

"But word has spread of your success. Every village, every kingdom, longs for something to believe in—a story of hope. You are offering them just that. A Dim who not only competes but outperforms those with magical abilities? It's unprecedented, and it's reshaping long-held perceptions and prejudices against Dims."

My chest tightened as warmth spread through my veins. His words were more inspiring than I had expected.

"It's not just them," he continued. "This evening, I overheard a Dim placing bets on your success tomorrow," Kaz said, a smile playing at his lips.

"What?" My mouth dropped.

I finished circling the settee and stood beside him.

Kaz stepped closer, and my heart thundered wildly in my chest.

What was he doing? My pulse fluttered anxiously.

He wrapped his arms around me.

"I'd wager on it myself, if it weren't such a conflict of interest."

I bit my lip as I looked up at him.

Kaz's rough knuckles brushed against my cheek, causing my breath to catch in the back of my throat.

My eyes met his.

His thumb slowly moved over the curve of my mouth. As it lingered on my lower lip, my heart threatened to burst.

When he spoke again, his voice had softened almost to a murmur. "Tomorrow, during the challenge, remember—you don't need magic. You are strong as you are."

CHAPTER

FIFTEEN

T he heat blazed on my skin, sending trickles of sweat down my spine. I wiped my damp forehead with the back of my hand, blinking against the bright sun.

The air felt thick and suffocating. I stood with the other Questlings on a sandy field, the coarse grains clinging to my legs. The sand had been flattened into the shape of a rectangle, creating a smooth surface for the second Quest.

Kaz hadn't exaggerated last night. Rows of wooden benches, filled with thousands of people, surrounded us, their voices filling the air. People had traveled from all the Spheres, including the Bleak Sphere, to witness the second Quest. Black lines were painted on the sand, enclosing us in a rectangle and marking the boundaries of whatever hell we were about to face.

My alliance wore azure leather pants, boots, and fitted sleeveless tunics. The other group wore the same, but in fire-blossom red.

Will stood directly to my right, his expression unreadable. Tada hummed distractedly to my left, her fingers twitching with nervous energy. Otto, ever the restless one, was throwing invisible punches into the air, practicing his swinging arm. Tada watched him move, her lips pressed tight as if absorbing his every action. I arched a brow at her.

"Oh, shut up," she mumbled, jabbing me in the ribcage with her elbow. It knocked the wind out of me. For someone as tiny as Tada, she sure was strong.

Sand brushed the back of my boots. I looked behind me. Hugh stood there with his head bowed, kicking at the sand.

The crowd stilled. Queen Catalina strolled onto the field, followed by Oak, Kaz, and Queen Nerian, stopping right in front of us.

"Questlings." Queen Catalina clasped her hands in front of her, her voice commanding the attention of the entire arena. "Welcome to the second challenge of the Sphere Quests." She paused, her eyes sweeping across us. "You will be evaluated in three distinct categories during this challenge. First, your ability to win the game." A ripple of whispers spread through the crowd, the murmur of curiosity growing louder. That was the first real clue we had about what the challenge might be.

"Second, your ability to effectively use your individual skill set—focusing on physical performance and analytical thinking," she continued, her tone unwavering. "And last, your ability to work with your allies. The second challenge of the Sphere Quests will be *Seize the Banner*." She let the words hang in the air.

The crowd erupted in rowdy cheers. I groaned.

"Coco, I've seen you play." Will's voice cut through the noise, low and teasing. "You aren't... terrible."

"Thanks, Will. That's super reassuring," I muttered, rolling my eyes at him.

His lips twitched, as if he was trying to suppress a laugh.

I punched his arm. I might as well have hit a boulder.

"Mother of Aridan," I hissed, clutching my hand to my chest.

Will grinned, clearly amused. "I'm pretty sure you did more damage to your hand than to me."

"You think?" I growled, rubbing my sore fist.

I glanced around at the other rulers, trying to gauge their reactions. Kaz was practically vibrating with excitement, a wide grin on his face. Queen Nerian gave a polite, close-lipped smile. Oak just stood there, hands clasped behind his back, and when his eyes met mine, they were intense and unreadable.

Light smoldered in his gray, gold-flecked eyes. I looked back toward Queen Catalina to escape the heat of his gaze. My pulse began to pound rapidly. I couldn't decide whether it was the weight of Oak's stare, the nervous anticipation of the challenge ahead, or both.

Queen Catalina cleared her throat, and silence spread throughout the crowd.

"*Seize the Banner* is a game of skill, intellect, and strategy."

She snapped her fingers to charm two banners out of thin air on opposite sides of the field, hanging from wooden beams in their teams' respective colors.

I turned my attention to my alliance, studying their reactions. Tada stood with her hands on her hips, chewing the inside of her cheek in thought, her brow furrowed. Otto bounced back and forth on his toes, a wide grin spreading across his face. Will was still, his arms hanging by his sides, his face tense with concentration, listening intently to the rules. Hugh's gaze remained focused on the ground, though the erratic kicking of the sand had ceased.

The moment was broken by the sudden snap of Queen Catalina's fingers as she charmed twelve spheres into existence, each roughly the size of a coconut. They rolled onto the field with a soft thud.

"The black spheres will cause temporary paralysis if they make contact with your body. If you are struck by a brown sphere"—she paused, her hand sweeping toward a patch of darker sand directly in front of a raised dais—"you will be transported to the quicksand pit, where you will have only moments to escape."

Escape. She said it so casually. Having my lungs filled with sand didn't seem casual to me at all. I had never played this version of *Seize the Banner*. This new element—quicksand—gnawed at my confidence.

I bit my lip, a nervous habit I had developed over the years. Whenever the anxiety crept up, my teeth would dig into my bottom lip until it bled. The pain was almost comforting, a distraction from the overwhelming sense of helplessness that threatened to take over.

Forcing myself to focus, I turned my attention to our opponents.

Aldo stood with his arms crossed, his biceps flexing. Rodor cracked his neck and knuckles, looking like he could crush me with his pinky if he wanted. Amabel shot me a hostile glare, her crimson lips pursed in both amusement and determination.

Severin looked distracted, his eyes scanning the crowd. Cecille's small frame trembled; fear was written all over her face. Her eyes met mine, and I gave her a reassuring smile. She hesitated for a moment, then returned the gesture, her shoulders relaxing ever so slightly.

I turned back to Queen Catalina.

"You may not step out of the perimeter, which is marked by black paint, or you will be disqualified. The game will end once an alliance steals the banner of the other alliance and crosses back over to their side. All magic is allowed, and Fire Elaryns will be evaluating your performance, as well as the Luxari. Ari Dust vials will be awarded to the winning team. Alliances, please head toward your banner."

Fire Elaryns appeared out of nowhere, hovering in the sky. Their fiery orange, translucent skin burned with deep red.

Amabel shot me a vicious smile, and my body filled with scalding irritation. Clenching my fists, I looked away. Our banner was on the opposite side of the field, but Will didn't hesitate. He started jogging toward it without looking back. One by one, the rest of our alliance followed. My heart pounded as I took the first step toward what was sure to be a brutal fight.

The Luxari took their seats on the raised dais. Kaz sat in the center on a sleek black throne. His Luxari Council were seated in the row behind him, along with Niko and Sabina.

Will stopped next to our banner, his jaw set in determination.

"Otto, how do you feel about throwing spheres?" Will asked.

"I was born for it!" Otto whooped.

"Tada and Hugh, how do you feel about defense?" Will questioned.

"On it," Tada said, rubbing her hands together. "I already have the perfect charm."

Will smiled and turned toward Hugh. "You are a gifted Swayer, Hugh. Don't be afraid to use your magic," he said in a soft but firm tone.

Pink crept onto Hugh's cheeks.

"I'll be causing a diversion so Coco can retrieve their banner," Will said.

My head snapped toward him.

"Alright, let's show these twig-snapping fools exactly why Aridan summoned us for the Luxari Councils," Will said, his voice filled with unshakable confidence.

We scattered ourselves across the sandy field, waiting for the signal to start the game. I bounced nervously on my feet, the anticipation of the challenge building in my chest. Sweat clung to my temples, and my stomach twisted in tight knots.

Kaz finally stood, holding his clenched fist in the air. He suddenly opened his palm, and fire—taking the shape of a cobra—slithered upward in a burst of yellow and orange. It coiled, stretching higher and higher, dark smoke trailing from its tail. The air crackled with heat. The cobra exploded, sending sparks across the sand as Kaz bellowed, "Begin!"

The ground shook violently beneath me. My hands dug into the dirt as I pulled myself up. Aldo had sent a massive tremor through the ground, knocking us all onto our asses. He had already reached our side. Tada and he were circling each other, tension crackling between them. Tada's back was to our banner.

A black sphere came whirling toward me, and I barely managed to dive out of the way in time. Rodor didn't hesitate; he threw another one. I dropped my body, rolling through the sand, narrowly avoiding it.

"Impressive for a Dim." Amabal's voice came from behind me, and before I could react, she crouched down right in front of me.

My mouth went dry, and panic wormed its way down my spine.

Her hands were engulfed with flames. I tried to rise quickly, but she slammed her fiery hand down on my neck, pushing my face into the sand. The sand muffled my screams as scalding heat burned my neck. I thrashed and struggled against her hand.

"Pathetic," she snorted.

The pressure on my neck released. I gasped and jerked up.

Will had hit Amabel with a black sphere. She collapsed to the ground, frozen in place. Her eyes were wide with shock, her body curled in on itself.

My heart thundered in my chest, my neck burning from where her flames had scorched my skin. I sucked in a ragged breath, tasting the grit of the sand that had pressed into my mouth.

"Will, look out!" I shouted as Rodor hurled a brown sphere at him. It cut through the air with a whistle, barely missing him.

Will cursed. I gritted my teeth as unbearable pain from Amabal's attack seared through my neck.

A hawk screeched from above. I looked up. Aldo had shifted into a hawk and was swooping down to retrieve our banner.

Panic thrummed through me as he dove for it. His large, sharp talons opened to grip it, but they rebounded off some invisible force.

Tada stood near the banner, her eyes closed as her mouth moved rapidly. She must have charmed the banner with an invisible force.

Hugh stood next to her, watching the scene unfold as Will and Otto ganged up on Rodor. With Aldo, Rodor, and Amabel tied up, this was my chance to steal the banner. I would only have to face Cecille and Severin.

Fueled by adrenaline, I broke into a sprint, beelining toward the red banner on the opposite side of the sand field. Sweat rolled down my cheeks as sand clung to my skin. I did my best to ignore the pulsing agony radiating through my neck.

I heard a small cry. My gaze shot toward the quicksand pit in front of the dais, just in time to see Cecille's face disappear beneath the sand.

My breath hitched, a cold spike of fear piercing through the chaos. *Run*, my mind screamed. But as my eyes snagged on her struggling form, the thought was gone, replaced by a sudden, fierce resolve.

I changed course, halting in front of the pit. I threw my arm over the edge of the quicksand and tugged lightly on Cecille's curly hair. Her fingers broke the surface. Desperation surged as I grabbed her fingers, then her hand, using all my strength to lean back and pull her up.

Her body slowly rose from the depths of the pit as I fell back onto the ground. She landed with a heavy thud beside me, coughing violently, but alive, gasping for air.

My heart pounded in my chest, and I forced myself to turn toward their banner once again.

I whirled around just in time to see Rodor barreling toward me, a black sphere clenched tightly in his fist. It looked like it might pop any second. I waited until the last possible moment, then rolled forward out of the way. He couldn't stop in time. He stumbled and crashed headfirst into the pit. He wasn't like Cecille—he was strong and experienced. I wasn't worried about him getting out.

Glancing over my shoulder, I found Tada on the ground, unconscious, a trickle of blood sliding down her temple. I took a step forward, but Otto was already by her side. Will and Aldo had both shifted into jaguars, poised to pounce.

Dashing toward the banner, I saw Severin pacing lazily beneath it. Fire Elaryns swam through the air, keeping pace with me.

I stopped a few feet from him. Clearly not seeing me as a threat, he continued pacing with his hands in his pockets. I chewed on my lip, weighing my options. A slight breeze stirred the air. The banner fluttered, almost as if it were waving me on to victory.

Hugh. I turned. He could control the wind, but he was young, unsure, and hesitant to fully embrace his powers. Rodor was nearly out of the pit, dragging his hulking frame across the sand. Hugh needed encouragement. I gave him a thumbs-up, which he returned with a brief nod.

As soon as I turned, a gust of wind picked up the red banner and sent it soaring through the air. I worried that Amabel would fry it to a crisp or Aldo would snag it before it made it to our side, so I jumped, reaching up and bunching the material in my hand. I spun around and bolted toward our side of the field.

High-pressure water slammed into my back, knocking me off my feet. The water engulfed me as if I had jumped into the Cobalt Sea. A sharp, biting sting tore through my burn. The air was ripped from my lungs.

Then, the strangest thing occurred—the voice of the Aurefly began to sing. Though I couldn't see it, its haunting melody filled my ears:

> Coco, Coco, brave and bright,
> Don't fall behind—turn and fight.
> You hold the fate of those now gone,
> And you'll be the one to right the wrong.
> Follow your heart, stay steady and sure—

The water ceased, along with the singing. I choked out water onto the sand, the banner still clenched in my fist. A little disoriented, I rose. Hugh and Severin appeared to be locked in a wind-and-water face-off.

I rushed toward our side of the field, but a ball struck me from behind. My limbs froze as I toppled onto the sand. The banner glided to the ground.

My body was completely immobilized. Amabel stalked forward, grabbed my hair, and wrenched my head back. Pain exploded across my scalp and burnt neck as she dragged me through the sand toward the front of the dais.

My pulse rattled in my ears.

I screamed wildly in my mind, urging my body to move. But

I was helpless. She released my hair, and my head hit the ground. I had never felt so powerless.

My head faced the dais. Oak and Kaz sprang to their feet. Oak's eyes flashed with outrage, his fists trembling at his sides, his nostrils flaring. Niko stood, placing a hand on Oak's shoulder. Kaz scowled at Amabel and threw his hands up.

Amabel's sinister, silky lips brushed my ear. "Say hi to your brother for me," she snarled. Then, with a malicious laugh, she heaved my body into the quicksand.

Pitch blackness consumed me.

CHAPTER
SIXTEEN

A silent scream tore through my head. Sand scraped against my skin and grated against my injury like ground glass, sending a flash of white-hot pain ripping through my flesh. My lungs burned, desperately seeking air that wasn't there. I was going to die. Icy fear twisted around my heart.

The panic choked me as much as the sand. My thoughts spun in circles... but then, Kaz's words from last night echoed in my head:

You don't need magic. You are strong just the way you are.

With every fiber of my being, I willed my fingers to move. One finger twitched. A wave of hope surged through me. Slowly, feeling began to return to my body, spreading through my limbs.

I thrust my arm up, and it exploded from the sand. A strong hand gripped mine and wrenched me from the hole. I frantically gulped in air, instantly awake and fully aware of my surroundings. My body jerked with each cough as I heaved air into my lungs.

Otto and Tada lay motionless on the sand. Amabel reached for our banner, flanked by Rodor and Aldo. A sharp, biting cold pain shot through my arm and I glanced up. Will stood with his hand in mine, his body encased in ice—frozen.

My head whirled to Severin, who stood a few feet back, aiming his open palms at me. Magic surged through the air, raising every hair on my arms. Severin collapsed to the ground, clutching his head.

I snapped my head toward Hugh—his eyes squeezed shut, his body trembling as he slithered into their minds. He hadn't tried this before—maybe because he wasn't sure what he could do, or maybe because he hadn't been confident enough. But now, as the challenge wore on, he was willing to risk it.

Amabel, Rodor, and Aldo were on the ground, clutching their heads.

I raced toward the red banner, scooped it up without pausing, and hurled myself across the field.

Applause erupted from the crowd.

I slowed down and rested my hands on my knees, struggling to gulp down air.

"Victory to the Ellipse Alliance!" a loud voice bellowed.

I straightened. Queen Catalina sliced her hand through the air, and all the magic disabling the Questlings lifted.

Sharp, searing pain roared in my neck, reminding me of the burn. I placed my hand on the wound, flinching at the sting. My knees wobbled beneath me, adrenaline still pulsing hot through my veins. But then I saw them—my team, alive, waiting, cheering. Relief crashed over me in a wave.

We had won. My alliance had triumphed, and I was a part of it. A smile spread slowly across my face as I jogged toward my team.

I stood in front of the square, black-framed mirror after hours of getting ready. Tonight was the Scorch Ball—another celebration thrown by the Luxari, one of so many that I could barely keep track.

A Charmer had treated me right after the Quest. I unwrapped the fabric from my neck, my fingers brushing the edges of the burn. It was a faint, slightly raised pink mark, a reminder of Amabel's power. I had expected it to be healed by now, but it wasn't. After what Oak had done to my wrist, I wondered if I should have gone to him to treat my neck. But I hadn't—I was too embarrassed to ask.

Hugh was ecstatic about his contribution. As we had walked off the field, he'd told me that he'd never been able to wield control over so many minds at once—and he owed it to the Ari Dust. He downed the next vial from our winnings right away. Will quietly tucked his away, while Tada and Otto were too caught up in their excitement to pay much attention to theirs.

I tried to recall what the Aurefly had sung to me, but apparently, when you're high on adrenaline, trying not to die, and something starts singing to you, those words don't exactly stick. Still, it was strange. It was the same song, yet with each Quest, more lines seemed to be added.

The shimmering specks of silver and gold in the Ari Dust caught my eye, glittering from the vial resting on the table beside my bed. As I had suspected, Queen Catalina admitted that Ari Dust would do nothing for a Dim. I'd tried to offer it to Will, Otto, Tada, and Hugh, but each refused, spinning their own excuses.

I glanced back at the mirror, taking a moment to admire the dress.

The top section of my gown had a bateau neckline and was sleeveless, made of sheer fabric. The silky skirt started at my navel, clinging to my curves before softly flaring out at the ground, the fabric smooth against my skin. Toffee-gold glitter shimmered on my eyelids, while a pastel pink gloss coated my lips, the color a perfect match to my gown.

Unlike in the Hush Sphere, Eda had asked if I had any preferences for the gown I wanted to wear. She had left a large trunk in my room, filled with gowns in the style I preferred. I couldn't shake the feeling that her cold demeanor seemed like a shield, hiding some type of hurt that she faced.

My stomach churned with anxiety as I wrung my hands together. I was nervous to see Amabel. She had tried to kill me in cold blood. And how did she know about Milo? Was his death just common knowledge now? My fingers brushed over the ring Milo had given me, offering the slightest bit of comfort and courage.

I stood outside the tall, dark doors of the library. The wide doors appeared to have no handles. Even though I knew the library was protected by charms, I thrust my hip into the door anyway, but it didn't budge. I placed my hands on my sides. I never thought sneaking into a library would be this difficult.

"I figured it out."

I jumped at the sound of the voice.

"I suspect you're attempting to break into libraries to steal the romance novels you claim to despise," Oak teased.

I blinked, a bit surprised. I guess I hadn't been as stealthy as I'd hoped.

I turned toward him and the cocky, smug grin on his face vanished. His eyes boldly raked over me. My cheeks flushed under the heat of his gaze.

His gaze slid downward, slow and deliberate, lingering just long enough to make my skin prickle and my stomach twist with heat.

"Coco. You look..." He swallowed. "Absolutely beautiful." His voice dropped to a lower, huskier tone.

Flames licked my cheeks as heat rushed up my neck. My heart fluttered wildly in my chest. *Did he mean it?*

"Thank you," I murmured, swallowing hard.

By Aridan's breath, my body felt ablaze with heat. Oak looked amazing. He wore a fitted, quarter-sleeve cream tunic. His thigh muscles made his umber leather pants taut.

"May I ask why you attempted to access the library at the Hush Sphere—and now, the Scorch Sphere as well?"

How did he know about my attempt at the Hush Sphere? Maybe he had watched me head to the second floor.

The way he looked at me made it feel like he cared—like maybe he could even help—which is why the words tumbled from my lips. "I need to see the *Ari Report*."

His eyebrows shot up in surprise.

"And why, exactly, would you need to see the *Ari Report*?"

"My brother Milo died over two years ago."

A flicker of unease passed across Oak's face, but I pressed on. "And I haven't heard from the Retired Luxari. And I only have one year left to figure out what happened to his soul before it dissipates. My brother was the most amazing person I know, and I have no doubt he has an Ari Soul. I just want to make sure he has moved on to the Unknown. The *Ari Report* can tell me if the ceremony has happened yet."

Oak studied me intently, his eyes softening.

The words hung heavy in the air between us. I waited, hoping Oak would say something, anything. But then Sabina's voice shattered the silence.

"There you are." Her throaty, sultry voice filled the hall. She wore a shiny silver dress with a neckline that plunged to her navel.

"I've been looking for you everywhere," Sabina drawled, wrapping a thin arm through Oak's.

Annoyance stirred inside me.

"Oh, hi, Bobo," Sabina said.

"It's Coco," I replied, a flicker of irritation rising in my chest.

"Oops, silly me," she let out a fake laugh. "Oak, you're needed in the ballroom."

Without waiting for a reply, she pulled him down the hall. He glanced back at me over his shoulder, but I turned and walked in the opposite direction.

I stood by Tada and Otto, my eyes scanning the ballroom as I took in the scene. The room was underground, yet a massive skylight dome above us revealed the vast night sky. Hundreds of stars sparkled down on us, and the full moon bathed the room in pale light. Lush green bushes and lunara trees dotted the space, making it feel almost like an exotic garden. In one corner, a fountain poured radiant blue water into a small, rounded pool.

Throughout the space, vaporous figures—dragons, snakes, scorpions—danced and twisted through the air, leaving trails of billowing, sizzling steam in their wake.

The room was packed with people, but I couldn't seem to find Amabel or Rodor. A wave of relief washed over me. I hoped

Amabel was off licking her wounds after losing the second challenge—and staying clear of me.

Aldo, Severin, Will, and Niko were deep in conversation. I looked for Cecille instead. She was chatting with a group of girls her age when her light brown eyes met mine, and she walked toward me.

"You don't need to leave your friends…" But before I could stop her, she wrapped her arms around me in a quick hug, then pulled away.

"Thanks for what you did for me today."

"It was nothing."

"I appreciated it," she said, her voice light. "And I just wanted to let you know that you don't have to look out for me during the next two Quests."

My brows knitted in confusion. She thanked me, but didn't want my help? I understood she was in a different alliance, but that didn't seem to explain it.

"I've seen my fate." She smiled. "I know that I will live past the Sphere Quests."

Before I could respond, she turned and skipped back to her friends. If she knew her fate, had she received a prophecy? How could she be so sure? That's when I noticed Will, his gaze fixed on us, his expression serious and unreadable.

Suddenly, the room quieted. Kaz entered, strolling confidently into the center of the ballroom. A hush fell over the crowd.

"Congratulations to the Ellipse Alliance on their triumph in the second challenge," he announced, his voice steady and commanding. Polite claps rippled through the room. "The next challenge will commence in the Daze Sphere in a few days.

Until then, let us drink, dance, and revel. I have enough alcohol to last us until the next Sphere Quests, so drink up."

Attendants immediately entered the room, carrying trays of golden liqueur with flames dancing on their surfaces.

Kaz took a seat on a throne that matched his obsidian crown. Around him, several people mingled—the Luxari Council of the Scorch Sphere, all tan and well-built.

Severin approached me with someone I didn't recognize beside him.

"Coco, this is my partner, Crispin," Severin said.

This must have been the person he'd been searching for in the crowd before the game.

Crispin had dark, glossy hair and a steady presence. He extended a hand. I took it—and paused. A square marked the inside of his wrist. He was a Dim.

My eyes widened. Severin smirked, like he could read exactly what I was thinking.

I wasn't shocked, not exactly, but it still caught me off guard. Most Embers were with other Embers. The fact that Severin—an Ember—was with a Dim made me like him more.

"You were incredibly fast, Coco," Crispin said. His deep blue eyes swept over me, assessing. "Honestly, I think you'd outrun any Dim in all of Aren."

"You're too kind."

He shook his hand in his pocket, and something jingled inside—coins, I assumed. He smiled.

He was the Dim Kaz was talking about—the one placing bets in my favor.

Severin gave a knowing nod. "He is. And painfully honest. And currently very grumpy. His orbs are in a knot."

"I'll keep them in a knot until the Quests are over," Crispin muttered.

He shoved a hand in his pocket and started walking, Severin falling into step beside him. Their hands brushed before folding together.

"Coco," Niko said, her voice a smooth drawl as she draped a toned arm over my shoulders. "Now listen, you were magnificent out there today, truly. However, I think you would benefit from some expert training." Her voice was warm and sincere.

"I agree. Where is this expert?" I asked, lifting her arm as I stepped out of her embrace.

"You wound me, Coco," she said, trying to frown but failing. Her smile, playful and teasing, made it hard not to laugh.

A melodic tune rose from the orchestra seated in the far corner of the room and the crowd slowly began to disperse, the soft hum of conversations blending with the music.

"Tomorrow morning, be at the fight pit," Niko called as she plucked a glass of beer off a moving tray.

Why did Niko suddenly show an interest in helping me? Was this just another "female thing" I was oblivious to, having grown up with a brother?

I quickly joined the crowd and moved off the black marble dance floor. The strings filled the room with harmonious music. I could really use extra help—it was sweet of Niko to offer.

Tada grabbed my arm, her fingers tight with excitement. "No, he is not." Her attempt at whispering failed, her voice rising just enough to be heard by the people closest to us.

"No, he is not what?" I actually whispered, trying to keep my voice low.

"It's customary for the host of the ball to have the first pick of whom he dances with. In this case, it would be King Kazimir, but..." She paused, her eyes widening with excitement. "King Oak is walking straight toward us. I think he's going to ask you to dance," she said, her face filled with giddy anticipation.

My heart skipped a beat at the thought of Oak approaching. I hadn't expected him to make a move. But as his tall figure moved through the audience, his eyes locked on me. A lurch of excitement ran through me, followed by fear.

"Tada, I can't dance. You have to get me out of here," I said, my eyes pleading with hers. My heart raced as the crowd swirled around us, but I couldn't seem to move. My feet were suddenly glued to the floor.

"Too late," she mumbled, a wicked grin tugging at her lips.

King Oak stood in front of me, his profile sharp and confident, as if the entire room bent around his presence.

He cleared his throat. "Coco, will you dance with me?"

CHAPTER
SEVENTEEN

He reached out his arm, his palm open.

"No!" I practically shouted, panicking.

Amusement flickered across his face.

"She means yes," Tada said, followed by a little shove. I stumbled forward, my hand falling into Oak's. His fingers wrapped around mine. The sensation sent sparks dancing up my arm.

Oak guided me onto the black marble to join the other couples. Fear knotted my stomach. I didn't know how to dance, let alone with a Luxari, and the thought of my first attempt being a spectacle for hundreds of eyes made my skin clammy. My gaze darted around the room, taking in the sea of faces. A ripple of whispers spread from a huddle of women, their eyes glittering with speculation. Niko choked on her beer, spraying those around her. Sabina's eyes, sharp as glass shards, pierced me through the crowd.

My heart slammed violently against my chest as my other

hand grabbed Oak's wrist. I looked up at him, panic rising in my throat.

"Please, Oak. I really can't dance. I'm just going to embarrass you." My voice trembled.

His gaze never wavered from mine. "Coco, I don't care about anyone else's opinion. What matters is *you*—and you have nothing to fear, not from anyone, not ever."

He tucked a curl behind my ear, his fingers grazing my skin in a way that sent a shiver racing through me.

He led me to the center of the dance floor, then released my hand as we took our places, facing each other. A dimple appeared on his right cheek as he lowered his head in a bow. I followed the movements of the other women, curtsying in return. As I lifted my head, my breath caught in my throat. The expression on Oak's face was unlike anything I had ever seen— his eyes sparkled brighter than the stars above.

The music grew louder as he stepped forward, motioning for me to follow. Oak slipped one hand into mine, the other settling at the small of my bare back. I shuddered. Struggling to keep up, my movements faltered as I tried to follow his lead.

Heat rushed to my face—not just from Oak's proximity, but from the way everyone seemed to be gawking. I stopped, my hand slipping from Oak's as I stepped back.

"I'm sorry. I can't do this," I whispered.

Oak's fingers curved under my chin, lifting my gaze to his. Goosebumps erupted on my neck. His gray-blue eyes lit up, the gold flecks gleaming like scattered stardust.

"Coco, nobody in this room matters but you and me," he said, his voice rich and husky. "Look at me. Forget everyone else." His breath lingered against my brow as he spoke.

His arm swept around my waist, and I was flush against him again. There, pressed to his chest, I drank in his scent. He was coconut and fresh rain and a safe harbor from all the scrutinizing stares in the room. Here, I was safe from everything, everyone—even myself.

His fingers splayed across the exposed skin on my back, leaving trails that seemed to light my skin on fire. I took the hand he offered. I wrapped my arm around his neck and shoulders. But it was his smile that held me.

My heart pulsed in time with the music as I gazed into Oak's eyes, letting him guide me across the floor. With each step, I felt an exhilarating closeness. I did as he asked, allowing the crowd to fade into nothingness. We didn't need words; our bodies spoke for us instead.

As the music quickened, he placed his firm hands on my waist, lifting me effortlessly into the air. His touch moved in perfect harmony with the rhythm of the strings. My feet found the floor again. His body pressed against mine, his gaze intense, and his strong hands sent a tingling sensation through me with every caress.

We floated around the dance floor. The feelings that had simmered in the pit of my belly now seemed to be boiling over, spilling through my veins with every second spent with Oak. I liked him, and the thought both thrilled and terrified me.

As the music slowed, our bodies followed suit. His lips brushed my temple, causing a deep ache to grow in my throat. Oak murmured in my ear, "You're more radiant than a thousand sunsets melting into the ocean." His thumb traced delicate circles over the curve of my bare back.

"Thank you, Coco," he said, his voice low and smoky.

Then he was gone. The crowd seemed to hold its breath, all eyes on me. A deep blush engulfed my face.

Wringing my hands together, I joined Tada and Otto. Both stood gaping at me.

Otto smirked. "Good thing you had a king showing you the steps... More like carrying you through the dance."

"Oh, I'm sure I made quite a fool of myself," I half-heartedly joked before pushing through people, desperate for fresh air.

A group of women spoke loudly, making sure I heard every word.

"Did you see him dancing with that Dim girl? There's no way he actually sees anything in her. Maybe it's just listed in the Luxari's responsibilities—to take pity on the less fortunate."

My stomach sank. I didn't wait to hear any more.

As I walked out of the ballroom, I turned sharply to the right, desperate to escape the suffocating weight of the palace. It felt as though I were drowning, the walls closing in on me. I followed a group of people who seemed confident in their destination. Anything that led upward.

I ascended a set of obsidian steps—smooth, glossy, and

dark as midnight. I gathered my skirt, bunching it in my hands to climb. My thin fabric slippers slid against the polished stone. The stairs leveled off, and the only light came from flickering torches mounted on the dirt walls.

A strong hand gripped my elbow, yanking me behind a swath of black sheer tulle. The alcove was cramped—barely big enough for two. My back pressed against the cool, damp stone wall.

Oak stood inches away. His eyes bore into mine—pools of blue and swirling golden hues, like a storm over a dark sea. A flame licked through my veins as his palms gently molded to my hips. My breasts pressed against Oak's solid frame, tightening my stomach. I could feel each breath I took against him. My heart fluttered with nerves, being this close to a Luxari.

His skin seemed to glow, as if lit by starlight. Following the glimmering light that illuminated Oak's features, I looked up. A clear dome curved above us, allowing unlimited access to a night sky filled with twinkling stars. It looked as if someone had hung thousands of glittering diamonds in the sky.

Oak's strong fingers cupped my face, pulling my gaze to his. His eyes dropped to my mouth, then he slowly lowered his lips to mine—a gentle press that deepened swiftly into a fierce, claiming kiss. The passion sent a shockwave through my entire body—hot and desperate. He tasted like sea mingled with coconut.

His arms tightened around me, drawing me into a storm of passion. His tongue, slow and deliberate, explored mine. Where our bodies met, spirals of sensation swirled, leaving my legs feeling like they might dissolve into nothing.

Each touch was a fresh breeze, whispering pure longing

through me. His teeth grazed my lower lip, a tender threat, while his hands traced the curve of my spine, a slow descent that only deepened the promise of more.

He slowed the kiss, his lips leaving mine. Raising his head, he gazed into my eyes.

"I shouldn't have done that." Oak shook his head, and a flash of regret crossed his features.

He turned and disappeared through the tulle, leaving me under the shimmer of the stars. A soft song drifted into my mind—tender and strange, like a dream half-remembered from another life.

> *The long day is gone,*
> *As the stars sing along,*
> *Glimmering brightly above.*
> *Reach out to the sky—*
> *Can't you see them shine?*
> *Sparkling, humming till dawn.*

I brushed my fingers over my lips, still warm. A shadow passed, stirring the tulle like a whisper of wind. I pushed the fabric aside—

But no one was there.

CHAPTER
EIGHTEEN

I barely slept. I tossed and turned all night, the kiss with Oak replaying in my mind over and over again. I was worried the memory would fade, and I wanted to remember every detail—the way his lips felt against mine, the intensity in his touch. I still couldn't believe a Luxari had kissed me. It felt like I was caught in a foolish girl's daydream.

But it wasn't just that. My failure—once again—to access the library gnawed at me, keeping me from rest. I tried to calculate a solid plan to break into a structure that was charmed, but with what? I didn't know.

I considered bailing on Niko, but I found the willpower to get out of bed. I refused to look like a fool in front of Amabel again. Niko could help me prevent that.

Niko and Oak were sparring as I approached the pit. Oak was shirtless. My mouth suddenly went dry as I watched Oak's movements. Defined muscles covered every inch of his magnificent frame, as if all he ever did was train.

Oak turned, and black swirls etched along his spine came into view. Like gusts of wind, they curved across his broad shoulders and traced the contours of his strong muscles, weaving with the wind pattern all the way down to his breeches. The dark markings stood out starkly against his sun-kissed skin.

Niko and Oak circled each other. Sweat gleamed off Oak's tanned chest. I told myself not to look, but my eyes betrayed me, tracking the glistening beads of sweat as they clung to his sculpted chest, slowly descending over his rigidly defined stomach muscles. My breath hitched as it slid lower, vanishing beneath the waistband of his tight leather pants.

I had to force myself to look away. I shouldn't have even entertained the idea that a Luxari would go for a Dim. Even if he had kissed me, it didn't mean he was truly interested. I mean, he said it himself—he shouldn't have done that. I wasn't sure what his intentions were, and I couldn't shake the thought that if the other Luxari found out, it would cause serious trouble. But then again, he had asked me to dance in front of all those people.

"Coco, you came." Niko turned toward me.

Oak snapped his head around the moment he heard my name, clearly surprised. Niko grinned widely and seized the opportunity. She punched him in the gut, then swept his leg out from under him, sending Oak sprawling onto his back. She pinned him down effortlessly.

"Looks like somebody got distracted," she taunted, eyes gleaming with mischief.

Oak shot her a nasty glare, but she just laughed, sprang to her feet, and wiped her hands on her pants.

With his head bowed, Oak shuffled to the far side of the ring.

Niko stepped beside me. "All right, Coco. Let's see what you've got."

She moved through a series of sharp motions, punching the air with precision. Her walnut-colored curls bounced with every strike.

I did my best to follow, sweat clinging to my temples as my breath grew short and uneven. A half hour passed. Oak continued his own training nearby, but I was too focused on Niko's drills to pay him any mind.

"Coco!" Otto's voice boomed as he strode up with Tada, Hugh, and Will trailing behind him. "How dare you train without us?" he said, mock offended.

"She's not training without you," Niko replied, her copper eyes gleaming. "She just needed a little extra help."

"Thanks for the vote of confidence, Niko," I laughed. She just winked at me.

Otto shrugged. "Come join us for some drills." He led us to the far side of the pit, where he began setting up a row of large hoops.

Otto's hands sparked with flame as he filled two of the hoops with fire. Tada added swirling water to another, then froze one into jagged ice. Hugh summoned a mini tornado in one, and then Will placed his palm on the last, sending the sand inside spinning in violent circles.

"This one's yours, Coco," Otto called with a grin, handing me an empty hoop.

"Har har," I muttered, setting it down.

"All right," Will cut in, turning serious. "We need to come

up with a strategy—how we're going to cover each other's weaknesses and work together as a team. Though we won the last team challenge, it's only going to get harder from now on."

"Tada, protect Otto as he runs through each hoop," Will instructed.

Otto's sapphire eyes sparkled. "Don't let me die, love," he teased before springing forward. He darted through the fire hoops with ease, but the moment his foot hit the water hoop, he dropped like an anchor, vanishing as if a hidden ocean swirled beneath.

With a sharp pull of her palms, Tada sent the water erupting from the hoop, spraying us all—and flinging Otto out. He coughed and spat out water as he lay drenched on his back. "By the rogue's curse, why'd you have to turn that into a lake?"

Tada winced. "We have to be prepared."

Otto groaned but nodded. "Yeah, yeah." He got to his hands and knees, then stood up.

Thundering footsteps echoed through the tunnel, and Kaz's presence filled the room. As he strode confidently to the center of the pit, he pulled his shirt off and tossed it to the ground. His eyes locked on Oak.

By Aridan's breath, he was just as ripped as Oak—maybe even more so. I swallowed, feeling the heat rise in the room. Fiery orange, red, and yellow flames twisted up his shoulder and down his back, morphing into a gigantic sun.

Kaz swiftly tied his hair back with a leather strap. "King Daze," he mocked, his voice dripping with venom. "Please do me the honor of a fight."

I couldn't look away. Was this the follow-up to the fight earlier?

Oak turned to face Kaz, the few inches of height he had over the other king evident. His jaw clenched as he stepped into the center of the ring, tension radiating from him. Every muscle in him was taut, ready to spring at the slightest provocation.

"You know, Oak," Kaz sneered, swinging his fist toward him. "You have a lot of nerve."

Oak smoothly leaned back, dodging the jab.

"How so?" Oak asked, throwing an undercut punch aimed at Kaz's upper abdomen.

The blow landed with a satisfying thud. Kaz let out a low grunt, stepping backward.

"Don't be coy. You sent Lerains to assault my ships," Kaz hissed, as he took another swing. The punch landed with a sharp crack against Oak's ribcage.

But Oak didn't flinch. His expression remained unchanged, as though the blow hadn't even grazed him.

"You had no right to deploy your Flameborne Legion along the border of my Sphere," Oak retorted, jabbing toward Kaz's throat.

Kaz's lips twisted into a sneer as he ducked, but instead of pulling back, he lunged forward and hooked his bicep around Oak's neck. Oak shoved sharply against Kaz's chest, but he held firm, digging his feet into the dirt floor. They pushed and pulled like Will and Milo wrestling as kids.

"I do—especially when your Stormwind Legion prowls the Cobalt Sea, right at the border of my Sphere," Kaz spat.

Heat flushed his cheeks, and blood pounded in my temples with the mounting suspense.

Oak's jaw clenched so tight I thought it might shatter. He twisted, trying to throw Kaz off balance, but he was too heavy.

Oak grabbed a fistful of Kaz's tied-back hair and yanked hard. They tumbled to the ground, rolling in the dirt as they grumbled and exchanged blows.

Oak shot to his feet, Kaz close behind—both coated in sweat and grime.

Kaz's face turned mottled red. He wound up his arm and threw a hook punch, landing straight into Oak's jaw. Oak recovered quickly and took a few steps toward Kaz.

"Relocate your ships, and I shall do the same," Kaz spat.

Oak's eyes narrowed as he glared at Kaz. "My Legion has been strictly ordered to patrol only the Depths of Delusion. I cannot be held responsible simply because it shares the same ocean as the Scorch Sphere."

Niko hesitated but then slowly approached the two kings, careful to stay out of their way.

"Oh, really? You expect me to believe that? It seems to me, Oak, that you're surveilling me, positioning your forces strategically should a conflict arise," Kaz said, eyes flashing. "And now that your Lerains have attacked my Legion, who can say—perhaps one of them will pay for it."

My whole alliance stood still, watching and listening to every moment of their argument.

"I will only say this once: my ships are stationed there to protect against the Void," Oak replied, his voice low. "It concerns neither you nor your Sphere."

Kaz's nostrils flared, and his fists clenched at his sides.

"Move them," Kaz bellowed.

"No," Oak said between gritted teeth.

Kaz's expression hardened. "You are going to regret this," he seethed.

Oak threw his head back and let out a nasty chuckle. "Your threats are as scary as an Aeralith's sneeze."

"Oak, I'm warning you. If you don't move your men, the Daze Sphere is going to need a new king." Kaz's voice was cold and sharp.

"Is that a threat?" Oak snarled, his fists tightening.

"It's a promise." Kaz's voice was filled with thunder.

Kaz clapped his hands together, and as he pulled them apart, a blazing blue ball of flames expanded between his palms. He threw his arm back and launched the fireball straight at Oak.

Oak's hand shot up, halting the sphere. He thrust his palm forward, and a powerful gust sent the orb soaring through the air. It slammed against the dirt wall and instantly extinguished, smoke billowing from the impact.

Power ripped through the room as it shook. Fire and smoke exploded around me, knocking my whole alliance off their feet.

A searing pain vibrated through me. A violent ringing started in my ears as I tried to sit up, but I didn't make it far. Dizziness swarmed my head.

"Damn it, Oak." Niko's voice was distant, her figure a blur above me.

Pain pulsed through my body.

I could hear cursing and arguing coming from Kaz and Oak.

"Half-wits with delusions of grandeur," Niko muttered under her breath.

My alliance followed Niko out of the arena.

I sat up, my head pounding. The room was dark, save for the soft flicker of a lantern casting golden light on the walls. The sheets were silky black, cool against my skin. A rich, spicy scent enveloped me. My mind was a whirlwind, replaying the chaos from earlier.

The door creaked open, and Niko's copper eyes met mine. Her face softened with relief.

"Oh, thank Aridan, you're awake. If something had happened to you, I would've been left for the Lerains."

She walked in and sat beside me. I glanced around, still disoriented, until I remembered that after Kaz and Oak's clash, I—and the rest of my alliance—had needed a Charmer. Niko's room was the closest, so I had chosen to recover here.

A slow, throbbing pain danced across my forehead.

"Do you need anything? Water?" Niko asked softly, her voice filled with concern.

"No," I shook my head. "What I need is answers. What happened?"

Niko sighed. "Ah, yes. You see, Oak had a considerable amount of magic built up in his system, and King Kaz has a habit of pressing the wrong buttons. You witnessed firsthand what occurs when a Swayer and an Enticer lose control."

Words evaded me. Kaz and Oak were Luxari, and yet they were absolutely terrible at controlling their emotions. I started to question their relationships with the other Spheres if they couldn't behave around each other.

"I've never seen either of them behave that way," Niko said in a low voice.

"What do you mean?"

"Well, don't misunderstand—I've seen Kaz angry more times than I can count. But Oak? He rarely ever loses his composure."

I scoffed.

"It's true!" Niko raised her voice.

"If you say so... Niko, I've been meaning to ask you something."

"Yes?"

"Why did you spit out your beer when you saw Oak and me dancing?"

She scratched the back of her neck and released a quiet sigh. "Oak has never asked anyone to dance before."

I raised an eyebrow. "Seriously?"

"I'm quite serious," she said, lifting her hand as though making a solemn vow. "I swear on my life."

Surprise rocked through me. He had never asked *anyone* to dance before.

The door suddenly swung open and Eda strolled in, her arms crossed tightly over her chest.

"Eda!" Niko said, her voice light. "Welcome, come join us."

"Coco, I simply wished to say—Oak and Kaz can both be insufferable at times. And, speaking as someone well-acquainted with their more immature tendencies, I offer you my sincerest apologies." Eda's jade green eyes glowed softly in the darkened room.

Eda had barely said more than a few sentences to me since we'd met, and now she was apologizing for something she wasn't even responsible for.

"Well, someone's skies are looking stormy," Niko muttered, staring at the ceiling.

Eda walked toward us and pinched Niko's side. Niko yelped.

"Someone must take responsibility for their actions. You"—Eda poked Niko in the armpit, and Niko flung herself forward to grab Eda's wrist—"were meant to keep them in line. You've done a dreadful job."

They started slapping each other, much like Milo and I would have when we were kids. It made me strangely amused to see two obviously powerful women fighting like children.

"Stop it!" I admonished. "Look, I'm fine, my alliance is fine, it's over."

Eda stepped back, and Niko rested her arm over her shoulder.

"Well, that settles it. You really need to start training." Niko paused, and her tone shifted to something more serious. "And after today's events, I'd suggest we do so in private. Fortunately, we're heading to the Daze Sphere—I know of several secluded spots where we won't have to concern ourselves with Oak or Kaz appearing."

THE DAZE SPHERE

AREN FOLKTALES

Where wind brushes
And light gently touches,
Breaking through the haze,
A flower grows upon the hill,
Inviting souls to play.
Swirling thoughts and swaying plots
Beckon toward the sea.
The mist rolls in,
And nothing's seen—
A daze, a place to be.

CHAPTER
NINETEEN

The ship rose over a large wave and plummeted down. The spray lifted, misting my hair and face, and I embraced it—the crisp, cool relief that settled over me, refreshing and soothing.

Both alliances had gathered on the deck. I didn't know how the captain knew we were close, considering the dense fog that surrounded us. I lifted my hands but couldn't even see them.

Not even Shifters could Sphere Jump into the Daze Sphere —there was a protective, enchanted shield over Oak's kingdom. The only way to reach it was by sailing through the Delirium Sea.

Earlier, we had passed Kaz's Legion stationed just outside the shield's boundary, guarding the edge of the Daze Sphere. With over twenty ships there, I couldn't help but understand Oak's perspective.

Our ship came to a halt as beguiling, chilling voices filled the sea air.

All of us are lost.
The sailors come our way.
They long for our embrace,
As we sing the night to day.
Time is often fast—
It leads us to our fate.
The ocean never lasts;
It simply starts to sway.

Lerains. People avoided the Delirium Sea at all costs in fear of the Lerains. Above the water, Lerains appeared beautiful—but beneath the surface, they were creatures of death.

"What in the scorching sun is that supposed to mean?" Otto asked loudly.

"Hush!" Tada hissed, placing a finger to Otto's lips.

"Lerains," Severin said, his voice cold.

Severin strode to the ship's edge and peered over the railing. We all followed. It was hard to make them out in the fog, but they were there. Bewitching Lerains bobbed above the churning, dark surface of the Delirium Sea.

The water lifted a Lerain to the railing of our boat, as if the sea itself were a chair for her. She had long, white-gold platinum hair that cascaded down to her hips. She swept her glossy hair over both shoulders, revealing bare, voluptuous breasts.

Otto's mouth dropped, and others followed suit. They stared, dumbfounded, at the Lerain.

"What can travel through time but never rests?" The Lerain asked, her hazel eyes glowing with a golden hue.

She was mesmerizing.

"We just need to pass," Severin explained.

"Answer the question, and you may pass," the Lerain responded.

"What if we don't?" Will asked.

The Lerain's eyes locked onto Will's. "Then your fate will show the way."

A gleam took over Will's eyes. He hurriedly shook his head, as if snapping out of a trance.

"This is stupid," Amabel complained from the corner of the ship, where she had been sulking. "It's not as if they won't let us through. King Oak will come and grab us. We can wait until then."

"Say it again!" Otto demanded.

"What can travel through time but never rests?" The Lerain repeated.

"The mind," I blurted, the words escaping before I could stop them.

All eyes fell on me. No one blinked.

"Correct, Dim," the Lerain said, her voice haunting. She disappeared beneath the sea—the foam bubbled where she vanished.

The fog immediately parted, as though someone had sliced it in half with a blade. The ship lurched forward, cutting through the opening. As soon as the end of the vessel passed, the fog folded back in on itself.

"That answer doesn't even make sense," Amabel whined.

"For once, I agree with her," Aldo muttered, stepping closer to me.

Will looked at me, waiting for a response.

"You can recall a memory anytime you want. That's the time-travel part. Technically, you can always visit a different time—you just need to call up a memory. The last part's simpler. Even when you sleep, your mind never truly rests because it's dreaming."

Will's face broke into a wide grin. "Brilliant, Coco," he said.

Amabel scoffed and stomped off.

Aldo stood still, rubbing his chin thoughtfully.

"Look!" Cecille squealed, pointing toward the shore.

The Daze Sphere's palace stood between two towering mountains, as if they themselves were holding it up.

"Where is the kingdom?" I asked.

"It's behind the palace," came a small voice—Hugh's.

This was the first time I had heard him speak since the second Quest. His tousled black hair whipped around in the wind.

"King Oak says the palace is a barrier to our kingdom. It's his job to protect us. If the Void attacks, they have to go through him first," Hugh said, his voice filled with admiration.

Hugh continued, his eyes fixed on the distant stone walls of the palace. "His father's palace is further back in the kingdom. As soon as King Oak came into power, he built this one," he added, jerking his thumb toward the palace.

"So the other palace just sits there?" Will asked.

"No. King Oak has turned it into a home for those living in poverty and for orphans like me," Hugh said. He stood a little taller than before.

My chest tightened at the thought.

I also couldn't help but notice Hugh growing more confident as the Quests continued.

"We're here!" he shouted, sprinting toward the front of the ship.

The palace was breathtaking—built from smooth, dusty-blue stones rising to the edge of the Delirium Sea. Algae clung to the walls where the ocean crashed against them, leaving behind a salty sheen. The harbor sat on an island where ships docked, their sails billowing in the breeze. A stone bridge connected the island to the palace.

Our ship eased into position, and we disembarked onto the bridge. As we walked, a fine mist fell upon us, carrying the scent of fresh rain.

The drawbridge lowered and the portcullis rose, allowing us into the palace's bailey—a large courtyard surrounded by towering walls crowned with battlements. At the center stood the elegant keep with its many towers and turrets. The hazy blue stones shimmered under the golden sun.

To the left, the clashing sounds of swords echoed from the barracks, where guards practiced archery and weaponry in an open grassy area.

Wandering to the right, I found a secluded courtyard garden hidden behind thick green hedges. A small bronze plaque read: "Aridan's Garden of Solitude." Stone paths wound between exquisite flowers—thornkisses, serian blooms, delicate moonbells, and wild starpetals. A graceful fountain bubbled softly in the center. Though concealed from the bailey, this lush oasis was still connected to the palace.

The guards' uniforms consisted of loose, midnight-blue tunics, revealing their wrists and the marking of the Daze Sphere: a Daze lily. Ash-gray pants and chestnut-brown boots completed the ensemble. The tunics were embroidered with spirals and swirls in silver thread.

We stopped before two vast, ebony wooden doors, intricately carved with Daze lilies and curling wind patterns. Two guards pulled open the antique bronze door handles, which twisted out like gusts of wind. The heavy doors groaned as they swung open, revealing the grand foyer beyond.

A crisp breeze brushed against my skin as we entered. Our footsteps echoed through the vast emptiness of the palace. The others rushed forward, following the guards down the hall, but I stayed behind, distracted by the grandeur.

To the right, the great hall stood cloaked in darkness. To the left, rich timber doors lined the stone corridor. Above, charcoal wooden beams arched across high vaulted ceilings, while banners in shades of blue and gray swayed gently in the draft. Tapestries of clouds and delicate flowers hung on the walls. The entrance was bathed in the soft glow of flickering candles, and an aged metal chandelier hung from the ceiling, casting warm light from its candlelit arms.

The palace was intimidating and daunting; the library could be behind any of the countless doors. I needed to be efficient with my time, so instead of wandering aimlessly for hours, I decided that I needed to ask someone who lived here where it was. Lost in my own thoughts, I was pulled back to reality by Will's voice.

"You coming, Coco?" He asked, looking over his shoulder.

"Yes." I sped up to join the others.

The walls were patterned with brocades of indigo, chambray, and cloudburst, while bronze sconces, woven into the shapes of swirls and lilies, added a decorative touch.

We continued down the hall through the sunlight that streamed through high arched windows. The corridor led to several mahogany staircases that all ascended toward various towers and turrets.

Each of us had been assigned an attendant, and Tada, moving in the same direction as me, was already hounding hers with a barrage of questions about the palace, overwhelming the poor guy before he could speak. My attention kept drifting to the oil paintings of landscapes hanging from the walls.

The atmosphere of the palace shifted as we climbed higher, transitioning from darker tones to lighter ones. The stairs led into a corridor with so many windows that I was certain someone below could make out the stitching on my dress.

Tada practically skipped into her room, slamming the door behind her. The loud thud made her attendant flinch, clearly unimpressed by her enthusiasm. I smiled at my aide as she twisted the elegant handle to the guest room. I brushed past her and stepped inside, and the door slowly closed behind me.

Wood beams stretched across the ceiling, and the cobblestone floor was adorned with a deep blue rug. A stone fireplace the color of frost occupied one wall, with a vase of blush pink Daze lilies resting on the mantel. In the corner sat a circular bed, its sides draped in sheer fabric, with dark blue and pink pillows scattered across it.

My fingers brushed the delicate tulle as I crossed to the glass double doors and threw them open. A small gasp escaped me. The balcony overlooked the mountainside, where hydrangeas splashed the landscape with vibrant colors, surrounded by hundreds of Daze lilies bursting in shades of white, yellow, and pink—their curling petals flowing like wind currents. To my left lay the Delirium Sea; to my right, the Daze Kingdom, nestled behind Oak's palace.

"Hey, there weren't any chocolates in my room," Tada complained, strolling in and plopping down on my bed.

"Where were they?" I asked as I closed the doors behind me.

"They were right here on the bed," she said. She opened the box of chocolates and popped one into her mouth. "Coco. You've *got* to try one of these." Tada moaned in pleasure.

Shaking my head, I stepped beneath an arched entryway. Gray tiles decorated the walls, while the sink and tub were crafted from white ivory marble. Navy blue swirls, reminiscent of mingling winds and intertwined with soft pink lilies, were painted across the high, arched ceilings.

An enclosed balcony featured two steps leading down to a glass-bottomed tub. The glass stretched over the Delirium Sea below, revealing the churning ocean. Smooth, cloudy, round stones lined the walls, and the ceiling was clear, offering an unobstructed view of the sky.

"Are you serious?" Tada said through a mouthful of chocolate. "My room doesn't have a glass-bottomed tub."

I shrugged.

"Did you sleep with King Oak?" she asked suspiciously.

"What?" I screeched. "Of course not! Why would you even ask that?"

Tada raised an eyebrow, a mischievous grin playing at the corners of her mouth. "Why *aren't* you all over that? He's hot." She fanned her face dramatically. "If I were you, I would've climbed that man by now. What I would do to..."

"Tada!" I groaned, covering my face.

209

"Okay, okay, I'm just saying," she smirked. "Not all of us get chocolates and glass-bottomed tubs."

I plopped onto the bed beside her.

Tada's violet eyes grew wide. "I'm waiting."

"For what?" I asked, raising an eyebrow.

"An explanation," she said. "It's long overdue."

I told her that Oak had kissed me—it felt good to finally say it out loud—but there wasn't much more to add. I left out the part where he had said he regretted it.

"Enough about me. What's going on between you and Otto?"

A blush crept onto her face, and she quickly tucked a pink strand of hair behind her ear.

"He's fun."

"That's all you're going to give me?"

"Fine." She scooted over to the bed and sat next to me. "He wants me to visit him after the Sphere Quests."

"Are you going to?"

Her eyes lit up as she leaned closer, practically bouncing with excitement. "I'd be a tide-washed fool to say no. Have you seen his muscles?" She waggled her eyebrows, then fanned

SOULSHIMMER

herself dramatically with one hand, a self-satisfied smirk tugging at her lips.

"Have you..." I trailed off.

"Maybe..."

I shoved her lightly and she rolled off the bed with a yelp, bouncing back to her feet with a wide, mischievous grin spreading across her face.

I chucked the pillow at her. "You didn't tell me?"

She caught the pillow and hugged it to her chest. "Well, both of us have been kind of busy."

"How was it?" I asked, already guessing from the gleam in her eyes.

She grinned wider. "Perfect. Best yet."

We both laughed.

"Come on. Hurry up and get changed," she said, throwing open the armoire.

"Why?"

"Dinner with all the Questlings. It's the feast before the third Quest. We need fuel for tomorrow, so hurry up and get ready!"

CHAPTER
TWENTY

We all sat in the Great Hall of the palace—the space illuminated by the roaring fire. The vaulted ceilings loomed high above. Tall candlesticks stood along the long, dark wood table. The Globe Alliance occupied one side of the table, while our Ellipse Alliance sat on the other. The high-backed chairs were upholstered in rich velvet.

An empty seat was to my left, with Niko beside it at the head of the table. Across from me, two seats remained unoccupied—one at the far end clearly reserved for King Oak. Will sat on my right, followed by Tada, Otto, and Hugh, whose fingers tapped restlessly on the surface.

"I'm starving," Otto whined. He slammed his head down on the table. "I might die if I don't eat soon," he grumbled into the wood.

Tada glanced at me and rolled her eyes, but she still placed a hand on his back and scratched it.

"Who are we waiting for?" I asked Niko.

"The rest of Oak's Luxari Council."

I glanced at the three vacant spots.

"There are only three people on Oak's Luxari Council?" My brow furrowed.

"Five. Don't forget me." Niko flashed a grin. "And one won't be here tonight."

"Every other Luxari Council in Aren has over ten," I said in disbelief.

Niko shrugged. "Strength and power aren't defined by numbers; they are reflected in the individual. True power isn't about quantity."

The comment sent a shiver down my back, and I couldn't help but smile.

"Niko," I teased, raising an eyebrow. "That might just be the most profound thing I've ever heard you say."

She chuckled. "I'm full of wisdom. Who knows, maybe I'll write a book one day."

Rowdy laughter echoed down the hall. The air in the room shifted as the Daze Sphere's Luxari Council entered. One man and two women walked in.

A woman with jet-black hair down to her shoulders sat next to me.

Niko leaned forward with a knowing look. "Coco, meet Zareen, one of our Luxari Council."

Just then, Oak walked into the room. I started to scoot my chair back, along with Will, to stand in respect, but we stopped short when we saw how casually Oak's own Luxari Council treated his arrival. They didn't even acknowledge him.

Platters of food drifted in on a breeze and settled gracefully onto the table. The savory scent of sky-roast, galebird, and honey-glazed roots filled the room. I stole a quick glance at Oak. His shoulders were bunched and tight. His gaze remained on his food.

"By Aridan's shattered legacy, you make the most absurd claim I've ever heard," Zareen said loudly, pointing her fork aggressively at the man across the table.

"I swear it's the truth," the man said, raising both palms in the air. His short hair gleamed with red-gold highlights, and his indigo eyes stood out against his fair complexion.

Niko met my eyes, an amused glint in hers. "Benedict here swears he saw a Shifter turn into a bear, at least twenty feet tall."

"Tell me, Benedict, where did you see this creature?" Zareen asked, leaning forward with a smirk.

"Don't encourage his fantasies," said Niko.

Ignoring everyone, Benedict pressed on. "It was near the Depths of Delusion."

Zareen barked out a laugh. "Hah! You probably saw a raccoon, and since your mind was addled from the mist, you turned it into a bear in your wild imagination."

"I wasn't *in* the Depths of Delusion," Benedict countered, his voice steady but firm. "I was *by* it."

"Everybody knows to get to the Void, you have to pass through the Depths. They say even the most grounded people go mad there. The mist that envelops the area is *possessed*, creeping into your thoughts and warping them. I think you inhaled some mist for sure," Zareen scoffed.

"If the Rogue Embers can travel daily through the Depths of Delusion without losing their minds, I think I can do the same," Benedict argued, his voice confident.

"You tread dangerously near lunacy," Zareen said, leaning back in her chair, as if she had already won the argument. "Rogue Embers can travel through the Depths of Delusion because they're already delusional. They work for the damned souls. Their minds are already twisted and corrupted."

"Niko, what do you think?" Benedict asked.

"Well, I don't think it's wise to test your theory. Anyone who's gone into the Depths—who isn't a Soul Snatcher or a Rogue Ember—doesn't return. The few who do return are completely deranged."

Benedict waved her off. "That's just a folktale parents tell to keep their kids away from the Void."

"It's not," a raspy voice said.

All heads swiveled toward the voice. The woman who spoke had pale yellow hair, like fields of grain. Her eyes were darker than sapphires.

"Oh, please, do enlighten us, Isabelle." Niko's lips twisted as she leaned back in her chair.

"I knew someone who went in," Isabelle said. "When he escaped, he was stark raving mad."

"Well, that settles that," Niko said.

"It's not like the Rogue Embers and the Soul Snatchers are just being run by the damned souls. Someone—someone you know—has been telling them what to do," Isabelle added.

A chill crept into the room.

"That is not possible," Niko said in a hardened tone, leaning forward. Her entire demeanor shifted. "That, Isabelle, is nothing more than a myth."

"What myth?" Will asked.

Niko sighed.

"You've never heard of the Myth of Arrow?" Benedict asked in disbelief.

"Obviously not," Will grumbled.

"Well, go ahead, Isabelle," Niko said with a nod, her tone now more clipped. "You brought this up."

Isabelle tilted her head toward us. Her gaze was fixed on us, but it seemed as though she was somewhere else entirely.

"You were taught that Aridan created Aren. Well, there's another version of the story. Aridan had a twin brother, Arrow, who helped him create Aren. Aridan assumed Arrow shared the same vision, but Arrow's views began to shift. He started to make decisions that directly defied Aridan's plans for Aren. As punishment for betraying him in this way, Aridan damned Arrow's soul to the Vile. The Vile is where souls go if they are corrupt—a suffocating black hole where they rot, never moving on to the Unknown."

I felt a cold rush of disbelief, my mind struggling to keep up. I had never heard the name Arrow. In all the historical books I had read about Aren, there was no mention of a brother.

Isabelle's voice broke through my thoughts. "Some of us were taught that Arrow controls the damned souls. He has convinced them to seek others who will help his cause—to rise back to power. That's where the Void comes in. The damned souls have taken the form of Soul Snatchers.

"Their cause is to steal Ari Souls for magic so they can bring Arrow back to life. They want to raise him from the dead and give him back his power. That's why the Void seeks magic; they need enough to raise a deity.

"Their cause has been crushed many times. Some of the

damned souls even hide in the Depths of Delusion, keeping others from witnessing what happens in the Void. The Void has been obsessed with stealing Ari souls, everyone knows that, but why? To raise a deity."

Will and I exchanged a look. His face was pale. My mind raced, a flood of information swirling in my head as I struggled to swim through it.

It took several sips of wine to quiet the roar of my pulse.

"This is a very uplifting feast conversation," Niko said sarcastically, lifting her glass to drink. "Why don't we do some introductions?" She raised her voice over the bickering whispers of Benedict and Zareen. "Zareen, why don't you go first?"

"What?" Zareen asked, raising her brows. Her grip on her fork tightened until it started to bend.

Niko's eyes narrowed, her tone taking on an alarmingly serious edge. "Introduce yourself," she repeated, her hand sweeping across the table. Sure enough, all the Questlings turned their attention toward the Daze Luxari Council, waiting for introductions.

"Oh," Zareen said with a wide grin. She scooted her chair back, tossed her fork onto the plate, and took a deep bow, her black hair falling forward. She straightened and, in a booming voice, declared, "I'm Zareen the Magnificent."

"The magnificent pain in my ass," Niko shot back. Zareen only grinned wider.

"I'm the Caretaker of the Sphere," Zareen continued. "In simpler terms, I'm responsible for both people and spaces in the Daze Kingdom. My days are spent evaluating lands for bridges and listening to everyone's complaints."

Benedict rolled his eyes. "Zareen, not everyone wants to hear you drone on about your role."

Zareen raised an eyebrow. "I'd beg to differ," she replied smoothly. "But since you now have the floor..." She sat back down in her chair and cast a wink my way.

Benedict stayed seated, his posture stiff and formal. "I'm Benedict, the Master of Commerce. I oversee trade and financial matters in the Daze Sphere."

Isabelle spoke next, her deep sapphire eyes glowing in a haunting way. "I'm the Guardian of the Assembly."

The rest of us exchanged glances, all but Hugh equally confused. Unlike the others, Isabelle didn't offer an explanation.

Oak's voice filled the room. "It's in poor taste for Luxari to make all the decisions," he said, wiping his mouth with a cloth. My gaze lingered on his lips for a moment, the memory of their softness and how they tasted... I quickly snapped my attention back to his eyes.

"The Daze Sphere has an assembly of elected officials who vote on all matters regarding the Daze Kingdom. Isabelle runs it."

A murmur of whispers rippled through the room. I saw Amabel shaking her head and leaning in to speak to Rodor, while Will nodded in agreement with Oak. I couldn't help but feel a surge of surprise at Oak again. Despite all my studies, I had never heard of any Sphere granting its people real influence—this was rare, a break from the strict traditions I'd read about.

"And Drogo, who is out on patrol this evening, is my

General of the Sphere. He commands the Daze Sphere's military."

I couldn't help but wonder again—if by some miracle I were offered a spot on a Luxari Council, what role would I want? My thoughts drifted back to my childhood, to the struggles Milo and I had endured because of selfish, neglectful parents. If given the chance, I'd dedicate myself to ensuring no one else had to suffer the way we did.

As I made my way to the library, the smell of spices and the clinking of dishes caught my attention. As I turned the corner, I found myself facing a wide kitchen where three attendants still worked. One washed dishes, another decorated pastries with Daze lilies, and the third, carrying a dark wooden tray piled with food— the same as our dinner—struggled with a thick, wooden door.

I rushed forward. "Let me help," I offered, pulling the door open.

"Thank you, my dear. Aren't you a sweetheart?" She smiled, the lines on her face softening as she walked down the rocky steps. She placed the tray onto an empty cart hitched to a horse and wiped her hands on her apron.

I quickly noticed the square marking on the inside of her wrist—she was a Dim living in the Daze Sphere. Curious.

"Is this all there is tonight?" a young man around my age asked, emerging from behind the horse.

"No, Charlie. There's more inside. I just need to bring them down."

"I wish I could—"

"Don't. You shouldn't be on that leg of yours."

Charlie limped as he pulled himself onto the cart. His face was obscured by the shadow of his hat, and the night made his expression unreadable.

"I can help," I said. "Just tell me what to do."

The attendant looped her arm through mine. "Well, you truly are a treat," she said, lifting her modest brown dress with the other hand. "I have about six more trays to bring down."

"What exactly is this for?" I asked as we returned to the warm kitchen. She led me to a table where platters of food lay waiting.

"King Oak donates all the leftover food from the day to the Calla Gale Palace."

My brow furrowed in confusion.

"The Calla Gale Palace was once the Luxari palace for the Daze Sphere. Now it's a place of refuge for orphans and others in need."

Hugh's home.

"Who named it?" I asked, lifting one of the trays.

"King Oak. Quite poetic, don't you think? At the dedication, he said, 'May this place serve as a fresh start as rejuvenating as a crisp wind. A place of beauty and elegance, grounded in refuge and renewal.'"

A lump formed in my throat, and my pulse quickened. Oak wasn't just a king. He was a savior to these people—a splash of light on a dark night and a breeze of hope on a hot day.

And I couldn't help but imagine a network of Calla Gale Palaces spread across Aren, where orphans could find a home and children who couldn't afford the local Halls of Knowledge could still receive an education. Maybe—just maybe—if, in some wild twist of fate, I were offered a place on a Luxari Council, this could be the duty I was meant to fulfill.

CHAPTER
TWENTY-ONE

With the celebration still in full swing, I slipped away from the kitchen unnoticed and made my way to the library. Earlier, I'd casually asked my attendant where it was—conveniently, it was just across from the Great Hall.

The heavy door groaned open. I stepped inside and let it shut behind me with a soft thud. A fire crackled in the hearth, casting flickering shadows across rows of towering shelves. Three arched windows lined the far wall, framing a view of the sea and the silhouette of the mountainside. The room smelled of old paper and cedar.

This could take hours.

And it did.

I scanned each spine, shelf by shelf, until the titles blurred together. Just as I was about to give up, something caught my eye—a tapestry that seemed to ripple slightly, though there was no breeze. Intricate Daze lilies, stitched in rich greens and golds, adorned the fabric.

I reached out, fingers brushing the edge. The cloth shifted aside, revealing a faint outline carved into the dark wood paneling—a hidden door.

Heart hammering, I pressed gently. A soft click echoed through the silence, sending a jolt of adrenaline racing down my spine.

The door opened into a small, hidden alcove. Frosted windows lined one wall, and a single blue chair sat beside a narrow desk. The room smelled of coconut and the sea, confirming my suspicions that this was Oak's private study. Three low shelves held worn books.

This had to be where he kept it. I scanned each spine but didn't see the *Ari Report*. About a dozen books lined the shelf. As I began rereading them, a darker, tattered paper caught my eye from where it stuck out. I opened the book. The parchment was folded in half, and it read:

Mother,
I love you. I miss you.
More than anything, I wish I could hug you.
Look to the moon
Feel my love in the stars,
And my arms in the mist.
Love,
Your Starry Flicker

I went to unfold the paper, but suddenly, it was snagged from my hands.

"What are you doing here?"

I yelped and spun around. Zareen stood in the doorway with narrowed eyes. She held the paper in her hands. Benedict leaned against the wall, arms crossed and amused.

"You know, it's not exactly polite to sneak around a palace when you're a guest," Zareen said with cool authority.

"I didn't sneak in. The door was open," I shot back.

"She has a point," Benedict said, voice light with amusement.

Zareen slipped the parchment into her pocket and crossed her arms. "You've got nerve, Coco. Just as you continue to shock the people of Aren with your ability to compete without magic, you're starting to impress me even more—with your blatant disregard for rules."

"It's not against the rules to explore the palace."

"She's right again—" Benedict began.

"Benedict, drift off," Zareen growled, circling slowly around me.

"What are you looking for, Coco?" she asked. "Trying to sell our secrets to another Luxari—like King Kaz, perhaps?"

I snorted. "I don't give a damn about your politics." I turned toward the hidden door, but Benedict moved impossibly fast, blocking the way with a half-smile.

"What kind of Luxari Council would we be if we didn't interrogate intruders?" Zareen said.

I turned to glare at her.

"Oh, Coco, I think you're trying to look intimidating, but you look adorable—like an Aeralith."

"Are you going to keep me here until I speak?" I asked. "Is that your brilliant plan?"

Zareen shrugged. "I just had an excellent meal. I've got hours."

"I'm comfortable," Benedict added, already sinking into the blue chair like it was his throne.

I sighed and ran a hand through my hair. I had been caught. I doubted they would believe any lie I tried to spin. They could potentially help me, and what did I have to lose?

"I'm looking for the *Ari Report*," I said quietly. "My brother died two years ago, and I haven't received any word from the Retired Luxari. I've got one year to uncover what's happening to his soul before it fades away forever. So when I was summoned to the Quests, I couldn't care less about the immortality prize—I just want access to the *Ari Report*."

They were quiet.

Zareen gave a low whistle. "Well, as daring as your efforts are, I hate to break it to you, Coco, but I'm not sure you'll find the *Ari Report* here," Zareen said.

My heart sank. "What?"

"Only King Oak knows where it is," Benedict answered, as his eyes softened—probably at my disappointed face.

Oak had already known I was looking for it when he caught me in the Scorch Sphere, and he knew what it meant to me— yet he still didn't offer it.

"There could be many reasons you haven't heard anything," Benedict added gently.

"Yeah," I murmured, though my mind was already drifting.

Where would Oak hide the *Ari Report*?

My chest ached—failure blooming like a bruise inside me —and I was growing desperate.

"Can you give me anything to go off of?" I asked.

Zareen shook her head.

A flicker of anger sparked in my gut. "Forget it."

"Look, Coco, I understand," Zareen said, placing a hand on my arm. I pulled away instinctively.

"No, you don't."

Her eyes darkened. "You're not the only one who's lost someone they love."

Guilt twisted in my chest as I watched her expression soften.

"Now, I'll admit—I don't know what it's like not to have closure about where a loved one's soul is. I can't relate to that. But whether they're an Ari Soul or not, it doesn't take the pain away. Because at the end of the day, they're still gone."

She turned and walked through the door. Benedict rose quietly from the chair and trailed after her. I hesitated, then stepped in behind them.

We moved back into the heart of the library, where firelight danced across the stone floor.

"I'm sorry," I murmured, fingers twisting nervously.

"You have nothing to apologize for," Zareen sighed, turning to face me. "If I could help, I would. And Benedict would too."

Benedict's indigo eyes glowed in the dimly lit room. He gave a single nod.

The main doors to the library groaned open. Will stepped inside, his face drawn with concern. Relief softened his shoulders as soon as he saw me.

"Coco. I've been looking everywhere for you."

Zareen and Benedict exchanged a glance, then quietly made their exit.

"What are you doing in here?" he asked.

"Oh, just bored—looking for something to read."

Will stepped closer. "I've known you since you were little," he said gently, a smile tugging at the corner of his lips. "You're a terrible liar. I know you're looking for the *Ari Report*."

Shock washed through me.

I let out a breath and shoved him gently, more out of disbelief than frustration. "Then why haven't you helped me?"

His smile faded. "I have. I just haven't gotten anywhere."

A lump rose in my throat. "What do you mean?"

He motioned toward the settee, and we both sat down.

"For the past two years, I know it's felt like I brushed off your worries about Milo's soul. And the truth is... I did."

He stared into the fire, rubbing his palms together slowly.

"But lately, something's been gnawing at me. A voice in the back of my mind telling me something isn't right.

"I got into the Hush Sphere library, but the *Ari Report* was enchanted shut with a nasty charm." He opened his hands to the firelight. Faint, jagged red lines crisscrossed his skin like lightning scars.

I hadn't noticed them before, but now, being this close, the marks were impossible to miss.

"Will..." I started, reaching out. I stared at him, stunned.

He had done that for me. For Milo.

A tightness rose in my throat, and warmth flooded my chest. I swallowed hard, eyes locked on the faint lines zigzagging his skin.

He shook his head, offering a small, reassuring smile.

"Don't worry about it. It's almost healed." His smile faltered for a split second, eyes narrowing as if weighing what to say next. "Now, the Scorch Sphere was a bit trickier. But I managed to slip in with one of the Luxari Council."

My eyes widened. "How?"

He smirked. "Nobody suspects a beetle."

I couldn't help but grin at his cleverness.

"But King Kaz is no fool. The moment I shifted back into human form, the doors flew open. I was thrown out—literally by an invisible force. Landed flat on my ass."

He laughed once, shaking his head. "This time, you beat me to the library," he said, glancing around the room. "I'm guessing it didn't go well."

I nodded slowly. "It's not here."

Will studied my face for a moment, then moved closer and wrapped his arms around me. He rested his chin on my head—just like Milo used to do.

"Why didn't you tell me?" I asked, the question mumbled into the fabric of his shirt.

"I didn't want to get your hopes up."

The thought that we'd both been summoned—and instead of chasing immortality or a seat on the Luxari Council, we were using this chance to bring peace to Milo's soul—spread a quiet warmth through my body.

"It's going to be okay, Coco," he whispered. "We're going to figure this out. Together."

Eventually, he pulled back.

"I'm so sorry I didn't validate your concerns about Milo's soul over the past couple of years. I thought I was doing the right thing, but I was wrong. You—and Milo—deserve better from me."

The ache in my chest was so sharp that it felt like my heart might tear straight through my ribs. I didn't have the words to match everything he'd just said, so I only nodded—hoping he could feel what I couldn't say.

"If we don't get some sleep tonight, we're going to be absolutely useless in the Quest tomorrow." He stood and held out a hand. "So. Shall we?"

I took his hand and let him pull me to my feet.

We left the library without the *Ari Report*, but it didn't feel like a failure. For the first time in a long time, I didn't feel alone. I hadn't found what I was searching for—but I'd found someone willing to search with me.

CHAPTER
TWENTY-TWO

T he air was thick with moisture. As I stood in the sandy marshes outside the palace, the ground felt spongy beneath my boots. Above us loomed the gloomy sky.

We'd been allowed to choose our clothing for the individual challenge. I had opted for tight black leggings, a light blue tunic, and boots—practical, given the soggy terrain. The dark clouds above hinted at the rain that would soon fall. Severin pulled out his vial of Ari Dust, drank it politely, then pocketed it once again. It was a good strategy, saving the Dust for the Quests, but I was beginning to wonder how much it really enhanced magic.

"Welcome to the third challenge of the Sphere Quests," Queen Catalina sang out.

Queen Catalina stood in front of us. One of her guards stood beside her, holding a tray with glasses filled with an umber-brown liquid. This was a change—not seeing all the Luxari with Queen Catalina.

"This is an individual challenge and should not be attempted with a team." Her gaze slid over each of us, lingering for a moment longer on me. "Breaking the rules and regulations outlined by Aridan is not only disrespectful to him, but also a direct challenge. Those who fail to follow the guidelines will face consequences.

"The ten of you will be transported to Blackwing Isle. Drink the Drowse Draft, and you will be delivered there." She gestured behind me.

We all turned. A couple of miles away, a small island stood in the mist. A swirling darkness hovered over the island.

"Your task is simple: return to this island. You have until dusk to do so. Wind Elaryns will be observing your every move and reporting back to the Luxari on your progress."

"That's it?" Amabel scoffed. Her platinum blonde hair clung to her skin from the dampness in the air.

"That's it," Queen Catalina said, her lips twisting into a smile.

We exchanged wary glances as raindrops began to fall.

The guard stepped forward and handed each of us a glass.

"Drink up!" Queen Catalina commanded, clapping her hands together.

"To not dying," Will said, raising his glass toward mine.

I clinked his, and we both drank the Drowse Draft. It tasted like beer and piss as it slowly slid down my throat. At first, I felt nothing, but then the light seemed to fade, leaving me in darkness.

Loud caws sliced through the air above me. My eyes snapped open, and I felt completely disoriented. Boulders, tangled bushes, and weedy grass lay in front of me, while a few thin trees stood in the distance. I tried to move my arms, but they were tightly bound behind me. I sat on damp, moss-covered ground. My back pressed against a boulder, and a dull fuzziness clouded my head. It took a moment for my mind to clear and to realize where I was: the third challenge of the Sphere Quests.

Panic churned in my belly, threatening to rise up my throat.

Following the sounds, I glanced up. A dark, swirling mass hung in the sky. It wasn't a cloud—it was a swarm of crows. Hundreds of them gathered, their black wings blotting out the sun. The caws of the crows were harsh and bloodthirsty. The cawing grew louder, more frantic, and the swirling mass seemed to quicken. A twist of anxiety filled my stomach, driven by the need to get off this island.

I stood, arms bound behind my back, and spotted the ocean through the trees. They must have tied us up after we had drunk the Drowse Draft.

Wind Elaryns hovered gracefully between the branches. Their long, wispy hair resembled clouds, and their pale blue eyes, along with their transparent forms, made them appear as if sapphires were floating in the breeze.

A big tree snagged my gaze, and suddenly an idea sprang to mind. I walked toward it and turned around so that my back faced the trunk. With a sharp tug, I ran my tied hands up and down the rough bark. My skin scraped painfully against the jagged surface, the friction from the tree slowly working at the rope. A slight burn spread across my wrists as I continued.

I bit my tongue as blood dribbled down my skin, leaving droplets of red to paint the ground. I squeezed my eyes tightly shut and continued the movement until I felt the ropes begin to thin. I wrenched my fists apart as the rope fell. My wrists looked as if someone had taken a blade to them, peeling the skin like an apple. Clenching my jaw, I fought back a wave of nausea.

As I moved toward the sea, a crow swooped down, its wings skimming the top of my hair. My heart jumped against my breast.

But then another swooped—and another. Panic clawed at my throat as I started to run. Crows from every angle and direction dove at me, their wings slicing through the air like sharp knives.

Their silken black feathers gleamed, mirroring the inky blackness of their eyes. Then I noticed something—red rimmed their pupils.

These crows were possessed. A Charmer must have bewitched them before the Quest.

They surged toward me. I ran, heart pounding, hands clutched over my head, desperately trying to dodge every crow that dove at me. They grew more aggressive. Their sharp talons grazed my skin. One clipped my arm, sending a searing sting through it. I tripped over my own feet, crashing face-first into the rocky ground. My legs and arms splayed out beside me.

I lay there for a moment, breath ragged, before I rolled onto my back, instinctively bracing myself to shield my face. But the crows were gone.

Ignoring the burn of my wounds and the ache in my muscles, I pushed myself up and staggered toward the ocean, arms raised in defense. The crows swooped again.

An idea sparked. Every instinct told me to shield myself, to hide. My wrists throbbed, the pain from the shredded skin still sharp, but I fought against it. I could feel the tremble in my limbs—the overwhelming urge to hide, to protect myself from the crows. Fear pressed down on me, almost unbearable. But I wouldn't let it control me. As soon as my arms dropped, the crows froze in mid-air, hovering like dark shadows.

It was the fear. They fed off it.

I forced my arms to my sides and continued walking, even though impulse told me to protect my head.

The swarm of birds moved away from me.

A trail of flames ran up the trees to my left, engulfing the crows in fire. Rodor's hulking body smashed through the trees, flames bursting from his palms. The muscles in his neck bulged from his roar of anger. The fire didn't kill the demon crows; if anything, it made them angrier. They dove at Rodor, and he began plucking crows out of the air, tearing their heads off with his bare hands, his biceps bulging with each head. The sound of ripping feathers, muscles, and bones filled the air. His whole body was splattered with red and black blood.

Otto came hurtling out of the trees, his light brown hair in disarray, black feathers jutting out of his scalp. His blue eyes locked onto mine. Without a word, we both turned toward the chaos erupting on the beach.

Five rowboats lay on the sand. The rest were already in the Delirium Sea, surrounded by Lerains. But these weren't like the ones from the fog. Their stringy black hair hung in matted strands, their webbed hands glistened with saltwater, and their translucent skin glowed sickly pale. The whites of their eyes were a deep, demonic black. They seemed cursed.

"These Lerains look like fish hags. Bring me back the pretty ones," Otto bellowed into the sky before flashing me a grin. Nothing seemed to faze him.

Otto grabbed an oar and stomped toward the rowboat, swatting Lerains away with it as he pushed the skiff into the sea.

Hugh was the furthest away, and none of the Lerains bothered him as he rowed. Amabel was conjuring fireballs that burned the Lerains alive. Their screams mixed with the crackling flames. Severin, calm as ever, froze the water near him, encasing the Lerains in glittering ice. I couldn't see Cecille anywhere, and I immediately began to search for her before reminding myself that she had asked me not to help her. I shifted my focus to Tada, who seemed to be faring well by creating a shield around the boat.

Up the shore, a brown wave surged, but it wasn't water—a living tide. Mice the size of pebbles, packed so tightly that they moved like liquid, crept closer.

The swarm split in two. Half plunged into the ocean, swimming effortlessly toward the boats like a storm rolling over the shore.

Panic crept into my mind.

The sand pulsed beneath my feet as high, piercing screams shredded the sky.

In seconds, the swarm overtook Amabel's boat. One moment it floated there; the next, only her creamy blonde hair was visible as the mice tore through the skiff.

Then rodents devoured the boats on the shore until there was nothing left but slivers of splintered wood dust.

They turned toward me.

I backed into the water, heart hammering. It was the only way to run. But the moment I looked toward the ocean, I froze.

These mice didn't drown.

They skimmed across the surf like foam, slipping into cracks in the hulls and chewing through wood.

Behind me, someone bellowed in agony. I turned.

Rodor lay sprawled on the sand, mice crawling over every inch of his body. Only his pale face showed—slick with sweat, mouth open in a scream as brown mouse tails brushed his lips.

I sprinted to an oar—one not yet gnawed through—snatched it up, and swung. Mice flew, their bodies smacking against the tree trunks with wet, dull thumps. But there were too many. They kept coming.

Rodor forced himself upright, fire bursting from his hands. He scorched the swarm off me until he suddenly howled.

I spun just in time to see him twitch—first an eye, then his jaw—and collapse.

I dropped beside him. His chest rose in shallow jerks, his skin covered in tiny, bleeding gouges. He looked terrible–barely alive.

If the birds fed on fear... what were these things after?

Sweat dripped down Rodor's temples. I looked at the mice he'd burned. They were still moving, shaking black soot from their fur like it was nothing. And they were growing.

Rodor was an Enticer and so was Amabel... They were drawn to salt. To warmth.

I needed cold. I needed ice.

I spun, searching for Severin and Tada, but they were too far out.

Still swatting rodents away, I scanned the island.

A memory surfaced of my time spent in the Frosted Peaks with Edur and Ava.

Edur and I stood in his Frigid Garden. He bent down gently, cupping a beautiful blue lily.

"These are rare, but you can find them in most climates—if there's a Charmer to look after them," he said, grinning up at me.

His fingers turned to ice, and frost spread over the petals like liquid staining a wooden table after a spill.

We were in the Daze Sphere—the land of lilies. There had to be one.

I bolted inland, toward the island's sunlit center. Pain was building inside my frame, my muscles sore, but I had to keep moving.

My eyes locked on a shimmering blue flower—a Frostblight Lily.

Tall and delicate-looking, the plant stood before me, its crystal-blue blossoms flickering with frost petals and a glowing silver core.

I rushed forward and snapped several blossoms from their stems. The stalk was rough and sharp, slicing my hand open and embedding fine ice crystals into my flesh.

Pain bloomed, quick and cold, but I didn't stop.

I ran back to Rodor and dropped beside him, the rocky shore digging into my knees as I whacked the mice from his body.

I held one blossom above him and squeezed.

It burst into a fine powder that coated his flesh like a blizzard—a veil of freezing silk threads wrapping around him, tightening, hardening—forming a second icy skin.

Rodor's eyes shot open. He gasped and jumped to his feet.

His eyes locked on mine—midnight-blue and burning—and for a moment, nothing needed to be said. Then he turned and ran for the water.

I crushed another blossom against my chest. It exploded in a cold pulse, and I felt power ripple off me. The mice scattered, thrown backward like leaves in a storm.

I stepped forward, breath ragged. Between the swarm and the Lerains still tearing into the boats, I had no idea how I was going to make it across.

But, at least for now, I'd taken care of one problem.

Suddenly, a giant eagle soared toward me, diving down before shifting into a human form—Will.

"I can't fly back to the palace. Bloody demon crows!" he hissed, clutching his arm, his face twisted in pain. "I can't Sphere Jump. Apparently, you can't Sphere Jump out of the Daze Sphere."

His arm was cut open, and it was deep.

I racked my brain for any ideas. The Lerains were attacking the boats—except Hugh's. But Hugh could control minds, and I had no doubt he was creeping into their thoughts.

What if they were just attacking the rowboats?

I walked straight into the water. The freezing cold temperature flayed my skin, while the salt from the sea seared the raw wounds on my wrists. My teeth instantly began to chatter.

"What are you doing, Coco? Are you insane?" Will asked, his eyes wide.

"Most likely. I'm testing a theory," I replied, my jaw clenched against the pain icing my veins. I waded in until the water reached my waist before Will joined me.

"Swim, Will. Shift and swim to the finish," I said before remembering the lily. "But wait—come here."

He took a step toward me. I pulled a blossom from my pocket, held it above his head, and crushed it. It burst over him in a flurry of frost. He shivered.

"What was that?"

"Demon mice," I said. "Just trust me. Shift and swim."

"What about you?" Will asked. His soft hazel eyes widened in concern.

"I survived the other Quests. I'll be fine." I didn't let the doubt creep into my words. He went underwater, and a shark fin emerged a few feet away. He was off. None of the Lerains went for him; in fact, they moved out of his way.

Aldo stood on the beach, taking in his surroundings. His eyes locked on the shark fin. Without hesitation, he dove into the water. Another fin emerged, swimming after Will.

I kicked as fast as I could, my legs burning from the effort. The chill stung my skin, but I had to keep going. I hadn't made it this far to let the sea's biting touch stop me.

The first stretch wasn't difficult since my adrenaline was pumping, but the second hit me hard. My legs were completely drained. The salt stung my raw and aching wrists, and agony screamed through my limbs, impossible to ignore. I swam into the fog, but my body collided with it as though I had tried to walk through a concrete wall.

A head emerged from the water. The Lerain's silver hair glimmered, and her eyes were the color of amethyst, not black, which meant she wasn't possessed.

Panic surged through my veins again as the Lerain began to speak.

She sang in an alluring voice:

> All of us are lost.
> The sailors come our way.
> They long for our embrace,
> As we sing the night to day.
> Time is often fast—
> It leads us to our fate.
> The ocean never lasts;
> It simply starts to sway.

It was the same song that had been sung to us on our way to the Daze Sphere. Back then, I hadn't realized it was a riddle, but now I understood.

I treaded water as I tried to decipher the riddle. I closed my eyes, humming the melody to myself.

All of us are lost. Lost in life, in time, in battle... Who knows? I needed to focus on the next line. *The sailors come our way. They long for our embrace...*

Sailors live for the sea, so that seemed like an obvious answer. But it was too simple. It had to be something deeper, something more cryptic. *As we sing the night to day.*

A shiver rippled through me. There was a rhythm to it, something beyond the obvious. The change from night to day. The sun? No, too literal... *Time is often fast; it leads us to our fate.*

Fate. Time. Destiny. All tangled together. What governs time, and what governs the ocean?

The moon. The moon pulls the tides. It controls the cycles.

I froze. The meaning of the riddle unfolded in my mind, slow and clear. It was the moon's embrace that guided the sailors, leading them toward their fate. The moon was a silent witness to the passing of time. It sang the night to day.

I was exhausted, and this was my only shot.

"The moon."

"Correct again, Dim." Her head vanished beneath the sea as the fog parted. I swam through, and off in the distance, I could make out the palace. A faint mist rolled over me, calming my ragged breaths.

The burning muscles in my legs verged on total exhaustion, but I kept pushing myself forward.

A soft humming noise rose from the depths, and once again

the water splashed upward, morphing into an Aurefly as it sang:

> *Coco, Coco, brave and bright,*
> *Don't fall behind—turn and fight.*
> *You hold the fate of those now gone,*
> *And you'll be the one to right the wrong.*
> *Follow your heart, stay steady and sure—*
> *For a Dim shall rise, both frail and pure.*

It burst into raindrops, showering the sea.

I wasn't sure whether I was slipping into delusion during these Quests, if it was part of the trials, or if somehow this was a message meant just for me—but my gaze immediately fixed on the land. It was so close.

Staggering toward the shore, Will came running to meet me. He clasped me tightly, and my trembling limbs clung to him for support.

"Coco!" Will made a sound that was half laugh, half sob.

"You're incredible," he said, pulling back to grasp my hand. We walked in silence toward a bench where Aldo and Hugh sat.

My body ached from the endless hours spent in the water.

Fatigue hit me like a wave, and I shivered from the chill of the sea.

A Charmer knelt before me, his touch light as he placed his hands over my wrists. A numbing sensation bloomed beneath his palms. The pain, once sharp and biting, dulled to a throb—then melted away. Before I could say thanks, the Charmer stood and moved on.

Will wrapped a fluffy towel around me. A bandage was wrapped tightly around his arm.

"How's your arm?" I asked.

"Just a flesh wound," he said with a grin. "The Charmer already healed it. I couldn't have done this without you." He glanced toward the others. "Hugh made it back first, then me, then Aldo, and finally you."

"Wait, where are the others?"

"They're not back."

"But they were all ahead of me!"

"You outsmarted them," he said, his eyes sparkling. "I can't wait to see the look on Amabel's face. Maybe she'll finally stop underestimating Dim strength."

I stared out at the sea. The wind tugged at my hair and the salt air filled my lungs. A new kind of confidence swelled inside me. It wasn't just the victory. It was the realization that I could compete against Embers—not just compete, but even beat them.

Kaz's words from the other night rang true. My power didn't come from magic like the others. It came from strength. From knowledge. From determination. I'd been focusing on the wrong thing. Magic doesn't make you smarter, kinder, or better.

My lack of magic was my greatest asset. It forced me to rely on what truly mattered: my mind, my heart, and my soul.

CHAPTER

TWENTY-THREE

The bubbles and salts soothed my muscles. I could see the sea below and the stars above. I gazed at them as they shot across the sky, leaving colorful dust in their path. The night sky was filled with diamonds and shimmering trails. I rested my arms on the edge of the tub and nestled my head atop my hand.

Shortly after I had returned, Amabel followed, then Severin, and finally Rodor. Otto, Tada, and Cecille hadn't made it back before dusk, so the Wind Elaryns had reported their location. Oak's Luxari Council had sailed out to retrieve the ones who hadn't returned. It turned out all three of them had gotten stuck in the fog; they couldn't figure out the riddle.

The Wind Elaryns spoke with the Luxari, and based on strategy and skill, they ranked Hugh first, me second, and Will third. Queen Catalina saw my "defiance"—my refusal to obey her rule by warning Will and helping Rodor—as a violation. As a result, I was bumped down to fifth place. Turns out Tada was right—she really was a stickler for the rules.

Still, I couldn't have cared less about my rank or the Ari Dust, which ended up buried deep in my satchel alongside the other vial—I had completed the task entirely on my own. Pride rose within me.

A swath of bubbles coated my knuckles, glimmering in pastel pinks.

A knock echoed through the bathroom. Probably Tada, wanting to get ready together.

"Come in," I called without thinking twice.

I heard faint footsteps, then they stopped.

I turned—and shrieked.

Kaz stood in the doorframe, averting his eyes—surprisingly modest for someone who was usually such a flirt—and staring at the ceiling. Luckily, the bubbles covered me all the way to my shoulders.

"What in Aridan's name are you doing here?" I bit out.

Kaz awkwardly scratched his head. A flush crept up his neck, blooming across his cheeks. I was surprised; I had never seen Kaz turn this red.

"Well, I..." he stammered. "I'll wait for you in your bedroom."

Before I could respond, he left.

My heart raced as I practically sprang from the tub, wrapping a towel around my body.

I walked into my room. Kaz stood by the fireplace, hands resting on the mantel as he looked up.

He slowly stepped toward me, deliberate and sure. He stopped inches from my face. I could see the muscles in his neck tighten as he gazed over my body, then back up to my eyes. The close proximity—and maybe the heat from the bath —made my heart flutter. His citrusy scent overwhelmed my senses.

"I won't be able to see you again until the Still Sphere. An urgent matter came up. I just wanted to say goodbye before I left and tell you how amazing you were today." He fidgeted with the hem of his tunic as if he was nervous.

But why would he be? And what was a Luxari doing here in my room?

"I'm sorry you got hurt because of our fight—again," he said, his voice dropping. "Sorry will never be enough for what I did to you and your alliance, but I wanted to apologize anyway."

The apology caught me off guard—I hadn't expected it. Was he apologizing to Will, Tada, and Hugh too?

Kaz came toward me and leaned down. His lips grazed my cheek and sparked a blush so fierce it that stained my skin with the deepest shade of rose. Without another word, he turned and walked away. The door closed softly behind him, leaving me lost in the silence.

I brushed violently through the tangles in my hair. It felt like a bird's nest, thanks to the crows and the Delirium Sea. My thoughts were just as tangled—caught between the search for the *Ari Report* and Kaz's unexpected apology.

A knock echoed through the room. After Kaz's surprise visit, I wasn't about to invite a visitor in so easily.

I flung open the door, but the hallway was empty. However, a cream box sat on the floor with a thick peach bow wrapped around it.

I picked up the box and placed it on my bed.

Hesitant, I lifted the lid—and gasped.

A midnight black ball gown, wrapped in delicate paper, lay inside.

I rushed to finish getting ready; the excitement of wearing the gorgeous fabric fueled the need to hurry. The dress fit perfectly.

It was breathtaking. The halter neck, midnight black gown had long sleeves and a deep V-shaped neckline made of hollow lace. The slit on the side rose to my upper thigh, while the rest of the material pooled in black silk to the floor.

My hair flowed down my back in waves, and gold glitter sparkled on my eyelids. A deep red gloss painted my lips. I felt absolutely beautiful.

The stars shone brighter than ever as I strolled onto the terrace. Flower petals danced on the breeze, swirling around each other in graceful spirals. Stardust drifted down from the sky in silver and gold specks, reminding me of the faint song still echoing in my mind—like mist clinging to memory. I could only remember one line:

glimmering brightly above.

The gentle hum of conversation pulled me back to the present. I absentmindedly spun my seashell ring around my finger as I took in the crowd. Guests mingled beneath floating lanterns, white Daze lilies and vines wrapped around the marble balcony, and a live orchestra stood off to the side.

"I might fall in love with you," Tada muttered from behind me.

"What do you think?" I said, as I twirled and posed.

"Seriously. I'm reconsidering who I'm attracted to these days. You look stunning, Coco."

I raised my chin with a confident smile and scanned the terrace.

Crispin's eyes lit up as he spotted me, and he strode forward with an eager grin. Severin followed behind, his steps far more leisurely.

"If I didn't know better, I'd think you were a Questling. You manage to be punctual for every Quest and all the celebrations that come with them," I said, amused.

A confident smile spread across Crispin's face. "These Sphere Quests would be far more epic if that were true. It's actually quite a hassle that I can't travel with you all. Besides, you'd enjoy my company far more than Severin's."

I chuckled, and Severin just rolled his eyes.

"Oh, right—I almost forgot. I owe you a thank you," Crispin added, his smile widening.

"For what?" I asked.

"You won me some more gold," he said, amusement flickering in his eyes.

Severin stepped up beside him, shaking his head. "I've told him to stop betting, but it's like telling a child not to look at something shiny—useless." He downed the rest of the wine in his glass with a sigh.

"Don't you want some more?" Crispin asked, clearly annoyed by the interruption.

"I can take a hint, Crispin," Severin said smoothly. He turned to me with a nod. "Coco, that dress is enchanting on you." Then he exchanged a glance with Crispin before strolling into the palace.

Crispin leaned in slightly, his voice lower. "I placed a bet on you finishing every Quest."

I tried to sound cool, but my voice cracked anyway. "You shouldn't have."

"Here's the truth, Coco," he said, eyes steady on mine. "Magic doesn't equal power or control. Half those Embers out there barely know what they're doing."

I raised a brow. "Sounds like you've got a problem with Embers. Funny, considering who you're with."

He shrugged, but his expression hardened. "It's not them. It's what they've always thought of us—Dims. Weak, stupid, incapable of success. For years, we've been the joke. The bottom of the pile."

Even now, standing on the terrace, I could feel those eyes —Embers watching, judging. Their stares were sharp, dripping with disbelief, even though I'd proven myself in three Quests.

Crispin's gaze softened as he studied me. Then he tapped his temple.

"You've got this. Heart. Grit. You think magic opens locked doors? Solves riddles? It doesn't. Your mind does. That's why I'm invested in you. My whole life, I've been fighting to prove that being an Ember doesn't define success. I've proven it to myself. But you, Coco... you're proving it to all of Aren."

I opened my mouth, searching for something to say, but words failed me. Before I could find the right response, Crispin gave a brief bow, a spark of humor in his eyes, and walked away.

All heads turned as King Oak and his Luxari Council walked in. His hair gleamed under the stars, and he wore a simple cream tunic, light brown pants, and leather boots—his attire understated, yet still fitting for a king. No crown rested on his head, but his presence alone commanded attention. His sun-kissed skin seemed to sparkle as the stardust fell onto him.

Niko walked next to him, while the rest of the Daze Luxari Council trailed behind.

"Come on, Coco, the meal is about to begin," Tada said. She looped her arm through mine as she led me into the palace.

We entered the Great Hall for the champions' meal, where three long tables filled with every imaginable food rested. Thornbeak roast, juicy rootswine ribs, and mistfin bits abounded. Sweet, glazebloom turnovers cooled on the far end of the table, their sugary scent mixing with the rich aroma of spiced wine. Tada squeezed my hand, then skipped over to Otto's table.

Oak entered the room and sat at the head of one of the tables. In an instant, a girl leaned in, whispering something in his ear.

A sprinkle of jealousy hit me as she tucked a strand of long, shiny, charcoal hair behind her ear, revealing the side of her face.

Sabina.

Looking away, I headed toward a nearby table. I pulled out a chair and sat down next to Zareen.

"Coco. What an honor," Zareen said, leaning toward me. Her jet-black hair brushed against her shoulders.

Seeing her again reminded me of my failed library search. I was growing impatient—there was still no sign of the *Ari Report*. Time was slipping away, and soon the Quests would end, taking with them my only chance to gain access to the libraries.

I downed my glass of wine, hoping it would numb the tight knot of frustration in my chest. It slid down smoothly and spread warmth through my veins.

"Coco, honestly, you were amazing today. I hope you'll join our Luxari Council," Benedict said.

"Slow down there, Benedict. There's still another challenge to go," I reminded him.

If I did get an offer, it would buy me more time to search for the *Ari Report*—but that was a big if.

I slumped back in my chair and swirled the deep amber liquid in my glass.

Benedict leaned back, his hands behind his head, looking entirely at ease. "Oh, I'm not worried about that. You keep doing what you're doing, and you'll have offers from every Luxari Council in Aren."

I couldn't prevent the blush that crept onto my cheeks.

"Thanks, Benedict, it means a lot," I murmured.

He simply nodded.

Zareen's chair scraped against the floor as she moved closer to me. She rested her elbows on the table, her head in her palm, and watched me intently.

"You have to tell us how you solved the riddle so quickly, Coco."

I shifted uncomfortably as all eyes at the table turned toward me.

"Excuse me, I need some air." Standing, I tossed my cloth napkin onto the table and slipped out the double doors leading to the veranda.

CHAPTER
TWENTY-FOUR

I stood on the terrace, my hands resting on the cool iron railing. The stars were beautiful in the midnight velvet sky above.

Stardust fell like fresh snow, frosting my skin and gown with silver and gold specks.

"I learned something," Will murmured from behind me. He gently tugged my elbow and guided us down the steps into the garden, where only the fountains bubbled softly. We stopped beneath a tree whose thick branches cast deep, concealing shadows.

"Niko had a bit too much to drink tonight," Will said, glancing around, "and let something slip. Not even on purpose —she just... rambled. All I had to do was ask the right questions."

"What did she say?" I asked, my pulse quickening.

Will leaned in slightly. "The *Ari Report* isn't even kept in the palace."

I blinked. The shock hit like a splash of cold water.

"If it's not here, then where is it?" I whispered. "It'd have to be somewhere protected."

He shrugged, watching my reaction closely. "Beats me. But I may have suggested that you were interested in exploring more of the Daze Sphere... with King Oak."

My head whipped toward him. "You did what?"

Will held up his hands. "Coco, listen. You're not going to get near that report without him. He's obviously... interested... in you."

"No, he's not," I retorted, a little too quickly.

He gave me a look. "Come on. You're really going to pretend you haven't noticed? He looks at you like you're the answer to a question he's been asking his whole life."

I folded my arms, but I didn't push further.

"We've got one more day here," he said. "If you get close to him, maybe you'll stumble on the report. Maybe not. But it's our best lead."

Little did Will know that my lips had already touched his—and that damn kiss kept playing on repeat in my mind.

I didn't answer immediately. Manipulating Oak—using his feelings, if there were even any—felt wrong. But the report could give me the answer I desperately sought.

"All right," I said quietly.

A spark of excitement flickered inside me at the thought of spending more time with Oak.

Will nodded. "Worst-case scenario, we've still got one more shot in the Still Sphere."

He cleared his throat, then hesitated. "Hey, um... you're a woman—"

I tilted my head, amused. "Excellent observation."

He laughed awkwardly. "No, I mean—can you tell me what you think of this?"

He reached into his pocket and pulled out a ring.

An ice-blue sapphire bloomed at the center, encircled by a stunning floral halo. Tiny diamonds paved the silver band, catching the moonlight like stars.

"It's beautiful," I breathed, my voice soft with awe. The way it sparkled—it was clearly chosen with care.

I knew who it was for. I felt a warm, swelling joy for him.

"Elizabeth is going to love it," I said softly, eyes still on the ring.

"I hope so." His voice cracked just slightly. "I got it from the Starfall Mines—they say the rarest stones in Aren come from there."

He looked down and nerves flickered across his features.

"I'm going to ask her after the final Quest," he said. "Being away from her this long... it's changed everything. I don't want to be away from her for another second. Not if I can help it."

I reached out and placed a hand on his chest. "Will. She loves you. You already have her answer."

His smile returned and he tucked the ring carefully back into his pocket.

I looped my arm through his as we turned toward the palace.

"Remember when Milo and I tried to trap Aeraliths so we could marry them?" Will asked, chuckling.

I laughed. "Yeah, you thought love was something you could catch if you just used enough sugar cubes and string."

He went on recalling the memory, but all I could think

about was that Elizabeth was marrying the best man in all of Aren. And somehow, knowing that Will had found happiness made me feel lighter too.

The next morning, I found Niko outside the palace, sparring in a small sandy area. Her curly hair clung to her forehead as she moved. She was dueling one of the Daze Luxari Council— Drogo, I believe his name was. He was massive and clearly from the Scorch Sphere with the trademark broad shoulders, sun-darkened skin, and that unmistakable fire in his eyes.

I couldn't help but wonder why Niko was looking out for me so much. I was used to Milo and Will—but having women as friends? I liked the feeling more than I expected.

Drogo walked toward me and reached for a towel on the bench. He stalked off without a word.

"He doesn't say much, does he?" I asked.

Niko paused to catch her breath. "Not unless it's necessary."

She motioned for me to join her.

"Drogo doesn't shut up once you get a few grogs in him," Niko said. Her copper eyes shone with mischief.

"So, what are you teaching me today?" I asked through a yawn.

"Oh, where to start... First, you need to build your arm strength." She gripped my arms with her hands. "I could break these like *that*."

"How are we going to do that?"

A grin spread across her face, and I followed her gaze to two empty buckets sitting beside the wooden bench.

"I need water for an exercise. Carry them down to the sea, fill them up, and come back," she said matter-of-factly.

"Did you wake me up to train me, or just to do your chores?" I scowled.

Niko chuckled. "Oh, Coco. Would I manipulate you like that?"

"Yes. You would," I said. But I picked up the two empty buckets, my fingers clasped against the rough, splintered handles. I brushed past her, making sure to ram my shoulder into her as I did.

She didn't move an inch, but her laugh followed me as I walked. "I'll keep you company, then."

I turned to tell her not to bother, but she had already stepped in behind me. The buckets rubbed against my hips as we followed the sandy path that led to the sea, listening to the waves crash in the distance.

"Aren't there Virelliths in the Delirium Sea?"

"Pardon me, Coco—was that a word, or did you just sneeze? I truly haven't the faintest idea what you said."

I grumbled. "Never mind."

Niko chuckled softly. "I'm teasing. I believe you meant to

say *Virelliths—vih-RELL-iths.* Fortunately, I've yet to encounter one myself, so I daresay we're safe."

Pink crept into my cheeks. As if being a Dim wasn't bad enough, mispronouncing words I'd only read in books—my only window into the real world—was humiliating. A subject change was much needed.

"Do you like it here?" I asked, my voice louder now as we neared the roaring waves.

"Coco, your attempts at small talk could use some refinement," she said with a teasing smile.

My eye roll didn't stop her from talking.

"I was raised here and chose to serve on the Luxari Council here. Naturally, I hold this place dear. Yet, I would follow Oak anywhere—even into the depths of the Bleak Sphere."

"Have you always been close?" I asked.

"Oh, yes. We were raised together, bathed together, and endured our first heartbreaks side by side." She placed both hands over her heart, her expression dramatic.

"Like anyone's ever broken your heart, Niko."

Niko smirked. "You'd be surprised," she said, flicking a pebble into the sea.

I raised an eyebrow. "Not buying it."

The waves lapped at my ankles, soaking my boots and socks as I filled the bucket with salty water.

Filling the first pail was fairly easy, but the second felt heavier. I glanced up toward the path leading back to the bench. It had been easy coming down, but it was going to be a pain going back up.

My eyes flicked over to Niko, who was smiling way too wide.

"Don't say a word." I grasped the buckets and slowly trudged up the sandy path.

As I made my way back up, the weight of the buckets seemed to grow with each step. Water sloshed down my legs, and the ocean breeze swept against my face.

Niko trailed behind me, enjoying every strained sound that escaped my lips. At one point, I had to set the buckets down to catch my breath—my arms ached and trembled with exertion.

"You were surprised when I mentioned I'd follow Oak anywhere?" Niko called from behind.

I turned and met her gaze.

"Well, I get you're friends, but I don't know... your dedication almost seems... unreal."

"Oh, Coco," Niko said. Her gaze lingered on me for a moment, and a look of sympathy crossed her features.

"What?" I asked, defensively.

Niko pulled me into a tight hug. "Get off me," I mumbled into her chest, breathing in a fresh, spicy scent.

She whispered, resting her chin atop my head. "I thought you might need a hug."

She released me and strolled around me up the hill.

"What's that supposed to mean?" I asked, my eyes narrowing.

"It means, 'Pick up the buckets and keep moving,'" she hollered over her shoulder.

As I made my way ahead, I was surprised to see Severin and Crispin at the top of the hill with a group of men—Niko was already there, chatting with them.

I set the water down and rubbed my sore arms. Niko smirked at me, her eyes practically glowing with excitement.

"Oh, no. Should I even ask?" I grumbled.

"Let's just say it's part of your training," Niko said. She gestured toward the men. "Crispin was impressed with you during *Seize the Banner*. Now, after Blackwing Isle, he thinks you're invincible."

"Get to the point, Niko." My chest rose and fell rapidly from hauling the buckets up the hill.

"He wants you to race."

"Now?" I raised an eyebrow. "I'm too tired." I waved my hand dismissively and stepped past the figures who were now eyeing me.

"Aww, come on, Coco. Why not? Plus, you owe me," Niko called after me.

I stopped and turned. "What do you mean, I owe you?"

"For all the extra time I spent helping you train," she replied, grinning.

I opened my mouth to argue, but Crispin cut me off, rushing over. "Just one quick race. I'm trying to prove a point. These men—" he gestured to the Dims surrounding us, "—won't believe me until you beat them."

All eyes were on me. I was too tired to argue. "Fine."

Crispin clapped his hands together, his smile wide. "All right, then." He walked to the path and stopped at the slope that led to the sea. "First one to touch the ocean and race back wins."

The crew of Dims laughed. All of them were bigger than me. It irked me more than I expected. I wasn't about to let them underestimate me, especially when running was one thing that I knew I could do well.

I shoved past them and stood next to Crispin. They followed, taking their positions beside me.

"Severin, could you please make sure they all touch the ocean?" Crispin called over his shoulder.

Severin nodded and jogged down the slope toward the beach. Niko took her place by Crispin and gave me two thumbs up, as if I were a child. I rolled my eyes and looked toward the sea.

Breathing in through my nose, I centered myself, then exhaled slowly.

"All right, you know the drill," Crispin yelled.

I shifted my weight, eyes locked on the path ahead.

He continued, "On flight. Take your stance."

I leaned forward.

"Sway the tide."

I prepared my arms.

"Race the winds—and take flight!"

I surged forward, sand flying beneath my feet as I raced down the path. Not looking back, I focused on my goal: the sea.

My pulse roared in my ears, but I focused on keeping my breathing steady. The salty wind whipped across my face as I hit the beach, bent low to touch the water with my fingertips, then spun and shot back up the path.

The wind and sea salt breeze filled my lungs, pulling me forward until I sped past Crispin and Niko. I finally turned and allowed myself to sit down. My heart raced, but I couldn't stop a grin from spreading across my lips.

The horizon was clear. Only Niko and Crispin stood at the finish, and the blue sky seemed to applaud my victory.

SOULSHIMMER

AREN FOLKTALES

The body once asked
For a heart that would last
Beyond the deaths of those who've
    passed.
A shimmering gleam,
Born from a dream,
Created the soul—
The SoulShimmer of old.

CHAPTER
TWENTY-FIVE

My stomach rumbled with hunger as I sat down in the Great Hall for breakfast. I'd worked up quite an appetite after going through Niko's training and Crispin's race.

Since the Scorch Sphere, I'd been doing the exercises and techniques Niko taught me three times a day, on my own. They were simple moves designed to build strength and sharpen reflexes. The training wasn't flashy, but it was making a difference—and, if nothing else, boosting my confidence.

Crispin was so thrilled after the race that he kissed me on both cheeks and said he owed me. I wasn't sure what that meant, but I couldn't help but relish handing those Dims their asses.

One by one, others began trickling in, and the hall slowly filled with the murmur of voices.

I felt Oak's presence before I heard him.

"I was wondering if you'd like to accompany me today," he

said. "I'm heading to one of my favorite places in the kingdom, and I thought you might enjoy seeing it."

I dropped my napkin in shock at his offer and the opportunity Will had so conveniently set up. As I bent down to grab it, he did the same. Our fingers brushed, sending a wave of heat through my entire body. I quickly pulled my hand back and stood up.

This was my chance to find out where the *Ari Report* was.

He extended his hand. His gaze was steady, inviting.

"If you're worried about being alone with a Luxari," Niko said as she joined Oak's side, "I'll be there."

"How long will we be gone? We still have the final Quest…" I asked.

"We'll be back by tomorrow afternoon, before the ship leaves for the Still Sphere. Besides, I'm the King of the Daze Sphere—I can be gone as long as I want. No questions asked. I even took the liberty of telling your alliance you were going."

I shot Oak a narrowed glance just as Niko choked on her apple, spraying apple chunks across the room.

"Come on, how could you refuse? You've got me—and this slob—coming along. What could possibly go wrong?" Oak said, a wide grin spreading across his face.

I made my way to the stables, where I was supposed to meet Oak and Niko. As I walked, I rehearsed how I might casually bring up the *Ari Report*—how to ask where it might be without sounding suspicious. That's when I heard it—a soft, deliberate whistle from the shadows.

I kept walking, pretending not to notice.

Then it came again. Louder.

I turned toward a stone wall just in time to see Zareen lurking in a dim corridor, motioning for me to come over with exaggerated secrecy.

I sighed. *Of course.*

Reluctantly, I approached her. Before I could say a word, she stepped forward, grabbed my elbow, and hauled me into the darkened hallway.

Benedict leaned against the far wall, arms crossed, watching Zareen with amusement.

Zareen's eyes lit up like a child about to unwrap a long-awaited present. She bounced slightly on the balls of her feet.

"What has you so giddy?" I asked, narrowing my eyes.

"Shhhh," she whispered, looking around. "Keep your voice down. We did something... almost treasonous."

"*You* did something rebellious," Benedict muttered dryly.

Zareen whipped her head toward him. "You stood guard. That makes you an accomplice."

I crossed my arms. "Can we make this quick? Oak and Niko are waiting."

Without another word, Zareen grabbed my hand, pried it open, and dropped something into my palm. A cold weight. I held it up, letting the filtered sunlight from a curtained window catch its surface.

A bronze key etched with two intertwined Daze lilies and delicate wind swirls spiraling around the edge sat heavy in my palm.

I raised an eyebrow. "What is this?"

Zareen shrugged, but her smile didn't fade. "Not entirely sure. But I have a good feeling. It might open something valuable—maybe even the *Ari Report*."

A wave of warmth swept through me, tightening my throat with unexpected emotion.

"Why would you do this for me?" I asked, voice low. Zareen just smiled in response.

I'd heard you made vows when you joined the Luxari Council, but I wasn't sure what those entailed or how strictly they were enforced. Would this act of kindness break an oath that Zareen and Benedict had taken?

I hesitated—just for a second—then tucked it into my pocket. "Thank you."

"Don't thank us yet," Benedict warned. "For all we know, it opens something random. Or worse—something dangerous."

Zareen clapped a hand on my shoulder. "Good luck."

With that, the two of them melted into the shadows.

"I'm not getting on that," I said brusquely, crossing my arms over my chest. Oak's lips twitched as if he were trying to suppress a smile.

"Coco, don't tell me you're scared of a horse. You've faced Rogue Embers, demon crows, and Amabel, yet you're scared of this beautiful creature?"

"Yes. Thanks for the invitation, but I'll be going now," I said, turning to walk away. A strong hand clasped my elbow. Oak pulled me toward him.

"I've got you," Oak said firmly.

My knees felt wobbly. His other hand cupped my cheek, gently pulling my gaze up to meet his.

"I had you when we danced. I have you now." His eyes bore into mine, making my breath catch. I simply nodded as he dropped his arms and walked toward the horse. He patted the silken black mare.

"This is Astra. She's my favorite horse," Oak said.

My hands trembled. I was going to humiliate myself in front of Niko and Oak. I could already see the smirk on Niko's face. I shot her a glare, but she only laughed. I stepped toward the horse. My entire field of vision filled with Astra's bulk.

"I don't know how to get on..." I started to say, but Oak immediately came behind me. He placed his hands on my waist, and his touch burned through me. He stepped closer, his powerful body pressing against mine. A fluttering sensation started in my stomach, as though an Aeralith had taken flight inside me, spreading warm magic dust through my blood. I felt Oak's breath against the back of my ear.

"Now, what kind of king would I be if I left a beautiful

damsel to climb onto a horse by herself?" Before I could react, he lifted me by the waist, as if I weighed no more than a Wind Elaryn, and set me gently on Astra.

He pulled himself up behind me, his body pressing into mine. He tugged me closer, leaving no space between us. I glanced toward Niko, whose smile was full of mischief.

"Enjoying yourself, Coco?" she asked cheerfully.

I shot her an obscene gesture, which drew a bark of laughter from Oak. His body vibrated against my back, sparking a tingle that ran down my spine. Niko's horse cut in front of us, and she rode ahead, kicking up dust as she went.

Oak's arm wrapped around my stomach, holding me firmly against him. He kept it there, his fingers tracing idle circles on my hip.

I felt as though my heart might give out at any moment. No Dim—or even Ember—should have this effect on me.

We rode in silence into Oak's Kingdom. Children played in the fields while their parents worked the patchwork of crops and tended to the cattle. It was quiet—peaceful. We crossed a small stone bridge that arched over a gentle river.

Everything was so green—a striking contrast to the red sands of the Scorch Sphere. The dirt path wound through the valley, climbing soft hills dotted with modest wooden homes. Laundry fluttered on lines, and flowers in vibrant colors—glimmerbuds, thornminds, and mistlace—decorated the hillsides.

Laughter and cheers rose over the hill as a crowd came into view, every face tilted skyward. I followed their gaze—and gasped.

High above the moors, Swayers sailed through the air on shimmering trails of silver-blue wind, gracefully gliding just beneath the clouds.

Astra slowed beside a cluster of Swayers. Across the grassy field stood a raised platform that held chairs draped in deep blue velvet and tilted back beneath the wind-stirred sky — where I assumed the judges lounged, eyes trained above.

One Swayer glanced at Oak, then did a double take and bowed. "King Oak." The rest followed in unison.

"How's the weather today?" Oak asked casually.

"Ideal for sailing."

"Anyone of note?"

"Seraphine," the Swayer said, gesturing upward. "The one dressed entirely in black."

I tracked his gesture and spotted her. She spiraled effortlessly through a vertical climb, loop after loop, ascending into the heights above.

"What is this?" I asked, awed.

Niko pulled up beside us, smiling. "Aetherglide Quests. Highlight of Spice Season—other than the Sphere Quests, of course."

"How do you win?" I craned my neck, my gaze lost in the endless sky.

"You're scored in three categories," she said. "Altitude, aerial display, and style—with a flair for elemental control."

A pack of children dashed past us, laughing as they tried to race the Swayers overhead. I couldn't help but smile.

Niko's voice dropped to a quiet murmur. "Many of the participants come from the poorer districts. They use these

Quests to showcase their skills and catch the eye of the Luxari —hoping for a chance at a better life."

Her words lingered in my mind as I watched the Swayers glide effortlessly.

"What do you win?" I asked.

"Nothing," Oak replied from behind me. "It's merely a matter of bragging rights."

The Swayers navigated the sky as if it were a dance, shaping the air currents around them—evidently steering the wind with thought alone.

"It takes a lot of concentration," Oak added.

I couldn't help but compare the Spheres. The Bleak Sphere's Quests were sloppy and crude. The Hush Sphere's were elegant and refined. The Scorch Sphere's were ferocious and competitive. But here, in the Daze Sphere, it felt different—joyful, dreamlike, fun.

The crowd was no less invested than the gliders themselves.

"We'd better get going," Oak said gently, steering Astra away from the field.

The dirt road turned rocky, and we passed a few mines, the sound of clinking metal echoing through the dark tunnels. A heavy canopy of birch, pine, and oak trees emerged, their thick trunks weathered and covered in moss at the base.

The key pressed cold against my thigh through the fabric— a sharp reminder of why I'd accepted Oak's invitation: for information. I needed to find a strategic way to bring up the *Ari Report*, but there wasn't exactly a natural way to ask him about it.

We veered off the main road and into the woods, where Niko rode about twenty feet ahead. Flickers of golden-yellow light danced in the air like fireflies.

"Milo would have loved this," I sighed.

"Tell me about him," Oak said, surprising me.

I hesitated for a moment. "Milo was fun. He was never in a bad mood—always joking, smiling, cheering people up. He loved being around people."

"What do you miss most about him?" Oak asked.

I swallowed hard. "His laugh. It was contagious. If he started laughing, you were doomed."

Oak's gaze felt like it was on me, even though I couldn't see his face. "What about your parents?"

"My mother and father are both dead." I cleared my throat. "And yours?"

"Mine are dead as well," he said.

"I'm so sorry, Oak. I didn't realize..." I trailed off, unsure of what to say.

"It's okay," he said, his arm tightening around me. "At least they're together." I nodded, feeling a pang of sadness.

It was now or never. There wouldn't be a more perfect moment—death made for the best possible segue into what I needed to ask about the report.

"I've always been curious," I said, trying to keep my tone light. "I wonder if all Luxari keep the Ari Report in their libraries."

He didn't answer right away, just shifted slightly behind me.

Great. I'd pushed too far, too soon.

But, to my surprise, Oak replied, "That is a matter of personal discretion."

I kept my expression neutral, careful not to show how hard I was listening.

It was the right call—he suddenly went quiet, almost eerily so. I instantly regretted bringing it up. I needed to say something. Anything.

"So," I said, aiming for casual, "tell me about your parents."

"My father was a natural leader—serious, focused. My mother... she made him laugh. She was funny, kind, and warm. My parents were SoulShimmer."

"SoulShimmer?" I asked, raising a brow.

"You've never heard of SoulShimmer?" Oak's voice was teasing.

"Clearly not, or I wouldn't be asking." I bit back.

He let out a low chuckle. "Okay. That was a stupid question.

"SoulShimmer is the radiant glow of two souls intertwined —bonded souls. It's said that Aridan couldn't keep the two souls apart before this life. They are destined to be together; they find each other in Aren, and after death, they continue into the Unknown."

The hairs on the back of my neck rose, and goosebumps skated up my spine.

"The SoulShimmer mark appears on the inside of your left wrist. It's called SoulShimmer because the mark is said to glow, shining under both sunlight and moonlight."

"What is the mark?" I asked.

"The mark of the Sphere your SoulShimmer is from." Oak lifted my left wrist and rubbed his thumb over the inside, sending a rush of heat through my arm.

"My mother received the mark. Two Daze lilies intertwined here." His thumb lingered for a moment, as if tracing a memory.

"Did your father?"

"He didn't. Not until my mother knew she wanted to be with him forever—that she loved him. His mark appeared the moment she told him."

"Why have I never heard of this?"

"SoulShimmer is ancient magic, and it's exclusive to the Luxari. Even among the Luxari, it's incredibly rare. Having that kind of bond goes beyond the Unknown."

"What if you don't accept it?"

"Once the mark appears, it's already been chosen by fate— it's out of your control by then," Oak said, his voice thoughtful. "But if you don't accept it, the other won't receive the mark, and the bond won't be completed."

"What do you mean, 'chosen by fate'?" I asked.

"A Fate Dancer gave my mother a prophecy, revealing who she would spend the rest of her life with."

"Like a seer?" I furrowed my brow, trying to make sense of it.

"Most seers are vague at best," Oak said. "Visions, riddles, dreams—half of it sounds like poetry. But Fate Dancers don't guess. They know. Fate Dancers are extremely rare; there are only a handful in all of Aren's history. Their prophecies aren't possibilities—they're certainties."

A branch snapped, startling Astra.

A sharp sting scraped against my arm. A streak of brown flew past and embedded itself into the tree beside us. The arrow dripped with blackened goop—magic repressor.

Oak jumped off Astra, yanking me down hard. Fear shot down my spine as I noticed an arrow protruding from his shoulder. The syrupy goop seeped around the entry wound as blood stained his tunic. He wrenched the arrow from his shoulder, letting it fall to the ground as he spun toward the forest. In one swift motion, he unleashed a burst of wind so powerful that it ripped the leaves from the trees, revealing hundreds of hooded figures hidden among the branches.

Terror pooled in my stomach. There were only three of us, and even though I was with some of the most powerful Embers in Aren, Oak's power would be dimmed for the next few hours thanks to the magic repressor.

Niko appeared beside us just in time, as Oak slumped to the ground, unconscious. She flicked out her hand, conjuring a strong gust of wind that lifted Oak's body and gently set him atop Astra like a sack of flour.

I grabbed a knife from Oak's hip and carefully wiped the leftover Darksap from the arrow that had hit him onto the blade. I hoped it would weaken the Embers I was about to face.

Then Niko slapped Astra's rear, sending her galloping into the woods.

She nodded to me, and together we slipped between the trees.

A figure emerged from the shadows, startling me. I plunged the blade into his back. His scream of agony rose sharply as I bolted deeper into the woods, panic rising.

My chest tightened with every step. Branches struck my skin as I ran through the forest.

A clammy hand clasped over my mouth. Fear flooded my mind. I threw my head back, crashing it into my attacker.

Stars exploded across my vision. He let out a grunt, and a surge of white pain throbbed against the back of my head. I could taste blood, sharp and metallic, on the edge of my tongue.

A sweaty palm yanked my head back by the hair, forcing a whimper from my throat. My eyes watered from the relentless pressure as the attacker leaned in close, his rancid breath hot against my ear.

Midnight wings swooped and dove at us. They looked like bats with smooth, flat wings extending from their backs and sides like a manta's cape. Their vertical pupils glowed with fury.

Skelrays. It was as if Aridan himself had sent them to me.

They glided through the air with grace. The man gripping me was distracted just long enough for his hold to loosen. I leaned forward, then ducked as a Skelray's tail struck him. Its venomous barbs pulsed poison through his veins.

Niko was still surrounded by attackers, but she seemed to be holding her own. If I could lure the Skelrays away from her, she could focus on finishing the attackers off.

I knew what to do.

I began to whistle—a slow, haunting tune. The Skelrays' frenetic flight began to calm, their movements softening as I began to sing:

> *Even when the night is here,*
> *I know he slumbers everywhere.*
> *He feeds off dreams,*
> *Devouring sleep,*
> *Wisping thoughts away through the air.*

What do they call him? The creature of
   sleep,
The lonely,
The bargainer,
The dealer of greed.
Come follow me
Before he steals all your dreams.
Come through the crook,
But don't make a noise.

They began to follow me, and I had no idea where to lead them. All I knew was that I had to draw them away from Niko —so I ran, plunging deeper into the woods. Mesmerized, they followed.

He is here.
Waiting.
Fearing.
Shh... shh... come closer now...
Sleep now... sleep now...
Come little ones,
Before he awakes.
One look from him,
And dust is all that remains.
Shh... shh... the shadows call...
Hush... hush... fade away...

I just kept running, repeating the lullaby Milo used to sing to me every night, though my voice was growing ragged.

A sudden gale slammed into me, hurling me to the ground.

The Skelrays shrieked—sharp, high-pitched cries—as their leathery wings rustled and they scattered into the sky.

I gasped and pushed myself up just as Niko emerged from the trees covered in blood, sweat, and dirt. She jogged toward me like she hadn't just sent a storm through the forest.

"Not bad for a Dim." She smirked and looped her arm through mine as we headed off to find Astra.

CHAPTER
TWENTY-SIX

By the time we made it back to the site of the initial attack and found Astra, Oak had regained his power—Darksap doesn't last as long in Luxari blood as it does in an Ember's. He was in a foul mood, but relieved we were okay.

We had been attacked by Timber Raiders from Whisper Ridge. It made sense they would have a supply—the magic repressor sap could only be found at the top of Wraith Peak and Whisper Ridge.

We rode for hours. My body still ached, stiff and sore from the fight, but I wasn't going to say anything about it. The scenery shifted from lush greens to dead trees. The only thing that seemed alive were the vines that curled around a massive boulder.

Oak hopped off Astra, and Niko followed. He raised his arms to help me down.

"I've got it," I said, already swinging my leg over Astra's side. My boots hit the rocky ground, and I stumbled.

"Oh, Coco. I truly don't know how you made it through any of the challenges," Niko quipped.

I punched her in the arm.

"Ouch! I think our training is actually making a difference," Niko said, grinning and rubbing the spot where I'd hit her.

Oak chuckled. His hand pressed lightly against my back as he brushed some vines aside. "After you," he said.

I stepped forward.

I pushed through the thicket, branches scratching my arms and leaving behind angry red lines. I emerged from the dense brush into a valley surrounded by fields of green alfa grass and golden straw. Color burst across the mountainside in hues of yellow, sepia, and russet.

I followed them down a narrow path beside a river.

We crossed a wooden bridge and strolled into a grassy field bordered by thick woods. In the distance stood a small stone cottage. Anticipation and hope surged through me—this had to be where the *Ari Report* was hidden.

"It's beautiful," I said, taking it all in.

"Why, thank you," Oak replied. "Now, please don't be offended by this, but I'd like to keep it beautiful. And I'm afraid all three of us are in need of a bath."

I glanced back toward the river, shivering at the thought of bathing in the cold water.

Niko, however, had already walked around the cottage. I followed suit, with Oak right behind me.

The back of the cottage opened into a dense forest. Just

outside the tree line stood a wooden shack, its door covered in moss and vines. Niko walked straight towards it.

Oak gently placed his hand on the small of my back, urging me forward. A tingle of warmth crawled up my spine from the contact.

I pulled the door open, and a wave of humid air hit me. Steam that smelled like fresh mint sprayed my face. Oak nudged me inside.

"I'll wait until you two finish," he said, then strolled toward the cottage.

I found myself standing at the top of a narrow wooden staircase. The steps creaked beneath my weight as I descended slowly.

When I reached the last step, a gasp escaped my mouth.

Starlight bubbles hovered throughout the cavern, each one glowing with golden Aeralith dust and casting a warm light across a huge pool of the brightest blue I had ever seen. Steam rose from the surface like smoke.

Niko's head shot up from the water, spraying droplets across the granite walls.

She glided over to the stairs and smiled warmly. "Get in—it feels incredible."

I wanted to scrub my flesh raw and wash away the memory of the Timber Raider's touch.

I shucked off my sweater and breeches, making sure the key was still tucked safely in my pocket first.

Hot water splashed around my ankles as I lowered myself into the pool. If I weren't on my tiptoes, it would have risen past my neck, submerging me completely.

Water cascaded from the cavern's smooth rock walls,

tumbling into the pool below. The sound was mesmerizing, comforting—like a familiar lullaby, soothing and magical.

The inside of the cottage was dimly lit and drafty. I clutched my towel closer to me. To the right was a small kitchen with a stove and a wooden table. Three doors lined the left side, and a hallway led to an arched room at the back of the cottage.

Where would he keep the Ari Report?

Oak pushed open one of the doors to reveal a small room: a simple bed, a table, and a dresser. He went to the drawer and pulled out a dark blue sweater, black pants, and soft, fluffy socks.

"Please make yourself at home. We'll be in the back of the cottage," he said. He turned and left, closing the door behind him so I could dress.

As soon as the door clicked shut, I dropped to the floor and began searching—checking under the bed, opening and closing drawers, scouring every inch of the room. But I came up empty-handed, finding nothing but dust.

Frustrated, I got dressed.

The black pants hugged my legs, and the cotton felt incredibly soft. I slid the key into the waistband of the pants. The sweater fell to my knees. It smelled like Oak: a mix of fresh rain and coconut.

My gaze drifted to the dresser, and my fingers hovered over the two initials scratched into the wood. *D.A.* I ran my fingertips over the letters, tracing the worn ridges embedded in the surface.

A flicker of unease brushed against my thoughts, but I let it pass.

I paused to peer into the kitchen and briefly scan for anywhere Oak might hide the *Ari Report*. Again, I found nothing. As I made my way to the back of the cottage, my feet slipped on the floor.

I stepped under the arch into a room with dark wooden walls. At the back, curved glass panels overlooked the forest.

The floor was bare of furniture. Bookshelves lined one wall, while the other had a massive stone fireplace. Dozens of pillows and blankets were heaped onto the floor in front of the fire.

Before I could start searching for the report, Oak appeared in the doorway, his arms full of wood.

He wore a black sweater and dark pants, his damp hair swept back from his face.

"Niko went to retrieve the horses," Oak said, bending down and adding logs to the fire. "A storm is coming. We'll need to stay the night."

He smiled. "That sweater drowns you."

I laughed, tugging at the hem of the sleeves that hung past my fingertips. "Well, I'm getting quite attached."

"You can have it, then," he said.

A smile spread across my face before I could stop it.

I stood awkwardly, playing with the sleeves of the sweater, unsure of what to do.

"You can sit down, Coco. I can tell you're freezing."

I hesitated, then walked over to the rug covered with pillows and blankets and sank down into the softness. Oak followed to drape a tan quilt over my shoulders. He handed me a mug.

The rich, sweet scent wafted into the air, and I couldn't help but grin. "Melted chocolate?"

He smiled, his eyes warm. "Yes. You're welcome."

The chocolate ran smoothly down my throat, instantly heating me. I leaned back, savoring the warmth.

"I'll be right back." Oak's voice faded as he exited the room.

As soon as he left, I set the mug down and stood. I scanned the bookshelves for the *Ari Report*—but found nothing. Maybe I'd missed it, but I had no idea how much time I had before he returned.

Defeated, I sat back down and stared at the stone fireplace. That's when I noticed the exact same markings as the key—carved prominently into the wooden wall on either side of the hearth. I glanced toward the arch; Oak and Niko were nowhere in sight.

I crawled forward and reached out to trace the delicate wooden carvings. Between the two intertwined Daze lilies was a small, perfectly round hole. My hands trembling, I pulled out the key and pressed it in. It fit—but wouldn't turn.

Frustrated, I glared at it, tapping my fingers against my thighs, searching for a new plan.

"I suspected as much." Oak's voice rang through the room.

I yelped and scrambled upright, mouth opening to protest —but he raised a hand, silencing me.

I clutched the ends of my sweater as he approached, goose-bumps prickling across my skin.

I'd been caught. And not only that—this was all for noth-ing. Oak knew I'd used him. He'd never believe me if I said I wanted to be here with him. But the truth was, I did.

Oak plucked the key from its hole, then dropped to his knees to the right of the hearth.

He pressed it into the slot. A soft click echoed through the room.

My eyes snapped to the stone above the mantel as it sank with a low grind, its swirling carvings folding into shadow.

CHAPTER
TWENTY-SEVEN

Oak stood, and his gaze locked on mine.

Shock rippled through me.

"You knew I came here for the *Ari Report*..." I whispered, disbelief weighing down my voice.

"Of course. You told me back in the Scorch Sphere you were looking for it." His tone was calm, but regret clung to the edges. "And believe me, Coco—I only wish I'd been able to give it to you then."

Anger swelled in my chest. "Then why didn't you?"

His jaw clenched. "I am bound by a vow, Coco. An old magic. The *Ari Report* is only for the eyes of the Luxari. We can't share what we see in it, nor can we open it for someone else. We're meant to keep it away, to hide it. If someone breaks through those magical forces, then they've earned the right to view it, and the vow is irrelevant. It was never about whether I cared, but about the rules that govern such powerful artifacts."

He shook his head with a faint, weary smile. "I was

surprised by how much trouble Zareen and Benedict caused, sneaking into my chambers to steal a key..."

A storm of confusion and frustration churned inside me. I crossed my arms, my voice tight. "So this wasn't some kind of test? Just watching to see how desperate I was to learn what happened to my brother?"

His gaze softened.

"No test, Coco. The forces at play here are far older than any of us. I'm in your corner. And the truth is, you possess more strength than you know. You've just demonstrated it—against powers you scarcely realized."

He stepped closer.

"You accomplished this on your own, guided by instinct and helped by the strength of your allies. Just as you did in the Quests."

I crossed my arms, some of the heat in my cheeks fading. "So you were just waiting for me to figure it out?"

"I merely sought to guide you—to steer you gently in the right direction. That's why I invited you to the cottage," he said, voice low. His eyes never left mine. "This..." he nodded toward the fireplace, "you achieved on your own."

I bit my lip, mulling over his words.

Oak pushed the stone farther back and pulled out a thick, leather-bound book. My heart thundered as he handed it to me. I sank down onto the soft blankets and pillows scattered across the floor.

My hands trembled as I held the book and brushed my palm over its smooth, black cover. The seashell ring Milo had given me caught my eye, and a sharp ache bloomed in my chest. A prickling sensation stung the back of my eyes. I couldn't look at Oak—I was afraid I might cry, and crying wasn't an option.

"It's updated by magic," Oak continued. "Every time a cataloger adds a name to their parchment, it appears in all the reports throughout the Spheres. If Milo has gone through the Ari Ceremony, his name will be there."

I couldn't speak. I didn't know what to say.

Oak immediately crouched in front of me. His fingers tucked a lock of hair behind my ear as he sat down next to me. He didn't say anything for several minutes while I mustered the courage to open the book.

At first, I read through the names slowly, but soon my eyes flew from page to page, scanning frantically for his name.

"He isn't here," I whispered, staring down at the report.

"May I?" Oak's voice was soft.

I nodded, and he gently took the book from me. He flipped through the pages, his brow furrowing as he came to the same conclusion. Milo's name wasn't there.

"I don't see it, either," he said quietly, not meeting my eyes.

I squeezed my eyes shut, fighting the sting of tears. Anguish and grief surged through me. I had hoped that there had been some kind of mistake. That the Retired Luxari hadn't yet contacted me or maybe there was a slowdown at the Soulari Hall like Will had suggested. I had so many questions. Why hadn't the ceremony been done yet? Was something wrong with Milo's soul? Would I ever receive closure?

The room felt heavy with unasked questions, but then Niko's voice rang out.

"Well," Niko swept into the space, "Oak, you owe me. The temperature is dropping by the second."

Niko's eyebrows shot up as she took in the *Ari Report*. She looked at Oak, understanding flickering behind her eyes.

Oak nodded, lips pressed in a hard line.

Niko lowered herself onto the edge of a pillow pile. "I take it his name wasn't there."

I shook my head.

"Damn," she whispered. For once, Niko didn't have a clever comeback. She just sat there with us, quiet.

It felt like a hand had closed around my heart, squeezing until I couldn't breathe. I stood up too quickly.

"I just need a moment."

I fled down the hall into the room where I'd changed earlier. The door clicked shut behind me and I sank to the floor, my back pressed against the dresser. I pulled my knees to my chest, crossed my arms over them, and dropped my head.

My eyes burned, but I couldn't let my tears fall. I clenched my eyes shut, willing the pain to stay inside.

Anguish rolled over me in a wave, sharp and suffocating. It felt like losing Milo all over again—like learning, once more, that he was truly gone. The certainty hit me hard: his soul was missing.

For two years, I'd been drifting through life—working at the Dreary Den, waiting—while he might have been lost, trapped, suffering.

He only had one year left before his soul would be lost forever.

The guilt was blinding. Milo had always been there for me. And now, when he needed me most, I'd been oblivious.

What if he couldn't move on to the Unknown? What if

something had gone wrong—something I'd never be able to fix?

A dull ache pulsed behind my eyes, then bloomed into a throb at my temples. I lay down on the floor and curled into myself, my arms wrapped tight around my body as if that might hold me together.

I had believed—truly believed—that the *Ari Report* would bring answers. That once I saw his name, the weight pressing on my chest would lift.

But it hadn't. The worst had happened: there was no name. No answers. No path forward. And only a year left to figure everything out.

The thought hollowed me out. Aching and helpless, I let the exhaustion take me. And as sleep pulled me under, I let it—anything to escape the weight of my reality.

Milo was packing a bag to visit the Hush Sphere with his friends —it would've been his first time there. But I didn't want to be left alone.

Father stormed into our room, telling me I needed to grow up. Then he left, like always, to drink himself into a sloppy stupor.

Milo left.

I crawled under the thick quilt, hiding from the ache in my chest. But moments later, the covers were yanked off.

Milo stood there. Without a word, he scooted me over and climbed in beside me. He'd ditched his friends—to stay. So I wouldn't be alone.

The next morning, Father said we were both weak. I was weak for needing someone. Milo was weak for caring too much.

THE STILL SPHERE

AREN FOLKTALES

Weaving through the dirt,
And soaring through the sky,
Appears the shifter's plea.
Crying through the woods,
Humming in the trees,
It leaves none behind
But still and silent peaks.

CHAPTER
TWENTY-EIGHT

I stood at the railing of the ship, staring out over the endless expanse of the Delirium Sea as Grizzly Landing —the harbor of the Still Sphere—loomed closer. The wind whipped through my hair, but my mind was elsewhere.

Milo. The truth—that he hadn't gone through the Ari Ceremony—throbbed in the back of my mind. What did it mean? Where was his soul? Had he been suffering this whole time while I waited, hoping for peace that never came? The sorrow sat heavy in my stomach.

Everything that I thought I knew about Milo was unraveling all at once. I didn't know which thread to hold onto to keep from falling apart.

The salty breeze clung to my skin as a faint mist curled around me.

"You've been avoiding me," Will said as he stepped up beside me and leaned on the railing.

I had been. I just didn't have the nerve to tell him the truth about Milo—but he deserved it.

"I know," I said. I met his hazel eyes, warm with concern.

A knot tightened in my throat. I drew in a breath, trying to steady it. "I found the *Ari Report*."

Will's eyes widened, and his lips twitched, as if he couldn't decide which question to ask first.

"He wasn't in the report," I said quickly, before he could get his hopes up.

Will's face fell, a flicker of shock and concern crossing his features.

"What do you mean? Are you sure?" he asked, his brows furrowed.

"He wasn't there," I replied, my voice tight with exasperation. I had been asking myself the same question since I found the report.

I turned toward the ocean, scanning the horizon like it could offer some kind of answer. But there was only wind and waves—no voice, no sign. Just silence. Milo's silence.

When I looked back at Will, he was shaking—his hands pressed over his face like he was trying to hold himself together.

"Will," I whispered, gently taking his hands and lowering them.

Jagged red lines marred his palms—the same ones from the Hush Sphere charm, only now they were darker, almost purple-black, and slightly swollen. My heart lurched, but before I could ask, I looked up to meet his eyes and saw the tears clinging to his lashes, slipping down his cheeks.

Something in me cracked. I had never seen Will this vulnerable before.

I wrapped my arms around his neck. He pulled me in, clinging to me like I was the only thing keeping him upright.

So I held him while he cried, the fissure in my heart widening with each quiet sob.

After a long moment, he pulled back and wiped his face with the sleeve of his tunic. "Sphere's curse, it's all falling apart," he muttered, voice hoarse. "I'm sorry, Coco. I just miss Milo so much that it physically hurts. Like there's this hollow in my chest that will never fill."

A hot ache swelled in my throat. I swallowed hard, nodding, unable to speak as grief and love tangled inside me.

Will's voice was barely above a whisper. "Milo was my best friend—my brother. He was always there for me. Not a day goes by that I don't think about him." Will cleared his throat. "But I do feel his presence."

This surprised me. I never felt like Milo was around.

"What do you mean?"

He shook his head. "It's hard to explain, but on my worst days, I can almost feel his presence. Like he's there, quietly reminding me to keep going, that I can handle whatever comes my way."

We both stared at the waves, lost in our thoughts.

"It doesn't make sense," Will finally said, frustration creeping into his voice. "Could Soulari Hall not be as protected as Queen Catalina claims it is?"

I turned to him. "What are you saying?"

He gave a helpless shrug. "I don't know... what else could it be? His soul is missing. Did it get lost on the way over?"

It was a haunting question—and one I had no answer to.

Before either of us could speak again, the soft toll of a bell echoed from the shore, pulling our attention toward the deck, where the other Questlings had begun to gather.

Will ran his palms over his face one more time, wiping away any trace of tears as he strode forward.

Someone tugged my elbow, and I glanced over my shoulder.

Crispin stood on the ship's deck, dressed in a cloak and a wide-brimmed hat pulled low over his eyebrows.

"What in the name of Aridan is this ridiculous getup?" I asked, motioning toward him.

"I think I look rather dashing," he posed dramatically. "Severin bet that I wouldn't be able to travel with you all without getting caught—so I had to come up with this outfit as a disguise. You know I can't say no to a bet." He grinned wider.

I couldn't help but laugh. "Clearly, you succeeded," I said.

"Severin should've never underestimated me." He fussed with his hat, then unbuttoned his cloak and draped it over my arms.

"You're going to want this," he said. Suddenly, he clutched my hand. "I didn't mean to, but... you see, I—"

"Overheard everything?" I asked.

He simply nodded, his shoulders sagging slightly. "It's awful, Coco. I'm so sorry. Please let me know if I can help in any way."

"Thanks, Crispin. That means a lot."

"Now"—he straightened his hat once more—"I must go fetch Severin and rub it in his face that I won."

We disembarked at the dock in the Still Sphere. I wrapped

myself in Crispin's cloak. It wasn't as cold as the Frosted Peaks, but it was cooler than I was used to. Queen Nerian's people hauled large nets brimming with fish onto their boats. As we walked along the pier, we passed barrels overflowing with crabs and lobsters.

Tada scrunched up her petite nose in disgust. "I hate fish. They smell awful."

"Now, come on, Tada, it's not that bad," Otto said with a grin.

He picked up a fish that thrashed in his hand. Tada shrieked and took off running, and Otto chased after her, the wriggling thing clenched tightly in his grip.

We entered the thick woods with Will and Aldo leading the way—since both of them were from here. The air was crisp, carrying the earthy scent of pine and damp moss.

We passed hunters hauling carcasses of deer, rabbits, and even a bear. Their boots crunched against the forest floor as they moved past us.

A line of Shifters stood outside a lodge, their voices rising in laughter and shouts. The queue twisted and snaked all the way to the edge of the woods. Most were men, but a few women stood alongside them—each dressed as though prepared to rough it in the mountains.

"What are they waiting for?"

"They're signing up for the Wild Quests. During Crisp, Frigid, and Fresh Season, there are three rounds of Quests in Hunter's Hollow—one for game, one for survival, and one for wit. It's pretty competitive. They sign up during Spice Season, and the list goes up later."

"How do you know all this?"

He shrugged. "My father competed in more than a few Wild Quests in his day."

"Your father? No. I can't even picture that."

He just shook his head, a small smile tugging at his mouth.

An image of Will's dad flashed through my mind: tall, very lean, soft-spoken, always reading a book—picturing him in a Wild Quest nearly cracked me up.

Will's family had shown Milo and me nothing but kindness. I remembered praying to Aridan as a child that Will's parents could be my own—and being disappointed every day when I went home to my drunken father instead.

They had never asked directly about our home life, but as I grew older, I suspected that they always knew. Sometimes it had felt like Milo and I really were part of their family, treated as warmly as Will himself.

The Still Sphere was nothing like I had imagined. The kingdom rested at the foot of towering mountains—their peaks lost in the clouds. We passed through a massive log fortress guarded by hundreds of soldiers. Some carried spears, others hefted crossbows.

The guards lined the entrance to the palace. They wore brown quilted tunics, deep forest-green breeches, and heavy leather boots. Fur-lined cloaks draped their shoulders, each bearing the embroidered symbol of the Still Sphere: two jagged peaks stitched across the back. Queen Nerian's timber palace stood high in the branches, nestled among the trees. Wooden bridges stretched between the trees, connecting different sections of the palace.

The entrance to the palace was carved into the trunk of a massive pine tree wide enough that it would take fifty people, with joined hands, to encircle it. As we stepped inside, we ascended steep steps that spiraled upward.

Etched into the inner wooden walls along the way were scenes from the "Story of Aren"—conveniently leaving out Arrow's role in the world's creation, which seemed to be knowledge known only in the Daze Sphere.

The stairs led us into the grand hall. The wooden flooring was carved with earth elements, such as roots, vines, and stones. The log walls were decorated with pelts, furs, and antlers from bears, wolves, and other creatures. Wooden furniture upholstered in hunter green fabric filled the space, while animal skin rugs scattered across the floor. Instead of paintings or tapestries, carvings adorned the walls, depicting scenes of forest animals and towering trees.

The platform room sat amongst the branches—its lumber walls opened to reveal pathways that wove between the trees. The scent of pine filled the air while Starlight bubbles floated lazily through the space.

"Welcome to the Still Sphere," Queen Nerian intoned. Her dark caramel skin glowed under the drifting bubbles as she stepped into the room, draped in rich furs. "Please, make yourselves comfortable. If you need anything, don't hesitate to ask. My attendants will show you to your rooms."

Ten attendants appeared, each assigned to one of us. The girl assigned to me had pale skin and dark, glossy hair. Without a word, she picked up my bag.

"I can carry that," I offered. She gave a slight shake of her head and gestured for me to follow.

We walked through an opening in the lumber wall onto a wooden bridge. It led to a new platform wrapped snugly around the trunk of a tree, from which we continued forward onto another walkway. The lush, jade-green leaves of the forest offered a sense of quiet comfort.

She stopped in front of a small, round door built into the tree. I pushed on the vine-wrapped handle—it creaked open, revealing a darkened room.

Starlight bubbles floated gently above me.

My attendant followed my gaze. "The Daze Sphere and Still Sphere rely on Starlight bubbles as their primary light source. Aeraliths thrive in these wooded regions—unlike in the Scorch and Hush Spheres, where the climate is too warm for them."

I gave a small nod and continued to take in the room.

A small, carved window sat high in the tree. The bedposts were crafted from intertwining roots that twisted and wove together, and sage-green blankets were draped neatly across the mattress. Aeraliths fluttered in through the open window, hiding in the branches above me. I sank into the softness and let the quiet hum of the forest soothe my restless mind.

Queen Nerian invited only the Questlings to dinner. We walked up a tall, spiral wooden bridge that led to a room in one of the highest trees. The branches tangled and curled above us, while the trunks of wide trees formed the walls around the dining room table.

The room was dimly lit by short candles. Hearth-roasted meats, thornroot wedges, and warm glacierloaf slathered with thistlebutter covered the table. My mouth watered immediately.

"Can you believe we only have one more challenge?" Otto exclaimed. Flecks of food sprayed across the table from his open mouth.

"I, for one, will be glad when it's over," Severin said. He dabbed his mouth gently with a cloth napkin.

"Me too," Hugh added, poking at his thornroot wedges.

Amabel rolled her eyes. She wasn't eating—she never did.

"Of course, you're eager for it to be over. You don't even care about being a part of the Luxari Council. Frankly, I think you should leave."

"Amabel, if you leave the Quests unfinished, you know the Ashen Death will mark you," Aldo said.

Amabel clasped her fingers together and rested her elbows on the table, her gaze shifting toward me.

"Well, you've been awfully quiet tonight, Coco. Or are you just too exhausted from screwing both Luxari Kings to even speak?"

"Amabel!" Aldo warned.

She leaned back, her eyes widening. "What? Do tell us, Coco, who's a better lay?"

I stood, fury rising within me. She didn't deserve to know she'd gotten under my skin—but she had. I set my napkin down and walked out of the room, stepping onto a small wooden deck that overlooked the treetops of the Still Sphere.

Will joined me at my side.

"Coco, come on. Come back in. Amabel is just trying to rile you up before the next challenge."

Will dragged a hand over his face.

My eyes were immediately drawn to the swollen, jagged lines zigzagging across his skin.

"Will, your hands... they look worse than they did in the Daze Sphere. Did you see a Charmer?" I stepped closer to get a better look, but his arms dropped to his sides as a wry smile curled at his lips.

"I went to a Charmer. Don't twist your roots over it."

I shook my head. "If you say so."

We stared out into the spellbinding Still Sphere.

"Where would you go if you were offered a spot on the Luxari Council?" I asked.

"I'd take any spot, as long as Amabel isn't on it."

We both laughed.

Will continued, "Honestly? It would be an honor to serve in any capacity. I just want to join. I want to have a family, and the Luxari Council would give me the stability to support them."

"Would you choose immortality?"

"Uh, no. I want to grow old. I want to get wrinkled and pruney and be completely unrecognizable. Wisdom comes with age, and I want people to see just how wise I've become."

We stared into the dense woods for a few moments in silence. It was so quiet out here.

"Let's finish this, Coco," he murmured. "One more challenge."

I nodded, and he slipped his arm around my shoulders as

we walked side by side, making our way down the wooden bridges toward our quarters.

My room lightened as the sun rose, casting rays through the small window. I changed into leggings, a burgundy sweater, and sturdy boots. I glanced at my reflection in the small mirror hanging on the curved wall. My eyes were bloodshot, with dark shadows resting beneath them. I braided my hair to the side, so it would be out of the way for the Quest. I just wanted to be done with the final challenge so I could go... home.

Sadness and uncertainty rushed through me. I didn't have a home. It was just me.

CHAPTER
TWENTY-NINE

We stood at the base of Wraith Peak. The open, grassy field was filled with observers, while the intimidating woods stretched out before us. Queen Catalina paced a few feet away. Aldo pulled a vial from his pocket, downing it in one gulp. I watched as a few others did the same. They had been saving them for the last Quest.

"Welcome to the final challenge of the Sphere Quests. It has been an honor to watch each of you push yourselves past your limits. We, the Luxari, are thrilled to witness you in this final event..." Whispers filled the air as Queen Catalina smirked, savoring the tension. She clasped her hands behind her back.

"The final challenge of the Sphere Quests is Wraith Peak." My stomach plummeted as chatter broke out. My heartbeat thudded in my ears. Will smiled at me, but the look didn't reach his eyes.

The branches and leaves of the tall trees created a thick shield that blocked out the sun, adding to the dark, foreboding atmosphere of Wraith Peak. A cold wind blew from the woods, sending a chill down my spine.

Queen Catalina continued. "You will have four days to journey through Wraith Peak. Wraith Peak is home to dangerous creatures—creatures parents warn their children about before bed. But only the best are summoned to the Sphere Quests. If anyone can face these creatures, it's all of you." She held out her hands. "The first alliance to reach the end and collect the most Wishing Veil Orbs will be declared the winners of this final challenge—and awarded Ari Dust vials."

"What is a Wishing Veil Orb?" I whispered to Will.

He only shrugged in response.

Queen Catalina continued, "To understand the prizes you seek, you must first hear a Starlight Tale."

She paused, then began:

> *In the days when the stars still whispered...*
> *Once, there was a wolf*
> *Who prowled through the woods,*
> *Seeking food and shelter, but never*
>   *lingering too long.*
> *But the wolf wanted more than survival.*
> *He wanted friends. He wanted a family.*
> *He wanted a human form.*
> *So he howled at the moon, asking for more.*
>
> *And the moon answered, though her voice*
>   *was soft and strange:*
> ***Find the tallest pine; pluck a needle***
>   ***from its branch.***

Find the scattered star, with dust in its
path.
Find the leaf, just bigger than the rest.
Find the cinder ember, glowing softly in
the ash.
Find the smoothest pebble, worn gently
by time's flow.
And bring me something veiled—wild
and full of breath—
And I will give you what you so dearly
desire.
The wolf set off at once—but not unseen.

The Wraith Peak Guardian heard every
word,
And he did not want the wolf to change.
So he unleashed his shadows:
The Threadling,
The Farsight,
The Twilight Maw,
The Silent Claim,
And the Dream Thief.
The wolf faced them all. He bled and limped
and pressed on.
He plucked the pine's needle. He chased the
dusty star.
He found the broadest leaf in the whole of
the valley.
He happened upon the ember. He claimed
the smoothest pebble.

And at last, he held all five tucked against
    his chest.
He found something veiled and wild, full of
    breath.

But just before he reached the lake where the
    moonlight shone down,
He heard a mother's cry.
A child, pale and still, lay in her arms.
She had no hope, no healer to fix the wrong.
But the wolf stepped forward
And placed the treasures at her feet:
The needle. The stardust. The leaf. The
    ember. The pebble. The veiled.
All that he had fought for.
The baby stirred, inhaling fresh air.
The mother looked up, tearful and grateful
    for the wolf.

That night, as he stood by the lake
Without the treasures he had won,
The moon appeared beside him—no longer
    a shape in the sky,
But a woman, cloaked in starlight.
Her eyes were full of wonder.
"You gave up everything," she said,
"Not for yourself, but for love you had never
    known."
And she touched his muzzle.
The wolf trembled, then changed.

His paws became hands, and his fur
  smoothed to skin.
He stood tall and blinking in the moonlight,
No longer a beast—but a man.
The moon kissed his cheek,
And the stars above rippled with light.

Some say they walked together for years—
A man who had once been a wolf, and a
    moon who had once been a mystery.
And if you look closely on a clear night,
You can see their story traced in stars, still
    dancing just above the trees.

"There are six Wishing Veil Orbs—each representing a treasure from the story: the Pine, the Star, the Leaf, the Ember, the Stone, and the Veiled. I don't expect any one alliance to collect all six, but the first to complete the task and bring back the most spheres will win the final challenge. The Wishing Veil Orbs are already hidden deep within the forest, but they look very similar to Lumen Orbs."

"Shall we begin?" she asked, nodding toward the ground.

Roots erupted from the earth, twisting and braiding themselves into two arches—one to the left, one to the right. Aldo's alliance moved toward the left passage, while ours veered right, guiding us toward our final Quest.

We were each given a knife, a fur-lined cloak, and a small brown leather canteen of water. Will was given a satchel—I assumed it was to carry the orbs.

The first few steps into the woods filled me with dread. Will led the group, followed by Tada and Otto, then me, and finally Hugh. Creeping fog slithered around us, as if trying to swallow us whole. Spiky, thick bushes clawed at the ground, intertwining with gnarled roots that clung to the forest floor. I rolled my ankle on a jagged root, and a sharp pain shot up my leg. I clenched my teeth, determined not to let the others notice.

Will glanced over his shoulder just as I winced. He looked down at the roots, then lifted his hands, palms facing the forest floor. Slowly, he pulled them through the air, as if parting something unseen. The ground trembled as the roots recoiled from him, snaking backward and sinking into the earth, leaving a clearer path ahead.

We turned a corner, and my breath caught. It was stunning —an unexpected mystical lake surrounded by towering Nightglow Aspen trees. The water was a deep, inky blue, so calm that not even a ripple disturbed its surface. I shook my head, almost in a trance as we pressed onward.

A sudden sting jolted me, followed by a crawling itch. I

looked down, horrified to see velvety, hairy spiders scuttling up my thighs and disappearing beneath the hem of my sweater. I yelped and swiped frantically at my clothes.

"Get them off!" I screeched.

Otto turned around. I froze. A spider the size of a large rabbit was perched on his shoulder. Slowly, I raised my trembling arm to point at it, just as Otto let out a high-pitched scream. A gust of wind sent the spider sailing through the air, crashing into a tree, and exploding on impact. Black blood splattered across my face, and the shockwave knocked both Otto and me off our feet, sending us sprawling onto our backs.

"Sorry, guys. Probably a little *too* much wind," Hugh said. He stood over us and offered a hand. I pushed myself up and turned to help Otto.

"I *hate* spiders," Otto spat through his teeth.

Suddenly, Otto vanished—there one moment, gone the next, as if someone had charmed him away.

"Otto?" I shouted, scanning frantically along the tree line.

Tada's eyes widened as we all yelled his name.

Twenty tense minutes passed before Otto finally emerged from a thicket, covered in ash and dirt. His knuckles were cracked open and bleeding, and a tooth was missing from his grin. Without hesitation, Tada rushed to him and cupped his cheek gently. When she pulled away, his smile was whole once more.

"Where were you?" Will asked. He tried to steady his voice, but a tremor of desperation betrayed him.

"I have good news and bad news," Otto said, catching his breath. "First—the good news: I'm pretty sure every time we kill a creature, we get a chance at one of the Wishing Veil Orbs."

My eyebrows shot up in surprise. "And the bad news?"

"I didn't get the Ember Wishing Veil Orb. Rodor beat me to it."

"What do you mean, he beat you to it?" Will asked, a little too sharply.

"It was surreal. One moment, I was here; the next, I was suspended high above the forest, trapped inside a massive, transparent bubble. I could see everything below, but the barrier held me in place. Rodor appeared beside me, just as confused, and then a Dirt Elaryn showed up, holding the orb with the ember glowing inside. Whoever broke through the barriers fastest would win it. Walls of ice and stone rose up around us—it was like an obstacle course. He was quicker."

"It's okay," I said in a soft but firm tone. "There are still five more orbs out there, but we have to be ready for the possibility that any of us could vanish at a moment's notice to compete."

"Wait," Will said, frowning. "If Hugh killed the spider, why did Otto get pulled in?"

We fell silent, pondering the question.

I shrugged. "Maybe it's random. Does it really matter who gets pulled in? The goal is to get the orb."

"True," Will said. He pressed forward as the rest of us followed close behind.

My feet ached as we trudged through the forest, and no matter how many times I shook my sweater, I could still feel phantom spiders crawling across my skin. It had only been a few hours, but blisters had already formed on my heels. Twisted branches wove above us, closing in like a canopy, leaving us trapped in the dense woods.

Wraith Peak was notorious for its demon creatures. Every time a stick snapped, my heart skipped, and I glanced around, expecting danger to be lurking behind every shadow.

"Can't you just Sphere Jump us to the top of the ridge?" Tada whined.

"No, I can't," Will replied, frustration edging his voice. "I've never been to the top of Wraith Peak. I can only Sphere Jump to places I've been. Even if I had been there, I'd still have to Sphere Jump each one of you out, one at a time, from the Still Sphere to another Sphere, and then back to the top of Wraith Peak. It's not as easy as you think."

"Well, that's not helpful," Tada muttered.

"Neither is your attitude," Will grumbled back.

"Why don't you just Shift into some kind of bird and fly to the top?" Tada suggested.

"I'd love to," Will sighed, "but our alliance has to make it to the top together. Victory means nothing unless we all make it. So instead of complaining, can you Charm us something to eat?"

"It doesn't work like that," Tada huffed.

"I can make fire," Otto piped up eagerly, "so whenever we have food, I'm on it."

Tada rolled her eyes, and she and Otto began to bicker.

It was as if the air itself were thick with tension, filling our senses with irritable mood swings. I was too tired to weigh in. Every muscle in my body ached with fatigue.

"We need to find somewhere to camp. The Dusk Demons will be coming out soon enough." Will's words brought me back to the task at hand. I dreaded the nightfall, but I swallowed my fear. I needed to offer something to this challenge, but I doubted any riddles would need to be solved up here.

A flicker in the sky caught my eye—a shadow of black and dark purple, gliding silently through the air.

"Sphere's curse!" Will muttered. "Get under the tree. Now."

We dropped to our knees, instinctively seeking cover beneath the branches. I could feel my heart pounding against my chest.

"What is it?" Hugh whispered, his voice trembling.

"It's a Murk Merlin," Will replied, his eyes fixed on the sky. "Deadly. And it's most active at night. It's not worth trying to kill for an orb—we won't succeed."

Dread pooled in my stomach as I remembered what I'd read about them—creatures native to the Still Sphere.

The creature descended, its wings spreading wide—five, maybe six feet. I tried to swallow, but my mouth was dry. Its eyes were like chips of polished silver. The beak, curved and sharp, was tinged with a sickly greenish hue—a warning of the venom it could deliver.

Will's whisper broke through the tension. "It's fast and impossible to track. But the real danger is in the claws and beak. When it strikes, it injects its blood. Demon blood. Corrosive. It'll burn you from the inside out, slow and agonizing."

The Murk Merlin circled higher, vanishing into the fading light of dusk. We stayed crouched. After a few tense moments, we moved.

"Stay alert," Will warned, his eyes scanning the tree line.

We continued farther into the eerie woods, all of us paranoid, waiting for the next attack or creature we might encounter. Eventually, we found a cave where we lay down for the night. We didn't have any blankets—just the moist ground to sit on. We couldn't light a fire, since it would attract the Dusk Demons. As soon as the sun set, wailing echoed through the forest, creeping its way into our cavern. Will sat by the opening, standing watch. As scared as I was, my body was exhausted, and sleep overcame me.

"Coco." A whispery voice filled my head.

"Coco. Milo needs you," the voice continued.

My eyes flew open. I sat up, my heart pounding violently against my chest. It took a moment to remember where I was: Wraith Peak.

I scanned the cave quickly, relieved to find everyone still asleep. A shiny orb glided into the room, filled with amber mist.

"Follow me to see Milo."

I was on my feet before I could think to stop myself. I followed the orb outside the cave and ran through the skeletal trees, their sharp branches like bones in the fog. Ignoring the scrapes on my arms, the cold on my feet, and the howling creatures in the distance, I kept my eyes fixed on the orb.

It shot up through the branches. A pointed limb, like the end of a dagger, extended out, clipping the orb as it soared by. A loud pop echoed through the trees, and a silvery wisp rained down on me. It spiraled toward the ground, slowly taking the form of a body. My breath caught as it landed in front of me. The familiar presence sent a chill down my spine.

CHAPTER
THIRTY

Milo.

I found myself blinking hard, goosebumps spreading across my skin.

His honey-blonde hair had grown since I last saw him; it rested on his neck, curling at the ends. His blue eyes were vibrant and clear.

"Milo?" His name tore from my throat. I took a step forward, then another. The closer I got, the further he seemed to go.

Breaking into a sprint, I chased him through the blackened, bent trees. My breathing grew rapid as branches nicked my skin, but I couldn't stop. Not when he was this close.

"Come join me, Coco."

Milo vanished around the bend.

I was running so fast that I didn't have time to stop before I toppled over the cliff. My chest constricted, and my stomach dropped. The ground disappeared beneath me. A scream erupted from my throat as fingers gripped my forearm, squeezing tightly.

"Coco. Don't let go." Will's face appeared over the cliff. His forehead creased with concern, and his arm trembled.

My legs kicked and dangled in the air. I looked down and froze. I couldn't even see the bottom—just swirling darkness.

He hauled me up. My breathing was rapid, and I was shaking.

"What in the howl of the forest were you thinking?" Will barked.

"I heard Milo, Will. I saw him," I said.

"You didn't see him, Coco. You saw a Mora. They lure you to death with dreams." Will sounded tired, defeated. "I guess I should have warned you about them beforehand."

I shook my head, frustration and embarrassment churning inside me. "It's my fault." My voice faltered. "I know what they are. I just... got so caught up in everything else that I forgot about the Moras."

My shoulders slumped with shame. I felt stupid. The cold wind sliced at my skin as we started to walk back toward the cave.

My legs shook with each step I took. Where Will had grabbed my arm, red, angry marks were left behind.

"You're going to get yourself killed, Coco." He abruptly stopped, turning toward me. "You can't afford to make mistakes like this. You almost died," he said desperately.

Guilt filled my entire being. He was right.

"It won't happen again," I promised.

"It better not." Will's words were clipped as he stalked ahead of me.

As we approached the cave, Hugh stood just outside, holding an orb in his palm. It shimmered with sparkling gold and silver flecks, like scattered stardust, and at its center gleamed a radiant star.

Otto was wrong. Will hadn't killed the Mora, but it looked like Hugh had been pulled into the bubble anyway—it must have been random who was chosen.

Hugh stepped forward. "It was just like Otto described. I appeared inside this bubble in the night sky—along with Severin."

"What did you have to do?" Will asked, eyes wide with curiosity.

Hugh scratched the back of his neck. "It was a Mind Duel, mixed with water elements. Hard to explain. Here." He handed the orb to Will.

Will slipped it into his satchel.

"One to one—not bad," Will said with a faint smile as we all settled back down.

I tossed and turned the rest of the night, hugging my arms around myself to create some warmth. My teeth chattered, and I felt lost.

Loneliness was isolating. After the Sphere Quests, who did I have left? Milo was gone. Will would go off to Elizabeth, and the friends I'd made would return home—Tada, Otto, and Niko.

An ache tightened in my chest at the thought of not seeing Niko again. Out of everyone, I'd grown closest to her.

I sat up, glancing at the others still asleep. The faster we climbed, the faster I could be done with the Sphere Quests—I could leave it all behind and only focus on finding Milo's soul.

As soon as the sun's first light crept into the cave, I woke everyone up.

Otto's groggy, half-lidded eyes met mine as he yawned and stretched his long arms, accidentally connecting with Tada's.

She let out a string of curses as she shoved him, sending him rolling across the damp dirt.

"We have a long way to go, so we might as well get moving." I tucked my knife into my boot as the others followed me out of the cavern.

The brisk breeze, mixed with pine, filled my nostrils as we marched over the frosted ground. As the sun rose higher, the air warmed, turning the icy layer into dew.

Will had hardly spoken this morning, and neither had Hugh. I couldn't help but wonder if Will was still mad at me, or worse, if he was disappointed in me for what had happened last night. The guilt gnawed at my chest, constricting my breath.

We approached a cluster of rotting tree limbs, broken and blocking our way.

"We can probably just cut through it," Will suggested. He pulled his knife from his pocket.

"That will take forever. Why don't you just move the branches like you did with the roots?" Tada whined.

Will's shoulders slumped as he dragged his palm down his face. "I can control dirt or elements that are part of the ground, which is why I could move the roots yesterday. But I can't control the tree limbs."

Will began hacking at the branches. Tada pouted, crossing her arms and letting out a dramatic sigh, her lips curling into a frown as she glared.

Will paused, his jaw tightening as he glanced at her. Clearly annoyed by her nonverbal disagreement, he shot back, "Got a better plan?"

Shrill sounds vibrated through the air—sharp and unnatural, just like the one I'd heard back in the Bleak Sphere. Will immediately dropped the limp branch and stood. The rest of us froze in place. Twigs began to crack, and a hissing noise emerged from the forest.

Why would Soul Snatchers be up here on Wraith Peak? Wraith Peak was void of human life. Soul Snatchers were only after Ari Souls. They had no reason to be on this desolate terrain. Was this part of the challenge? Or maybe it was another creature of Wraith Peak.

"There wouldn't be Soul Snatchers up here, right?" I whispered to Will.

"Looks like there are," he said, pointing. I followed his finger in the direction of the trees.

Rotting hands reached from the brush—skeletal, decayed. A Soul Snatcher.

"Run!" A hot rush of panic flooded my body. Every head snapped toward the Soul Snatcher.

We all started sprinting up the steep slope of the mountain, our feet stirring rocks and sending them tumbling down the cliff.

The Soul Snatcher clawed at Otto's heels, but he sent his foot ramming into its skull, giving us time to get ahead. I dared a glance back, and my toe stubbed a rock. The impact sent me sprawling, and before I could react, the Soul Snatcher was upon me.

Its decayed hands reached for me, and in an instant, its slimy, twisted fingers clasped my throat and hoisted me into the air. My legs dangled beneath me as I struggled to gulp down air. A ghastly chill swept through my skin from the contact with the creature.

This was the end. I felt the warmth of my body leaving.

Suddenly, the Soul Snatcher released me.

I came crashing down on top of it. The feeling of its brittle body beneath me disgusted me. I hurriedly scooted off.

My palms were scraped, a hole was torn in my pants, and clumps of my hair hung around my face. I looked up to see Hugh.

The Soul Snatcher's paper-thin fingers clasped its mummified skull, withering on the ground as if Hugh had sunk invisible talons into its mind. He released his hold just long enough for the creature to rise and flee, wailing.

"Thank you, Hugh," I gasped. My heart pounded violently against my chest, and my fingers trembled.

He walked over to me and held out a hand. I grasped it as he helped pull me up. The others were coming down to us, with Will stumbling quickly to reach me.

"I'm fine. Everything is fine. Hugh took care of it," I said, my voice shaky between stifled breaths. Will came to a halt, sending dirt into the air.

He bent over to catch his breath, a crease forming between his brows.

"Giant spiders, Soul Snatchers... what's next?" Tada grumbled.

"Don't even ask," Will said. "Coco, are you okay to move forward?"

"I'm fine," I reassured Will, giving him a look he knew all too well—the one I'd used since childhood to make sure he didn't ask me again.

His jaw tightened in response, but he turned and moved forward.

My skin was torn right under my chin, my bones ached, and I felt shaky from the encounter with the Soul Snatcher, but babying me wasn't going to get us to the top of Wraith Peak.

Suddenly, my stomach churned and my vision blurred, then it felt like someone had zapped me with lightning. The next thing I knew, I was squinting up at the blue sky—through a glimmering barrier. I looked down, and my stomach dropped.

Birds flew below me. I was high above the forest, the green tops of the trees stretching beneath me. I didn't dare take a step forward; I was certain the bubble would pop.

"Of course," a voice purred from behind me.

I turned to face the one person, out of all the Questlings, I least wanted to duel with: Amabel. Her amber eyes locked onto mine.

"Why you?" I asked, taking a deep breath to keep my temper in check.

Amabel scoffed. "Come on now, aren't you supposed to be

the smart one?" She traced her slender pointer finger along the glimmering barrier. I tensed—worried she'd burst the bubble with her nail and send us plummeting to our deaths.

She slowly inched closer to me. "All the creatures we're encountering originate from different Spheres. When one is killed or defeated, it pulls someone from its own Sphere."

Of course. The monster spiders came from the Scorch Sphere, like Otto. Moras originated in the Daze Sphere—that's why Hugh was called. Soul Snatchers were closest to the Bleak Sphere.

"Then why are you here?"

"Because my team doesn't have a pathetic Dim. It seems as if Aridan fated us to go against each other. Luckily for me, this challenge will be easy."

THIRTY-ONE

A little creature with pale skin and short hair like twisted roots appeared inside the bubble: a Dirt Elaryn.

"Welcome." A popping sound filled the bubble as the Wishing Veil Orb appeared, floating gently in the air. A single pebble rested inside as it drifted away.

But the glimmering barrier above us began to rise. My neck strained to follow it. Stone platforms emerged, splitting into two paths: one ascending to the left, the other to the right. They stacked upward to the very top, where a cloud of teal mist surrounded the Wishing Veil Orb. Pillars of flame flared at the corners of each platform.

"What do we do?" Amabel hissed at the Dirt Elaryn.

"Retrieve the orb, of course," the Elaryn responded before drifting toward the top.

Amabel didn't hesitate. She tore to the right, effortlessly lifting herself onto the first platform.

I ran left and hauled myself onto the cool stone. Swinging my legs up, I barely caught the edge before flames erupted across the platform beneath me. I jumped to the next, clutching with trembling fingertips. As soon as I pulled myself up, it began to swing, teetering dangerously.

I glanced to the right, struggling to keep my balance as dizziness swarmed me—Amabel's platform rocked just as wildly. The next platform had risen so high that neither of us could reach it.

Then a light, high-pitched voice echoed throughout the bubble:

> Tick tock, ding dong—look around, but do
>   not frown.
> Be sure to whisper so the other doesn't hear.
> Get it right and move on with cheer.
> Living then, living now, moving up, moving
>   down,
> Spinning, twirling, dreaming deep,
> Walking, running, waking sleep.
> What could it mean? I ask of thee–
> Unlock the secret, tell it to me.

Another riddle? Irritation bubbled in my veins as I tried to sort through my thoughts. It was talking about time—something that moves with it? Maybe it was speaking about different stages of life: motion, emotion, and even death. But "life" felt too simple and too literal as an answer.

What stays with us through all of this? Even if we're dreaming, dying, or barely conscious?

The soul.

I was growing nauseous with every sway, but it had to be right. It felt like a mocking reminder that Milo's soul was missing. With clenched teeth, I whispered so Amabel wouldn't hear: "A soul."

Immediately, the rocking stopped, and my platform moved closer to the next one. I ran and jumped, grasping its edges and pulling myself up.

My chest rose and fell rapidly as I wiped the sweat from my brow. This bubble felt like the Scorch Sphere, with the heat radiating from the pillars of flame on every platform. I took a step forward, but a wall of smooth obsidian erupted from the stone. It twisted and wove together like roots, creating a fence. I could see through it, but it closed around me, trapping me in a cage.

I looked toward Amabel. She had solved the riddle as well and reached the next platform. The wall of ebony rose around her, too, but with a sharp bang and the sound of shattering glass, she obliterated the cage with her enhanced strength. She gracefully leapt onward.

I struck the obsidian, but it did nothing except tear my skin open. Blood bloomed. I scanned the edges, searching for markings, symbols—anything. I tried slipping my hand through the cracks, but all it did was slice my palm, leaving crimson in its wake.

The thought of failing left a bitter taste in my mouth—along with the sting of how unfair this all felt. I was a Dim with no powers. This task had someone like me at a complete disadvantage.

I heard Kaz's voice in the back of my mind. He had said that

I didn't need magic. I had already proven to myself—and to all of Aren—that I was perfectly capable of competing and winning.

I lifted my chin. I could do this.

I paused and looked over my shoulder, narrowing my eyes toward the previous platform—the riddle and its cryptic directions.

Be sure to whisper so the other doesn't hear.

Could it be that simple?

"Umm..." I mumbled, unsure if I was completely delusional to think this might work. "Open up, please?" I whispered to the cage. At first, nothing happened, making me feel like a globe-smashing idiot. Then it let out a groan, and the cage lifted—and disappeared.

Heart pounding, I climbed to the next platform. Amabel was almost at the top, while I still had at least four more to go. I needed to be strategic. Hands on my hips, I looked down at the gray stone.

Could it possibly work a second time? There was only one way to find out.

"Take me to the Wishing Veil Orb," I whispered. The platform lurched forward, making my arms flail as I struggled to steady myself. Then it rose swiftly, soaring to the top of the bubble. I glanced back at Amabel, who, furious, erupted into red flames, her shrill cries piercing the humid air.

The moment cost me. Amabel conjured a fiery blue sphere, a blazing snowball aimed with deadly precision. Time stilled as it hurtled toward me, the flames of death threatening to incinerate me. I felt the searing heat on my skin and squeezed my eyes shut as I dropped flat onto the platform.

Fire erupted on my left arm, and agony roared through me like nothing I'd ever known. The stench of burning flesh and hair made chills of trepidation race down my spine. I stared at my arm, charred and smoking. A churning sensation filled my stomach. The orb gleamed directly overhead, within reach. I had to be fast. I sprang upward, even though the air stung my open flesh and my body screamed with pain.

My fingers wrapped tightly around the orb, and I clutched it against my chest. With a sharp pop, my vision blurred, and a zapping sensation shook my body.

CHAPTER
THIRTY-TWO

My feet landed firmly on soil. I peeled an eye open, just to glance at the damage. My sleeve was fused to my skin. I swallowed hard, trying to suppress the bile rising in my throat. Amabel's firestorm had utterly ravaged my arm.

My allies rushed toward me, but all I heard was a buzzing noise in my head. My arm, where it wasn't charred black, was a gruesome display of raw muscle and bone. I moaned in agony as my heart began to pound faster.

Tada shot forward and gently took my arm, cradling it in her palms. She mumbled, and a cool, numbing sensation spread through me. The pain slowly evaporated as she continued to chant, until all that was left was a light throb and healthy, pink skin.

"Amabel," Will said through clenched teeth. A tremor ran through his jaw.

I nodded and held out the Wishing Veil Orb. All my alliance's faces lit up.

"Now we have two. They've only got one." I smirked.

We continued up the mountainside.

The terrain was steep, with rocks jutting out at every angle. Pain throbbed through my every limb. The higher I climbed, the stronger the gusts of wind became, biting at my cheeks and stinging my skin.

The wind ceased. I could still see the branches swaying, but the strong gusts were no longer hitting me. I turned to face Hugh. His head was bowed, but his arms were restless.

"Is this you?" I asked, still in awe of his abilities.

He nodded silently.

I turned my gaze forward, and a surge of gratitude washed over me.

A Dirt Elaryn flitted through the air, her translucent skin shining in hues of pale brown. Wispy, short hair, resembling strands of roots, fluttered in the wind. She wove through our alliance, bouncing through the sky, before disappearing into a cloud.

A deep, terrifying growl echoed off the cliffs, halting our footsteps.

Will's muscles tensed. Veins bulged in his neck as he instantly shifted into a grizzly bear and charged into the tree line toward the vicious growls.

A blur of black sprang toward me and knocked me off my feet as pain erupted in my shoulder. Razor-sharp teeth sank into me, causing excruciating spasms throughout my body. Thick, pointed claws tore through my sweater and flayed my skin. I screamed in agony as the animal was wrenched off me, ripping my skin with its clenched teeth.

It flew through the air and struck a tree with deadly force. As I stumbled back, Otto crouched down to help me up.

"Sun-blasted spheres, Coco. Your arm!" Otto's voice was tense.

I glanced at my shoulder. But before I could say anything, a shriek tore through the air, and another monster slammed into Otto.

Terror seized my breath, and sweat pooled at the base of my neck.

The impact staggered him. Otto roared as he erupted into raging hot fire. The uncontrolled inferno forced the demon to recoil, growling as tendrils of fire licked at its dark form.

It lunged again—a desperate, clawing attack that Otto met with another blast of heat, incinerating the demon to a crisp. The flames extinguished as Otto crouched down in front of me, his eyes blazing with fury as they took in my shoulder. I followed his gaze.

It looked as if someone had taken a blade to me. My skin was shredded, hanging in tatters from my exposed muscle and tissue. Blood dripped down my arm, pooling at my elbow before spilling onto the ground.

My vision began to blur. I staggered back from Otto, forcing my gaze away from my mangled arm.

"What...was...that?" I asked between rapid breaths.

"That is a Dusk Demon," Otto said, his eyes wide on my injury. "Turns out they don't only come out at night."

"Why do all these creatures always come after me?" I said through gritted teeth.

Otto winced. "I thought you knew. Sorry, Coco." He raked a hand through his hair. "You're a Dim. Your blood's sweeter. To demon creatures, it's like ringing a dinner bell—they'll sniff you out faster than any Ember."

I clenched my jaw. *Of course.* That actually explained a lot.

Sinister, barbaric screeches rang through the air, filling me with dread. A pack of Dusk Demons burst from the tree line and skidded to a halt when they saw us. They stalked back and forth, their milky yellow eyes piercing into us. They resembled wolves, but much larger—and the only word that came to mind as I looked at them was *haunting*. Their bodies were scarred and marred with decay, fur patchy and so thin that it looked almost translucent.

A flurry of activity broke out. The Dusk Demons swarmed us. Will's paws pounded the ground as he snuck up behind them and sank his jaws into their flesh, but more came to close in around him.

My heart pounded as I threw myself forward. My hand darted toward the small knife tucked in my boot. The sudden movement sent a shockwave of pain through my shoulder, and I clenched my teeth so hard that I thought they might shatter. Will shifted again, rocketing into the sky as an eagle. He swooped down and landed in front of me before shifting back to his regular form, his breath coming in heavy pants.

"Run!" he commanded. Our whole alliance broke into a mad dash away from the monsters.

Except Tada was missing. How long had she been gone? Otto had killed the Dusk Demon—terrible timing. Just as the thought crossed my mind, Tada appeared out of thin air.

"That was quick," I said, noticing her empty hands.

"I don't want to talk about it," Tada said through gritted teeth, her fist clenched tight.

Like we had time to discuss it anyway. Two to two—we were tied so far.

I grasped my shoulder, trying to stem the bleeding. My fingers were covered in sticky blood, but the Dusk Demons were fast, and it was only a matter of time before they were on us again.

Immense, towering trees stood just a few yards ahead of us, clustered together.

"I can't get into their heads!" Hugh's voice cracked with desperation, panic flashing in his eyes.

"Don't worry about that. Everyone climb—fast!" Will hollered, his voice sharp with urgency.

Tada scrambled up one of the trees, Otto right behind her. Will climbed effortlessly, with Hugh following close behind. I grabbed hold of a low branch and glanced over my shoulder just in time to see a Dusk Demon lunge—its jaws wide, aiming for Otto's ankle.

"Otto! Look out!" I cried, my voice straining as trepidation laced my veins.

He looked just in time and threw his hands out. Flames erupted from his palms in a raging blast of fire at the Dusk Demons. They shrieked as the molten shimmer ignited their fur, but the flames didn't stop there. The fire caught the brush and began spreading quickly.

I hauled myself up with one arm, quick and efficient—a move I never could have managed before Niko's training—as Hugh reached down. A burning Dusk Demon jumped, and I narrowly missed one of its thrashing claws as Hugh tugged me up. An inferno swallowed the monster. The smell of incinerated spoiled meat and smoke left a sickening feeling in the pit of my stomach, and my mouth soured as I struggled not to gag.

I looked down—the entire ground below us was engulfed in fiery tendrils. Thick, black smoke billowed through the air.

An encroaching wave of flames singed the branches below us.

"Orb-rot!" Otto yelled over the choking smoke. "Um, guys, I think I messed up."

The forest around us burned as the blaze rapidly swept through the trees. Sweat started to drip down my back and roll down my face. Every breath I took was filled with fumes and ash, and my eyes stung from the soot.

The heat exacerbated the pain in my shoulder.

"Tada, drop down! I'll catch you!" Otto roared. The embers didn't seem to affect him, but the rest of us would be torched. I wasn't sure how Tada's mixed heritage—half-Enticer, half-Charmer—would play out in this situation.

Water poured from Tada's palms, dampening the flames until they turned to ash—for now. Who knew how long it would last?

Tada fell gracefully into Otto's strong arms. He set her down and yelled at Hugh, who followed suit. Will shifted back into an eagle and glided down to the ground.

The branch holding my left foot creaked just as Otto was placing Hugh down next to Tada. It gave way, sending me barreling out of the tree.

My wounded shoulder hit the ground first. I bit the inside of my cheek to cope with the pain—blood pooled in my mouth.

Will grabbed my good arm and hauled me to my feet.

"Can you run?" His eyes searched mine.

I nodded, afraid that if I opened my mouth to speak, screams of pain would be the only thing to escape.

Otto and Tada led the way, with Hugh, Will, and I bringing up the rear. Heat singed my clothes when I glanced back.

Blistering waves of flames rapidly began to close in on us as the fire blazed a trail up the mountain.

The heat was unbearable. Every inch of my skin was soaked in sweat, smoke burned my nostrils and throat, and my open wound stung painfully.

"There's a ravine this way with a river!" Otto yelled.

As he turned, I saw Tada go down.

Tada's ear-splitting screams filled the air. Otto ran to her side. I didn't know if it was adrenaline or sheer panic, but I bolted toward her. Fear seized my heart as I took in the scene.

A branch protruded through her leg. Dark blood spewed from her thigh. Otto dropped to his knees and cradled her head gently with trembling fingers.

"No, no, no," Otto groaned, his deep voice breaking.

He let out a roar of fury, the sound merging with the crackling and popping of the fire. A whooshing sound pulled my attention. I glanced back just as the trees snapped behind us, their burning trunks toppling and adding fuel to the already raging flames that hurled toward us.

"Otto," I snapped, my voice sharp. He didn't respond.

I grabbed his face with both hands, forcing him to meet my gaze. "We need to go now. We don't have time to wait."

Recognition flickered in his eyes as I released him.

Tada's wails felt as if they could rupture eardrums, slowing down time as her screams turned into sobs. Otto swept her into his arms and ran toward Will.

Will went over the ledge first, followed by Otto—Tada clutched to his chest—and then Hugh.

I halted at the edge, sending pebbles tumbling into the dark depths below. A river flowed beneath, but the fall would be long.

I glanced back at the approaching wall of fiery orange and knew that I didn't have much of a choice. I took a deep breath, and I jumped.

CHAPTER
THIRTY-THREE

My body smacked into the chilling water—it felt like hitting stone. The bitter cold numbed my limbs. Every muscle ached as I drifted toward the riverbed. The bite on my shoulder burned fiercely, and the shock of the icy river only deepened the sting.

A hand clasped mine, pulling me toward the surface. I broke through the water, and the air prickled against my skin.

Hugh released me. Droplets clung to his dark hair as the river sloshed against his chin. Both of us treaded water, looking up at the ledge from which we'd just jumped. The flames roared down the ravine, but halted at the edge of the glacial pool.

Will stood over Tada's small form, while Otto knelt beside her on the far side of the river. Hugh and I swam toward them. The current was slow but steady, nudging us in their direction, though it didn't make the effort much easier. I could only propel myself with my good arm, and every stroke burned.

Hugh dragged himself over the stones and turned, reaching back to offer his hand.

My body scraped against the jagged rocks that sliced into my abdomen, cheek, arms, and legs. I staggered to my feet and rushed to Tada's side, my heartbeat thundering in my chest.

Tada's face was pale, her lips tinged gray-blue.

Nerves racked my body. She had to be okay. Tada was going to be okay. I kept repeating it in my mind.

"She keeps losing consciousness," Will said, his voice steady but strained as he looked at Otto.

Otto grasped his hair so tightly that he tore out strands. He stood and stalked toward a nearby tree. Swinging his arm back, he buried his fist in the trunk—again and again. The sound of splintering wood cracked through the evening air. His shoulders sagged as he turned and walked back.

Agony radiated off him as he looked down at Tada's suffering.

"I'm sorry, Will. I'm sorry, everyone. I wasn't thinking." Otto dropped to his knees in front of her, his face twisted with devastation. "She's burning up."

"She needs to be healed. She can't keep moving like this," Will said, his voice urgent.

"Tada can't heal herself. She's not strong enough." Otto's gaze locked with mine. "This is all my fault."

"It's not your fault. No one's blaming you. We just need to figure out how to help her," I said, forcing my voice to stay calm.

I wished more than anything that Hugh could heal her wounds like Oak could. But Oak was a Luxari, and his gift was rare—unheard of.

339

"If only we had Starshade berries," Will said, his voice low and hollow.

Starshade berries. They were incredibly rare, and the only reason Will and I knew about them was because his grandfather loved to tell us—the three of us, including Milo—the story of how they had saved his life. He always said they could heal any wound and that he would've died young if it weren't for them.

"I saw some berries yesterday," Hugh said, suddenly at my side. "But I didn't think anything of them."

Will turned sharply. "Where, exactly?"

Starshade berries grew only on Wraith Peak. If Hugh had seen berries there, they were most likely the ones we needed.

Hugh hesitated. "The first was near the spider attack. The second... close to where the Soul Snatcher showed up." He shoved his hands deep into his pockets. He looked embarrassed—ashamed that he hadn't thought to tell us or bring them.

I gave Hugh a small smile. Not much, but just enough. I hoped he'd understand—it was okay.

"I'll go grab them," Will said, his voice final.

He moved toward Tada, lifting her fragile body and cradling her against his chest. Otto began gathering logs and branches to quickly construct a shelter around them.

After a moment, Will gently set Tada down on the ground to rest against the soft bedding of branches Otto had arranged. She'd lost a lot of blood—enough to kill a Dim outright. But Tada was an Ember. They could survive more... though even Embers had their limits.

Hugh stared at the river, his gaze distant. The temperature plummeted as the sky filled with stars.

Tada started thrashing, her body jerking violently. Hugh rushed to her side and pressed his palm to her forehead. Slowly, she went limp, her movements easing into stillness.

"What did you do?" Otto's voice was barely a whisper.

"I just rested her mind so she could sleep, so she wouldn't feel the pain. It won't heal her, but it's all I can do."

"It's enough." I wrapped my arm around Hugh and squeezed his shoulder in quiet reassurance.

The gesture sent a hot spike of pain through my own shoulder. I bit my tongue, willing myself not to flinch as it roared through me.

Will didn't have to carry everything. I could help. He always took responsibility for everyone, shouldering more than anyone should. He didn't need to do this alone—Tada was my friend, too.

Will wiped mud from his pants as he brushed past me.

"I can help," I said, stepping forward. "If we split up, we'll be faster—and we'll have a better chance of saving Tada."

Will didn't even slow down. "I can do both," he said, his voice flat, over his shoulder.

I bristled at the suggestion that I was incapable of helping.

I followed him, feeling like his shadow. "I know you can, but we can't afford to waste any time. You can fly to the berries near the bottom of the mountain, and I'll take care of the ones nearby."

Will spun around so quickly that my feet skidded, and his arm clasped around my elbow.

"Coco, you're injured. Not only that, but you'd have to climb back up a different way than we came down, since we jumped into a river." His eyes softened. "Please, remember

341

what I promised Milo. You need to make it out of this." His voice dropped to a near whisper.

"I know what you promised, Will, and you've kept that promise." I kept my voice steady as I pressed on. "But if Milo were here, he'd go. He'd go even to save a stranger, and you know that."

Will's jaw clenched as his gaze shifted to Tada. Sweat beaded at her hairline, and her body shook. Otto rocked her gently, his face a mirror of helplessness.

Will sighed. "All right.

"Hugh, watch them. We'll be back as soon as we can." Will lowered his head and whispered in my ear, "Coco, be safe. Run like your life depends on it—because it does."

My eyes shot up to meet his hazel-brown ones. He pressed his lips to my forehead, and I closed my eyes. When I opened them again, Will was gone.

I tore off the hem of my tunic and wrapped it around my arm before plunging into the woods, sprinting faster than any Dim had a right to—and maybe fast enough to matter.

I ran the entire way, each step driving me harder, my breath growing ragged. Sweat slicked my brow, and my hair molded to the damp skin around my neck. Moisture slid down my spine and pooled at my lower back.

I passed the spot where the Soul Snatcher had attacked us, pausing for a moment with my hands on my hips in front of a gnarly tree. Its skeletal branches twisted and spiraled toward the night sky. I stepped into a wide field of grass.

The basil-colored expanse reminded me of the size of the field where we had played *Seize the Banner*. Trees bordered the space, acting as a fence—a shield from the forest itself. The silence of the night pierced my ears. Not a single branch swayed; the wind seemed to have vanished in this vast space.

In the center of the field stood a thin tree. Its glossy, ivory trunk shimmered under the moonlight. Its branches hung perfectly still, as if sculpted to remain in place. Leafy greens covered each limb, and white Moonlight Blossoms sprouted along the branches. Their soft petals glimmered in the dark.

I pushed through the whispering grass, moving cautiously toward the tree. My adrenaline-fueled heart thudded in my chest after running for over two hours, and I was still paranoid, expecting an attack at any moment. I took deep breaths, the scent of jasmine and vanilla from the blossoms filling the air as I stepped beneath the tree's branches.

My neck craned as I scanned the tree for the Starshade berries. My gaze snagged on the clusters of small lavender-blue berries that clung to the tallest branch—just enough to fill my palm, and hopefully enough to heal Tada.

A breathy growl rose from the bush. Two yellow eyes locked onto mine as a Dusk Demon crawled out of the underbrush. It lunged, a blur of teeth and shadow, and my blood ran hot as I leaped out of the way, narrowly dodging its strike. Twisting around, I yanked the knife from my boot.

We circled each other, poised and ready.

I gripped the knife tightly, pointing the tip directly at the Dusk Demon.

It moved faster than air and buried its fangs into my calf. I gritted my teeth as seething pain burned up my leg. I hacked at the creature, and it yelped as the blade nicked its skull. I heaved the knife, sinking the point into its flesh and causing enough damage that it released me. Backing away, I assessed my leg.

Blood covered the grass around me from my wound. The entire left side of my body was out of commission. The demon twitched and dragged its injured body towards me. I was starting to feel lightheaded, but I knew it was building up for its final attack. Its mouth twisted into a blood-chilling grin, and burgundy blood sprayed from its throat as it let out a howl.

Tada needed me, Hugh needed me, Otto needed me—they would need me to survive this ordeal. I clutched the handle of the knife, steadying my pulse and focusing on what had to be done. The Dusk Demon howled and was instantly answered by distant shrieks that sent shivers down my spine. Animalistic roars sliced through the air like shattered glass.

The situation had just become even more dire—more demons would be coming now. The Dusk Demon ran toward me and leapt into the air. I waited until I could see its underbelly before plunging the blade into its chest, hitting my mark with precision.

The force of the Dusk Demon slammed me to the ground, but suddenly, its weight was gone.

I scrambled to my feet, each movement sending a fiery

spike of pain shooting up my leg. Severin stood in front of me. His chest rose and fell as he wiped the soot-black blood of the Dusk Demon onto his pants. Ash-blonde strands escaped his bun, curling at his temples.

"Thank you, Severin," I panted.

A faint smile flickered across his face. "I didn't do anything. Just moved the corpse off you."

"Regardless, thank you."

He glanced at my leg. A sharp line appeared between his eyebrows as he took in the mess of torn skin, pink muscle, and clawed clothing painted with crimson. His attention shifted to the Starshade berries, his eyes widening in realization.

My heart dropped. We were both after the Starshade berries. With his powers and my injuries, I didn't stand a chance.

A cold knot twisted in my gut.

Scarlet globs oozed like a spout from the open wounds on my leg. Garnet blood soaked through the bandage wrapped around my shoulder and arm, staining the cloth dark.

He jogged toward the tree, reaching for the Starshade berries. With a smooth, quick gesture, he charmed the branch to lower toward him and plucked the lavender berries into his palm. Feral howls echoed through the trees as I began moving, dragging my limp leg behind me.

I turned to leave the meadow, but a firm hand gripped my elbow, halting me. I looked up to meet Severin's gaze as he cupped my hand, pouring the few berries into it. His eyes were full of kindness.

His jaw tightened as he stepped back and dropped to his

knees. One hand gently curled around my wounded leg—the other wrapped around my arm.

"We don't need them," he murmured. "Amabel wants them as a safeguard—just in case I get hurt or killed. That way, they'll still be able to heal themselves without me."

I swallowed hard, feeling a heat rise in my chest. Severin had seen me—really seen me. Not just as a Dim, but someone capable. Someone worthy of saving.

He began to mumble, his voice slowly shifting into a hum. Gradually, the pain started to ebb, as if his fingertips were drawing it away.

But the night's sounds—howls, cracking branches, leaves crunching—filled me with a sense of wariness.

Amabel's shrill voice cut through the air. "Severin! Get the damn berries and let's go!"

Severin rose quickly, leaving my injuries tingling with numbness. He mouthed "run" to me, and I didn't hesitate.

My legs moved, carrying me away from the meadow. I didn't dare look back—not when I could hear the growling and screams of violence from the Globe Alliance.

Severin hadn't just saved my leg and arm—he'd given me the Starshade berries, too. His compassion fueled me with hope, filling me with the energy and adrenaline I needed to race back to my alliance.

CHAPTER
THIRTY-FOUR

Tada ate the berries, and within an hour, she was completely healed. Otto, overwhelmed with relief, wept. Will returned not long after, empty-handed—he'd flown off in search of the berries but had to cover far more ground. He had worried that if he had Sphere Jumped, he would have wasted time trying to guess where they were. We were all exhausted, so we slept as much as we could, rotating shifts to keep watch through the night.

The next morning, we woke before the sun, making up for lost time as we climbed the mountainside. The higher we climbed, the thinner the air became, and every step forward seemed steeper. My legs trembled; my toes were numb from the cold. My fingers felt like icicles, and my face stung from the bitter bite of the wind.

We only had two Wishing Veil Orbs, while the Globe Alliance had two as well. But who knew if another opportunity would arise to claim the remaining two?

"I can check on how much longer we have," Will said. "Keep moving forward. I'll keep an eye on you from above and swoop down when I can to keep you updated."

Admiration swelled inside me. Will was a natural leader, always thinking of others. He didn't need to fly down to keep us posted—he could stay aloft, watching for threats or tracking our path, but he was going to check on us anyway. Tada needed reassurance, and Will was going to give that to her.

Will shifted into a hawk and soared toward the peak. The air grew eerily quiet as we continued forward. The temperature dropped with each passing minute, and the wind howled through the trees. Finally, the sun disappeared behind the mountain peak.

"Will's been gone for a while," Tada said, her teeth chattering. "I hope he's okay." Fear edged her voice.

Otto and Hugh glanced at me, their eyes silently expressing their concern.

"Will is strong," I said, keeping my voice steady. "The flight is probably just taking longer than he expected. And it's getting dark—maybe the fading light and thick canopy are making it harder to spot us. Or he might've seen something and went to check it out. We should keep moving. We've already lost time because of the..."

My voice faltered when I noticed Otto staring at the ground. I hadn't meant to make him feel worse.

"If it gets any darker..." Hugh said, his tone grim.

"Let's start looking for somewhere to camp for the night. I know he'll find us," I said, mustering as much confidence as I could. My composure couldn't crack—not with all eyes on me.

Otto gripped Tada's hand as they ventured deeper into the woods, with Hugh and me trailing behind.

We found a small overhang of rock jutting from the mountainside, offering just enough shelter for the night. Otto had to duck to avoid hitting his head, but it was the best we could do this late.

I paused, hands on my hips, as dampness crept into my socks. I pushed the discomfort aside and stepped out from under the overhang. We needed a way for Will to find us.

Tearing off more fabric from the bottom of my sweater, I walked into the dense woods and climbed a tree. Sap stuck to my fingers as I scaled it as high as I could until I straddled a branch near the top. I tied the strip of burgundy cloth to the highest point—distinct enough for Will to spot from above.

Back at our shelter, I sat down and pulled off my boots. My socks were soaked with blood. I didn't dare look at the damage —I was afraid it might stop me from moving forward. I just laced my boots back on and stood up.

"Go to sleep, guys," I said firmly. "I'll take the first watch."

Otto lay on the ground and wrapped his arms around Tada's tiny frame, pulling her to his chest and cocooning her with his hulking body.

I crossed my arms and scanned the dark forest, eyes searching for any sign of Will—or Dusk Demons.

All I wanted was to lie down on a warm, fluffy mattress with thick blankets wrapped around me. I stifled a yawn as footsteps approached from behind.

"I can't sleep," Hugh said quietly. "Do you think Will is all right?"

Hugh was usually hard to read, but in that moment, his concern was plain on his face.

I kept positive thoughts marching through my mind: *Will is okay. He's going to find us.*

"Of course he is," I said, placing a hand on Hugh's shoulder. "Everything's going to be fine."

We stood in silence as the night brought forth sounds only found in nightmares.

Eventually, Hugh lay down, leaving me alone with my thoughts.

Dawn crept in slowly, just as I heard a branch snap. I grabbed the knife hidden in my boot and snuck toward the sound, my body taut with fear and the instinct to protect my friends.

When Will emerged from the trees, I let out a shaky breath and slid the blade back into my boot. He looked exhausted; gray mud splattered across his face, and one arm wrapped protectively around his midsection. Relief surged through me—then faltered when I saw his hand clutching his stomach.

"Thanks for the marker," he said with a weak chuckle. "Brilliant as always." A wry grin tugged at his lips, but I knew Will—he was trying to distract me from the injury.

"What happened to your stomach?" I asked, stepping closer.

"Oh, nothing," he waved me off. "Just a little squabble with a Murk Merlin." He wiggled his eyebrows.

A shiver of unease coursed through me. But before I could press him for more, he continued, "I come bearing good news. If we keep moving now, we'll reach the peak before dusk."

Joy jolted through me as I met Will's eyes. They danced with a flicker of amusement, but also hope.

"Should I wake the others?" I asked.

He gave a curt nod. "Yes. The sooner, the better. I passed the Globe Alliance on my way back down. They're not far behind, and I think Aldo noticed me."

Amabel's gleaming, beady eyes flashed through my mind. She wasn't going to win this challenge—not if I had anything to say about it.

I sprinted to rouse the others. We needed to finish our Quest.

I thought I knew cold, but Wraith Peak made the Frosted Peaks feel like the Scorch Sphere.

Snow slammed into our faces, and ice-cold wind coiled around our bodies. We all shivered uncontrollably. Hugh tried to control the wind for a while, but it was draining him.

"This is by far the *worst* quest of them all," Tada said through chattering teeth. Her petite frame could barely withstand the chill.

Otto scooped her into his arms. "You're so warm," she murmured.

"Yes, I'm an Enticer. My blood runs hot." He set her down gently, but kept hold of her hand as we continued up the mountain.

Something had been bothering me throughout the entire Quest. Something felt off, and an uneasy chill trickled down my spine the higher we climbed.

What did Queen Catalina say? Did she say *to the top*, or did she just say *journey*?

The incline leveled out, and before I knew it, we were walking across flat ground.

"Where is it?" Otto asked. "We're at the top. Where's the end?"

Dread washed over me as it all clicked—the tale of the wolf, the grieving mother, and the moon that didn't shine from above, but appeared beside a lake, cloaked in starlight.

My breath caught. "The end isn't here," I whispered to myself. "It never was."

All heads swiveled toward me—apparently, I hadn't whispered as quietly as I thought.

"In the Starlight Tale... the moon wasn't in the sky. It was reflected in the lake."

They stared in stunned silence.

"The Veiled Orb is the moon, and it's at the bottom of Wraith Peak, along with the finish."

An owl hooted, then burst through the branches of a tree, gliding downward—but I didn't think it was just any owl. It had to be Aldo.

"He heard everything, damn it," Will said. "We'll need to hurry, but Tada...."

Tada lifted a brow, her violet eyes shining bright.

"Now I can Sphere Jump us out of here one at a time, since we've already been to the lake."

A big smile spread across his face, and soon we all grinned —relieved we wouldn't have to journey back down Wraith Peak.

CHAPTER
THIRTY-FIVE

ill Sphere Jumped us one at a time. My heart pounded with the anticipation of finishing the Quest.

But something was off with Will. He was drenched in sweat, his breaths sharp and uneven, and I could've sworn I heard a faint rattle when he inhaled. Still, he assured me he was fine.

As my alliance stood before the stunning, mystical lake, my thoughts wandered. If I was wrong, I had led my team straight into failure.

I really hoped I was right.

The inky blue water was as calm as ever. The Nightglow Aspens looked as if they were standing guard.

"Where is it?" Otto asked impatiently.

"In the lake," I told him.

"I'll grab it," Will stepped forward. The moment his foot

touched the water, steam hissed from his toes, and he inhaled sharply.

I pulled him back. Then Otto crouched and reached toward the lake, placing a finger in the water before yanking it back—his skin bubbled and smoked.

Tada giggled and Otto smirked up at her. "You try, Tada."

She stretched her palms apart, trying to summon the orb from the lake. The water trembled violently before a geyser shot up, splashing her in the face. She screamed, clutching at her scorched skin.

"I'll pass," Hugh muttered.

I stared at the lake. Maybe this Quest was fairer than I'd thought—and this was the advantage of being a Dim.

I stepped forward. Will grabbed my arm, but I met his eyes and said, "Trust me." He released his grip.

The water was cool beneath my fingers. I plunged under the surface. The lake wasn't very deep, and resting on the rocky bottom, glowing faintly with pale hues, was the Wishing Veil Orb. A misty moon pulsed from within.

The water stirred in front of me, spiraling into a swirl—then morphing into an Aurefly. Once more, it sang:

> *Coco, Coco, brave and bright,*
> *Don't fall behind—turn and fight.*
> *You hold the fate of those now gone,*
> *And you'll be the one to right the wrong.*
> *Follow your heart, stay steady and sure—*
> *For a Dim shall rise, both frail and pure,*
> *To release death long kept obscure.*

Panic began to creep in—what did it mean, that I would release death? But a pulse from the Wishing Veil Orb reminded me of the task at hand.

I dove deeper, and my fingers closed around the orb. It felt alive—cool and soft, like mist settling on skin. I kicked off the lakebed and swam toward the surface. Breaking through the water, I rose and stepped onto the shore, clutching the sphere tightly.

My alliance cheered as Will placed the orb carefully into his satchel alongside the others.

Just then, the ground trembled beneath us.

A stone arch emerged at the far end of the lake. Sunlight glistened through the cream-colored vapor that swirled in its center.

"All hail Queen Coco, the greatest Dim of them all! Hear ye, hear ye!" Otto bellowed, his voice echoing through the trees and sending birds fluttering into the sky.

All I could do was grin.

We began walking around the lake toward the arch, but voices rose in the distance, carried by the wind. The Globe Alliance was closer than we thought.

I snapped my gaze to Will. He met my eyes, then glanced at the others.

"Run!"

The wind sliced through me as we bolted forward. Will led the way, Otto and Tada followed hand in hand, Hugh close behind, and I brought up the rear.

Will stopped and motioned for us to hurry. Otto ran through the vapor first, Tada disappearing right behind him. Will gestured for Hugh to go next—and he vanished too.

That's when I noticed Will clutching his midsection again, his eyes wide with pain.

Then, an excruciating jolt shot through my shoulder. I turned just in time to see Amabel's grin widen as she lowered her arm. Severin, Rodor, Cecille, and Aldo flanked her.

The handle of a knife protruded from my shoulder, lodged deep in my flesh.

The arch was a scant few feet away; our only task was to reach it. Ignoring the lancing agony, I stumbled forward. I yanked the blade out, a brutal tearing of muscle and tissue, and flung it to the ground, biting back the scream that was waiting to burst through my lungs.

I reached out my shaky hand to Will, and our fingers interlaced. Together, we bolted through the vapor. It felt like rose petals being rubbed against my skin, and a churning sensation filled my stomach.

Warm air kissed my body as Will and I toppled onto soft, luxurious grass. The crowd shrieked with applause. I glanced toward Will—his face drained of color. His eyes widened with shock.

I blocked out the noise and the faces, zeroing in on Will.

"Are you all right?" I asked, my heart beating faster.

"Yes. I was just scraped by some branches," he teased, but something was off.

Without warning, he collapsed. The force of his body hitting the ground jolted through me. Any relief I had felt vanished, swept away by a torrent of dread.

He moaned in agony, and a frantic thrumming started in my chest.

"It's okay, Will. It's okay," I whispered, my voice trembling.

"My chest," he hissed, his voice strained, eyes squeezed shut.

I tore open his tunic, my hands trembling. Four ragged claw marks marred his chest—marks from a Murk Merlin. Beneath the skin, angry copper veins writhed, bulging as though desperate to break free. The poison pulsed beneath the surface.

"Somebody help him!" I shouted, desperation thick in my voice. People rushed toward us, but fear kept them just out of reach.

Will took my hand, his grip firm yet weakened by the poison. His hazel eyes locked onto mine, shining with a clarity brighter than the bluest sky on the sunniest day.

"Coco, it's okay," he said, his voice steady despite the pain. "This is how it's meant to be. We did it. We finished."

His trembling hand reached into his pocket and pulled out a small paper package tied with twine. He hissed through clenched teeth, slamming his eyes shut as a wave of pain hit him.

"There's a note for you," he whispered, "and... the rest is for Elizabeth."

A single tear slipped down his cheek. "Promise me you'll give it to her."

I nodded, but a fog of panic crept into my mind, curling around my thoughts. Terror rose in my throat, choking me.

"Don't you dare talk like that, Will. Help is coming. We'll —" My words were cut off as his hand tightened around mine, his grip growing colder by the second.

"I see Milo," he murmured, craning his neck as though Milo stood just behind my shoulder. I automatically turned to look, even though I knew Milo wasn't there. His gaze began to slip away, drifting toward something distant.

My heart stopped. Time froze. Will's eyes glazed over, and a faint smile spread across his face.

No. Not Will. Not like this. He couldn't leave me. Not after everything we had been through together.

I grasped his cold hand. "Will," I whispered, my voice shattering.

My eyes darted through the crowd. "I need help! I need a Luxari!" The words choked out of me.

Will's grip suddenly tightened, his breath shallow, his lips parting again. "I see Milo," he repeated, his voice almost peaceful now. "He says they need you. They need you at the Void."

"What?" My voice was strangled. His words didn't make any sense.

Just as I pulled back, his eyes fluttered closed. With a soft, final exhale, his body went still.

"No!" I screamed, shaking him.

My eyes blurred as a scream of grief consumed me. I looked up to see all the Luxari gathered around me.

"Bring him back," I demanded, tears clouding my vision.

Queen Nerian knelt beside Will, her features somber. "He is gone. Demon blood. There is nothing we can do."

The last shred of hope vanished. *Will was gone.* The world seemed to collapse around me. I looked over at him. He lay still, his hand still in mine, but he was gone. I could feel it.

I pushed myself to my feet, forcing my way through the crowd. Kaz reached for my arm, but I wrenched it away. I started to run, stumbling through the trees. My vision blurred with each passing second. My legs grew weak beneath me, and I fell to my knees, pressing my hands into my eyes. My chest burned with grief. This couldn't be happening. Not Will. This had to be some prank by Aridan—because out of all the Questlings, Will was the best.

My breath grew rapid as someone knelt beside me. I didn't need to look to know who it was. I could smell him—rain-soaked ocean and coconut.

"Coco, look at me," Oak's voice was commanding, but tender. His calloused hands lifted my chin gently. His gray-blue eyes locked onto mine.

"Crying isn't a weakness, Coco. Crying is a strength." He paused, swallowing hard. "It shows you care. You love. Compassion is the greatest magic anyone can possess."

Will was gone. Milo was gone. A hot tear burned down my cheek, and a sudden rush of anguish filled me.

I broke down, weeping. Oak swept me into his arms as I wailed—for Will, for Milo, for everything I'd lost. My whole body trembled against him, my throat raw from the screams. I was alone. I had nobody.

Oak cradled me against his chest, and for a moment, I let myself mold into him. I let every wall I had ever built around my heart fall until I was exposed and vulnerable, trembling against him.

His strong arms tightened around me, reminding me who was holding me: a Luxari. I needed to escape his embrace, to leave, to run. I needed to untangle my sorrow somewhere private.

Exhaling slowly, I pulled myself up and drew my body away from his. Sorrow pierced my stomach.

Oak stood, his mouth drawn, his eyes scanning mine with a look that held uncertainty—and something deeper, something haunted.

CHAPTER

THIRTY-SIX

I forced myself to walk back to the palace. A swarm of people tried to speak to me, but I ignored them, each step taking me further from the crowd. I climbed the wooden stairs and went straight to my room. Aeraliths fluttered around the space, their wings sprinkling golden dust on the sage comforter, but their presence did little to ease my heartache.

I carefully placed the small package on the bed. With shaky hands, I pulled the string and gently unfolded the paper, revealing the sapphire ring meant for Elizabeth. My heart pounded, and tears rolled down my cheeks. It was as if he had known he was going to die...

I lifted the ring, setting it aside with care, then pulled out the parchment labeled *Coco*.

Coco,

If you're reading this, then you know I'm gone.

I didn't tell you about the curse that took hold of my hands when I tried to access the Ari Report in the Hush Sphere palace. It spread faster than I expected, and by the time I realized the extent of the danger, it was already too late.

The night before our last Quest, someone visited me in a dream. Not just any dream—a prophecy. Clear. Undeniable. She said:

"His soul cannot find rest while yours walks the earth. Only beyond the veil can his voice reach yours."

So, I chose to face what was already coming. I embraced the cost, hoping—maybe—that it would bring you the answers you've been aching for.

I love you, Coco. I pray this brings you the peace and closure you deserve. My journey isn't over—not yet. Even in death, I'll keep searching for Milo.

Always,
Will

A wave of grief clogged my throat. I'd known something was wrong with him, but I hadn't pressed—and I should have. As I lay down, fresh tears soaked my pillow. So many questions twisted inside me like thorns, unanswered and sharp. But no amount of doubt could change the truth I had to accept: he was gone, and nothing could bring him back.

I cursed Aridan as I shouted into my pillow, the cotton rubbing against my face. My sobs tore through me until my inflamed throat gave out. I had no more tears to give. I ignored the persistent knocks on my door. I locked it and shoved the dresser in front of it. Finally, I fell into a dreamless sleep.

The sounds of birds chirping woke me. Surely, I had dreamed of Will's death. But as I tried to open my swollen eyes, the reality of it crashed over me. My lips quivered as more tears flooded my face.

I had nobody. Why couldn't Aridan take me? I clasped my hands over my face as my body trembled with grief. A knot of sorrow formed in my throat.

A light knock sounded on the door, but I ignored it. Then came a click and the scraping of wood against the floor that broke the silence. Eda's voice filled the room. "Coco?"

Warm, smooth hands covered mine, pulling them away from my face.

Concerned jade eyes met mine. "I thought you might want some water."

She stood and walked to my side, setting a glass on the nightstand.

I didn't need water. I didn't need anything. I especially didn't need Eda—to whom I had barely spoken—seeing me like this, at my lowest.

"Go away," I muttered. I flipped onto my stomach and buried my face in the pillow, making it difficult to breathe.

"No," she replied firmly, though her voice was gentle. Her stubbornness reminded me of Ava, insistent on helping me after Milo passed away.

I didn't respond. I was too emotionally and physically drained to push her away. The mattress dipped, a silent confirmation that she hadn't left the room.

Hours passed—or maybe minutes—time blurring together. She didn't leave me once; her presence surprisingly brought me comfort.

"You really need to bathe, Coco," Eda finally said. "Your wound is going to get infected."

My stab wound. My entire shoulder had gone numb with pain, just as I felt inside. It was stiff as I tried to move it.

"I can't." My voice was barely a whisper. I couldn't get out of this bed.

She left the room, and for a moment, I thought she had given up on me. But the door creaked open again. She stood directly in front of me with a steaming bucket of water. Gently, she took my arm, rolled up the sleeve, and dunked a cloth into the water.

The pleasant warmth of the cloth against my skin was the

first relief I'd felt in days. She wiped away the dirt, blood, and remnants of tears from my body. Then, with careful hands, she peeled the fabric of my sweater away from the raw, open wound. The water stung as it touched the gash, and I flinched involuntarily. Slowly and painfully, she cleaned it out, then smeared a cold, green slime over the area. The sensation pricked, but also soothed.

She screwed the lid onto the jar that contained the slime. "This was given to me by Queen Catalina. It won't provide immediate healing—a Charmer could accelerate the process. However, it will eventually heal on its own."

I didn't have the strength to thank her, but I knew she wasn't expecting it. She finished cleaning me, then laid out fresh clothes and stepped out as I changed.

When she returned, I sat on my bed, gazing out the window at the forest in sunlight, my thoughts consumed by Will. After Milo died, I had started to forget little things at first—the way he would snort when he laughed, the exact shade of his eyes—and now, looking back, I wished I had branded every memory of him into my brain. I was trying to do that with Will, before his image, the memory of him, began to fade.

"I'm sorry, Coco. It's awful what happened."

A fresh wave of grief swept through me. Heat rushed to the backs of my eyelids.

"Awful?" I choked out. There wasn't a word worthy of describing what had happened, nor any explanation that could justify it. Unfair? Cruel? Evil? I was at a loss for words.

"I'm not going to tell you it gets better, or that you need to move on. I just want you to know that I'm here. If you want to talk, I'm here."

The gesture was kind, but confusing thoughts burst in my mind. I looked at her. "Why do you care?"

Her eyes softened. "Someone was there for me once, when I needed it. We all need someone, sometimes."

There was so much I didn't know about Eda, so much I didn't understand, but the sincerity in her gaze washed the other thoughts away. We sat there together, watching the room darken as night came once more.

THE DEPTHS OF DELUSION

AREN FOLKTALES

Lost in smoke, the terror rises—
Panic, despair, all compromises.
Alone in the clouds,
Grief and doubt shroud,
Revealing the cursed, the worst.

CHAPTER

THIRTY-SEVEN

Over the next few days, I couldn't stop replaying Will's voice in my head: *They need you at the Void.*

And the prophecy he had received echoed in my thoughts: *"His soul cannot find rest while yours walks the earth. Only beyond the veil can his voice reach yours."*

Because Will had been dying, Milo had been able to reach him, and through Will, Milo had sent me the message that I needed to go to the Void.

I didn't know much about the Void, except that the Rogue Embers and the Soul Snatchers lived there. It had to be connected to Milo's soul. I thumbed his old ring. He needed me.

I couldn't let Will's sacrifice be in vain.

The only thing that managed to pull me out of bed was the overwhelming need to leave the Still Sphere—to leave this place behind—and to help Milo.

I picked up a tray of food Eda had left outside my door, and although it made my stomach churn, I forced myself to eat every bite. I dressed quickly. If I snuck out now, hopefully no one would notice I was gone. I packed my satchel and braided my hair tightly.

The village was quiet in the early morning light. Small log cabins dotted the tree line with smoke rising from their chimneys. Wooden stalls lined the rocky road, selling meats, furs, and fish. I passed the dock we had arrived at just days before, where the scent of saltwater and fish wafted into the air. I broke into a jog, heading south along the coastline of the Cobalt Sea. I didn't know how I'd reach the Void yet, but I had to keep moving—I had to push as far as I could within the Still Sphere until I found a way across the ocean.

I didn't stop running, even though my shoulder throbbed and my legs felt like they might snap from the strain I'd put on them through over the past week. I had to get far away from the palace before anyone realized I was gone.

"For the love of Aridan, Coco, I need a breath!"

My head whipped around so quickly that my neck cracked.

Crispin stood twenty paces away, bent over and resting his hands on his knees. Sweat lined his brow.

"What are you doing here?" I asked, my tone sharp, irritation bubbling in my belly.

Crispin straightened and met my eyes with a wry grin.

"Remember when I offered to help? Well, I meant it, and the only reason I can fathom that you would try to sneak off would most likely be because of Will or your brother."

I turned and kept walking, my boots stamping down pine needles.

"I'm going to the Void," I called over my shoulder, refusing to look at him. "So now is your chance to run back."

Crispin stepped in front of me. His eyes met mine, unwavering.

"Coco, I'm coming." He sighed. His deep blue eyes softened. "I'm here because I care. You lost someone you loved, and I thought I could keep you company. Maybe even help."

His words struck deeper than I wanted to admit.

"All right," I conceded. "You can stay—as long as you keep up."

I'd never admit it aloud, but... not being alone was kind of nice. Crispin became a helpful distraction, even if only for a few minutes at a time. In those fleeting moments, the sorrow and grief that consumed me felt a little lighter.

The wind picked up as we stood on the edge of the Cobalt Sea. Waves crashed against the rocks below. The sun dipped toward the horizon—we'd been running all day. I didn't know how we were going to cross the ocean efficiently.

"Well," Crispin said, like he was reading off a list, "we could get a boat. Swim across. Or walk around it."

"Thank you for your contribution. I don't know how I made it this far without you." I rolled my eyes.

"Well, you suggest something," Crispin teased, nudging me with his shoulder.

He looked around, and his eyes lit up. "Aha! See that?" He stepped behind me and pointed over my shoulder. "There's your way across."

"An old man in a fishing boat?" I raised an eyebrow, my patience hanging by a thread.

Crispin grinned. "I've been able to observe your skills—now you get to see mine." He jogged down the hill toward the beach.

I sighed, sat on the grassy beach, and tried to focus on anything besides the hollowness in my chest. Hopefully we would be able to set sail before sunset. I squinted toward the horizon.

About ten minutes later, the fishing boat appeared, gliding across the waves like rain running down smooth glass. The old man steering it headed straight toward Crispin. They exchanged a handshake, and after a brief word, the fisherman nodded and walked north toward the kingdom.

Crispin jogged back up to me. "Well, I got us a ride."

I stood, impressed but skeptical. "How?" I asked, crossing my arms.

"My charming personality and good looks. I simply persuaded him to let us borrow his boat and promised to return it by tomorrow night." Crispin's grin could melt hearts —something I was sure he knew. "Impressed, yet?"

"We'll see," I said, walking toward the boat.

My boots kicked up sand as we neared the water. Seaweed

and mussels clung to the wooden hull. It was smaller than I expected—water leaked from the frame, and there was barely enough room for the two of us.

Crispin pushed it off the sandbank, the water sloshing around his knees. With one final shove, the boat lurched forward. He leapt in with ease just as the sun dipped below the horizon.

The water was unnaturally calm—no breeze, no pull—more like a lake than the open sea. Only the soft lapping of waves against the sides broke the silence.

I grabbed a paddle and moved to row, but Crispin plucked it from my hands before I could get a stroke in.

"I can do that," he said.

We soon glided across the ocean, carried by Crispin's rowing.

"Well, it appears you've already been helpful," I murmured. I slouched forward as I studied my hands.

Crispin pulled a packet from his pocket and handed it to me —dried meat and fruit. He gestured at me to eat. After a minute of slow chewing, I passed them back. I didn't have much of an appetite.

"You should get some sleep, Coco. You're starting to resemble a Soul Snatcher," Crispin said lightly, though his eyes held sympathy.

I tried to sleep, but the constant rocking of the boat left my stomach unsettled. People crossed the Cobalt Sea regularly, but not to the island of the Void. What would be waiting for me there?

By the time dawn broke across the horizon, we had reached the far side of the sea. The sky looked like an oil painting—soft strokes of pink and orange brushed the clouds. We stepped off the boat onto the rocky shore.

A glimmering black mist swirled a few feet ahead, obscuring everything beyond.

Anticipation thrummed in my veins.

I reached into my satchel and pulled out a strip of torn fabric from the sheets at the Still Sphere's palace.

"Try to cover your mouth," I said, "so you don't inhale the mist."

We tied the cloth over our faces.

"All right, let's stick together," I muttered. My voice sounded faint behind my makeshift mask.

Without another word, we plunged into the black, chalky haze.

Cracks crisscrossed the dried mud, as if the fissures could tear wide open at any moment. The ground stretched flat and desolate—no trees, flowers, or any sign of life. The mist curled into my nostrils and crept into my ears. I felt normal. I couldn't see very far ahead, but it was as though I knew exactly where to walk, as if Milo were pulling me forward with an invisible thread.

The fog barely seemed to affect me—instead, it wrapped around me like an old friend. Oddly comforting. Almost familiar. I wasn't hallucinating or convulsing like the stories I'd heard.

I glanced at Crispin to see if it was affecting him, but he looked just as alert as I felt.

"What do you think?" he asked. "From what I've heard, the Depths mess with your mind—unless you're a Rogue Ember who's taken the Void Oath. That's the only way they can make it through without losing their grip."

"I wonder if it doesn't affect Dims. Only Embers."

I noticed the crinkle around Crispin's eyes; he was smiling. "Aren't you glad you invited me along?"

"I didn't invite you along," I pointed out.

"Funny. I could've sworn a raven delivered a very *official* summons for me. Maybe it got lost in the wind."

I couldn't help but grin.

CHAPTER

THIRTY-EIGHT

I lost track of time. I didn't know how many hours had passed. The mist pressed in around me, but the soft, cooling haze settled over me like a strange comfort. No demons. No sign of anyone. Only the silence, which rang louder in my ears with every passing moment. I opened and closed my mouth, trying to pop my ears, desperate for some relief, but it didn't work.

Crispin followed me quietly, almost as if he didn't dare to speak, as if it would awake the Depths.

The mist suddenly dispersed. The ground shifted beneath us, jagged rocks jutting up from the earth. The rough terrain made it difficult to walk. The sky seemed different from Aren's —there was no moon, no stars, just dark, coal-colored clouds hanging in the air. Ash piled around my feet, as thick as snow.

A pointed peak towered into the clouds ahead. We moved toward it. Smoke and cinders swirled around the top, accompanied by the shrieking screams of demons. As we drew closer, shadowed tents appeared, filled with thousands of Rogue Embers, stretching all the way to the base of the volcano.

I caught myself wondering whether any Rogue Dims were among them. It was hard to distinguish who had magic and who didn't without seeing their wrists.

Fiery red lava flowed through the earth, snaking its way down the mountainside. The volcano called to me. My body hummed with the certainty that Milo needed me there. I chewed on my lip, staying hidden in the darkness, trying to come up with a plan. I needed to blend in, and all the Rogue Embers wore hooded cloaks. If I could get my hands on one, I could slip past them easily enough and make my way to the base of the volcano.

I was about to share my plan when Crispin beat me to it. "All right, Coco, here's the thing—I've been studying the lore of herbs, and it's opened my eyes to the subtle magic woven into nature's greenery."

I raised an eyebrow. "That's nice, Crispin, but where are you going with this?"

He leaned in, eyes sharp. "We both lack magic, and soon we're about to venture into territory crawling with Embers and Soul Snatchers. We can't just stumble in blind. We need a plan. Luckily for you, I already have one."

I didn't feel scared or uncertain; it was as if the mist fueled me with adrenaline, erasing any trace of doubt. Crispin's plan sounded solid, and I silently prayed to Aridan that it would work. The part about us splitting up had my nerves on edge, but I forced myself to push through the fear.

I wasn't the same Coco who had been summoned to be a Questling. I thought of the night I'd hidden under my covers, trembling at the thunder while the storm howled outside. Milo had ditched his friends just to stay with me. Now, I almost laughed at the memory. That girl was long gone. I wasn't weak. I wasn't pathetic. And I *knew* I had what it took to face any creature that dared to stop me.

Muffled voices grew louder as one by one, the Rogue Embers emerged. They were leaving. I crept to the back of one of the tents and prayed one of them had left a cloak behind. Quietly, I lifted the tent flap and slipped inside.

My heart lurched. A single Rogue Ember lay on a cot, breathing softly.

A sharp snort froze me mid-step. My gaze locked on the Ember as he rolled onto his side to face me. Even from a few feet away, his rancid breath curdled the damp air.

His hooded cloak and boots lay crumpled on the ground beside each other. I crept forward as the muffled sounds of the camp pressed in. Sweat dripped down my spine.

I bent, fingers clasping the fabric. As I pulled it toward me, he stirred again. My pulse spiked.

I yanked the cloak over my head, choking down a gag as his stench clung to me—rank and oily. I quickly lifted the hood to conceal my face.

I left the tent, keeping my head low as I wove through the

Rogue Embers toward the volcano. More Rogue Embers crowded the base of the volcano, murmuring in low voices or huddling in dark groups. Looking up, I was mesmerized and intimidated by its greatness; the peak loomed high above, reaching into the night sky. There was no visible way to climb it. I circled the base—the rocky surface was difficult to navigate, filled with sharp stones and gnarled roots.

Then, I heard it—a distant chanting that grew louder as I neared the far side of the volcano. I tensed and scanned my surroundings. Dark thorns twisted and curled into a maze of bushes. The chanting intensified and I moved closer, my breath shallow. The ground opened just beyond the thorns to reveal a cave-like opening. Vibrant orange light radiated from within.

I crouched low, moved toward the opening, then froze. Below me, hundreds of Soul Snatchers circled a vast pit. Their chanting hummed through the space and vibrated with power. A chill prickled my skin as the realization hit me: a ritual had just begun.

An enormous Rogue Ember—at least seven feet tall—stood at the head of the pit. His veins bulged from his skin, straining against the flesh as though they might burst at any moment. His pupils, rimmed with red, stood out like two glowing rubies suspended in the air. His hands gripped a leather-bound book and his voice silenced the room as a dark, sinister tone poured from his lips:

> *Ancient Spirit,*
> *Hear the call*
> *Of loyal servants*
> *Sent to maul.*

Feed the souls
Of those who passed—
Awake the chosen one at last.

The swirling ball of darkness began to shimmer with a red hue. The chanting accelerated as the Rogue Ember repeated his words.

A soft glow near the pit caught my eye. Hundreds of orbs glistened with silver and gold specks surrounded by silvery vapor. They bobbed gently in a long black net that lay on the ground, keeping them tethered, preventing them from floating away.

I had never seen a soul before, but I knew that's what I was seeing. As soon as the thought crossed my mind, goosebumps spread across my skin.

Something deep inside me knew: Milo was here, somewhere among the souls. Will's words about feeling Milo's presence suddenly made sense to me—something I had never understood until now.

Dread settled in me like a boulder resting on my chest. The Ari Souls swayed in the net. I didn't know exactly what the Rogue Ember planned, but I could connect the dots. He was going to dump the Ari Souls into the pit. I had to reach them before it was too late.

I pulled a knife from my boot and clamped it between my teeth, biting down hard to steady my breath as I lowered myself to the ground. I used my arms to drag my body across the rocky surface, paying no attention to the way the rocks scraped against my skin or the dirt caked under my nails. I had to reach the net before they dumped the souls into the pit—without alerting the Soul Snatchers to my presence.

I hauled my body over the rocks, keeping low. The scent of sulfur filled my nostrils as a bead of sweat ran down my temple and slid off my cheek. More moisture gathered at my hairline as my arms tired. The chanting continued, growing louder by the second, and my heartbeat quickened to match the pace.

My body brushed against the desiccated flesh of the Soul Snatchers as I wormed my way between them, holding my breath when one of them shifted. I made it a few feet from the net and halted as two Soul Snatchers stepped toward it. I had one advantage: every single Soul Snatcher in the space was fixated on the Rogue Ember's chanting. Shrieks of delight erupted from their mouths, as if to encourage whatever was trying to emerge from the swirling madness.

The Ari Souls bobbed frantically in the net, as though they were screaming for help. This was it. I had to act now. I closed the distance between myself and the net. Pulling the knife from my teeth, I began to saw at the thick ropes. My blade was dull, and every second that passed brought me closer to being noticed. I had no idea how much time I had left.

The blade sawed at the fibers, breaking individual strands at an excruciatingly slow rate. Sweat poured down my temples, as if a bucket of water had been dumped on my head. The tip finally cut through, but the opening was too small—no bigger than a mouse hole, let alone large enough for a soul.

The room felt stuffy, the air thick with the smell of ash and sweat. I moved my fingers as quickly as I could.

Suddenly, slippery flesh clasped my ankle with a grip so strong that it felt like an anchor had been chained to my leg. I glanced over my shoulder to see a Soul Snatcher grinning at me. Black globs dripped from its mouth as its smile widened.

I was going to die. Fear surged within me, as though someone had thrust their hand through my chest and gripped my heart, squeezing it until it might burst. But the fear wasn't for my life; it was for Milo's soul.

The Soul Snatcher yanked my ankle, and the force slammed my chin against the rocky ground. I dropped the knife. It dragged me away from the net as I clawed at the rough soil, desperately trying to stop, but it was no use. I kicked and hollered, my free leg flailing, until its other hand clamped down on my other ankle.

The ground tore at my skin as I was dragged. My shirt rode up and the rocks cut into me. The open wounds immediately filled with dirt, causing a searing, stinging pain. The grip on my ankles loosened, and I rolled over, scrambling to my knees in a desperate rush.

I tried to escape the Soul Snatcher only to come face-to-face with the Rogue Ember leader. His ruby-red irises met mine and a sickening smile spread across his flaking face, baring yellowed teeth covered in black mold with blood—deep red—dripping from the corners of his mouth. He bent down, chanting as he jerked his burly arm toward me. His thick, meaty fingers gripped my neck. In an instant, my body dangled like a rag doll from the Rogue Ember's hand.

A furious thrumming filled my ears, drowning out the chanting. His fingernails dug into my skin; I could feel the blood, hot and seeping down my neck.

I cringed at his foul breath—a mix of rotten eggs and decay. I racked my brain for a plan, anything, but I couldn't think straight. I tried to inhale, but all I felt was the tension in my throat and the piercing torment exploding through my body.

I clasped the Rogue Ember's hands, trying to pry them off my throat, but I only scraped at his skin with no effect. Dark fog crept into my vision as his face became nothing more than a smudge. My eyelids suddenly felt heavy, and I could feel my body slacken.

A thunderous burst of dust exploded around us and crackled like fire. The grip on my throat ceased. I tumbled to the ground, gasping for air. I heard a snap, as if a stick had been broken in two. Pain seared through my leg. I looked down, my stomach clenching—a grotesque misalignment of bone and flesh. Terror gripped my heart. I sucked in a deep breath and stood, putting all my weight on the other leg.

Panting, I dragged my gaze from the mangled mess of my injury. All around me, grotesque, mummified forms scattered in lifeless heaps across the ground, covered in dust the color of brineberries. Crispin stood beyond them, panting. The Rogue Ember howled, clawing at his eyes. I breathed in the chalky particles that hung thick in the air and coated my lungs and throat. Crispin's skin was veiled in it—but it was only impacting those who had magic.

The Ari Souls needed to be freed. Even the scathing hurt from my lacerated leg wasn't going to stop me.

A ruby-red vapor rose from the pit, swirling into the air. The Rogue Ember inhaled deeply, and his nostrils flared as the steam filled his lungs. I watched as the veins in his neck darkened, taking on an angry shade of dark purple. Blackness crept across his pale, flaking skin, like a spreading stain.

The vapor amplified the Rogue Ember's magic, flooding him with raw power—untamed, unstoppable.

The ground shuddered. My eyes fell on the taut net straining to contain the souls. I clenched my teeth as my legs threatened to buckle. I put weight on my injured leg, and a jolt of agony shot through me as I grunted and shoved myself forward.

The ground shook violently as I stumbled, arms flailing as I desperately tried to stay upright.

The Rogue Ember boomed:

> *Ancient Spirit,*
> *Hear the call*
> *Of loyal servants*
> *Sent to maul.*
> *Feed the souls*
> *Of those who passed—*
> *Awake the chosen one at last.*

His arms spread wide, as if to embrace a friend. His voice deepened, rumbling like thunder as it echoed off the walls and filled the cavern:

> *The time has come*
> *To aid the fall,*
> *Open the Vile,*
> *And damn them all.*

He tugged the hilt of a knife from the waistband of his breeches. His colossal body stalked toward the pit as the vapor continued to swirl, accelerate, and take on the form of a human body.

Terror gripped me as I realized he was headed toward the net that held Milo's soul. He was going to feed those souls to the frightening form taking shape in the fumes.

I lurched forward before I could process the ache radiating through my shattered leg. I flung myself at the Rogue Ember and yanked the net from his hands; its rough fibers burned my palms. Then I desperately scanned for a weapon. My knife from earlier lay inches from me. *Thank Aridan.* I just needed to release the souls from the netting. I turned and ran toward the cave opening. Each step sent agonizing torment through my leg. I gritted my teeth, pushing through the burning sensation as I stubbornly dragged the souls behind me. A sharp blow to my back sent me sprawling forward, and my body slammed against the hard ground. I gripped the mesh like it was my own lifeline.

I hastily sat up, muscles screaming, adrenaline pushing me past the physical discomfort as I shredded the netting. Its coarse fibers tore, nicking my own skin in the process. The vaporous figure turned toward me. The Rogue Ember hurled himself forward, his arms outstretched to grab the netting, but his fingers grasped only air.

He hadn't seen me as a real threat; he'd let his guard down. He realized his mistake too late.

The Ari Souls burst through the openings in the net. They glided through the air, rose, and drifted out of the cave. I glanced back as the vaporous figure fell back into the pit.

One orb lingered behind the others, floating a few inches above my head before it soared out of the heated cave and into the starless night sky. Calmness filled my being as I recognized the soul. It was Milo's, lingering behind to thank me. A wave of peace settled over me.

I turned just in time to see the Rogue Ember howl in fury.

Then, through the haze of pain, I saw Crispin. He bolted toward the Rogue Ember. Without the red vapor, the Ember was no longer all-powerful. Crispin hurled out both arms, releasing dark smoke from the pouches in his hands. The blast hit the Rogue Ember in the chest and knocked him to the ground.

Crispin ran toward me. "Hop on my back, darling, please—and no arguments this time. We only have a few minutes."

I smiled dazedly. Both of us were covered in blue powder as he effortlessly lifted me onto his back and took off, sprinting away from the volcano.

A chilling, tingling sensation spread throughout my body. Flames of agony engulfed me. The ringing in my ears turned to silence, and I drifted into the dark.

CHAPTER
THIRTY-NINE

I was running through a sunflower field, squinting into the glaring sun. Over my shoulder, I glimpsed Milo and Will chasing me with wide grins on their faces. I quickened my pace, the cool morning air rushing past as the sweet scent of honey and vanilla filled my senses.

"Run, Coco, run!"

They sped past me, and their hands reached out to grab mine, pulling me along.

But the vibrant colors began to fade. Their fingers slipped from mine, and the sweet scent of honey and vanilla gave way to a fresh, cedar aroma.

It was familiar, but I couldn't quite place it... until it hit me. *Crispin.*

My eyelids felt heavy, but I forced them open. I stared up at a low, wooden ceiling. Spider webs stretched from beam to beam, and sunlight filtered through a small oval window. My mouth was dry, my lips parched when I tried to lick them.

I sat up slowly, my arms trembling.

"Well, look who finally decided to wake up," Crispin drawled. He stood from his chair and gently propped a pillow behind my back.

My head throbbed, and a dull ache pulsed through every inch of my body. It felt as if I had been asleep for years—or had woken up from death. Crispin offered me a tin cup of water, which I drank greedily.

"Where are we?" I asked, still raspy.

"A village town in the Hush Sphere, near the Depths of Delusion," Crispin replied. He sat up straighter on the edge of the bed, leaned forward, and rested his elbows on the mattress. His blue eyes held a strange kind of hope, though the dark shadows beneath them spoke volumes.

The Depths of Delusion. The memories came crashing down, intensifying the ache in my head. But then a wave of peace surged through me, burning brighter than the Void.

Milo.

He was free. I could still see the silver and gold specks of his essence flickering in that orb and rising into the night sky— toward the Unknown... or Soulari Hall.

"How did we get here? Are you all right?"

Crispin cut me off gently, placing his hand over mine and squeezing it in quiet reassurance.

"I managed to run us straight to the Depths without inter-ruption, then carried you back to the boat and rowed all by myself. I know you're impressed," he said with a wink. "After that, I ended up here, where a kind old Charmer healed both of us. I also had a few nasty scrapes I couldn't afford to ignore."

I smiled softly. "Thank you, Crispin. Truly.

"We need to tell the Luxari what we saw."

His gaze locked with mine.

"Do you think they'll take us seriously?" he murmured, his voice softer than usual. He rubbed his thumb over my hand before standing.

"What other choice do we have than to try?"

Standing outside the Hush Sphere's palace already felt like a precious memory. Though only weeks had passed since Will and I had been summoned, the world felt entirely different now. The moment seemed branded in my mind—embracing Will, both of us facing the Sphere Quests. Crispin and I walked between the marble moonstone pillars and entered through the arch of the open-air palace.

An attendant appeared in a sand-colored dress that glimmered under the beams of the sun. "I can escort both of you to the Queen," she said.

Crispin and I exchanged a nervous glance. I gave a small nod of reassurance as we followed her.

"I'm more nervous to see Severin at the banquet tonight than the Luxari," Crispin teased.

The banquet. I had completely forgotten the ending ceremony of the Sphere Quests amidst all the chaos—and the pain of losing Will. I swallowed hard. Grief burned my throat —the stabbing reminder of Will's death consumed me all over again. Tonight, the Luxari would offer some a spot on their Luxari Council. It meant nothing to me—not without him.

The ocean breeze carried the salt of the sea, mingling with the scent of fresh water in the air. I closed my eyes for a moment before taking a step forward.

Our footsteps echoed across the marble, the hall stretching endlessly ahead as we followed the attendant into an arched alcove. We stepped into a room full of murmurs. The windows revealed the Cobalt Sea, while the sun brightened the room. A large, narrow table stood in the middle, surrounded by high-back chairs upholstered with turquoise silk. Murals of Aridan covered every inch of the walls, painted with vivid, reverent detail.

The Luxari sat at the table, along with some of their Luxari Council.

We were guided to two chairs positioned on the opposite side of the table, facing Queen Catalina. Crispin took the seat to my right and gripped my hand beneath the table, giving me the strength I needed to face whatever was about to happen.

We had originally sent a letter to Oak and Kaz—mostly because I felt comfortable confiding in them—detailing the events of the Void. After that, this meeting had been arranged.

Queen Catalina's voice snapped me from my thoughts. "Colette and Crispin," she chirped. "Thank you for joining us." Her dirty blonde hair was pulled tightly back into a high bun, making her features appear sharp and skeletal.

I felt a wave of nervous energy and avoided eye contact with Kaz and Oak on my left.

"Well, as Rulers of Aren, we wanted to thank you." She pasted on a forced smile, and the whiteness of her teeth felt blinding.

I had never seen Queen Catalina look anything but composed. But now, she appeared utterly haunted, her once-regal presence replaced by an aura of dread. It radiated from her like a shadow, thick with something dark and evil.

My body trembled, but Crispin squeezed my palm, grounding me.

"Aridan, the Dazzling, believes magic is a gift—something that must be earned. Ari Souls fuel the magic in Aren, and without them, magic would cease to exist."

I was surrounded by the most powerful Embers in Aren. As Queen Catalina continued speaking, I listened intently, locking eyes with her.

"When someone dies, their soul leaves the body as an orb." Queen Catalina stood from her chair and rounded the table, her movements slow and precise as she continued. "The soul journeys to Soulari Hall, where it awaits its ceremony to determine whether it is a Pure Soul or a Damned Soul. If deemed an Ari Soul, it ascends to the Unknown; if not, it is cast into the Vile.

"Those souls remain at Soulari Hall, guarded by powerful spells and charms. After the ceremony, the Ari Soul bursts, releasing its shimmering magic into the pools of Aren, which then spreads across the land. The person moves on to the Unknown, but their magic stays behind."

She stopped roaming behind her tall chair and gripped its

side, her fingers turning white. Her voice filled with annoyance and anger. "After your... incident... at the Void, Queen Nerian and I went to Soulari Hall, where we discovered that Soul Snatchers had infiltrated its borders. They stole Ari Souls slowly to avoid detection and bring them to the Void. The breach has been dealt with, and we've implemented measures to protect the souls."

Will had been right about the "security" of Soulari Hall. The fact that Soul Snatchers had been stealing Ari Souls unnoticed was more than cause for concern.

Her shoulders straightened even more, if that were possible.

"It would appear that the Soul Snatchers were trying to retrieve Ari Souls to bring magic to the Void. After that, we aren't sure what their purpose was."

I snapped my gaze to Oak and Kaz. I had shared everything in detail in my letter, but it seemed they left out some of that information when speaking to Queen Catalina and Queen Nerian. Kaz shifted uncomfortably in his chair. Then Oak's deep, rough voice slid into my mind.

Don't say anything about the Rogue Ember's ritual.

The words cut through my mind as clearly and sharply as if he had spoken them aloud. My eyes widened, locking onto his. The gold flecks in his eyes stood in stark contrast to the blue-gray that surrounded them, and a surge of panic jolted through me. I had never heard Oak's voice in my mind before. He had truly been holding his power back.

"On behalf of Aren, we want to thank both of you for your service," Queen Catalina continued. An attendant pulled her chair out as she sat down, her fingertips rubbing her temples, as if the inconvenience of having to explain the situation had drained her.

"It was nothing," Crispin said confidently, speaking for us both.

"Regardless, Aren is in your debt." Two attendants entered, carrying a heavy trunk between them. "We want to show our gratitude." Queen Catalina stood and unlatched the trunk to reveal jewels and gold. The treasure glittered with ruby-red gems and diamonds. The gold gleamed like warm honey, smooth enough to lick.

I blinked, and the appeal of the treasure vanished more quickly than a snowflake in the Scorch Sphere. *This was wrong.* I would not be rewarded for returning Ari Souls to the Unknown. We were being offered payment for something sacred, and from Crispin's clenched jaw, I knew he felt the same.

I stood quickly, my chair scraping sharply against the marble floor as I clenched my fists. A surge of defiance rose within me. "I can't take this," I said, my voice firm.

Crispin stood as well. "Me, neither."

Queen Catalina's eyes narrowed, a flicker of something dangerous in her gaze. Her smile was thin, practiced. "Of course you can," she replied.

"We can, but we won't. We appreciate your gratitude." I turned, hoping Crispin would follow, forcing confidence into my stride. But Queen Catalina cleared her throat, stopping me. I turned back around.

Her brow arched. "Correct me if I'm wrong, Coco, but from what I've heard, you could use the help."

Crispin stiffened at her remark.

This was a pity payment, or worse, a way to keep us quiet.

My stomach soured. Kaz glanced over his shoulder, his expression unreadable, his flaxen blonde hair shining under the chandelier. Oak's back was to me. I'd hoped for support—at least from one of them—but neither spoke. Oak didn't look back. Not even a glance. I swallowed hard and pretended it didn't sting.

"We won't take it." My voice didn't waver as I stood my ground.

"Don't be silly, girl," Queen Catalina spat. The veins in her neck bulged with irritation. Her voice was full of venom.

"No," I said, taking a step toward her. The anger in me boiled my blood. "We did what we needed to do. Not for glory, fame, or some gilded box of bribes. Tell me, Queen Catalina, are the jewels and gold for our service? Or are they meant to keep us quiet, so that the people of Aren feel confident that Soulari Hall is safe?"

Her lips pursed and her eyes narrowed into slits. The jewels began to lift from the trunk and hover in the air, trembling with her barely contained rage.

"Cute trick. Is that it? For an all-powerful Luxari, I expected something more impressive." I scoffed at her.

With that, she flicked her bony fingers out. The jewels vibrated in the air, shaking violently. I stood my ground and didn't flinch. It would take more than trembling gems to intimidate me.

One second, the jewels were suspended, their pointed tips shaking—the next, they crashed to the floor in a chaotic clatter and melted into steaming puddles of blue and red. My heart pounded in my ears, confirming I was right in her true intentions for having us take the chest.

Kaz sprang to his feet so suddenly that his chair clattered to the floor. I blinked—he was steaming, his body radiating heat. The air thickened with the scent of burning wood. His short-sleeve tunic clung to his muscular frame, revealing every golden-tan curve of his arm, each flexed muscle straining toward Queen Catalina. Queen Nerian stood, watching the events unfold.

"Have you lost all sense?" The rage in Kaz's voice sent a chill down my spine.

He shoved the table with such force that it pinned Queen Catalina against the marble wall, tilting her crown and sending strands of her hair tumbling from her tight bun to cling to her face. Kaz strode toward the alcove that lead to the sandy beach. His footsteps were swallowed by the sounds of crashing waves.

I wasn't shocked that Kaz had defended me—I was shocked that he'd attacked another Luxari. And Oak? He just sat there, taking up space. It was too much to process. I turned and retreated from the scene, bunching my dress in my hands as I stormed down the hall.

CHAPTER

FORTY

S teady footsteps followed, but I didn't care to see who was behind me. I moved forward, increasing my pace as I passed dozens of arched windows opening to the Cobalt Sea. The ocean breeze licked my skin, leaving a sprinkling of salt.

A strong hand gripped my arm and tugged me into a shadowed alcove. My back pressed against the wall, and Oak's eyes blazed down at me. His towering frame made me feel so small.

"Are you mad, Coco? To speak to a Luxari in such a manner?" His voice was a low growl.

His face was mere inches from mine. I hated that even now —especially now—his nearness unraveled me.

Being this close to him was overwhelming. Every breath I took was filled with the scent of fresh rain and coconut. I couldn't ignore the hardness of his body pressed up against mine. That damn curl resting on his forehead only made my pulse quicken.

My heartbeat accelerated, pounding harder than it had in weeks—harder than when I'd stared death in the face. The cool smoothness of the marble sent goosebumps skittering across my skin as my breath hitched, rising and falling.

His gaze locked with mine.

"I'm not out of my mind. I don't even see why you care, considering you sat there and did nothing while Queen Catalina lost her temper."

"If you believe for a single moment that I stood idly by, you are gravely mistaken."

Time stilled. I stared at him, letting his words sink in.

"You compelled Kaz..." I meant to ask, but it came out more like a statement.

His sculpted jaw tightened as he pressed his hands against the wall, framing my face between them and cocooning us in a whirlwind of emotion.

"He didn't need much. He was already about to go all infernal. I simply nudged him to act more quickly."

"Why didn't you do something yourself?" I demanded, frustration coating every word.

He lightly chuckled. "Coco, you're a Questling—doing anything would look like favoritism," he said in a ragged, deep tone.

I scoffed. "And how is taking me out on an afternoon adventure to your cottage, asking me to dance, and kissing me *not* showing favoritism?"

"I told you that I shouldn't have kissed you." His jaw tightened.

"Thanks for the reminder," I bit back.

"I don't regret kissing you. I regret the position it put you in —if anyone were to find out, it would look like I was favoring you in the Quests." Concern flickered in his eyes.

"Then why did you?" I whispered, excited and nervous to hear his response.

His jaw hardened. He lowered his lips, but then stopped, his forehead resting against mine instead.

Oak's eyes fluttered closed for a moment, his dark lashes casting shadows on his features. "Coco, I am striving to act with honor and do what is right, but you are making it difficult." When his gaze finally met mine, it was hungry—a look that made my knees tremble.

His words—an accusation—snapped the breath from my lungs. "*I'm* making it difficult? You have me pinned against a wall, after you just told me you can't show favoritism."

A grin tugged at his lips, a dimple appearing in his cheek.

"Please, just say what you need to say," I said, my voice strained.

He immediately pushed off the wall. The space between us felt like a jagged crack, widening in my chest.

"I'm sorry I used my ability to Mindwhisper on you tonight," he said quietly, his tone sincere. "I've never done it to you before—I want to make sure you understand that."

A deep crease appeared between his brows, his concern clear.

I blinked rapidly at the sternness in his voice. Mindwhisper? Was that what he'd done? Knowing that he could invade my thoughts sent a cold shiver through me. If he was powerful enough to compel a Luxari King, how could I be sure he wasn't slipping messages into my mind without me realizing? I couldn't quite process it. I knew he was telling the truth, but a knot twisted in my stomach.

Every muscle in his expression was tight. "I merely wished to provide you with context. Kaz and I believe that someone within the Luxari—or the Luxari Council itself—is in league with the Void."

I wasn't shocked. It made sense now—the breach at Soulari Hall. "To do what?"

"To bring back Arrow."

Pure horror vibrated through me. The vaporous figure struggling to rise from the pit took shape in my mind—had that been Arrow?

"How would anyone do that?"

"With Ari Souls." He raked a hand through his hair, sighing. "But it's complicated. I have people looking into it." He waved it off as if that were the last we would speak of it.

"Until we uncover the culprit, we must keep our knowledge close. Only you, Crispin, and Kaz know what happened." He shot me a look, like he could see straight into my soul.

It was terrifying to think that someone supposed to lead Aren could betray it. But at least only a few knew.

"How is Catalina still queen after such a major screw-up? My brother's soul was nearly destroyed because she didn't do her job. Can't you do something?"

"I cannot, but after this, I'm certain Aridan will keep a close watch on her. He values Ari Souls, and Queen Catalina's negligence has put her in a precarious position."

"Well, thanks for filling me in," I said, stepping around him.

He moved aside as I rushed away. I didn't stop until I reached the guest room on the upper level, where I collapsed and cried.

The worst part was, I couldn't even tell if the tears were for Milo, for Will, or for something I didn't yet understand.

CHAPTER
FORTY-ONE

I sat in the bathtub so long that my skin wrinkled—I felt as though I'd lived a hundred years. I scoured my flesh, desperate to erase any trace of the Void.

My skin was raw, rough from the constant scrubbing. My gaze drifted to the lavender bubbles that floated lazily on the water's surface. Bottles filled with bright shades and lush aromas lined the rim of the tub.

I wrapped myself in a towel, soft as a cloud. Standing before the armoire, I combed through the gowns, searching for something to wear to the Reveal Feast. The Questlings of the Sphere Quests had arrived late this afternoon at the Hush Sphere's palace, ready for the gala where we would finally hear the results of our challenges.

Earlier, when Tada and Otto had arrived, they had hugged me so tightly and for so long that I felt I'd never need another hug again.

I tapped my bare foot on the cold marble floor, glaring at

the gaudy gowns. After a minute, a soft, low voice drifted into the room, drawing me away from the armoire. I stepped into the shallow hall and passed under one archway to a second one, where I opened the door.

I arched an eyebrow in surprise. Severin stood there, his ash-blonde hair pulled neatly into a tight bun. His cream tunic and black, form-fitting pants made him look evocative, yet deadly. But what held my attention was what he cradled in his arms: a champagne-gold, glittering gown.

"Severin," I murmured, still in shock at why he was seeking me out. "What brings you here?"

A small smile tugged at his lips. "Ah, yes. This may seem random, but Crispin says he owes you for the race—and for letting him accompany you to the Void. I, however, am not too thrilled about that last part." His eyes gleamed with amusement.

"That gown in the Daze Sphere—was that from you two?"

"Yes. Crispin loves secrecy. Says it 'fuels his creative juices.'" Severin rolled his eyes. "He's a designer. He made the gown you wore at the Daze Sphere—and this one, too."

I felt warmth spread through me.

"I won't keep you—but Crispin insisted I deliver this tonight, or else I 'wouldn't like the consequences.'"

Before I could protest, Severin draped the gown over my arms.

"Thank you."

He genuinely smiled, then turned and walked away.

I stood on the sandy beach of the Cobalt Sea under the night sky and adjusted my glittering gown. The dress was breathtaking—strapless, with a corset that wrapped around into a lace-up open back. Its long skirt swept to the floor in a flowing A-line shape, opening at the side in a dramatic slit. The champagne color complimented my skin tone perfectly.

I followed a path of teal fabric that looped out of the palace and across the beach, leading to a rectangular platform lined with torches. Lanterns dotted the path, and tideblossoms and brineberry shrubs framed it. The night sky seemed alive with silver specks scattered across the vast dark. Trails of gold and silver dust streaked overhead, as if the stars themselves had been charmed to dazzle. Gentle waves lapped against the shore, and the smells of the tropical paradise overwhelmed my senses. A mix of creamy coconut, sunlime zest, and moonvine filled the air.

Will's absence struck me like a wave—grief in my veins, guilt in my chest, my heart aching with the loss. He should be here. He was the most gifted, courageous, and outstanding of us all who were summoned.

I emerged onto the Arenwood platform filled with guests merrily drinking and conversing. The other Questlings were easy to spot—they stood crowded in the dead center of the platform.

The Luxari Council from every Sphere were scattered around the floor, but I couldn't spot Niko or Eda.

The crowd parted for me like I was a Luxari, and I strolled forward.

"Coco!" Tada sprang forward, clapping her hands together as she shook her pink curls in wonderment. "Damn, Coco. Just damn. You look sexy." She winked, her violet eyes shining with amusement. Otto joined her, wrapping his arm around her waist.

"You clean up well, Coco." Otto grinned. His sapphire tunic matched his eyes perfectly.

"Same to you," I teased back.

Amabel's glare pulled my attention away from Otto and Tada. She stood in the center of the floor, wearing a transparent silver gown so thin that it revealed undergarments crafted from diamonds and caused more than a dozen men to openly drool. Her bright blonde hair gleamed against her deep tan. The only thing she lacked was a smile. Her eyes narrowed at me, and puffs of steam rolled off her arms.

I smirked at her as I brushed past to speak with Hugh and Cecille, who were openly giddy that the Sphere Quests were coming to an end.

As soon as I approached, though, their faces fell, and a wave of sadness washed over their features.

"I'm sorry for your loss, Coco," Hugh mumbled, but he looked me in the eye as he said it, which I knew was difficult for him.

Cecille gripped my hand tightly. "Will was of the utmost character. I have no doubt he is resting in the Unknown."

I gave her a small, shaky smile as my throat tightened. She gently released my hand.

"Can you believe it's all over after tonight?" Hugh awkwardly inserted, trying to change the subject.

Cecille caught on quickly.

"I know everyone is trying to figure out why I was even summoned," Cecille said. Her tight brown curls bounced as she spoke, and her tawny eyes filled with sadness. "Pretty sure every person in Aren is dumbfounded by it."

"Why *were* you summoned?" Hugh asked bluntly, before I could stop him.

Her voice lowered, barely above a whisper. "I'm a Fate Dancer."

Hugh's head snapped up. We stared at her, stunned. This was why she had known she was going to make it through the Sphere Quests—she had foreseen it.

"Cecille, do you understand how rare and powerful this ability is? There have only been five documented Fate Dancers in Aren's history." Hugh's voice grew urgent. "It's more than just receiving and giving prophecies—they are always correct, unchanging facts of the future. Pure fate."

"Of course I know. Why do you think I haven't told anyone about this, besides you two?"

"Why us?" I asked. A chill slid down my spine, making the hairs on my arms rise.

"Because our fates are intertwined—all three of us."

Hugh's jaw dropped.

She smiled and held out her palm. Water stirred at the

center, rising in a quiet spiral that rippled upward. From the swirl, an Aurefly took shape. She lifted her hand and the Aurefly landed gently on her finger, humming softly. My eyes met hers.

"The prophecy..." I whispered.

Cecille's eyes gleamed, her gaze distant, as if seeing a place far beyond this one. Then she spoke:

> *Coco, Coco, brave and bright,*
> *Don't fall behind—turn and fight.*
> *You hold the fate of those now gone,*
> *And you'll be the one to right the wrong.*
> *Follow your heart, stay steady and sure—*
> *For a Dim shall rise, both frail and pure,*
> *To release death long kept obscure.*

"What does that even mean?" I asked, my voice rushed.

"You... you released death. You set the Ari Souls free in the Void. The souls of the deceased."

My heart pounded so loudly that I could feel it in my ears. Cecille had to be the "she" Will had mentioned in his letter—the one who had delivered the prophecy in his dream.

Just as I opened my mouth to ask a dozen questions, hundreds of bubbles floated through the air from the Cobalt Sea, glistening in shades of pastel pink.

All at once, the bubbles burst and showered the Arenwood floor with glimmering, colorful dust. The Luxari emerged through the haze.

CHAPTER

FORTY-TWO

Queen Catalina stood on the raised platform, her skin sickly pale, her gaze locked onto me. I raised my chin in response. She wore a ball gown of seafoam green, and her seashell diadem had been replaced with moonstone crystals and pearls. The metal swirled into ocean waves that glistened with hues of aquamarine.

Queen Nerian took her place beside her, wearing a modest, light gown. Her crown, however, was different from what I had seen her wear before. It was crafted from wooden branches and vines, with carved leaves and moss woven into spirals that mimicked mountain peaks.

Kaz leapt onto the platform to Queen Catalina's right, commanding instant attention. He wore a tightly fitted, slick black leather tunic and pants that showcased his toned arms and golden tan. His flaxen hair was pulled back, and his obsidian crown drew my focus. It matched the style of the one I had seen him wear before, but this one was embellished with molten amber glass that flickered with red and orange flames. Red sand speckles coated the surface. He shot the crowd a sensual smile that could melt the gowns off every woman in the room.

I glanced over at a woman fanning her face, boldly taking him in. I hadn't spoken with him one-on-one since the Daze Sphere, and I couldn't help but feel a pang of regret for not seeking him out or trying to spend more time with him. But he was a Luxari—even though he had shown me kindness, I couldn't mistake that for interest.

The creak of the wooden platform brought my attention back to the Luxari. Oak slowly ascended to join the others. Kaz instantly took a step closer to Queen Catalina, leaving extra space between himself and Oak. A hush fell over the crowd. Only the sound of crashing waves filled the night.

Oak wore midnight black—unlike Kaz's leather, the fabric looked like it was made of soft cotton. His loose tunic flowed gently, paired with polished boots and tight breeches that hugged every muscle of his legs. But it was his crown that caught my attention. A platinum circlet rested on his coffee-colored hair. It rose in soft, fluid waves, spiraling into elegant wisps of wind. White Daze lily petals were delicately sculpted into the metal itself, curving gracefully around the silver, their sweeping shapes glowing with an aura of dusty blue.

His gold-flecked eyes met mine, and I quickly looked away.

Queen Catalina cleared her throat, and to my horror, I realized I was the only one from the Sphere Quests who hadn't joined the others in front of the Luxari. I rushed forward to stand next to Hugh as a flush crept into my cheeks.

"Thank you for gathering with us this evening to celebrate the end of the Sphere Quests." Queen Catalina's voice rang out.

Cheers and applause erupted from the crowd, the sound wild. I stood frozen, fists clenched, nails biting into my palms. I felt my heart rate accelerate, though I didn't know why. I had never wanted to be part of any Luxari Council, but the possibility of not even being offered a position filled me with dread.

An attendant stepped forward, handing over a scroll, its parchment etched with swirling golden patterns.

"If I read your name, please step forward," Queen Catalina's voice sliced through the noise.

"Aldo."

The audience applauded as he stepped forward and clasped his hands behind his back.

"The Hush Sphere, the Still Sphere, and the Scorch Sphere have all offered you spots on their Luxari Councils." He bowed in gratitude, then took a step back.

"Severin."

He stepped forward, like Aldo had.

"The Hush Sphere and Still Sphere have extended offers to you as well."

Severin smiled and stepped back.

"Hugh."

Hugh stepped forward slowly, his gaze fixed on the ground.

"The Hush Sphere, the Still Sphere, the Scorch Sphere, and the Daze Sphere have all offered you spots on their Luxari Councils."

Hugh looked toward Oak. He gave him a small smile.

"And Colette."

My heart jumped against my chest at the sound of my

name. I took a hesitant step forward as Queen Catalina gave me a stern look. She paused before saying, "The Daze Sphere and the Scorch Sphere both offer you a spot on their Luxari Councils."

I felt my stomach tighten as I searched the faces of Kaz and Oak.

"You may step back now," Queen Catalina's smile looked anything but friendly as she rolled up the scroll.

I took a step back.

"Thank you, Questlings," Queen Catalina continued, her voice now softer, more somber. "We also wish to honor Will, our fallen Questling. Will would have received offers from the Hush Sphere, the Still Sphere, the Scorch Sphere, and the Daze Sphere."

Would have. The words echoed in my mind, and before I could stop it, my vision blurred. A few tears escaped, slipping down my cheek. Oak's gaze met mine as I wiped them away, brushing the wetness from my jaw.

I couldn't do this. I couldn't be here right now. It was all too much.

"Thank you again," Queen Catalina said, her voice faltering slightly before she was cut off by a sharp, shrill shriek from Amabel.

"That's it? You've got to be kidding me." Amabel marched toward me, her heels clicking sharply against the polished Arenwood floor. "You'd rather have a pathetic Dim than any one of us who are actually Embers?" The words slammed into me like a cold gust of wind, knocking the breath from my lungs.

I held my chin high. "I know ten Dims better than you'll ever be."

"You're nothing but a Void-sucker," Amabel hissed.

"That's enough." King Oak's voice was low and commanding, laced with authority, prickling my skin with unease.

He stepped off the platform, his boots barely making a sound on the floor.

"You just proved to everyone why none of us wanted you on our Luxari Council." His sharp gaze tightened my core as he stared down at Amabel.

The air thickened with intensity and tension, but it was broken by Otto's barking laugh. "Well said, King Oak. Well said."

Others hesitantly started to laugh as the crowd dispersed toward tables laden with food. The heavy scent of spiced meats and sweet fruits filled the air.

I pushed through the crowd, fleeing down to the shore and kicking off my shoes. Barefoot on the sodden sand, I tried to catch my breath as the sea drenched my feet. The hem of my champagne-gold dress trailed in the water.

The roar in my ears created a pounding sensation in my head. I held my stomach tightly, trying to breathe through the squeezing corset. I was the first Dim in Aren's history to be offered a seat on a Luxari Council—and I had no idea what I was going to do.

"Coco." Kaz's voice was low, like silk brushing against my skin.

I turned, water splashing at my ankles as the ocean soaked my dress even more.

He gave me a faint smile and stepped closer. The salt of the sea clung to my lips. He ran a hand through his golden hair and his sleeves bunched at the elbows, exposing the muscular curve of his arms.

"I'm truly sorry for your loss. Will was a good man," he said, his voice rough.

The sympathy in his emerald eyes sent a sharp ache through my chest. I stared at him, my fingers brushing the damp fabric of my gown.

"Thank you," I murmured as my vision blurred.

The only sound between us was the crash of the waves as we faced each other.

He took another step forward, his citrus scent wrapping around me like a hug.

A stubborn tear slipped down my cheek, burning before I had the chance to stop it.

In a quick motion, he gathered me in his arms and held me snugly against his chest. I wrapped my arms around his broad shoulders and buried my face in the curve of his neck.

Finding so much comfort in a single embrace was terrifying, but I soaked it in.

He was strong, effortlessly powerful, lifting me like I weighed nothing. His warmth radiated through me, heating every place our bodies touched.

"He was fortunate to have you," he whispered in my ear, brushing a soft kiss across my cheek.

I smiled as heat crept up my neck. A flutter of nerves swept through me—like Aeraliths had taken flight in my stomach. I wasn't even sure why.

He gently set me down.

"I'm uncertain how best to say this." He raked his fingers

through his hair. His eyes flickered toward the sea, then back to mine.

I felt a cold chill slide down my spine as I shifted uneasily from one foot to another.

"I'd advise caution with Oak—and be mindful of where you place your trust." His voice was calm, but carried a note of seriousness.

A rush of surprise swept through me.

"Why would you say that?" I asked, my voice shaky, heart pounding. The air around us thickened with tension.

I watched the muscles in his neck tighten, his jaw clench. Kaz fell silent. The only sounds were the distant hum of the party and the crashing waves of the Cobalt Sea.

My chest constricted, and knots of anxiety formed in my stomach.

"Why can't I trust him?" I said, more firmly this time, pursing my lips. Kaz's words weighed heavily on me, but the thought of not trusting Oak lingered like a dull ache in my chest. "Why are you trying to turn me against him?"

His face hardened, but he said nothing. The silence stretched between us, and I was too emotionally exhausted to face any more complications. My heart couldn't take it.

I gathered my soggy gown, dragging the wet fabric through the sand, and turned away, the ache in my chest deepening as I climbed back from the beach.

I approached the party with the intention of saying goodbye to my alliance—and to the friends I'd made—but something made me pause, rooting me in place. I couldn't bring myself to interrupt their joy. Otto held Tada in his arms, his grin lighting up his face as they swayed together on the

Arenwood dance floor. Hugh, standing nearby, smiled as he chatted with Severin. They all looked as if they didn't have a care in the world, and I was jealous of that, but happy for all of them. They deserved it.

I knew not saying goodbye would infuriate Tada, but grief and confusion were swallowing me whole.

As if Aridan had read my mind, Aldo appeared at the end of the path leading to the palace. I gathered my gown in my hand and quickly jogged to catch up with him.

"Aldo!" I called, my voice louder than I meant.

He stopped and turned, arching a brow.

"Coco?"

"Can you do me a favor?" I asked, meeting his mahogany eyes.

"Depends on the favor." He crossed his arms, looking me over.

"Can you Sphere Jump me to the Bleak Sphere, then to the Frosted Peaks?" I didn't give him time to ask questions; I just needed to leave.

His gaze softened. "Sure. When?"

"Twenty minutes?"

His brows rose, surprised. "All right. Meet you at the back of the palace."

"Thank you, Aldo. I owe you," I said sincerely.

I wasn't sure if I was running from the mess I'd left behind, but at that moment, it didn't matter. I just needed to breathe, to escape the weight of Will's death.

FORTY-THREE

THREE MONTHS LATER

I stared at the knife—Milo's knife—where it rested on my soft pink comforter. The silver glinted in the sunlight streaming through the window of Ava's mansion. Aldo had taken me to the Bleak Sphere the night of the celebration, just as I'd asked. I had buried the knife at our pond after Milo died, but the Bleak Sphere was no longer my home, and it felt wrong to leave it behind. It had taken me half an hour to dig it up, and once I had it in my hands, Aldo had Sphere Jumped me to the Frosted Peaks.

Ava and Edur had welcomed me as they always did, but after three months in their home, I couldn't shake the feeling that I had overstayed my welcome.

Within days of my arrival, Otto and Tada had showed up. Fiery as always, Tada had chewed me out for leaving without saying goodbye—a lecture I'd earned, no doubt. But before I'd left the evening of the celebration, I had carefully wrapped three vials of Ari Dust in delicate brown paper and placed them on her bed, along with a note asking her to give them to her brother—so he wouldn't be quite as jealous of her.

Tears had welled in her eyes as she told me how much her brother loved the gift and how thoughtful it was.

We had spent the day together, laughing and sharing stories. She'd filled me in on who had joined which Luxari Council, and they both warned me that I had until the next Sphere Quests summoning to decide, or my offer would be rescinded.

After their visit, I had summoned the courage to deliver Will's package to Elizabeth. It had to come from me—but by the shattered ground, how I wished it didn't. The sorrow etched into her face would haunt me for the rest of my life.

There was no quick remedy to cure the grief that clung to me after Will's death. No distraction could silence the ache. I tried my best to keep my mind occupied—playing with Holly and North, tidying things that didn't need tidying. But even the distractions couldn't keep the ache at bay.

I couldn't bring myself to visit the Scorch Sphere or the Daze Sphere. I wasn't ready to face the decision of whose Luxari Council I should join.

The truth was, I had never believed I'd have a real chance at being offered a spot on a Luxari Council. Immortality and power were nothing more than trying to grasp mist with your fingers. But now, I had two offers. And I couldn't ignore the low, thrilling buzz deep in my belly at the thought.

Would I choose immortality? I could never age, or get sick, but remain young and full of energy.

But at what cost? Outliving everyone I loved... watching friends grow old and fade, while I kept living.

Yes, immortality played its part in the excitement. But what really stirred me was the chance to make change for the better. I could help influence Aren's future—making sure all children received an education and safe places to rest and eat. Building Calla Gale Palaces across Aren. I could do something that actually mattered.

And I couldn't shake the voice in my head that maybe everything I'd endured growing up hadn't just been to teach me sympathy and empathy. Maybe it was meant to ignite something deeper: a purpose. A calling to make real change.

I absentmindedly twirled the hem of my sweater, my eyes fixed on the knife once more.

"A woman is here to see you," Ava's attendant said, standing in my doorway.

There were only a few people who would venture to the Frosted Peaks to see me.

A flicker of hope bloomed in my chest. I descended the staircase, bracing myself—

And then I saw Niko, leaning casually against the doorframe.

Niko flashed me a smile.

"Miss me?" she asked, her copper eyes sparkling with mischief as she opened her arms wide.

I arched an eyebrow at the over-the-top greeting. "Well, it's only been three months," I said.

She took a step forward, grabbing my arms and yanking me against her. "Three months too long."

The smell of her—a rich, spicy scent—seemed to steady me. I had missed her. Her tight curls had grown, now drooping more over her forehead and down her neck in walnut waves.

"I'm freezing. I don't know how your cousin lives here."

I crossed my arms. "You should have known it would be cold. Why are you here?"

"Always straight to business, huh, Coco? No time for pleasantries?" she quipped.

"Why are you here?" I tapped my foot, not amused.

"I'm here on official business," she said, mock formal. "You've got two Luxari Councils still waiting on you—Daze and Scorch. Time's ticking."

I raised an eyebrow. "And?"

"So, I'm here to invite you to a game night at the Daze Sphere and deliver a message from Kaz..." Niko mumbled under her breath, "the cowardly bastard." She shook her head. "He'd like you to visit the Scorch Sphere after your time with us."

His name alone brought to mind our private moment on the beach, and my cheeks flushed crimson at the memory of his arms wrapped around me.

I'd been avoiding this moment for three months. It had been only a matter of time before someone came looking—especially since I'd been dodging two Luxari Council offers.

"You came all the way to the Frosted Peaks to invite me to a game night?" I asked, skepticism lacing my voice.

"Yes," Niko said with a smirk, looking proud of herself.

I couldn't help but wonder how a game night would help me make any decisions.

"Is this the Luxari Council's idea or King Oak's?"

Niko's lips curled. "Funny you should ask. King Oak doesn't even know we invited you. He's busy with kingly duties, and frankly, I'd rather he stay away from game night. He's been insufferable lately."

"I feel like this is just a recruitment event," I said, crossing my arms.

Niko held her hands up in mock surrender. "I, for one, will not pester you about joining. But I can't promise the others won't try. You're the only Questling of the Sphere Quests who hasn't accepted their offer from a Luxari Council."

I knew this. Aldo had joined the Still Sphere, Severin the Hush Sphere, and Hugh the Daze Sphere.

"Benedict and Zareen miss you. Hugh, too. And spheres above, I'll admit it—even I miss you." Niko added, a touch of sincerity breaking through her casual manner.

I chewed on the inside of my cheek. I wanted to see Hugh. And as much as I tried to deny it, a part of me wanted to see Oak again.

"She would love to go," Ava chimed in, walking up beside me and wrapping an arm around my shoulders.

"Ava!" I hissed, pulling away from her embrace.

"Oh, buck up. You've been so gloomy here. You need to get out. Go be with some friends. It'll do you good."

"I'm not packed," I said, my stomach churning with anxiety at the thought of having to make a choice on a Luxari Council.

"Oh, don't worry about that," Ava said, raising her voice. "Edur!"

A bag floated down the stairs and landed at my feet.

"Ava," I huffed, rolling my eyes.

Niko immediately picked it up and turned toward the door. She glanced over her shoulder, her eyes crinkling from the grin she wore.

"Do you always get your way?" I sluggishly followed her.

"Of course," she said confidently.

A sleigh awaited us on the freshly fallen snow, blinding under the sunlight.

"How will we get there?" I asked, settling into the black sleigh.

"The long way," Niko replied with a smirk. She tossed my bag into the sleigh and hopped in, sitting next to me. Her arm instinctively wrapped around my shoulders, pulling me close. At first, I tensed, but then I melted into her embrace.

CHAPTER
FORTY-FOUR

The journey through the Delirium Sea passed without interruption, and soon enough, I found myself in the Daze Kingdom, dining with the Daze Luxari Council.

Hugh was pleased to see me. After most of the group had stuffed themselves with food, we gathered around the fireplace, sipping wine, as Niko began suggesting games.

I surveyed Oak's Luxari Council. Hugh, Niko, Zareen, and Benedict were all Swayers—Isabelle was the only Charmer, and Drogo the only Enticer. I found it curious that there wasn't a Shifter, but I was sure Oak had a strategy behind that decision.

Isabelle looked bored, absently playing with the ends of her yellow hair. Drogo made the sofa look ridiculously small for his hulking frame, and it creaked under his weight. Zareen and Benedict argued loudly a few feet from Niko, while Hugh quietly joined me at my side.

"Why don't we play *Seek and Shadow*?" Benedict suggested.

"*Seek and Shadow*? I haven't played that since I was four," I laughed, shaking my head.

"But have you ever played it in a castle?" Benedict shot back, grinning.

"No..." It could be fun in a palace—so many places to hide.

"Well, great." Niko set her glass on the mantle. "Then it's settled. *Seek and Shadow* it is."

"Niko, you have to go over the rules!" Zareen interjected. "Because that one"—she pointed at Drogo—"likes to cheat."

Drogo flashed a beastly grin but remained silent. He was massive and unnervingly quiet. I couldn't recall him speaking a single word.

Isabelle inspected her nails, acting as if this were one of the dullest moments in her life.

"All right, fine," Niko muttered in a rushed tone. "First rule: *no magic*. No mind tricks, no wind, no fire, no strength, no charms." Her eyes lingered on Isabelle as she spoke.

"We're sticking to the main floor of the castle," Niko continued. "Understood?" Everyone nodded, except for Drogo.

One moment, Drogo was slouched on the settee; the next, magic surged violently through the air, emanating from Niko's direction.

Dorgo winched, clamping his hands over his ears.

"Understood!" Drogo bellowed, and the magic instantly vanished.

"You prick," Drogo growled, standing abruptly from the couch.

I tried to stifle my laughter. Some of the first words I heard from Drogo were, "You prick."

"Martha," Niko called to the woman who was clearing off the table. "Which one of us is the biggest thorn in your side?"

She looked up. It was the woman I had helped carry trays of food. She pinned Zareen with a look only a mother could give. "Zareen," she scoffed, hefting a tray of plates before walking out of the room.

Niko chuckled under her breath, but I couldn't help myself —I giggled. Not because of Martha's sharp response, but because of the look on Zareen's face.

Zareen stood there, her mouth hanging open wide enough for a grapefruit to fit in, her eyes enormous—as if she had never, in her entire life, been called unpleasant.

"That settles that," Benedict said.

A sudden breeze swept through the room, plunging the palace into complete darkness.

Instantly, Benedict, Niko, Drogo, and Isabelle scrambled from the room, leaving Hugh and me standing alone. Zareen remained in the corner, facing the wall, muttering and counting under her breath.

"You two had better hurry," Zareen grumbled from her corner.

Gathering the fabric of my gown in my palm, I moved quickly. The main level of the palace was cloaked in shadow, and I tiptoed down the hall, every nerve tingling with the rush of adrenaline. I glanced into one room and spotted a boot peeking out beneath the curtain. I hurried on to the next.

I reached the end of the hall, my heart racing. I peered inside a room, praying it was vacant. The curtains were drawn back, allowing the moon to cast a soft glow over the floor. I turned toward the fluffy fortress of a bed that took up most of

424

the space. I wanted more than anything to run and jump onto it. Dozens of ivory pillows were piled high on the mattress.

"Here I come!" Zareen bellowed in the distance, yanking me out of my reverie.

I instantly dropped to the floor, flattening myself so my cheek rested on the hardwood. I used my arms to pull my body under the bed as dust greeted the inside of my mouth and nostrils.

I tried to control my breathing. A pair of boots appeared in the doorway. *Sphere shit.* If Zareen found me this quickly, nobody would want me on the Daze Luxari Council.

The boots came nearer to the bed, but stopped just a few inches from the frame. I stilled. Oak's smooth, deep voice filled the room.

"Damsel, can you come out from under there, or must I drag you out?" Oak drawled.

"Shh! You'll give my hiding place away!" I hissed.

Oak crouched down, peeking beneath the bed.

He gave a half-smile, displaying his perfect teeth.

"Either leave or join me. You're going to blow my cover, so please, shut it," I whispered.

Relief surged through me when he stood, but it quickly morphed into disappointment. I wanted him to respect my cover, but seeing him for the first time in months stirred something deeper within me.

He lowered himself again, and suddenly, he was lying on the floor, gliding his body against the ground to join me under the bed. Oak watched me with a bemused expression.

I heard a commotion echo down the hall—Zareen must have found someone.

Oak's side brushed against mine.

"You look beautiful," Oak said in a hushed tone.

He wasn't understanding the need for silence. I tried to shake my head in annoyance. Instead, he scooted closer to me. I stared ahead, fearful that if I turned my head, our lips would touch. I was a whirlwind of confusing emotions. Footsteps grew louder, and our breathing synchronized. Another pair of boots walked into the room.

"Pathetic," Zareen mumbled.

Zareen's face appeared in front of me.

"Good evening, Your Majesty. Coco."

"Damn you. You gave away my position." I shoved Oak as I crawled out from under the bed.

"I would have found you either way," Zareen said, glancing over her shoulder as she left the room. "I could smell the sexual tension wafting off you two from the Great Hall."

Oak joined my side.

"What do you want? You spoiled the game for me, so you'd better have a good reason for seeking me out," I said, hands resting firmly on my hips.

Oak chuckled, his fingers lacing with mine. A spark of heat shot up my arm at the touch.

"Come on." He tugged me down the hall into a small room with a desk. He dropped my hand as soon as we entered.

Candles flickered in his office, casting a soft glow that revealed his face. His features were sharper, more defined. He looked more tanned, his hair a bit longer, but there was a tiredness in his eyes that didn't escape me.

His tunic was untied, revealing his chest. My throat went

dry. I quickly looked away, focusing on the paintings on the wall to avoid the urge to look back at him.

Each painting depicted the Daze Sphere. I lingered on one in particular because of its familiarity.

It was a wooden bridge over a stream, covered in bright leaves. The russet and golden colors of the foliage were as vibrant as if I stood there in person. The painting next to it showed a grassy field, enclosed by large trees. The third painting took my breath away.

Three children chased each other into the woods, smiles lighting up their faces. Their familiar features were captured in the paint. Oak led from the middle, Kaz close behind, and Niko grinned as she ran alongside. A fourth child appeared at the edge of the frame—taller than the rest—but only the back of his head was visible.

I studied the painting, my fingers grazing the edge of the frame as Oak stepped up beside me.

"Who's that?" I asked, pointing to the boy.

Oak's eyes drifted, like they were looking at something far beyond the painting.

"An old friend. I haven't seen him in years."

His voice carried a quiet finality—enough to make it clear he didn't want to say more.

"You guys were close."

"Yes, we were."

"What happened?" I asked, meeting his gaze.

Oak's expression darkened slightly, the smile fading as his eyes drifted to the painting.

"It wasn't just one thing; it was a series of small things that piled up. The first time we felt a rift was when Niko joined my

Luxari Council. Kaz didn't understand—he felt like Niko was choosing me over him. But Niko explained it to him—said it just felt right, that she was a Swayer and all. Kaz tried to understand, but it never sat well with him. It ate at him, and it ate at us."

I tried to put myself in Kaz's shoes. Growing up with your two best friends and having one of them choose to spend eternity with the other? It would hurt, and I would feel snubbed.

He walked toward his desk.

"I have something for you," he said, turning.

He was holding the *Ari Report*.

Surprise surged through me; this was the last thing I had expected from him.

His eyes met mine, soft and serious. "I thought you might wish to look. Since you already broke through the magical forces, you've earned the right to view it at any time... to see if Milo's name is there.

"I didn't check. I felt you should be the first to see it," he said reverently.

I swallowed the lump in my throat. The thoughtfulness of his actions made my chest feel tight. I reached out and grasped the book, my fingers brushing against the rough texture of the cover. Milo's ring caught my gaze, its seashell surface polished and almost glowing beneath the flickering flames.

Flipping slowly through the pages, I read each name until I found him.

Milo Darroway.

My throat thickened, and for a moment, I couldn't breathe.

I looked up to find Oak studying my face. The heart-rending

tenderness of his gaze stirred something in me. I simply handed him the open book, my hand trembling slightly.

He held eye contact with me, then scanned the same page. "He is here."

"Yes," I choked out, a tear escaping my eye.

Oak read Milo's name, a faint smile crossing his face. Then he flipped through the pages and turned the report toward me so I could read the name above his finger.

Will Ashford.

Pressure clamped down on my chest. Will and Milo were both Ari Souls. They had moved on to the Unknown.

Oak walked toward his desk. I assumed he thought I needed space to be alone, but that only sent more tears sliding down my cheeks.

He set the report down gently, and in one fluid motion, he had me in his arms. I nestled deeper into his embrace. The feeling of his touch—something I hadn't realized I missed until now—flooded me. His arms tightened around me. His fingers curled into my hair as he held me close.

We stood there, our foreheads touching, alone in the shadows. I felt something I'd never known before: peace.

CHAPTER
FORTY-FIVE

I leaned against the railing as the sea spray misted my face. I was on my way to the Scorch Sphere to visit their Luxari Council.

While digging through my satchel for a book to distract myself from seasickness, I found one that wasn't mine.

Carefully, I cracked it open and flipped to the page marked by a parchment slightly larger than the book itself. I unfolded the paper and read what was written there:

> Coco,
> Here is the version of "The Damsel in Distress" that I read to you the first night we met in the library:

> There once was a damsel in distress
> Who found herself in a mess.

She struggled with fear
As the night brought near
A victor to wrangle her foe.

There once was a damsel in distress
Who suffered through tears and woes.
He swept her away,
As she prayed through the day,
Thanking her God for a man.

I had never heard that version of the Damsel in Distress until that night we met in the library. This is the version my mother used to read to me when I was small.

I opened the book to the page marked with a leather strap and began to read the poem:

There once was a damsel in distress
Who found herself in a mess.
She swallowed her fear
As she brought forth shears,
Slicing her demons away.

There once was a damsel in distress
Who conquered her fears through a test.
She battled the cause,
As her heart sang along.
The damsel—a hero at last.

The weight of his words sank in. All this time, he'd been paying me a compliment—calling me a damsel because he saw me as fearless, as a hero. He had always seen me for who I could be, even when I couldn't see it myself.

I suddenly felt a prickling sensation on the inside of my left wrist. I looked down, and iridescent shimmering dust glowed, weaving through my veins. As the dust evaporated, it left behind two intertwined Daze lilies etched into my skin—a mark, a bond. SoulShimmer.

But before I could fully comprehend what had just happened, a burst of golden dust swept across my wrist again, forming two radiant suns slightly overlapping. Their warm light flickered beside the glittering lilies—swaying my fate between a Luxari Enticer and a Dazed King.

To my Starry Flicker,

Shimmer, shimmer, shimmer—
The souls can hear you whisper.
Glimmer, glimmer, glimmer—
The heart flows like a river,
Swirling and twirling,
In shadows unfurling,
A glance with a spark
That once left its mark.
Shielding and building,
The cracks are healing,
Taming the pain,
Washed clean from the rain.
Even through strains,
A fire still remains,
Learning to love again.

Queen of the Daze Sphere

END OF BOOK ONE
THANKS FOR READING

Thank you for reading SoulShimmer, by Dawn Merchant.

If you enjoyed the book, we encourage to leave a review on Goodreads or your preferred book retailer online.

ACKNOWLEDGMENTS

If you had told me a couple of years ago that I'd be writing fantasy fiction, I would've laughed hysterically—yet here I am. This has been such an amazing adventure, and I have so many people to thank for that.

To my editor, Kenneth A. Baldwin: Thank you for taking a chance on me and for being patient with all of my questions, emails, documents, slideshows, and texts. Your honest feedback and thoughtful suggestions made this book possible.

Thank you to Eburnean Books for the opportunity to be published.

To my marketing agent and older sister, Amberly Asay Janke: Thank you for all your support and hard work in promoting my book.

Paige Johnson: This book would've been an absolute disaster without you. Thank you for uncovering the gem buried beneath all the rubble.

Danae Templeton: Thank you so much for your careful proofreading and close attention to detail.

Emily Young: Thank you for the incredible cover, symbols, and map.

To Mandi West, Jennifer Absher, Jocelyn Chatman, Kayleen Smith, Rose Nguyen, and Whitney Moss: Thank you for being my focus group and beta readers. And a special thanks to Whitney for reading the entire book, sharing thoughtful feedback, and helping with the second one.

To my students—you are my daily inspiration. Your curiosity, humor, and joy make me a better teacher and a better person.

To Ethan, Heather, and Amberly: Thank you for being my very first readers. Ethan, thank you for diving in first and for all your help with social media. Heather, thank you for your feedback and energy—especially for reading the entire manuscript right after having a baby.

To my family, for your endless support and encouragement:

Peaches, Amberly Asay Janke, Collin DeRosier Janke, Hallie Janke, Harvey Theodore Janke, Heather Kramer, Nathan Kramer, Beckett Kramer, Samantha Day, Troy Day, Millie Day, Tiffany Judkins, Josh Judkins, Joe LeBron Asay IV, and Ethan Cole.

To my favorite aunt, Sherene: Thank you for being my best friend since middle school and for introducing me to a world of books. Thank you for the phone calls, texts, words of wisdom, and all the time you've spent with me. You showed me I could write a book—because you did. Thank you for the drinks, the Oasis time, and for dreaming with me. I know you say you don't have kids, but you do—and on behalf of my siblings and me, we love you from the bottom of our hearts. And thank you to Keith Funk for letting me steal her away for countless hours.

To the reader: Thank you so much for picking up my book.

And lastly,

Chayce: There aren't enough words to describe how amazing you are. If every person had a Chayce, there would be world peace, endless happiness, and happily-ever-afters for everyone. I don't know what I did to deserve you, but thank you—for laughing with me, loving me, and making every second of every day worthwhile. I can write about love because you've shown me what true love is.

ABOUT THE AUTHOR

Dawn Merchant is a high school social studies teacher by day and a fantasy romance author by night. When she's not writing or teaching, you can find her out on a run, lost in a book, or taking long walks with her husband, whom she has known since kindergarten.

To keep in touch, join Dawn's newsletter at her website, DawnMerchant.com.

instagram.com/dawnmerchant.author

tiktok.com/@dawnmerchant.author

threads.com/dawnmerchant.author

www.ingramcontent.com/pod-product-compliance
Lightning Source LLC
Chambersburg PA
CBHW030329120726
47901CB00007B/1724